DUSK

MY CHILDREN FROM ANOTHER WORLD

BOOK 3: DUSK

PAYTON FLETCHER
AKA _GLASSES

Podium

To you, dear reader, for making this journey worthwhile

Published in 2024 by Podium Publishing
www.podiumaudio.com

Podium

DUSK

1

All that existed was darkness, a darkness that I felt I had acknowledged endless times before it had taken such self-reflection away from me. No truth existed for it had been held sway by inky webs.

And within darkness, all was darkness. There were no lines that distinguished the world around me, no changes, nothing that encouraged focus or interest.

In the brief moments that I realized I was surrounded by obsidian dreams, I could only recognize that this felt old and familiar. Faint thoughts of an old enemy surrounding me before I knew nothing else.

And yet, even as I existed within this darkness, there were moments where the world was alright.

"I'll learn it so fast, you're gonna have to teach me another one!"

Small pulses of something that fought against the darkness around me. Sights and sounds that were so unlike the inky fog that I hated with all my heart when I was capable of doing so.

"I never had a debut before . . ."

I loved them, I felt it. I was not sure whom I loved, but I did with all my being. Every little bead of light that I collected over the eons of nothing, making me feel warmer in the moments before the darkness subsumed me.

"It's quiet, peaceful, and the air is fresh. It's fine. Tell us about the fish."

The darkness took them from me, but I was left with the gift of knowing that I had something taken from me. An emptiness that gave me strength, that I held on to.

Even as the pulses came for me once more in anger, as if I had insulted them by my inability to protect them from the darkness, I welcomed their light.

"I'm not your fucking son! I'm not your fucking child! None of us are! We never fucking were!"

I loved them, as well, even as I felt hurt and pain. I welcomed the knowledge that something beyond the darkness had hurt me, that there was something, no, multiple somethings that I could yearn for in this place of nothing.

"They feel like the enemy."

The concepts behind the words were fleeting. The frustration I felt at being unable to answer the pulses was eternal. Eternal, of course, until the darkness once again came and all was wiped away.

"I'm smarter this time. I'm prettier this time. So how come I'm not the favorite, huh?"

It was a cycle, I realized a thousand times. An endless rotation of drowning beneath the deluge of onyx reality and clawing my way toward the pulses only to meet the realization that it was all a cycle.

Like a whirlpool, it all circled around words that continued to flow over me like the echoing bell of a temple, each word pounding through my existence with meaning I barely understood.

Three souls from beyond
Born to a hero and a pawn
Death and destruction
Peace and function
Lies within the strength of a bond

All for it to begin again and again and again.

Until the moment came that I clawed through the darkness, the realization coming to me once more that it would all be for naught. That there was no end to this, that I was doomed to failure.

And yet, I held on to the light in my arms, and I never let go.

"It was nice feeling like a hero one last time."

In what felt like a shock that reverberated through the eternity of my lifetime spent within the darkness, I felt something crash over me that was not darkness, nor was it a pulse of light.

Instead, it was a voice.

"Your mental fortitude is laudable, Rakta of Derra," the very first words I had heard in my entire existence said. "I believe it is important that we speak before the conscious world takes you."

And then a blinding light took me.

The sounds of birds and crickets welcomed me as I opened my eyes to see a clear cerulean sky above me, the feeling of soft grass underneath my form. My physical form that I felt for the first time in forever.

My name was Rakta Velbrun, no, Tribus. I was the father of three amazing children, the widower of the most beautiful woman in the empire, and Slayer of the Warlock King.

Coming back to myself in what felt like moments, as if the darkness that I had wrestled with for centuries was naught but a bad dream, so many emotions flooded through me.

A hotness stained my cheeks as I cried, pulling myself up and smiling as I looked around at the meadow I was in, a familiar one. The one behind my keep, my home.

In the distance I could see the familiar grave of my beloved Lydia.

The darkness felt like nothing compared to the brightness that surged through me from all that I was once again, feeling hope in my chest at having finally regained myself.

"It truly is wonderful to have you back." That same voice that had saved me from the darkness spoke up from behind me. "There was no saving on my end, Rakta of Derra."

I turned my gaze toward the voice, feeling emotions still lodged within my throat even as I spoke. "Who are you?"

Standing there, slightly turned away from me but with their velvet eyes turned to focus on me entirely, was an individual of slight build but ample presence. As if a star had stepped upon the earth, a light shimmered underneath their gray skin, and flowing tresses of white hair fell to the ground behind them.

"Depends on the world, I suppose," they said, but they shook their head slightly. "No, no, this is no time for being coy. I apologize."

I felt the apology rest at my feet, but the weight of even this entity's forgiveness felt beyond me. My people had stories of gods. Did I truly speak to one such entity?

"I am no god. I am Overseer," they said, some quiet amusement pulling at wrinkles I hadn't noticed around the eyes of this being. "Merely the one who keeps every watch ticking."

"Ticking?" I fell to my knees, feeling something hit me. Not a physical force, but the memory of my children screaming for me as they were teleported away, of Zactrik standing before me.

Shawn's death and the moments I'd had before falling into darkness.

"I'm sorry for your loss," Overseer said. "Shawn Hanchett was full of potential, and he squandered little of it in Derra. It was a good choice, I believe."

Those words, no matter the strength behind them, did little to fill the hole in my heart that hollowed out at the memory of Shawn's death. And yet, the way they spoke of him was familiar in its own right.

"You knew Shawn?" They spoke of him with unmistakable fondness.

Overseer nodded. "I was the one who plucked him from his first death, one of many little acts of rebellion that I've done over the years for those that had far more to do in life."

"Shawn died," I said, mystified, "and you brought him to Derra? And you have done this before and again?"

That would mean that this entity had done the same for my children, would it not? The one to take them from their previous lives . . .

"Yes," Overseer said. "I was the one who plucked those pained souls from Earth and brought them to Derra, delivering them to you in the form of your children with Lydia Velbrun."

To have it said so forthrightly made me weak with gratitude, but I nodded, giving my silent thanks. I'd noticed it seemed to read my thoughts and feelings as clearly as my words, my lead tongue saved by Overseer's insight.

"Now, however, you begin your return to the waking world, Rakta," Overseer continued, "and I come to warn you that the souls I delivered to you have fallen to darker paths in your absence."

"What?" The words sent a chill down my spine. "Do you mean the prophecy?"

For a moment, Overseer said nothing, and a chill breeze blew through the grassy meadow we stood in. The very idea of Daka, Natakia, and Dalton, any of them, being led astray by their own pain . . .

"The strengths of their bonds have withered, their darkest fears and impulses made true." Overseer closed their eyes, speaking somberly. "I'm glad you have awakened, for they will need you. The world needs you."

"How long . . . have I been gone?" I asked, fearing the worst.

Overseer did not speak, but with a small imperceptible twitch of their fingers, I felt the truth of the matter splash across my consciousness.

I had spent eight years within the darkness, my friends and family crumbling around me as I lay unconscious and unable to move by my own strength or will.

Overseer nodded. "You never succumbed to Zactrik's sacrilege, not fully. Never giving up, your mind has retained itself as much as one could. Once you wake, the damage to your mind will begin to heal."

"Zactrik." I asked, focusing on that monster, "Is he still alive? Is the world safe from the danger he poses?"

"Good questions, Rakta of Derra," Overseer said, but I was suddenly confident that there would be no answers from this entity on such matters. "Zactrik's gift was a brilliant one, but one that has been used to stain the world."

"Gift?" Was Overseer speaking of the inhuman monstrosity that Zactrik had become? His intelligence and genius when it came to splicing his wretched volunteers into murderous monsters? "What gift?"

"The gift I give all those I meet with," Overseer said. "Although it is not up to me what it becomes."

Overseer had met with Zactrik? I found myself digging my nails into the palms of my hands as I suddenly felt a great anger at this thing before me. "You brought Zactrik to my home?"

"Yes," they said. "I did."

I felt anger clouding my thoughts, but I pushed through it, trying to keep a steady mind. I had held anger within me for years, but the darkness had made old things feel new.

"Why?" That was the only question that mattered.

Overseer smiled. "The same reason I brought Shawn and your children here. The potential for new things, for those of great potential to pollinate new worlds with ideas, innovation, and leaders."

And then their smile dimmed, and I saw them look away for a moment. I was struck with the sense that they had never wanted Zactrik to do as he had, but he was not the first to do so.

"Some souls never grow past their pain," they continued. "I hope you'll be able to help them, Rakta. Your lights have always been treasured ones."

So many thoughts flew through my head, but I nodded and put my concerns aside. My children needed me, and that was all that mattered. The world may have moved on without me, but time had not weathered me fully. I would not crumble at the weight of this purpose.

"Then it is time for me to go, Overseer," I said, turning away. "I cannot move forward here, not in a direction that matters."

"Of course, but there remains one more topic of discussion between us, Rakta of Derra," the voice called for me, stopping me in my tracks as I began to head off toward my wife's grave. "As I said, all who meet me receive a gift."

I turned back to the smiling entity, my thoughts going to Daka's sight and aptitude, Natakia's insight, and Dalton's strange power through value. Esoteric and powerful abilities that had always impressed me.

"What would you like your gift to be?" Overseer tilted their head slightly.

"I thought these gifts were not decided by you, Overseer," I said, having returned to the entity's side. "You spoke as if the gift was decided by other means."

"That is true." Overseer nodded. "I rarely give specific gifts, nor do I usually ask the recipient what they would like. Oftentimes, they are not in any state to respond soberly, nor would they remember the decision regardless."

"They forget their meeting with you?" Was Overseer the origins of Lydia's prophecy? The spell that she had had similar ramifications on those present around her. "Will I?"

"I was not the source of Lydia's prophecy, no," Overseer answered my unasked question, "but the gods of Derra are aware of, well, not me, but the phenomenon that I represent. Most remember their discussion with me in feelings and emotions, no tangible memory."

For a moment, they looked at me with a consideration that seemed to look far deeper beneath the skin than any gaze I had ever set upon someone.

"I believe you will be an exception," Overseer said. "That, however, is secondary to what I ask you now."

The air around us changed, and if it were any other situation I would have prepared for a fight. In this, however, I simply stood and prepared myself for all that tried to take me.

"What do you desire, Rakta?" Overseer's words were stoic, unrelenting. A determination to their harmonic voice that demanded an answer that pleased them. "Should I return you to your prime? Should I grant you the ability to call upon gods? What if I gave you the power to go back in time?"

It was a testament to the feeling of being in the presence of this entity that I wholly believed all the increasingly ridiculous suggestions to be true and terrifying.

"Is there anything you cannot do?" I asked.

Overseer shook their head. "Nothing that you could conceptualize."

The moment stilled between us, and I felt the weight of their attention grow heavier and heavier, as if pressing me to come to my decision.

"I could bring Lydia back," Overseer said.

Years of fighting against Mortum within my own mind and those words did more to almost break me than such trials and tribulations ever had. The thought of Lydia coming back, of being with me as we sought out our children and helped them with their pain, made me want to accept instantly and entirely.

And yet, would Lydia's return be for my children's benefit or mine? Could it be both? And could I truly rip her back from the stories she existed within? Or the Great Beyond she had entered gracefully?

The answer was obvious.

"No," I said, shaking my head. "I know what I want."

There was something that had always eluded me, but perhaps, in these circumstances, it would elude me no longer.

Overseer knew my request as I looked up to meet their eyes, and they nodded, looking pleased by my choice of gift. "I believe I can make that work."

"I want to understand my children."

And then the meadow disappeared, and I found myself coddled by heavy blankets and resting upon the comfort of a mattress, the birds and crickets replaced by the sound of crying.

I looked over, feeling the weight of my true physical body, the absence of my arm, and saw Doh. "It's alright, Doh. I'm okay. I'm awake. You don't have to cry."

She looked at me, tears staining her cheeks, and as I hazily began to recollect myself after so long, my thoughts feeling like anchors, I realized that there was something unfamiliar about Doh.

"Oh, oh fuck." Doh started crying even harder, looking embarrassed and much younger than I remembered, but perhaps that was . . .

I felt like I had made a mistake.

It was good to be back.

2

At a brief glance around, time had seemingly not touched my room, but there was plenty of difference once my gaze had tempered and shrugged off the remnants of my time asleep.

The green-and-gold decorations of House Velbrun had all but disappeared, the colors of my wife's family having been overcast by a deep blue and sturdy brown. And emblazoned upon all I could see was the triangle made of bound rope, knots at each angle.

The symbol of House Tribus. A distant memory in all I had endured.

"Are the curtains new?" A banal observation, but one that would hopefully keep my attendant from driving herself mad as she was currently trying to do.

Macy paced back and forth, as she had for the last several minutes, biting her lip. "What do I even do? Who do I get first—What? The, uh, the curtains? The curtains. Yes, uh, the curtains are new."

She stopped, focusing on the curtains as I had, before she gave a sharp little whistle. I watched the curtains draw themselves across the rails, dimming the room.

"They open and close at a whistle," Macy explained. "Neat, huh?"

I nodded, waiting as she finally seemed to collect herself after a time. Every muscle in my body was burning to move, to be used after so long, but it would do me no good to rush and hurt myself.

"Dalton," Macy finally said, a certainty. "I need to go get Dalton, even if the Donn of Neve has arrived already, he'd kill me and then fire me if he wasn't the first to know his dad woke up."

"I think getting Dalton is a fine idea," I agreed, a touch of impatience in my tone. Any amusement at Macy's fear at being fired was waylaid by how very real it felt.

Macy nodded, gulping, before she headed for the door, before she stopped and looked back. "Do you, well, want anything, Lord Tribus?"

"My son," I said as politely as I could to the frazzled girl. "And my daughters."

The pained look that flickered on Macy's face didn't inspire a particularly good feeling in my gut, but she nodded nervously. "I'll, uh, go get Dalton."

And so I was left alone to truly begin to feel the weight of my body and the lack of use heavy in my limbs, the lack of sensation in my right arm. No, it wasn't quite lacking, but rather a distinct void in the shape of my arm.

As if my Vitae still flowed from the stump of my arm into the shape of what I had lost below my elbow.

And as it flowed, I could feel my Vitae was stirring only slightly slower than my mind. As if a storm was beginning to brew under my skin, but just as I could feel my age in my joints, I could feel it in my Vitae. Not as bright as it once was, tainted by time and the scars of those I had fought.

Zactrik and his horrid Mortum. What kind of terrors had plagued the world while I was gone? What tragedy had visited my children in my absence?

My dwelling on the enormity of my duty as a father was paused for a moment as I felt a faint burning creep across the back of my left hand. Pulling my sole remaining arm out from underneath the heavy blankets was more herculean than I would have liked it to have been.

Soon, my arm was in the air above me, and I could feel the slight strain of atrophied muscle, but my attention was held taut by the new sight before me.

"And what are you?" I asked.

There, engraved upon the skin on the back of my hand, was the symbol of House Tribus in black. Each knot tied at the ends of each angle, but I could feel a power within the art.

Something that did not feel like Mana or Vitae. Something that had not been noticed and felt like it never would be noticed by another person.

"The Overseer . . ." I said, feeling a power to even utter the title of that which had bestowed this upon me. A gentle reminder from beyond Derra and the gods that the knowledge I held was sacred.

There was so much to consider, but my thoughts pulled back from the world with every second that closed the distance between me and my son.

"Hurry, Macy," I begged to the ceiling. "I want to see my son."

After some time, I was tired of begging. I was also tired of lying down. My body, stiff as it was, was still my own to command, and I was no longer willing to say no.

I began to flow my Vitae through my body, swirling as I'd done so many times before but taking care to ease its way into my joints, before beginning to twist my body and sit up for the first time in eight years.

"Adoabi would be laughing at me right now." I shook my head. "Struggling with something as simple as getting out of bed."

Letting my Vitae relax as I sat on the edge of my bed now, I craned my neck around to see more of how my room had changed in so many years before I paused at the portraits on the wall.

My family through the years, some I recognized, commissioned pieces to be cherished for ages, but others that I didn't. I wasn't familiar with them. I saw my children age through the portraits on the wall, and I felt a deep well of grief hit me as I realized how alone each of them had been.

Dalton became a fine young man as he trod toward adulthood, each of his portraits looking more formal and official than the last, the sharpness of his gaze never dulling.

And Natakia, although her portraits were fewer, looked to have grown ever more beautiful. The newest one looked as if she had been born to pose, her green-and-gold dress . . .

"Why is she wearing . . . ?" I almost finished my thought before my gaze settled on the only portrait of Daka in the room. "Why is there only one . . . ?"

Perhaps it was the skill of the artist, but I mentally took a step back at the sight of Daka's visage, flinching at what I saw in her painted gaze. A deep sadness and anger, her body tense as if she had been lashed down for the painting.

A sense of wrongness clashed with the swelling of love I felt at the sight of my children, even as portraits, but as my gaze went up to the largest portrait on the wall, my resolve hardened.

A portrait commissioned in the week of my children's tenth birthday, all those years ago, of all of us together, all of them sitting down on my lap, surrounded by the forests of Gelvurt.

"I'll find you all," I said. "No matter what dark paths you tread, no matter what kind of monster you believe yourself to be, I'll find you."

I felt my hand burning for a moment, and I glanced down to watch the emblem of House Tribus on the back of my hand glimmer with a fluorescent energy.

And then the door to my room clicked open.

A portrait had not done my son the justice that I felt he deserved. He stood in the doorway with purpose, as if with every movement he carried a mission to fulfill.

His eyes stared into mine before they broke off their gaze and scanned me up and down, as if trying to ascertain the legitimacy of my person. Perhaps I wasn't the only one who had dealt with waking nightmares.

"Father," Dalton said, as if greeting me after a long trip. His hair was pulled back into a ponytail, a utilitarian knot that kept it out of his professional gaze. A long robe of blue and brown around him, the fineries of a noble expertly tailored to his form.

With a grunt of exertion, I stood up, stumbling forward as I felt my Vitae surge to enhance my weakened muscles enough to do just that.

"Father!" Dalton took a step forward, and I felt my strength surge as I heard the worry and uncertainty shake at the edges of his words.

I straightened my posture and found my balance before I turned to look my son in the eyes straight on and began walking forward even as my body argued with me.

I would brook no rebellion from the physical in the face of what needed to be done.

My son met me halfway, coming up to me with a thousand thoughts in his stare, and I wrapped my arms around him with all the might I had scrounged up at the sight of one of my children in the flesh.

"Dalton," I said, feeling his arms slowly wrap around me. "I love you, son. I'm sorry I was gone for so long."

The silence at my statement was warm and stretched on and on, even as my strength began to waver. My little boy had grown up to be a man who came up to near my own height, a man who had endured so many burdens in my absence.

"This is so sweet," Macy sniffled, rubbing her eyes. I'd barely noticed her enter the room behind my son.

Dalton sighed at her words, and as if the magical spell on the moment had been broken, my strength left me, and I fell back onto the bed, my son aiding my descent.

"Oh, uh, sorry," the maid said, before she backed out of the room. "I'll, uh, go dust . . . something."

My son kept his eyes closed as the door shut before he sat down beside me, opening his eyes. They glimmered, an unshed wetness in his stare as he watched me in silence.

"Father, I . . . I love you too," Dalton said, his voice wavering. "I was never sure you'd come back, and I'd . . . I thought I . . ."

No matter how old he got, no matter how different he was, I knew the meaning behind my son's unsaid words. It was hard carrying words for those you weren't sure you'd ever get to speak them to.

I put a hand on his shoulder. "I know, Dalton. I always knew."

Dalton's posture went slack, as if a great weight had been lifted off of him, but that moment of relief was seemingly too much for him as he regathered himself.

"Now that you're awake, there's much to discuss," Dalton said. "A lot has happened since your battle with Zactrik."

"I'm sure the world's changed a lot." I nodded. "First, where are Natakia and Daka?"

"Daka ran away five years ago to the Ruskan border," Dalton said, his expression and voice betraying nothing. "And then three years later, Natakia forswore her ties to House Tribus and has since become a member of House Velbrun."

The swift and clinical explanation saved time but left me little room to breathe as the revelations were dropped in my lap. I nodded, swallowing at the idea of my child being in a place so dangerous.

And for Daka to be somewhere in Rusk boded only a slight bit better.

"And so, you've taken up the role of High Lord Tribus, then?" It was always a role more suited for Dalton than it would have been for my eldest. Daka wasn't meant for that kind of lifestyle.

Dalton nodded, not even seeming proud of his courage in stepping up to such a task at such a young age, before something seemed to shake him, his gaze becoming wary. "I am still capable of acting as High Lord Tribus as you recover, Father."

For a moment, I was confused before I let out a gentle sigh. It seemed my son was worried that I would take away all that he had worked on in my absence.

"Dalton." I tightened my grip on his shoulder. "Let's leave such matters for later. Perhaps I could get something to eat? You can tell me more over something warm."

"I'll have Macy bring something in," Dalton nodded, not looking completely mollified at his business being put to the side. There were so many more important things to talk about than who was in charge, however. "Give me a moment."

He stood, and my grip slackened as he walked over to the door before a thought occurred to me. Something I'd heard as I slowly came to my senses.

"Dalton," I said, my son pausing at the door. "Did I hear Macy correctly about a Donn of Neve visiting? Coming here to Gelvurt?"

For the first time, I saw satisfaction sharpen the features of my son as he looked back over his shoulder at me. "I have so much to tell you, Father. Gelvurt is getting a bank."

And with that, he walked out. The distant sounds of his orders to Macy falling to the wayside at the enormity of my son's words.

3

The Donns of Neve were the wealthiest of all of Derra, said to hail from a once-powerful island confederation of which only they remained. They were great travelers and merchants, unifying Derra under their own personal currency and retaining control over the minting and distribution of it.

And their banks were the focus of all of it. Not only were they the greatest collections of sil, they were also where sil was manufactured. For Dalton to have the prospects of a bank in store for Gelvurt, it was tantamount to the Donns of Neve considering my son for membership.

"This food is still delicious as ever. Zao hasn't gotten out of practice," I said, absently wondering just how far Dalton had brought Gelvurt into the future.

I was also having to pay extra mind to not accidentally attempt to pick up the fork with my missing arm. I was already feeling a tinge of frustration every time I fooled myself into trying.

Dalton was eating his own food across from me, a simple table having been brought in to eat in the comforts of my room. There hadn't been much confidence in my ability to walk, and I'd preferred to eat before dealing with the concerns of Dalton's alchemists.

It was unfair to them, but I was a tad wary after Zactrik's duplicity.

Dalton shook his head, taking a bite of chicken. "Zao no longer works for us. I hired some exceptional cooks from Cerula to properly make our meals in his stead."

"I see." Perhaps Zao had found employment elsewhere? "How have you been, Dalton? You've done so much while I've been gone. Have you been well?"

"I've been busy," Dalton said, meeting my gaze with indifference. "After the king died, Daka was in no state to take up responsibility for Gelvurt, so I did so with her support and the support of the other High Lords Tribus."

"That must have been difficult." The food was tasting worse by the second.

"Not really." Dalton continued to eat, unabated by the subject matter. "I knew it was always a possibility with your lifestyle and Derra's penchant for surprises. There were some difficulties, yes, but nothing I didn't nip in the bud before they became legitimate issues."

Unease began to unfold in the back of my mind at his words, but I nodded. "I see. I'm thankful, then. I'm sure the people of Gelvurt appreciate your hard work."

"Those with intelligence, yes," Dalton said before he paused eating for a moment. "I have a lot to show you, Father. Gelvurt now competes with Cerula itself in terms of population and prosperity."

That was difficult to even imagine, but I trusted my son. He was never one to exaggerate about such matters.

"That's amazing, Dalton." I felt like I'd been complimenting him endlessly as we spoke, but I had years of acknowledgment to make up for. "How is the empire? What happened to Zactrik?"

"He escaped." Dalton was quiet for a moment before he shook his head. "Zactrik has become a phantom since your fight with him, although we still deal with remnants of his work. After you fell, CAD mobilized with aid from other nations to begin uprooting hidden laboratories around the world."

"So he's still biding his time?" It was hard to imagine that we had actually managed to kill Zactrik. The monster had seemed impregnable, although I could only remember the fight in pieces.

Dalton shrugged. "I suppose. I was more concerned with a civil war brewing after the houses began to accuse one another of assassinating the king. Don't worry, that was dealt with."

"That's, well, that's good." A civil war? I'd never thought that was possible, but I suppose that with Zactrik's machinations anything was within the realm of possibility. "You did not misspeak, Dalton. I have much to catch up on."

Both in my knowledge of the changed world around me and the weakness that plagued my limbs. There was little I could do to help my children if I couldn't even take care of myself.

As if taking notice of my inner concerns, Dalton wiped his mouth. "I had the alchemists prepare for your awakening in advance, Father. I have a magical healer on retainer, as well, ready to aid in your recovery."

"That—" I took a moment to consider what I'd just heard. "I appreciate that, son."

The Overseer had said that my son had gone down a dark path, but what was so dark about all that he had done in my stead? Dread began to pool in my stomach at the possibilities.

There was something bitter about being taken care of by strangers. Beyond the medicine, being in a position of weakness with so much to do, with so many concerns, it was a venom in my veins that was difficult for even these fine alchemists to find a remedy for.

"That should set you on the path to recovery, Lord Tribus," the healer, a woman by the name of Jaya, said. She was of a stouter figure and had a gentle touch. She'd barely uttered a word while lacing my weakened muscles with her magic, a testament to her expertise.

I nodded, already beginning to feel my limbs shake off the years of neglect. "I'll make sure to stick to the regimen you prescribed."

"I'm more worried about you overdoing it, Lord Tribus," Jaya scoffed kindly before she smiled. "I'll be checking in on you for the next couple of weeks, so don't think you can rush this, alright?"

Rushing was exactly what my heart wanted to do, but I soothed it for the time being and nodded once more. With that, Jaya was seemingly appeased for now and left the room, leaving me alone with my thoughts.

"Jaya's really sweet, huh?" Macy asked, a shadow in the corner of the room that I'd forgotten in the flurry of tests and concoctions that had been shoved in my face in the past hour.

I looked over to her. "Dalton's done a fine job in finding capable people."

Macy tucked a stray frizzly bang away from her face. "I, uh, yeah, he's done a great job. He's really dedicated to . . . you know, Gelvurt."

She made a strange gesture, as if to fill in her own words with motion, and I was struck by how little I knew this girl, even though I'd watched her grow up alongside my own daughter.

The quiet girl that was Natakia's best friend had grown up to be an anxious, rambling young woman, so like her mother, but in so many ways not.

"Macy, how have you been all this time?" I wanted to ask where her parents were, if she knew why Natakia had left for the Velbruns, and many other things, but . . .

She startled at the question, looking as if even she didn't quite know the answer herself, before shrugging and giving a shaky grin. "I, oh, I've been great. You know, um, Dad is still around. He's actually out on a patrol today, so, you know, he may come visit later . . ."

"And . . ." My words faltered as I saw the fear in Macy's eyes grow, both of us knowing the next inevitable question on the tip of my tongue.

"Mom." Macy knitted her hands together, letting out a breath of air. "I don't know where she's at. She went off to go find a cure for you, said that since there was something wrong in your head, um, no offense, that she could fix it . . ."

I never imagined that Doh would feel so dedicated to my condition that she'd leave to go find answers for it, away from her family. I looked up to Macy, another question on my tongue, but she cut me off.

"Years," Macy said, glancing away as if she were telling me a secret. "Her trip started before Daka left, so more than five years back . . . Crazy, right? Mom's been gone for a long time, but . . . you're back! Maybe . . . Maybe she found a solution somewhere?"

Any assurance on that matter would have been empty. The circumstances of my revival were a mystery even to me, beyond the fact that Overseer had made it clear that they had not been my savior.

"Your mother is clever, Macy." I smiled, speaking as truly as I could. "If anyone could have figured this out, I would not be surprised to learn that she did so."

"Ha." Macy nodded. "I appreciate that."

For a time we were silent before she began shifting around, red beginning to tinge her cheeks. She rubbed the back of her head, looking to the door and around the room.

"Are you alright, Macy?" She looked very uncomfortable for some reason.

Macy looked at me with a lot of concern. "I, uh, you didn't hear anything while you were, uh, sleeping, right? Like, conversations that I, well, people had around you?"

Macy never looked more like her mother than when she scrunched up her nose at the thought of being caught in something embarrassing or, more likely with Doh, mischievous.

"No, Macy, I . . . wasn't aware of my surroundings at all." Perhaps if I had been, the time I spent would not have felt quite so grueling, so painful . . . So real.

I felt a hand on my shoulder, and looked back up from that thought to see Macy looking truly concerned now. "Lord Tribus—"

"Macy." I cut her off lightly. "We are family. You don't have to treat me so formally."

For a moment I feared that I had spooked her with the interruption, but she seemed to finally relax, her lips twitching up into a smile. "Oh, uh, thanks . . . Rakta."

I smiled, and she seemed to think for a moment, regathering her courage from before, and sat down next to me. I could tell she had a question, one I suspected I knew.

"What was it like?" Her head faced down into her lap, but her eyes met mine, shining with hesitant curiosity. A macabre interest in the unknown that had almost been as much a part of her life as it had been mine.

Jaya and the alchemists had danced around the question during their examination, speaking of my time spent away from the waking world with emotionless terms and focusing on the physical.

"I'm trying not to think about it," I said honestly. "It was dark, Macy, like an ocean . . . I think I . . . I'm sorry. Thank you for caring, but there's too much to do now that I'm awake to focus on what I've endured."

Macy swallowed, nodding, before she got up abruptly, her eyes flitting to a nearby clock on the wall. "I think Dalton's probably done with his meeting . . ."

I was happy to hear that. Dalton had seemed annoyed at the reminder of his busy schedule, interrupting our reunion, but that was the life of a noble.

"I think I'm feeling well enough to walk, if you'd lead me?" I was getting quite tired of this room of mine. It was time to stretch my legs.

Macy smiled, nodding. "Sure, Rakta, just let me send word ahead."

As she went to alert another servant, I watched her go and felt my heart clench at the thought of how much Macy had lost to time and circumstance. Why did Natakia leave her here? What could Macy tell me? So much that I wanted to ask her, but would there ever be a good moment to do so?

"Alright." Macy peeked back in. "Let's get you moving. Dalton is waiting for you in the courtyard."

I nodded, standing up, before a thought struck me. *We have a courtyard?*

The Velbrun Keep that I had been familiar with, now garnished with the blues and browns of House Tribus, was larger than I remembered, with hallways and rooms made of fresher stone that had been expertly attached to the older building.

Two entire new wings expanded outward, wrapping around the property I had been expecting, with an open courtyard in the center of it all, a beautiful garden arranged all around me as I stepped out onto the cobblestone path that spiderwebbed throughout it.

"These flowers . . ." I admired the bright colors of the different Certillian breeds, feeling somewhat at a loss at identifying them all, but stopped and knelt as recognition blossomed at the sight of some of them.

They were beautiful teal rose-like flowers scattered throughout the garden among the brilliant arrangements. Jagged petals with thorny stems, like those of a cactus.

"Those are my favorite," Macy said, kneeling right beside me but sounding distant.

They were natakias, the flowers that my daughter was named after. They were so popular in Rusk that in some tribes it was considered dishonorable to propose without one in hand as a gift for your lover.

I swallowed, feeling my eyes burning wet. "How are these here?"

The natakias were frustrating flowers to grow, often needing ample room to truly flourish but requiring just the right amount of rain and heat to not die before they bloomed.

"Dalton had them brought here." Macy sighed. "It was before Natakia, well, left. The gardener is high-class, apparently has dryad in his blood or something."

Dryad? No, that wasn't of importance at the moment. I admired the beauty of the flowers and silently sent my thanks to all the hard work that brought them here.

"I will find them, Macy," I said. "No matter the paths they walk."

4

Taking my time enjoying the fresh air of the courtyard and feeling my muscles move easier with each step, I noticed Dalton in the distance, speaking to another. Approaching, I felt familiarity bubbling in the back of my mind.

She was tanned, standing strong with broad shoulders, almost half a foot over my son's own stature, with long brown hair that flowed down her shoulders, over the blue-and-brown noble gown that she wore. And by the way she stood, her fist clenched and her teeth gritted into the barest facsimile of a smile, I could tell that this noble was angry.

"Dalton," she spoke, a mix of frustration and exhaustion in her words, "Alwur is already having difficulty procuring the lumber that was promised to House Taine. We simply can't afford this additional project!"

"Is it a lack of manpower, High Lordess Tribus of Alwur?" I had never heard Dalton's voice so cold and authoritative. "Has your population suddenly decreased since your last census? I'd enjoy not having the same baseless reasoning plague me after the meeting has already ended."

I slowed my approach, my interest catching on to the conversation as Macy began to look more and more nervous. I knew that voice and that face, but it had been so long, and the darkness . . .

"It is not a question of manpower," the high lordess said, continuing despite my son's wishes. "It is a question of the resistance we face, the dishonor we invoke, if we continue to expand our operation. The risk—"

"There is always a risk." Dalton shook his head. "Yet, the risks you speak of are simple trifles that we've already dealt with before, time and time again. Do you need a refresher on how to deal with them?"

The noble paused, a flash of fear in her eyes, but she stood stalwart. "No, High Lord Tribus of Gelvurt. Do you need a refresher on the deals and promises we made in writing?"

"I remember them." Dalton nodded, looking like he was going to continue until he seemed to finally notice my approach, his form stiffening before he continued, "I'll send one of my men later to once more explain the particulars of the past agreement. That will be all."

The noble seemed surprised for a moment at the dismissal before she followed my son's gaze and met my own, her eyes widening as recognition shot through both of us at the same time.

"Caitlyn," I said, the beginnings of a smile on my lips, "it's been quite some time."

High Lordess Caitlyn Tribus, the cursed noble of the wooden city of Alwur, seemed to shimmer for a moment, briefly looking much younger, before reverting back to her present form.

"Rakta?" She took a step forward, looking completely taken off guard. "Is that really you?"

Dalton looked distinctly displeased as I approached, for reasons I couldn't put my finger on, before I nodded. "It's me, Caitlyn."

"When did you . . ." Caitlyn blinked before turning a burning glare at my son. "How long were you going to wait until you informed us he had woken up?"

My son's own look was glacial, but I swiftly spoke up in his defense. "Caitlyn, I woke up mere hours ago. I'm confident Dalton wouldn't keep such a thing secret, but we've barely had time to talk as it is."

"Is that so?" she asked, swallowing down her anger at my words, but my son's displeasure barely abated. Why were they fighting? What project had they been talking about?

"I'm glad you're back, Rakta," Caitlyn said, stepping forward and giving me a hug. I reciprocated as best I could, but it was a tad difficult with my missing limb and her new height—she was even taller than I.

I nodded, hugging her with my recovering strength. "So am I. My son and I have much to speak about, but will you be staying in Gelvurt for a time?"

"I'll make new arrangements." Caitlyn nodded. "I'll send to Jorge, let him know—"

"That won't be necessary," Dalton spoke up.

She turned to my son, already looking ready for a fight. "And why is that?"

"I've already had the news penned and sent to those with a need to know," Dalton said, his arms held gracefully behind his back. "I'd rather keep a finger on the pulse of this information rather than it spread like wildfire. My father doesn't need that kind of excitement while he recovers."

Caitlyn looked at my son with distrust, but I was beginning to feel the old chains of politics beginning to show their ugly head once more, threading themselves through every relationship.

"High Lord Tribus of Niers will receive a letter, then? About your father?" Caitlyn stood as officially as she could, the contrast of her formality with my son and her lack thereof with me being readily apparent.

My son didn't speak for a moment, glancing at me, before nodding. "I'll have one penned to him as well. I promise."

As soon as he promised, Caitlyn relaxed. I supposed that meant that, no matter their friction, my son's given word could still be trusted.

And yet, I felt like I was only scratching the surface of House Tribus's inner politics.

After some brief conversation, it was clear that Caitlyn had to depart to make her own arrangements to stay in Gelvurt for some additional time. It was sad to see her leave so soon, but I was happy to finally have spoken with an old friend, especially one that time had seemed to have forgotten.

After the farewells, Dalton finally turned to Macy and frowned. "Did I not make myself clear to keep my father unburdened by my business, Macy?"

Macy, who had been keeping distant from our conversation, flinched. Her hair whitened at the tips, as though she were a deer spooked in the forest by the cracking of branches.

"Well." She glanced at me and around the garden, as if trying to look for something. "I sent word, uh, I'm sure I sent word. I talked to Levile, and he said he'd go on up ahead and, and, uh, let you know . . ."

Dalton continued to stare at her.

"And, uh, I thought you'd be done with business because, um, I was told you were done and that, well." Macy let out a bit of nervous laughter before shrugging. "Oops?"

Dalton closed his eyes before taking a deep breath. "I will speak with Levile. If this blame is truly his, he'll find new employment elsewhere."

"Well," I said, both of them looking at me as I spoke, Macy untensing. "I was happy to see Caitlyn. It seems like she's refined her curse into a respectable technique, very impressive."

"Yes, very impressive." Dalton said the words, but there wasn't much heart in them. "I wish she would spend her time refining her policies."

From everything I remembered, Caitlyn was an admirable leader of her people, truly caring for those under her care. Something that few others within House Velbrun had ever expressed.

There was some silence between us for a moment as we walked through the garden before I noticed Dalton turn his head toward Macy from the corner of my eye.

"Oh, well, look at the time." Macy shakily giggled. "I better go, uh, check up on Rakta . . . I mean, uh, clean up his room, not that it's dirty or anything, but—"

"Macy," Dalton said, his tone brooking no further conversation.

She beat a hasty retreat, as hasty as she could without looking too unrefined, leaving my son and me alone in the courtyard, surrounded by naught but the flowers and the insects that trod on their stems.

"She's scared of you." I looked toward my son, measuring his response.

Dalton nodded. "I know. If she were anyone else, she'd have already been fired."

I frowned, thinking that was somewhat harsh of my son. I hadn't noticed any sort of mistake from her during my time with her, albeit quite short. Had the standards for servants risen?

"Anyone else, hmm?" It was good that Dalton had some affection for Doh's daughter. The Booker family had always made for good friends to have in hard times. I would have to ask Macy about a chance to see her father after so long . . .

I believed that Dresden and I would have much to talk about.

"It isn't a case of nepotism." Dalton interrupted my thoughts. "While her skills as a servant are lacking, her natural talents with memory magic and shape-shifting are good skills to have on standby."

For a moment, I thought about those words before I smiled. "It is good to have those you can trust, isn't it?"

My son almost missed a step, startled by my words, before he shook his head. "I don't trust her. I just don't think of her as a threat."

"Someone with her talents is always a threat to those who don't trust them to be otherwise," I said. It had been the same for some time when I had first met Doh. Despite the circumstances requiring me to risk trusting her far sooner than I might have had otherwise, only a fool would discount her.

"Perhaps," Dalton said noncommittally. "If there is anything I trust about Macy, it is her incompetence."

"And yet, you trust her talent enough to see her skills as assets." I knew that was a word he would pay attention to. "You believe her capable enough to keep on as a servant due to these skills but believe her not to be a threat due to her incompetence in using them."

"Father." Dalton's irritation was leaking into his words. "How was your time with the alchemists? I'm confident Jaya treated your fatigue and muscle atrophy?"

I nodded, no intention to hammer on the earlier subject. "I was given strict guidelines on exercising for the next few weeks to supplement her magic. She said I'll be healthy to travel within less than a month."

"To travel?" Dalton asked, and I nodded. I wasn't sure when I would depart on my trip to find Daka and Natakia, but I knew that I would eventually need to leave.

We continued to walk and talk about lighter things, with Dalton explaining the renovations of the Tribus Keep, the genius design of the garden and the hard work of the gardener, and many other things that weren't loaded down with the friction of our lost time together.

Until finally, as we reached the end of our walk, sitting down on a stone bench together, Dalton looked off into the distance, away from me, before turning back and meeting my gaze.

"I think going after them is a waste of time, Father."

* * *

We sat there for a while, his words lingering in the air between us. My son thought that his sisters, and pursuing them, were a waste of time. Perhaps I had merely misunderstood or misheard his words?

"Daka is likely dead," Dalton continued, stalling my deliberations. "Skilled or not, could she truly have survived so long out in Rusk alone?"

Daka had run away once before, I remembered now. A rainy night that had shown me one of the first cracks in the happiness that my little warrior had worn so openly on her chest.

I had been there to chase her then, talk to her and be there for her.

My son continued, "Natakia is the Velbrun Oracle now, so even if she wanted to return, the politics involved make it impossible. Of course, she's never visited in the years she's been gone. The last gift we received was her coming-of-age portrait."

I remembered a warning from someone, someone a long time ago whom I knew I barely trusted, even now. A warning that House Velbrun would come for my children, even as House Tribus rose in prominence. A warning I hadn't had the time to heed.

"Do you"—my mouth was dry, my words scratchy with emotion—"not want to see your sisters again, Dalton?"

"It isn't . . ." Dalton went silent for a moment, and I dared not look at him. I kept my focus on some nearby flowers. "I have a responsibility as the High Lord Tribus of Gelvurt. When your responsibilities fell to me, I was not as . . . prepared for them as I thought. I had to focus to keep House Tribus from being strangled in the crib. I still have to."

The political enemies that I had accrued during my time as Lord Velbrun of Gelvurt would not have disappeared after my descent into the obsidian nightmare of my mind. They would have pestered my family, my people, and everything I had fought for.

Did I not have such thoughts before? Times when I had to weigh the importance of fatherhood against the importance of nobility? The responsibilities I had not only to my children, but to the people of the empire? Could I truly fault my son for such thoughts?

No, I realized, there was no fault here. There was no need for fault or judgment. My children had struggled in my absence, but I was here now.

"Thank you, Dalton," I said, reaching out with my arm and hugging him close to my side. "I'm sure words can never truly show how difficult it was for you and your sisters. You've done an amazing job."

"Father?" Dalton looked at me, confused.

I continued, "Daka might be dead? Natakia has no desire to return? I feel it in my heart that they are out there, that they want to come home. And I know that you want to see them again."

"You're being foolish, Father." Dalton frowned, standing up and out of my grip, looking down at me with an uncompromising gaze. "You've only just woken up, and you're already making designs to waste your life. You're making a mockery of all the work I've put in for you."

"Dalton, I love all of you so much," I said, standing up and putting a hand on his shoulder. "And I know you never stopped caring for your sisters."

"You can't possibly think that," Dalton said, frowning. His body was still, barely an inkling in the language of his movements regarding how he felt.

Perhaps he had changed—perhaps all of them had—but I trusted that there were ever-present truths that had not been marred by time.

"You never stopped having the natakias cared for," I said, looking at the beautiful desert lilies around us. "And I know you would only have such confidence in Daka's demise if you had sent out search parties."

My son sighed, rubbing his forehead. It was the only hint to his growing frustration, Dalton shaking his head as he finally bit out his rough words. "Even if you're right, that doesn't change what I said. My sisters were the ones to leave, not me. I stayed. I made Gelvurt great. That was how I endured."

He moved away, my hand sliding off of his shoulder, and began to walk off and out of the garden, before stopping and looking over his shoulder back at me.

"Let me know how your recovery goes, Father," Dalton said, a determined edge to his words. "I'll show you just how far Gelvurt has come once you're able."

And then he was off, but I was relieved even in my sudden loneliness. My son was a hard man, but in his heart there was still love for those around him, no matter how much he denied it.

I agreed with my son. I would learn much about all that he'd done for Gelvurt.

5

Recovery was a familiar pastime; an adventuring lifestyle was rife with moments of downtime for the sake of keeping healthy. And yet, no story ever spoke of such moments—for a reason.

Plain and simple, it was very boring and made worse by the knot of impatience that had nestled its way into my heart over the last week. My son had scant time for me except for in the evenings, leaving me often alone with my personal attendant, Macy Booker.

"I'm not used to you being awake yet," Macy spoke as she came into my room without knocking, bringing in with her a platter of fruits and meat that smelled heavenly.

I nodded, doing some final stretches as I felt the medicine in my system bolstering my Vitae. It was a new medicine, not one I'd ever heard of before, but it was effective and certainly expensive.

"I suppose neither am I." I had not just made efforts to recover physically, but also mentally. It was difficult, however. It had been difficult to sleep, a fear gripping me every time I almost found rest. No matter my resolve, there was no ease in comforting that terror.

Macy put down the platter on a small table for me, before she seemed to register what I had said. "Hmm?"

"Hmm?" I echoed back, unsure of what she was questioning.

Macy blinked before she paled as the tips of her hair went a familiar white once again. "I, uh, I said that out loud?"

"Well, did you,"—I almost struggled to even respond to the bundle of nerves that Macy had become—"not mean to?"

She stood frozen, and I could see her reassessing her every movement before I chuckled at her misplaced fear, making her jump slightly, nervously giggling along with me.

"Macy, calm yourself. You didn't say anything wrong." Of course, Macy was one of the few who spoke candidly to me within these halls. The last thing I wanted was to taint her honesty with anxiety.

Her fingers wove together nervously as she nodded, swallowing hard as her hair shifted back. "I, yeah, sorry. I'm just really used to speaking my mind here."

"You still can," I assured her. I'd never faulted Doh for speaking her mind, perhaps in part from knowing the futility of admonishing her for such a thing, and would give the same benefit to her daughter.

Macy nodded hesitantly before she began to arrange everything for my meal. Dalton had insisted I take my meals in my room to keep the rumors of my awakening to a minimum.

In fact, solitude had been a constant plague on my return.

"I should be joined for lunch by Caitlyn, yes?" It had been a week since our reunion in the garden, and she had only just recently been granted an audience with me, another of Dalton's insistences.

Macy nodded, putting down the second platter, obviously meant for my incoming companion. "Uh, yes, absolutely. One of the servants just mentioned seeing High Lordess Tribus of Alwur."

Good, that was good. It was difficult to learn about how much the world had changed from the books that Macy had brought to me, although I'd gotten some interesting information. Apparently, there had been a stirring of civil war after Shawn's death, prompting a lot of maneuvers from the queen.

Including the announcement of Dalton Velbrun, Lydia's brother, as the Warlock King and the utter political incineration that had followed. They had even lost some of their land. I mourned the broken promise made to Lydia, but it had stitched the fractured empire back together.

Furthermore, my awakening had only come a few months after the official crowning of King Winfred Certimov-Hanchett, who had finally come of age. Tracy had swiftly abdicated the throne for her son's benefit.

So much had changed, a lot that I was still digesting, but I pushed such thoughts aside as a knock came at the door, Macy taking a deep breath as she went to answer.

I would finally get to talk to Caitlyn.

"And ever since, Julian has been pining after the baker's daughter like she doesn't have plenty of other better choices." Caitlyn giggled, currently in her adult form. She seemed far less stressed than she had a week ago, but her Vitae was far less composed.

I pushed my cleaned plate to the side, wiping my mouth with a bit of cloth to wipe the last trace of sauce away. "I missed these conversations."

Caitlyn stilled, and her thin facade faltered as she nodded solemnly. We sat in silence for a moment, the only sound being the rustling of cloth and clattering of ceramic as Macy cleaned up the table for us.

"There's so much to talk about, Rakta," Caitlyn said. "About Gelvurt, Alwur, the state of the border . . . and your son. I don't even know where to begin."

I swallowed back the protectiveness that stirred at the idea of her speaking of my son, but I had been curious about such things myself. How does one even begin to learn about eight years of change?

"How is the academy?" Despite everything, I felt that learning that would be the quickest way to get to the larger picture.

Caitlyn sighed, looking away. "It's still very popular and a great benefit to our lands. Education, I'd say, is something that House Tribus is most known for."

It sounded very rote and practiced, tinged with a bittersweetness that curdled the warm memories of getting the academy together so many years ago for the sake of my children.

"What happened?" Perhaps I should not have declined the wine that Macy had offered.

"Like I said, it's very popular," Caitlyn said again, but continued, "Dalton has done a lot to expand the academy, even making smaller branch academies in Alwur and Niers, but . . ."

For a moment, she was at the edge of rage. Her Vitae was powerful and free, which made it easy to feel the swirling maelstrom it was at risk of becoming.

"I should have seen it coming." She squeezed her fist hard. "Of course it's more convenient for families of our lands to go to these branch academies, I have no doubt of that, but that left vacancies here. Vacancies that Dalton auctioned off to the nobles of other houses."

Macy was quiet in the corner of the room, watching on with a worried expression as Caitlyn took a drink of her own glass of wine.

"And then, funding became an issue when Queen Certimov's support dwindled. Bigger things on her plate than the academy after her husband died," she muttered the last bit before sobering. "Dalton began footing the cost himself, but the branch academies started to falter. Our funding goes straight to Tribus Academy, but it's the Tribus Education Council that decides the budget and where the money goes."

I understood quite clearly the venom that laced the title of this council as it left her lips. This council was not doing well to give these branch academies the support they required and, if I understood correctly, something must be preventing Caitlyn and Jorge from supporting their branches directly.

"They even dismissed teachers deemed unworthy of their positions," she whispered, as if at the end of her wits on the subject. "Marge was one of the first to go."

My stomach twisted at the news of the alchemist's dismissal. I remembered her opening up to the students, seeing them all as the children she had lost that night when I'd first arrived in Gelvurt.

"I suppose Dalton is not unaware of this," I offered diplomatically, but it felt dry leaving my lips. It was hard to imagine such a thing slipping by his attention. Rather, I imagined that he implicitly supported much of what had occurred.

Caitlyn sniffed, almost sneering at my son's name. "Who do you think formed the council? Who do you think puppets them around? Gelvurt is the heart of House Tribus, and Dalton decides where the blood flows."

"These failing branches of Tribus Academy," I began, still digesting the delicacy of this subject. "Can the families not return to Gelvurt?"

"Absolutely," Caitlyn frowned. "Of course, there's a fee."

"A fee." I wrapped my head around the idea of having to pay to attend the academy. The original idea had been to keep the academy cost free, to keep its doors open to all who wished to attend.

"Not for the people of Gelvurt, of course." Caitlyn grinned sardonically, glancing over at Macy before turning back to me. "And the ones who stayed at the main academy when the branches were built, oh, they've been grandfathered in, but those who left? Hoping to get a similar experience at their homes? There's a relocation fee, not one that common folk can afford."

It painted a grim picture. Tribus Academy was seemingly of higher quality than I could even imagine, but it was now simply bait for those beyond Gelvurt, to draw them in and exploit their interests.

"I'll speak to him about this," I said, knowing how hard Caitlyn must be fighting for her people. Jorge, I'm sure, was suffering under this as well. They were the roots of the academy, working with me to get it running, and to have it be taken from their hands by my own son . . .

Caitlyn nodded, but I felt her appreciation was tinged with doubt. Doubt that I could change my son's mind? Doubt that I could ever side against my own son? I wouldn't deride her lack of faith either way.

"I hope you do, Rakta," she finally said. "Jorge and I are high lords, just like him, but Dalton has done more in the last eight years than I could do in my whole lifetime. He is the only reason House Tribus survived, no, thrived in your absence. Alwur and Niers pale in comparison to Gelvurt now. We just don't have . . . We can't do what he's done."

For as long as I had known her, Caitlyn had been a proud woman who cared for her people and the good of her lands far more than the average noble. And yet, that pride fell to the wayside now.

Perhaps it was the waning hours and her curse that made her seem older, but in this moment, I saw the weight of the last eight years in her wrinkled eyes and her weathered fingers. How did she feel, I wondered, about the success of my son who, by all accounts, had been unceremoniously thrown into his position?

"My son," I said, "has always had the capability of doing great things. I'm sorry that he hasn't spared a thought for Alwur and Niers. Our lands have always been stronger together, but Gelvurt should not be claiming a seat at the top by standing on the bloody shoulders of its siblings."

Macy was fidgeting as Caitlyn closed her eyes and took a deep breath. She opened her eyes, glancing at the shape-shifting maid again before meeting my gaze. "That's good. I'm glad you're back, Rakta."

"I am too." I was finally starting to learn more about my son, but there was so much more to know. How many stories had I missed? "I want to know about the timber situation in Alwur."

Neither Caitlyn nor Macy looked pleased as they registered my request.

I had asked Overseer for the gift of understanding, to know my children, but it had yet to reveal its inner workings to me as I arrived at Dalton's office hours later, documents in hand. They were wrinkled and folded, having lost their crispness in the time I'd spent going over every inch of copy.

I went to knock, but the door opened before my knuckle met the wood. Macy bit her lip as she met my gaze briefly before she ducked her head and whispered an apology as she left Dalton's office. She hurried away without another word before sharply turning down the first hallway she came across.

"Father," Dalton called from his office, "I think we have a lot to talk about."

Walking in, I inspected the room, remembering faintly when it was where I did my own similar work, but as opposed to the notion of a room getting messier over the years, more full of history, Dalton's office was empty. Only a few quaint reminders that someone worked here, a portrait or two and a large bookshelf and a small side table with a glass decanter of wine.

And in the middle of all of it, a large wooden desk, inlayed with bronze and gold that shimmered with Mana. My son, sitting behind the desk, had his eyes on the document before him but his attention on me.

"Please sit." Dalton motioned to one of the chairs in front of his desk. I was sure that Macy had just stood up from it moments before, the furniture half-askew.

Pulling the chair up and sitting down, I wondered if the gift of understanding was an understated one, one that would benefit me in the act of learning over time, rather than through a great revelation. Perhaps, I considered, that was for the best. Prophetic insight often lacked any kind of obvious nuance.

And yet, it would be nice to know what was going on behind my son's cold, emerald eyes. Once again, his body language was erased, his posture was cold and mechanical, and there was no insight to garner from his gaze.

From this cold facade, I could make out one thing for certain. Dalton was expecting an enemy, some kind of plot or scheme. If Macy had told him all of what Caitlyn and I had discussed, then perhaps he had reason to believe I was here to trick him or manipulate him.

Was that what I was here to do? There should be no politics between family and yet here I was with clear opposition to my son and his pressure on Alwur. And yet, in my heart, I knew . . .

"I always knew this was going to happen," I said, reclining back into my chair, feeling the weight of age. "An effective plan, efficient in every corner, but . . ."

Dalton frowned, making no other movements.

"The spirit of the promise is being held hostage for a few extra acres worth of lumber," I said, my eyes gliding lightly over the inked parchment.

It was a deal with the forest near one of Alwur's newest lumber camps, full of dryads and nymphs. Forest monsters that were generally peaceful unless disturbed, but years ago, they had well and truly been disturbed by the growing timber requirements from Alwur.

"They seemed perfectly happy with the deal when it benefited them. The Alwur Nature Preservation Agreement saved lives and profits while giving the forest denizens safety in land perfectly suited for them," Dalton said. "However, I made it very clear in the agreement that a time may come when those protections would need to be moved. Alwur must meet their deadline, Father."

I'd heard about this deadline in much detail. Caitlyn had made it very clear that this deadline was unlike any other, with little time to properly acquire the needed materials from Alwur's exhausted lands.

"House Taine may want new ships, but this agreement speaks of necessity." I rubbed my head, trying to figure out my son's labyrinthian logic. "I see no necessity other than the expedient deadline, which, from my understanding, you accepted without delay. Why is this sacrifice necessary beyond preference?"

That was the heart of the issue. Perhaps in a time of crisis, this would all be reasonable, but there was no crisis that I knew of, nor was there one that Caitlyn or Macy could provide for me.

"House Taine's offer is extraordinarily profitable, but they were adamant about the timeline." For the first time during this conversation, Dalton seemed bothered. "I made the deal, however, because right now it is vitally important for Gelvurt to boast financial excellence."

For a moment, I was confused at such importance before I remembered one of the first things I learned after waking up.

"This is about the Donns of Neve," I said.

Dalton closed his eyes and nodded. "I have a representative arriving near the deadline to take the final steps for my membership, something that will bring influence and power to our city that has only ever been witnessed in the capitals of great nations."

There was that zeal again, that desire to make Gelvurt greater and greater every day. I wondered if the city would ever shine bright enough for him.

"That is why it's necessary," Dalton finished. "This support could affirm House Tribus as a player in the empire without question. Even the king could not question our legitimacy."

I doubted that he ever would, our position lacking legitimacy or not. It was his father who had given us this land and our titles, but . . . one issue remained.

"Perhaps this truly is necessary, Dalton." I nodded, looking at the agreement in my hand. "If it truly is so important, what about your . . . other capabilities?"

Given to him by Overseer just as all my children's abilities had been, his was the ability to buy and sell from an esoteric shop that only he could perceive. Years ago, he had bought the knowledge of a surgeon and rare and exotic poisons, and that had only felt like the tip of the iceberg.

Dalton was quiet for a moment, matching my gaze with his own, before turning his head to the side. "It is Alwur's responsibility to meet the quota before the deadline. Why would I hurt my personal profits to aid them in their lands' issues?"

"Because they are our allies? Their people are kin to our people? Why must we set the wrath of the forest on Alwur just so Gelvurt can prosper?

Will we aid them with the trouble we pressure them to bring upon themselves?" I felt an anger stirring in my chest, knowing that this was wrong. I had made plenty of deals in my time, but none had cost the lives and safety of my people. "Why do you push them and yet give them no aid?"

There was silence before Dalton stood up out of his chair. I instinctively followed suit before he went over to his decanter of wine and silently poured himself a glass.

"Because, Father." He took a sip. "The other high lords of House Tribus, the ones you remember so fondly as friends and political allies, plan to have me killed."

6

During the war, at Lydia's behest, I slew many under the cover of darkness. I was no true assassin, not by training, but moving as swiftly as the wind through the night saw me amply capable of ending the lives of many without a struggle.

And yet, her aim had been pure. To save her brother, to truly bring him back to their family, no one could know his true identity. Witches and other higher-ups in the Warlock King's army never saw me coming, and only their remains were left to greet Shawn and the others when we arrived.

"That can't be . . ." I was without words, struck by the pure and honest accusation that had left my son's lips. The very idea that Caitlyn and Jorge would plan such a thing against my child . . .

Instinctively, it made me suddenly so angry that I could rend all of Alwur and Niers down around their heads, but the chill of reason calmed me. I breathed, letting the sudden rage leave me in puffs of hot air.

"I've already dealt with one assassin," Dalton said, drinking his wine as he watched me rein in my anger. "It's just how it is. Success is a bright light that others either want to have or to snuff out."

He walked back over to his desk, putting the glass of wine down on the reinforced wood. He rubbed his finger around the rim, staring amusedly down at the liquid.

"I'm effectively immune to poison, one of the first purchases I made once you were gone," Dalton said. "I still check for it, of course. You can never be too cautious."

"You are immune to poisons?" That was a relief, but not one that I was relieved to feel. Attempts on my children? By the gods, was Natakia alright!? House Velbrun basically signed their contracts with poison.

Dalton nodded. "I'm not a fighter like you and Daka, Father. I don't train. I invest, and I do it wisely. Spells and techniques to aid in any situation, cheap combinations that keep me alive."

Both spells and techniques? That was, well, I . . . I sat back down in my chair. This conversation was somewhat overwhelming, but at least I was getting answers. I could deal with the new questions later, but for now, there was one thing on my mind.

"How are you sure that Caitlyn and Jorge are involved in these assassination attempts?" That's what I needed to know. I needed to know where my son's suspicions had come from.

He sat down in his own chair and seemed deep in thought himself for a moment. A distant voice in the back of my head was relieved to see that his expression was no longer guarded.

"Evidence wise, I have little physical or definitive proof," Dalton admitted, not looking happy to say it aloud. "However, gifts from Jorge have had poison in them recently. If it were only once, I'd assume it was just an opportunity taken by a third party."

And yet, apparently it had happened multiple times. There was no telling who was behind it, but Jorge was the clearest suspect.

"Have you confronted him about it?" That was the next step. A man had sent multiple poisoned gifts, if Dalton's suspicions were true, so there should be some reaction to a confrontation, right? Jorge had never been one for pressure, and my son seemed skilled at intimidation.

Dalton sighed. "I've dabbled in some light insinuations, but he's so soft, Father. It isn't easy to know what's a sign of guilt or a sign of anxiety. It's just like dealing with Macy."

"And Caitlyn?" It seemed my son at least had reasons to believe it was Jorge but nothing truly incriminating. Obviously, my son knew that this could still be a ploy, or he would have been more direct now.

"Jorge's poisoned gifts began arriving around a month ago," Dalton said, raising a finger before raising a second as he continued. "And I believe that Caitlyn has decided to be more direct, hence the assassin. They failed and perished in the act. Now, I believe this whole Alwur business is just an excuse to get me out of the safety of Gelvurt to somewhere more vulnerable."

I wasn't sure which was harder to believe. That Jorge was sending poisoned gifts or that Caitlyn was directly trying to have my son killed, and yet that anger I had heard in her voice . . .

"Why do you think they want to kill you?" The question broke from my train of thought and passed my lips before I could give it another moment of consideration.

Dalton blinked before shaking his head. "I don't suppose that really matters. Like I said, success attracts enemies and, even worse, friends."

"So you think their attempts are born from simple envy?" It had led plenty to murder, but something about this wasn't right. Something about my son's suspicions didn't fit together well.

"I'm leading House Tribus to a golden age," Dalton bit out, a fierce anger and frustration suddenly clipping his words. "Only fools would find that a reason for murder. In fact . . ."

He rubbed his finger across one of the bits of metal on his desk, and I saw golden motes of magical light suddenly blend together as they rose from the metal before kaleidoscoping into the facsimile of an old clock, the time ticking as if it were the real thing.

"There should be enough light still." Dalton smiled. "Your recovery has been going well, Father. I think it's time to finally see Gelvurt. Perhaps you can find their reasons for trying to have me killed."

The weight of the seriousness of the conversation lightened slightly as I rose from my chair, feeling the first beads of excitement beginning to collect in my chest. There was still so much to talk about, but I was interested in making up for lost time with my son.

Once upon a time, a widower came to the small village of Gelvurt with his three newborns in tow, looking for a simple life with his children. He hadn't thought much of the place at the time, but it had quickly become a home for him and his younglings.

And now, right before my eyes, I could see just how much Gelvurt had grown while I was asleep. From the beginnings of cobblestone that I remembered only eight years ago, I now saw proper streets as far as the eye could see.

Once, the estate had been a decent walk from the town proper of Gelvurt, but now it surrounded the holdings of House Tribus, businesses and temples alike, with the chimneys of blacksmiths and simple family homes churning soot into the air all around.

It was cold. Was it winter? It had to be winter. A proper winter that had me flexing my Vitae to keep myself warm as I took my first steps with my son into his city, our city.

It was like I was in Cerula, the capital of the empire. I could see in the distance a proper wall, rising high above the rooftops of Gelvurt and all throughout the streets I could see so many people, more people than I ever imagined even visiting my fair town at the peak of trading season.

"I'm glad you like it." Dalton put a hand on my shoulder and pointed into the distance, and I felt a bittersweetness as I saw the familiar towering structure of Tribus Academy.

It was not much taller than I remembered it being, but it now spiderwebbed outward, with its own walls erected around it to keep others out of it.

I looked at Dalton, remembering Caitlyn's words. "Is it still a place for all of Tribus's lands to learn?"

"There have been changes," Dalton admitted somewhat evasively, "but there are bright minds still growing there, new doors opening for them every day."

There was so much to say to that, but I acquiesced to the moment and smiled at my son. He was proud of all that he had done, and simply put, so was I. To think that this had happened within so few years . . .

"Gelvurt has changed so quickly." Even the clothing that some of the passersby were wearing looked different, with finely stitched weaves and new colored designs catching my eye.

My son began to walk with me, pointing to various things as we talked. "I was awarded for my efforts to save the late king and invested a lot of that into businesses abroad and locally. The wall was a yearlong project that I brought in an experienced group of stone magicians to get done expediently."

"Was there a reason for the haste?" A wall was a strange thing for simple luxury, as far as I saw it.

Dalton waved his hand lightly. "Simple Ruskan banditry and the monsters that sometimes migrate nearby. Nothing too notable."

I felt like he was downplaying the severity of the danger but continued to follow his finger as he showed me the extent of his work and the businesses of others. I felt something almost childlike as I saw so many new things in my home, only tempered by the mature assessment of how monetarily impressive each new sight was.

And then the familiar sound of something large ripping through the sky above me filled me with a surge of adrenaline as I reached for my weapon . . . with an arm I no longer had and with a weapon I no longer possessed.

The unease of my vulnerability was quieted as I saw what had alarmed me: the underside of a flying galleon, the ship's bow piercing the air in front of it like it was surging through the waves.

"I had heard that ships fly now," I said, amazement in my voice, "but to see it in person is entirely different."

There was a story of a Ruskan who sailed the winds in a ship of ancient make, but to see such a thing in person, it was a dream that I thought was certainly one I had put to rest in my boyhood.

Dalton and I watched the airship begin to fly to the edge of the wall before beginning to dip down. My son pointed in the direction it had gone. "That's where our airship unloading bay is. If anything has made the world move quicker, it's Penelope's airships."

I nodded before blinking. Penelope's name had yet to come up in all of our discussions about these amazing achievements of magic. Why had I not heard of Penelope's involvement before now?

The question plagued me, and I was about to ask my son more when we rounded a corner and I saw it, all thoughts of airships leaving me for the moment.

A familiar sight that made my heart swell with nostalgia I hadn't realized I'd been aching for. With a bright new paint job and its windows larger than I remembered, giving passing common folk a peek inside, was the general store that had greeted me nearly twenty years ago.

"Orion's general store," I said, beginning to approach the building. "Although, I suppose it's just called Orion's now."

The sign above the door frame confirmed it for me. I supposed it was a proper name for the business, having come far from when it was simply a store for deliveries and the odd assortment of delights.

"Father . . ." Dalton followed me into the storefront but seemed far less invested than I was. I supposed that made sense. I was perhaps a little too excited to see an old, familiar face.

Walking inside, I saw a young man behind the counter, currently putting away sils that he had been counting before I walked in. "Excuse me. I was wondering if Orion was in town. I'm an old friend."

"Oh?" The young man, with golden curls and bright-green eyes, blinked. "I'm sorry, sir, but I believe he works out of Cerula these days. That's what I've heard at least."

Ah, that made sense. Orion had been turning out to be quite the opportunist years ago when Gelvurt had begun to grow. He was probably the enterprising type that fit quite well in Dalton's massive upheaval of the local area.

"Ah, I see. Thank you for the help." I made a passing glance at the goods of the establishment, noticing a few new sweets and general amenities, before making for the door alongside my quiet son. The offerings of the store were far less interesting than getting to meet my old friend.

I smiled at my son, who seemed lost in thought. "I'm sorry for the sudden detour. I suppose you already knew Orion wouldn't be around."

"Ah, yes." Dalton nodded. "He's overseeing some of my holdings in Cerula."

I blinked. "I see. I thought he might be doing some of his own work."

There were implications that I let fall silently between us as we walked, my eyes flitting to the buildings around us, before Dalton put a hand on my arm.

"Father," Dalton spoke, no discernable emotion in his words, "I bought out all Orion's businesses after he went bankrupt years ago. I own that general store. He works for me now; so does his son."

There was a moment of disquiet between us, and I tried to parse my son's words, no, not just the words but, rather, the intent. Why was he telling me this? Why was he being so forthright with this?

"You gave him a job during a dark moment, Dalton," I said, smiling at him. "I wouldn't mind getting to see him right now, but I'll have to keep it in mind the next time I'm at the capital."

I could tell there was more that he wanted to say, but he gave a rough nod and continued onward, beginning his tales of the rise of Gelvurt once more.

My son would have made a good, but very dry, storyteller. He efficiently carved out the story of Gelvurt's rise as if he had practiced it, but there was little mystique to his words. And yet, there was a subtle passion in his voice as he spoke that I imagined gave pause to all whom he shared it with.

"And finally, we come to the most recent site of Gelvurt's development," Dalton said, rounding a corner. "We would be nowhere near this level of development if it weren't for one person, in particular."

A single person? I wondered what kind of support Dalton had gotten in the early days of his administration if one person had seemingly been the pillar of all of this.

I rounded the corner myself and felt the breath leave me for a moment as I saw the grand building before me, not much bigger than the storefronts around, but the architecture was . . . It wasn't Certillian or, rather, not entirely Certillian.

The staple Certillian foundations and window panes were of obvious note, but the drapery of color and brilliant design, the arching entrance with no doorway, and the smooth domed roof were . . . They were Ruskan.

My eyes were eventually pulled down from the roof to the intricately carved sandstone sign that was erected out in the street in front of the building that read *The Tribus Museum of Rakta the Dancer.*

This was a museum dedicated to me.

7

In Kakrel, the capital of Rusk and one of the few standing cities in my home nation, there was a grand bazaar where all things were sold. And in the center of the merchantry was the oldest building in all of Rusk, the first palace of the Grand Cipher, a majestic monument of ancient Ruskan artifacts.

"I don't deserve something like this," I said, digesting the existence of an entire museum dedicated to me, to the stories of a single man. How could any single man deserve this?

"You don't," Dalton said, coming up alongside me. "It's terribly invasive, but the people of Gelvurt deserve to remember the reason why they enjoy the life they do."

Common folk passed us by in silence, some of them glancing at Dalton and me in interest but quickly moving along. Did they recognize me? They must recognize Dalton; he had been their leader for years.

"Do you want to go inside?" He took a small step toward the open door, motioning inside.

In all honesty, I wasn't sure. Did I want to go inside? Did I want to see the stories I'd left behind? How much of my life was truly on display within this building? Did it speak of Lydia?

"I suppose it couldn't hurt." There was a slight chill of death running down my spine as I entered the museum after Dalton. It was like looking down into my own empty tomb after getting out of it.

And yet, the museum smelled of home. Not just Gelvurt, but of Rusk. Dalton led me through the welcoming room, making subtle motions to the servants of the establishment, and I noticed so much flora that I knew would never blossom so elegantly in Certillian soil without the work of magic or expertise.

Flowering cacti of beautiful hues and colors were artfully on display in every corner, with flowers I recognized from my journey throughout as we entered deeper in.

And as Dalton silently strode through the halls of the museum, I began to see them, the display cases with my things in them. Clothes that I had worn in the past, gifts that I had been given by officials, and so many more remnants of my life as an adventurer and as a noble.

And above them, I noticed these metal plates, no, they were plaques, plaques with fine script engraved into the surface of the material. One spoke of a time that I had saved a small family from some bandits, while another spoke of a time when I was the only reason a soldier survived a sudden ambush by invisible monsters.

These were stories, stories of me collected throughout the empire.

"It wasn't difficult," Dalton said, motioning to the many plaques on the walls, arranged over the glass displays. "I offered a small reward for any who had known you to come forward with their stories, purchasing the right to have them engraved and put on display here in perpetuity."

Ruskan belief was that stories were to be shared by word of mouth, to keep the spirits held with them free to wander the world. To put stories down onto paper, or in this, metal, was often seen as trapping the spirit within. And yet, that was not why I felt a rising discomfort in my bones as I read more and more.

These were stories and things meant to be shared in my passing, to remember me once I had left this material plane, and yet I, still breathing, looked upon them. I was getting to peek at a small way the world would remember me, but I had yet to see any curse or criticism upon my name.

"Where are the times I lost or fled?" I idly looked around, wondering aloud for only my son to hear. "These all speak of my heroics, but did I not have enemies? I doubt that none held a grudge against me."

Not to mention the years that I had been a simple bandit for the Kroterruk Tribe. There were faces that still haunted me, fathers simply trying to protect their loved ones from our assault.

Dalton looked faintly amused. "I didn't have a museum commissioned to insult your name, Father. Of course, we have more thorough archives of stories documented in storage; that's where we've put less flattering tales. That was where we decided to put Penelope's stories."

Penelope had shared stories about me? That was the most comforting thing I'd heard since entering this building. If anyone were to put forth an honest retelling of my virtues and failures, it was her.

"I would rather be remembered than honored," I said, walking over to one of the other display cases and seeing that it was none other than my weapon, Crow, within. "I may need this one back."

It was still just as I remembered, it's onyx-black metal unmarred by time due to all the powerful enchantments that Penelope had inlaid into it during its construction. I was somewhat out of practice with throwing using my left hand, but that was what training was for.

"That can be arranged," Dalton said, sounding somewhat less excited than when we had first entered.

Ah, I realized what I'd done. Dalton had done all of this for me, and I was, well, I seemed to have only shared my criticisms of his hard work.

"Dalton, thank you," I said, turning to him and hugging him suddenly to my chest with my remaining arm. "In Rusk, it is a father's greatest joy to hear stories of himself from his own children. It means they were worth remembering. I'm grateful that this is how you wished me remembered, even as I wasted away."

Perhaps it was only due to the privacy afforded to us by the empty museum hallway, but Dalton's arms came to wrap around me, a tinge of hesitation in his affection that could not be hidden.

It was over dinner, hours later, when Dalton finally spoke once more about what had taken us out onto the streets of Gelvurt.

"So, what problems did you see, Father?" Dalton took a bite out of his food, a pristine-looking salad. "The people are happy, the businesses flourishing, and crime is at an all-time low. Why, I ask, would someone wish to kill me?"

It was a question that had been in the back of my mind as we walked, but one that I had pushed aside to enjoy the time with my son. There was no place to wonder why my trusted friends wished to assassinate my son while enjoying the sights of all his hard work.

And yet, now, I had the time to center myself and truly consider it. I already had some answers to his questions, motivations for such a thing, but that wasn't where my mind wandered. It wandered to my son's suspicions, that feeling of incorrectness.

"How long have you been expecting them to assassinate, Dalton?" I set my fork down, finally beginning to settle on what was bothering me. "When did you first believe them to be threats?"

Dalton paused before smiling with lidded eyes that seemed to glisten with bittersweet satisfaction. "I knew they'd be threats the moment Daka signed away her claim to your status."

That confirmed my suspicions. I imagined that perhaps this was a remnant of his time on Earth, from his life before, but my son truly trusted those who came to him with friendship less than those who openly opposed him. That was why this didn't make sense.

"Dalton, I don't think Caitlyn or Jorge mean you harm," I said firmly. Dalton seemed to blink in surprise before his expressions were wiped away by whatever strange talents he had purchased. "I think they have issues with your actions, your duplicity, and your seeming lack of concern for the lives of their people."

Unless Jorge had changed an unfathomable degree while I slept, I could not imagine the jolly friend of mine, who was certainly willing to butter people up for politics, would go so far as poison.

Perhaps Caitlyn had the edge to do so, but out of simple envy? No, she would do so only to protect her people. She would never take pleasure in it though. She would never kill my son and feel nothing but victory.

"I don't know who is trying to kill you." I imagined the possibilities could be quite numerous. "But I will put a stop to them and find the answer in all of this. I want you to be able to trust your allies, not fear them."

He listened to me, at least, I assumed he did. He stared at me with an expressionless face before nodding. "Then I suppose we'll see. There's a gathering in two weeks. Jorge and Caitlyn will be in attendance, a perfect opportunity to see for yourself."

"And this deadline for timber? Will you continue to pressure Alwur to the brink of conflict with the forest?" I would be a poor father if I simply allowed my son to do so without question.

"And what," Dalton asked very carefully, "do you think I should do, Father? Or rather, what will you do if I say yes? Do you think your wisdom would benefit Gelvurt more than my intelligence?"

I knew this would come eventually. My son had been worried about his continued position since my awakening. Power and wealth—Dalton was so worried about losing all that he had worked for.

"Dalton, just because I think you are making a mistake does not mean that you are unfit as a leader," I said, frowning. "Since before House Tribus, the lands of Alwur, Niers, and Gelvurt have always worked together and benefited from it. The single man that helped build Gelvurt would have failed were he truly alone, and that is why I insist that they, if no one else, are worthy of trust."

I took a sip of wine before picking up my fork to take a bite of chicken. The servants had very kindly prepared my food to allow for easier consumption with one arm.

"We must acknowledge our mistakes in the same breath as we honor our victories," I said. "That is the importance of being remembered, the wisdom in all that is recorded and learned from."

To that, there was no answer from my son. We ate in silence before my son retreated to his office for the night and I was left alone, except for the quiet presence of Macy. I finished my own meal before leaving for my room, noticing that Macy was quick to follow.

"Rakta, I'm sorry." Her words were quiet but earnest.

I was confused for a moment before remembering that it had been quite obvious that she had spoken to my son about all that I had discussed with Caitlyn. Likely not the first time such a thing had happened, remembering Caitlyn's glances to the young maid during our meal.

"No, Macy," I said, smiling at her. "I appreciate you being there for my son."

Macy blinked. "I warned him about everything, though, about what Caitlyn said, about your questions, about the documents you asked for afterward..."

"I would never want to ambush my son, Macy," I said. "I wanted to speak to him about important matters, but I'm not here to undermine him. I'm here to be there for him, and I'm relieved that, for all he says otherwise, he trusts you."

"R-really?" Macy looked stunned for a moment before she smiled. "I, uh, I would never have thought that . . ."

With everything said, I began to depart down the hallway once more before she spoke up once again. "Rakta, I . . . I want to be there for you too. I want you to know things, to help Dalton."

I looked over my shoulder back toward her, noticing how badly she was shaking in the hallway. Her fingers wove together, and her cheeks were flushed with anxiety.

"I . . . I have to tell you," she whimpered. "Natakia. I heard Dalton say that she'll be at the upcoming gathering."

That news was a strike to my system, but before I could respond, Macy ran off with a frantically whispered farewell, looking like she was shifting as she rounded the corner.

"That's . . . good to hear," I said to the empty hallway.

I had been staring at the portrait of Natakia for a while now. She had come of age two years ago, the last painting she ever sent to the Tribus Estate. The last time, to my knowledge, she had ever had anything to do with Gelvurt or her brother.

She was beautiful, just like her mother. She held herself with a confidence that befitted the oracle of House Velbrun, a vaunted position that her mother had held herself. And yet, Lydia had never spoken fondly of it; rather, she had never spoken of it at all.

And her eyes, her eyes shimmered with the glow of being alive. It must have been a talented painter, for now, in my time of quiet contemplation, I almost felt watched by them.

How had my desert flower fared in that pit of vipers? Had Markus aided her in her pursuit of whatever had led her to join with House Velbrun? Or had Lydia's brother been yet another whispered venom now flowing through my daughter's veins?

"I'm so glad I get to see you once more, Natakia," I said, whispering to her painted visage. "I just hope that the life your mother ran away from has not consumed you."

And with that, with one last aimless prayer to the gods and my ancestors to grant me strength and wisdom, I clambered into bed and drifted off into a fitful sleep.

8

Great Slash Technique!" The guard lashed out, his blade practically singing as it cut through the air, brilliantly glowing with the power of Vitae as it surged toward me in a side swipe.

I jumped back, feeling the strain of my **Grace Stance** pulling at my Vitae, and flipped through the air, landing lightly but with solid footing, on the training-ground dirt behind me. There was no time to waste, however, as two more figures dashed toward me.

I flipped forward this time, letting their blades pass through the empty air below me as I lashed out with Crow, sending half-real duplicates at the swordsmen of House Tribus and letting the weight of my throws knock the weapons out of their hands before I twisted midair.

"**Spiral Kick Technique!**" I roared, letting my body suddenly swirl as I lashed out with both of my feet, my heels burying themselves into the sides of the two guards, sending them sprawling.

Landing from the use of the technique, I sighed before stepping to the side and letting the blade of the first and final standing guard slice through empty air once more. Tired as I was, these guards hadn't seen the kind of combat that I had, and their forms were standard with little to surprise me.

Sharply knocking the sword out of his hands with Crow's handle, I threw his arms up into the air, throwing him off-balance before channeling my Vitae into my feet once more, leaping before kicking down into the stomach of the combatant, letting the **Fierce Kick Technique** send him flying into the dirt.

Landing once more, I was finally able to rest for a moment as I took in a deep breath. My movements were slower, I could tell. My Vitae was not quite as vast or potent as it once was. I had yet to even feel comfortable attempting my **First Dance Stance** or any of the stance's deadly techniques.

And yet, I assuaged my frustration with the growing wear and tear of my body with the comfort of still improving, getting somewhere near my original strength. My encounters with Mortum had left indelible stains on my Vitae, but it still withstood the test of time better than I could have hoped for.

Having spent the last few days gathering my thoughts on Natakia's arrival and the beginning of my own investigation into the assassination attempts on Dalton, it was good to finally spar once more. I only wished that Caitlyn had not had to depart for Alwur before the gathering. She would be back, but I was left with no chance to ask her questions leading up to the day of the event.

"They say worrying about age makes you grow older faster," a familiar voice called out to me from beyond the fence surrounding the training field.

I looked up from my thoughts, feeling the slightest grin pull at my lips instinctively at the older but still boyish face of Dresden Booker, the captain of Gelvurt's guard and Macy's father. He stood with far more confidence than I remembered him having, but there was also something much more somber in his gaze.

"Well," I said, "I suppose that's why I feel as young as ever."

He absentmindedly leaped over the simple fence, kicking up a small plume of dirt with his landing. Unsheathing his blade, he approached with purpose, but not an unkind one.

Dresden smiled. "I hope I'm not imposing?"

"No," I said, motioning to his defeated men as they dragged themselves out of the area. "I was actually hoping to see you. Macy said you're not one for meetings, but training was a different story."

We assumed our stances, each of us holding our weapons still, but neither one of us made the first move for a few moments. I could tell there was much on his mind, as there was on mine. There was so much to say, but it was clear that neither one of us could move with it all weighing so heavily on us.

"I'm sorry about Doh," I said, tensing my body as I readied myself. "I can't even begin to repay the debt I feel toward her service and friendship."

Dresden nodded, swallowing hard, readying his own blade. "I'm sorry about Daka. If I'd kept a better eye on her, then maybe she would be here with you."

And with those words said, we both blurred into motion. Dresden's slashes were coated in his glimmering Vitae, each faster than the last as I dodged and wove through the attacks, before throwing out quick, testing throws, duplicates of Crow swishing past my opponent as he blocked them with his blade, shattering the facsimiles.

I jumped back, attempting to gain distance, but blinked in surprise as Dresden dashed forward with incredible speed, forcing me to jump again midair, using my **Air Dance Technique** to flip over the swift strike and land behind the swordsman.

I felt the force of the sudden backward blow from Dresden reverberate through my arm, having brought up Crow to catch the sword that would have otherwise slashed me in the side. It was an awkward position, not one that was proper for distributing the weight of the blow. One arm was quite the handicap for a fight of this caliber.

Feeling the strain in my arm, I jumped back, circling my Vitae throughout my body to keep my speed enhanced before blocking numerous more blows from Dresden as he doggedly pursued me.

"You seem rusty." Dresden smiled. "Been sleeping on me?"

It was a joke that screamed of something only he and Doh would have the irreverence to say, making me smile as I threw out a Crow straight at his feet, making him jump back to reposition from the strike, giving me a chance to catch my breath and finally align myself into my **Dancing Star Stance**.

"Still feeling somewhat groggy, yes," I admitted before my arm blurred as the unfamiliar strain of using my **Swift Throw Technique** began to burn at me, sending numerous Crows into the air.

They danced through the air, swirling around Dresden as suddenly he was on the back foot, deflecting and dodging numerous Crows that continued to plague him even as he knocked them out of the sky. And yet, even as he looked outmatched by the speed of my attacks, I suddenly had to take a knee.

The Crows fell, fading as the Vitae that gripped them was released, and I let my Vitae rest from the strain of my stance. Dresden caught his breath alongside me, but there was a clear difference in our exhaustion.

"You've gotten faster," I said between heavy pants that I tried to keep even. It was hard to imagine that I had fallen so far from my original strength, to think that even the **Dancing Star Stance** could be so tiring.

Dresden came over, sheathing his blade. "When Kingsley retired, I knew it'd be up to me to keep the standards high. Otherwise, all the guards would start slacking."

"I'm sure Macy is proud." I certainly was. I remembered Dresden when I'd first arrived in Gelvurt, and he had grown leaps and bounds. He was certainly a master of the basics, with pragmatic strikes enhanced by his astounding speed and strength.

He looked bothered for a moment before he nodded. "I'd hope so. What I said about Daka, I truly meant it, Rakta. If I had just . . ."

I raised up a hand as he paused, giving me a moment to think and finish catching my breath. I felt a connection with Dresden now, one that went further than friendship. I saw the same look in his eyes that I had seen within my own gaze many times.

"Dresden, do you believe Doh is still alive?" I said the words carefully, understanding the nature of what I spoke.

He seemed surprised himself, swallowing hard before he sat down on the ground next to me. The young man I had seen grow into a father and an exceptional fighter stared off into the distance for quite some time.

"I believe for Macy's sake, Rakta, that Doh will come back to us," he said, his fingers rubbing the hilt of his blade. "I don't know if Doh still being alive is a good thing though."

I was stunned by his words but reined in my shock as best I could. "I don't understand. Why do you think that?"

"I want Doh to come back, don't get me wrong." Dresden shook his head. "There's a hole in my life, in Macy's life, that can't be filled by any-one else."

"So why?" I asked again, feeling like I was prying at his heart too hard and yet unable to keep my need to know from pulling at my actions, needing to know why Dresden thought so.

Dresden sighed, suddenly looking far less boyish and far more the stern guard captain that I had heard rumors of. "I don't know what happened to Doh, what she found or what found her, but if she hasn't come back yet, and if she's still alive, then there's a chance . . . the reason she hasn't come back is that she forgot."

As his words settled, I understood his fears entirely. Doh had the blood of a doppelgänger in her, giving her incredible shape-shifting abilities, but her memories disappeared. Doppelgängers were thieves of identity, taking from others what they could not possess, but Doh was robbed of her identity by time.

"If she hasn't been using her memory magic to keep her mind together," I said, following Dresden's concerns, "then she might not even remember who she is."

My friend nodded, looking pale. I wondered if this was the first time he had ever shared such concerns with anyone else, perhaps even Macy . . .

"Does Macy . . . ?" The question pulled at me to ask, to know if Doh's daughter was plagued with the horrible curse of not knowing if her mother would even recognize her the next time they met.

"We've never talked about it," Dresden admitted, looking torn. "I don't know if she's thought about it herself, but if I have . . . Macy's a lot smarter than I am; she always has been. If I talk to her about it, though, I feel like . . . I'll make it real."

It was unenviable and so near, yet far from what I had experienced with Lydia. Would I have preferred her alive but amnesiac? Perhaps if she remembered her children, but the pain of being forgotten would not have been an easy one to overcome.

"I can hardly imagine, Dresden." I wished he knew. To not know was a burden that kept them from even beginning to truly grieve.

We were silent for a time, both of us dwelling on our own thoughts of those we had lost. We were companions in loss, despite the differences in our woes. For all the comfort it brought, I would have preferred to be the only one who felt the pain of losing a loved one.

"I'm going after Daka," I said, breaking the silence.

Dresden looked up from the ground. "When?"

That was a very good question. Daka had gone off to Rusk and had been there for years at this point. Rusk was a very expansive nation, but there was still much to do in the empire. I could not simply leave Dalton or Natakia here sinking into their own fears and insecurities.

"Soon," I said, thinking back to Natakia's upcoming visit. "I have much to do here, but I cannot stay for long."

Perhaps it was because of the eight years I had lost to Zactrik's horrid powers, but I felt like I was on a clock. As if every moment were a precious one to be spent doing the best for my children. It was a dreadful premonition in my bones that I needed to do all that I could before I could do no more.

"Doh," Dresden said suddenly, looking at me with determination. "I'd like you to look for Doh too."

That was a very serious request, but I could not deny him. "I will do that, Dresden, but what of you? Do you not wish to search for her yourself?

"Of course I want to." Dresden shook his head, a hard edge of regret in his eyes. "I have responsibilities though. Not just to Gelvurt, but . . . Macy deserves to have a parent. If I go out looking for Doh . . ."

He may never come back. That was a hard risk to even consider, leaving Macy with no family and, from what I had observed, few friends.

"I'll do my best, Dresden, to bring you closure, one way or another," I said, knowing that it was the least I could do for the man and his family. Doh would want her family to know, for better or worse, what had happened to her.

He nodded before standing up. "The Mana Wastes, that was where she was heading. That's just beyond Rusk, right?"

The Mana Wastes were a neighbor of Rusk, yes, but only through a small stretch of land not cut off by some of Rusk's more mountainous terrain near the southern border. And yet, once I found Daka, there would be no harm in venturing there for the sake of Dresden's answers.

"That gives me a direction at least. Did she mention anywhere in particular?" I'd learned that she had originally left to find an answer to my condition but nothing in detail.

"A place called Rainwater," Dresden said. "I have to be on my way. It was good talking to you, Rakta. I'm glad you're back."

I nodded, appreciative of the sentiment, before he walked off toward a different training ground. I supposed it was now his duty to keep his men from slacking in their routines.

"Time has certainly changed us all," I said, reaching up to feel the empty air where my missing arm would have been. I could distantly hear the dying cries of a dear friend and the pain of black flames.

9

The servants of the Tribus Estate were spectacular workers, some of the finest stylists and organizers that I had ever met. The attire they had fashioned for me was dyed in the colors of House Tribus, but the noble flair was subdued, as if they recognized that I was, for all intents and purposes, retired from my role.

Today was the gathering that, ostensibly, should only involve other members of House Tribus, a relatively small affair with the small number of nobility actually among our lands. The few regular lords and lordesses of House Tribus were landless, owing to the size of our borders, and were often just uplifted merchants within Dalton's employ.

Such uplifting was a very ceremonial and traditional function of the empire's legal system, not often done, but the doors that it opened economically were of much greater value to my son than tradition.

Today, I agreed that tradition was weak in comparison to other matters. For it was through disregarding tradition that my daughter, Natakia Velbrun, the oracle of House Velbrun, would be attending in celebration of my awakening.

"How are you feeling, Macy?" It was only the two of us in the room, the servants having left after aiding me in getting ready for the event. I was appreciative, not yet used to putting on such finery with one arm.

Macy started, having been staring at the portraits on the wall, one in particular. "Oh, I, well, how you're feeling is probably a lot . . . more important."

"Will your father be in attendance?" There certainly were enough important individuals here that having the captain of the guard in attendance wouldn't have been strange.

Macy shook her head, seemingly lost in thought. I supposed that I had noticed plenty of guards elsewhere in the estate to make up for his absence. And yet, with an assassination plot afoot, I would have appreciated his company.

"Macy." I finished adjusting my attire and focused on her, noticing how white her hair was. "It's been quite some time since you've seen Natakia, correct? Do you have words for her?"

"Oh, no, I could never, that would be . . . This is a gathering, not somewhere that I can just . . . say something to her, you know?" Macy was tapping her fingers together, looking lost as to what to say.

Truly, I wasn't sure what I wanted to say to my daughter either. I had so many questions and concerns about her motivations for joining House Velbrun, but I also didn't want such concerns to get in the way of our reunion.

"I think it would be good to try," I said, focusing on Macy's plight for the moment rather than my own. "I don't know why she left, why she's distanced herself from you, but maybe now things can change for the better."

Macy was quiet for a moment before nodding. "That would be nice, Rakta."

It would be nice, but it was up to me to make sure it all worked out. There was only one problem that I'd heard about that I couldn't even begin to formulate an answer to.

Natakia Velbrun's near-constant companion, Esmeralda Velbrun, the monster that had once taken on the form of my wife while fighting my friends and me, and fought alongside us against Zactrik years prior.

Jorge Tribus was a rotund man with a jolly smile that belied a meticulous mind for politics, but with little of the cutthroat, backstabbing spirit of the Velbruns. That, of course, is why they had originally exiled him into the outskirts of their lands, just as they had me in similar circumstances.

"I can't believe I've lived to see the day you woke up, Rakta." Jorge shook my hand with both of his, his eyes wet with unshed tears. "I thought there was utter insanity about, rumors of you walking around when I get word from your son that it's no lie!"

"I'm glad word got to you," I said, happy that Dalton had actually sent word to him. "How is the family?"

Jorge smiled, laughing. "Right back to the same old same old, eh? They're doing wonderfully! Got a proper education and made good use of it. I think I'll have a relaxing retirement to look forward to."

He seemed to pause for a moment before glancing around us. We were currently in the great hall of the Tribus Estate, filled to the brim with nameless faces and servants attending to them. I had been accosted by many new names and fans of my adventuring background, but things had calmed down.

Dalton was currently getting the beginnings of the gathering together, with Macy alongside him. I'd seen them directing people, from chefs to waiters, to keep the guests of this party entertained and content.

"You, uh," Jorge said, keeping his voice low, "I don't suppose you're interested in taking the reins from your son now that you're back? He's been doing incredible work, but there are some concerns . . ."

"Well." I wasn't sure how quickly I wished to burst Jorge's bubble. I truly had little desire to resume any sort of influential role. There were far more important matters to concern myself with.

Before I could answer, Jorge cut me off. "I'm sorry, no, this isn't the time for that. I'm just so happy to see you back! Oh, I bet this'll be a rock in the shoes of some of those House Kire fools. Do you know what they did just last month?"

And on and on he went, making me smile as he began to jovially talk about the politics of the empire. Out of the three of us, Jorge was certainly the most politically inclined, but it was such an innocent knack that it failed to discomfort me like others discussing such matters would.

That was why it was so strange to listen to these familiar words with the accusation of assassination attempts against this man lingering in the back of my mind.

"My lord." A new voice interrupted his detailed rant on the horrors of House Kire's trade routes. "I imagine that Lord Tribus would be interested in that matter you asked me to remind you of."

I turned to see a woman with long black hair and a veil over her face, dressed in a black gown that billowed out and concealed her feet. It was as if she glided across the ground to us, and it was with a small tinge of guilt that I noticed the skull brooch on her headdress.

A lady of the Depth of Death. The followers of a god that had, ever since my adventuring group's defeat of the Warlock King, been vilified and ousted from power throughout the empire. A false accusation from Lydia that I had corroborated and none from our group had rebutted.

Jorge blinked at the lady, snapping his fingers. "I did! Yes, ah, thank you, Noelle. Rakta, this is Noelle, a disciple of the Depth of Death from their lands north of us."

Ah yes, I remembered now. That, with the reveal that House Velbrun had been the true origins of the Warlock King, Queen Tracy Certimov-Hanchett had given a small part of House Velbrun's lands to the Depth of Death as an apology, with the Church of Radiance issuing its own gifts and favors in recompense.

"It is good to meet you, Noelle," I said, unsure of how to even begin to address the woman whom I had ultimately spread falsehoods about. "I am no longer of any noble position, so please, feel free to refer to me as you wish."

A small dip of her head was all that I could make of her reaction to my greeting before Jorge began to rifle through his robes before procuring a few documents.

"I was recently presented with a very interesting proposal by House Iriend; you see, there is an excavation of some ravines near the edge of the border of Cerula that—" Jorge's words were cut off as the sound of a herald's trumpet called for attention to the entrance, a guest of worth having arrived.

I turned, having listened to each and every call of the horn as they came throughout the evening, waiting for the arrival of my daughter with growing impatience. A painting was no substitute for the real thing.

"Let us rise and greet the respected guest from afar," the announcer of House Tribus proclaimed, a touch of Vitae to his voice allowing it to carry throughout the large room.

The sitting among the crowd stood, annoying me slightly as my vision was immediately plagued by the odd assortment of nobility that blocked my view of the entrance. I began to gently push my way to the front, feeling an energy in my fingertips as my instincts pulled at me.

This guest felt important, far more so than those who had come before them. Was this my daughter having finally arrived?

"Presenting," the announcer continued as I broke through the crowd, many of them making way as they seemed to register who I was, "the respected and educated Mistress of Machinery, Grand Master of Innovation, Defender of the Empire, and Champion of Cerula, Penelope Iriend!"

The sudden applause and whispers echoing all around me distracted me naught as metal clinked heavily against the ground, my eyes widening as I took in the visage of one of my dearest friends or, rather, what remained of her.

She wore a dress of stark white that went down to her ankles, but nothing could distract from the metal prosthetics that had replaced her arms and legs, her eye sockets having been fitted with glass casing, surrounded by metal that seemed to be drilled into her skull.

Coils and tubing arched from a bulky fixture on her back, plugging into the bases of her replaced arms and legs, with one seemingly each plugged into her collarbone and back.

"Penelope?" I asked in shocked horror.

She was taller now, her fake legs slightly longer than they had once been while real, but height did not matter as she looked around the room, a distinct arrogance about her, before our gazes met and I saw her body relax in relief, even the metallic parts looking less tense, before she approached.

"Rakta." Penelope smiled, something near fondness in her tone. "It's been quite some time."

When I had first arrived in the Certillian Empire, I had experienced a stark confusion over the customs and culture that I had escaped into. New words, new hierarchies—it was all I could do to keep myself from going mad while learning the particulars of the new land around me.

And still I felt the oddity before me was something I truly had no basis for comprehension of, no common ground as foundation upon which rest this new truth before me.

"You haven't touched your tea," Penelope reminded me, having been watching me as I slowly digested her new appearance. The lenses of her strange new eyes were hard to not stare at.

I nodded, taking a sip of my tea. "Please forgive me, Penelope. I'm still reeling from all that you've told me. I don't think I'm even close to understanding well enough to respond."

There had been so many eyes upon us in the great hall, the reunion of two of the empire's greatest living heroes meeting once more after years apart, it was a grand spectacle for the common nobility. It made me appreciate our first reunion so many years ago, despite the bitter-sweetness it had tasted of then.

Dalton had secluded us quickly, calling attention elsewhere while he settled us in for a more private conversation. There was so much to talk about, but Penelope seemed possessed with even more initiative than before, an almost manic efficiency tinging her gentle words.

"I understand the confusion," she said, as if she were talking about simple arithmetic. "I made this decision a few years ago and haven't regretted it since. I'm sure you've felt the rigors of age?"

Penelope was talking about enhancements. A recent innovation by her hand, magically constructed implants and prosthetics that would invigorate the body and mind, according to her practiced pitch on the matter.

The very same enhancements that she had replaced a large majority of her body with over the years. And from all that she had spoken of it, it was clear that her loss of limbs was very much voluntary.

It was so bizarre that this was the first conversation we were having; we'd barely spoken a few pleasantries before she'd gotten straight to the point that I would be in need of aid. Aid that she was happy and willing to provide.

"How is Ulric?" That was a name I hadn't heard much after waking up. It was hard to imagine he was keeping a low profile.

Penelope blinked, or rather, an inner layer of apertures shuttered closed for a moment before reopening. "Ulric, oh, he's doing fine. I believe he's acting as the king's personal guard."

Ah, that was certainly a fine place for him to be. After the attack on the palace so many years ago, I didn't doubt that they were in need of someone of Ulric's caliber.

"You haven't gotten used to your lack of arm yet, have you?" Penelope was now looking at my right side, where it was obvious that, despite the symmetry of my outfit, there was far less beneath the clothing.

There was no way to deny that. There was just so much more to account for with only one arm. No matter how much I regained my former strength, there would always be a part of me gone.

"I remember that night so clearly." Penelope was no longer smiling. "Shawn dying, you recklessly trying to avenge him, my failure to finish Zactrik off."

"He was a monster, more than we ever expected from him," I said, reaching out and placing my hand on her metal hand. "There is so much more to be proud of than to mourn, in large part thanks to you, Penelope."

She was quiet for a moment before giggling under her breath. "I was really looking forward to you waking up, Rakta. It's hard, dragging this empire into the future, but I'm glad you're back. You're someone who can understand the necessity of advancement. If you just accept it, I'm sure you'll appreciate my gift."

"I appreciate the offer, Penelope," I said, unsure of how to put my words correctly, "but the sheer depth of what you offer is . . . unthinkable to me right now."

A full-body conversion is what she called it, one that she had tested on a few other willing individuals. It was different from her own changes, which were outfitted for her Mana production, but the details, she had made clear, wouldn't matter much.

"I see." Penelope frowned. "I suppose that wasn't an unsurprising response, but it was still very disappointing. Ulric said much the same, but he wouldn't even look at me."

There was something instinctively strange about Penelope's appearance. I could certainly sympathize with Ulric on that, but I felt that there was so much being left unsaid, that had gone unsaid for too long, that I wasn't sure how to even bring up the right words.

"I don't know what the future holds, Penelope. I can't say I understand what is best for the people of this empire or what they are ready for, but I know there are those who have and will continue to benefit from your work," I said, keeping my hand firm on hers. "You are still my friend, and I am here to listen and speak about anything."

Before Penelope could respond, the doors to our private chamber were suddenly opened with a harsh wrenching, Macy stumbling in with a flushed face. "Natakia's here! Very sorry for the interruption!"

And then she dove out of the room, faster than we could even negotiate a response between the two of us. Penelope squeezed my hand back. "I suppose the rest of our chat will have to wait."

"Thank you, Penelope," I said, smiling gratefully before my impatience dug itself out from deep within my chest and began to run wild as I stood up and departed for the main gathering once more.

I was to see my daughter, and no one would stop me until I had done so.

10

Lydia had once joked that her skin was as pale as it was because it was a gift of the full moon that she had wished upon nightly as a small child. The rare portrait I had seen of her as an even younger child claimed otherwise, her milky skin being from birth.

It was testimony to her beauty that such a story was oftentimes believed without a second of hesitation by those who heard it. And it was like watching that same story step out from the ether as my daughter stood at the center of the gathering, all eyes on her.

"It's been far too long, brother," Natakia said. "I do so appreciate the invitation."

Even as, unfortunately, she was staring down her older brother, the both of them the focus of everyone in attendance. She looked so much like her mother, espccially in her cold anger that revealed little.

"You invited yourself," Dalton said, expressionless. With his arms behind his back, he was the absolute paragon of decorum as he faced his sister.

The crowd parted around me as I moved forward toward them, feeling my heart pounding in my chest. "Natakia? Is that really you?"

She turned to me as I stepped out from the crowd, and the portrait, while expertly done, had not done justice to the graceful beauty that my daughter had become. Even in the green and gold of her dress, there was a power in her stance that was quiet but obvious.

I was relieved, convinced that however life had been with House Velbrun, it couldn't have been as tragic as my worst fears.

"Dad?" Natakia's voice was thick with emotion before she took a step forward. "It's been . . . a long time."

That was putting it far, far too lightly. I came up to her in great strides, thankful that I was not quite so physically challenged as when I'd reunited with my son.

My heart beat loudly as I went to hug my daughter before I paused as I felt the gentlest touch of her hand against my chest, stopping me in my tracks. Her eyes were shiny with emotion, but her face was untarnished by any expression, only a subtle glance around the room giving me an insight into her cause for worry.

"Perhaps we should find a more private arrangement?" A familiar voice slinked out from the entrance behind Natakia, my hair raising instinctively at the wrongness I felt once I recognized it.

Esmeralda, the result of some failed attempt at walking in Zactrik's footsteps, swayed into the room, wearing a dress nearly identical to Natakia's, with the only addition being the ebony embroidery on the golden shawl wrapped around her neck, falling loosely down to her waist.

While I did not feel the weight of the eyes upon us, I had to agree that Natakia was not the same, her stance still that of confidence, but one that seemed to be growing bolder, as if in the face of a challenge to it.

Dalton spoke up. "I'll have a servant guide you. I must get back to my guests."

We shared a glance, my son and I, as he motioned for us all to follow a young man who seemed quite eager to show us around. There was something about him that tickled the back of my mind, but I shed my curiosity for the moment as I eventually found myself in a room much like the one Penelope and I had shared mere moments before.

"I suppose privacy does have its—" I was interrupted as Natakia hugged me, her grip surprisingly tight as she clung close to me, all of her decorum suddenly disappeared.

"Dad." Natakia's voice was dripping with joy and sorrow. "I missed you so much! I'm so sorry! I . . . I thought you'd never wake up, and . . . and . . ."

I quieted her with a gentle shushing as I wrapped my arm around her, gathering her as best I could into my embrace. Despite my misgivings,

if Penelope's enhancements would let me hold my children properly
again . . .

"No need for apologies, my little desert flower," I said, feeling her
shake and shiver in my arm. "I'm just happy to see you've grown up to be
a beautiful, capable young woman in my absence."

No matter the soil she grew from, I was proud that my daughter had
weathered the hard landscape that Lydia had spoken so cautiously of.
There were few honest allies within House Velbrun; everyone had their
own plans predicated on their own personal divinations and gathered
information.

She pulled back slightly, carefully wiping her face without smudging
her makeup. "I couldn't have done it without Esmeralda. She's . . . I've
just been scraping by every day, terrified that I . . . I . . ."

I smoothed out her hair as she began to hug me tightly once more,
my eyes falling off of my daughter and landing upon Esmeralda in the
corner, her presence hard to miss and yet minuscule. Whereas Natakia
naturally favored her mother, the remnants of Esmeralda's past mockery
of my wife remained in the clear mimicry of her features, her nose, her
smile.

My attention swiftly went back to what truly mattered in this moment,
however, holding my daughter even more fiercely.

"I'm sorry I was gone for so long, Natakia," I said, feeling a burning
in my eyes as I shed tears alongside her, regretting all that had led to my
daughter crying in my arms like this. "I'm here now, I'm here. I'm not
going anywhere."

For a while, I simply calmed my daughter down, letting us enjoy the
moment we now had together. It was so similar to seeing my son after so
long, a sense of reunion tinged with the bittersweet wonderings of what
Overseer had whispered to me as I awoke.

That my daughter was on a dark path, and yet I had little knowledge
of what that darkness looked like. I had my suspicions, though, knowing
now who had kept her company in all my time away from her.

"And then, she tried to say that I was the one who had poisoned the
biscuits, not that there was any evidence." Natakia giggled, lounging on
one of the more comfortable couches of the private room. "Esmeralda

stepped in, Dad, and she ripped Diana's dress off in one motion to reveal the hidden vial!"

"I'm very proud of that little impulse of mine." Esmeralda smiled impishly into a polite hand over her mouth. "I only needed a small taste of her Vitae to know that she was up to something horrid."

Nothing could have prepared me for the gossip of two young ladies of House Velbrun, Natakia having seemed eager to regale me with stories after she had calmed down. Esmeralda was in all of them, as I'd suspected, but they painted a clear picture of friendship throughout.

The friendship between the two of them, from all that Natakia had said, was clearly strong. And yet, I was unconvinced by how honest such aid truly was.

"Oh, Esme, remember that time you chased off that one man? What was his name?" Natakia was staring at me determinedly, as if daring me to not listen. The intensity had grown over the course of her stories. "The one who tried to give me a gilded turtle for my birthday last year? You remember?"

I had been convinced, however, that my wife had not exaggerated the stories she had wove for me about her experience with House Velbrun. It was far different from my own brief experience, perhaps because of either the protections I'd had at the time or how far I was from the capital of their lands.

"Ah, yes, Victor." Esmeralda nodded sagely. "I suppose he was unprepared for you to deny him even a simple brunch after such a gift. The oracle's time is far more valuable than a turtle though . . ."

"It is; it very much is." Natakia seemed very proud of herself, watching me. "Of course, I already knew he just wanted some dirt on Ashford, but to think he'd get so irate when I declined!"

Esmeralda spoke up, as if in sync with my daughter. "I kept him from getting too handsy, of course. Him and all those low-brow assassins who made themselves a nuisance afterward."

"Like I said, Dad," Natakia said, "Esme has been a great help."

There was certainly a lot of evidence for it, but it was hard to put my finger on exactly why Natakia was so adamant on the subject.

"Well, it's good that you've had such an admirable companion," I said, nodding to Esmeralda, but my heart wasn't in it. While I did appreciate all this aid, it was hard to imagine Esmeralda as genuinely benevolent.

And, I realized with a sudden starkness, Natakia probably realized that. Her expression grew dour at my words, her arms crossing as she stared at me.

"Natakia," I said, feeling like I was being dissected. "I am genuinely glad that you found companionship in House Velbrun, but forgive me for having my doubts. I've found little reason to trust House Velbrun, much the opposite, and Esmeralda and I have . . . We have some unresolved issues."

I felt like I was doing a disservice to the innocent lives that she had taken and the danger that had been wrought upon my friends and me by her hand. Was it wisdom or weakness that stayed my hand from openly questioning my daughter's choices so heavily? Was it the same with Dalton?

"She wasn't in her right mind. You can't blame her for that," Natakia said, but her expression was softer, more understanding. "I just don't want you to think that she's led me down some . . ."

A dark path? I'd forgotten that Natakia was highly insightful, most likely as a part of whatever her gift from Overseer had presented itself as. There was little I could say to assuage her without truly meaning it.

"I'm just worried, Natakia, but I don't want that worry to taint our reunion. I want to share a drink and hear all that has happened in my absence," I said, letting my honest feelings take root in my words. "If Esmeralda truly is your friend, or more, then I'll keep an open mind and see for myself."

Natakia had the faintest blush bleed through her cheeks at the mention of her friendship with Esmeralda being something more, but the signs were certainly there. In all the stories Natakia had told, not one spoke of any interest in the courtship offered by the men of House Velbrun.

I believed the topic was of some complexity within the empire, depending on where one lived within it, but Rusk was quite open about such things. Or rather, such things were paid little mind.

"I understand, Rakta," Esmeralda said, nodding. "I've also been looking forward to your return and am eager to show you how I've grown as a person."

It was said so guilelessly, with Natakia nodding in agreement with her companion, but those words from her lips, with only the faintest emphasis, made my skin crawl.

Eventually, it was time to return to the larger gathering still ongoing within the estate, my daughter and I walking side by side as we traced our way back through the unfamiliar hallways of our old home.

"Dalton has expanded the estate quite a bit, hasn't he?" It was the only time I'd brought up my son to my daughter, unsure of what their relationship was like.

Natakia hummed in agreement, but I could tell that her tension was growing as we walked closer and closer to the gathering. Instead of any thoughts toward her brother being revealed, it felt more like she was distracted by the slowly growing sounds of chatter.

"Natakia," I asked, pausing for a moment, "are you alright?"

My desert flower blinked, glancing at me before turning to look back at Esmeralda a couple paces behind us. "I'm just nervous. Large crowds are . . ."

She paused, glancing at me again. My thoughts went back to that day the Rose Gala was attacked, rendering all Natakia's preparation null and endangering her life. My daughter had always seemed eager to be the center of attention, and yet now she hesitated.

"As long as I have Esmeralda and Dad," Natakia continued, more to herself than me, "I'll be fine."

The aforementioned companion simply smiled quietly, but it was due to years of recognizing danger that I could feel her gaze lingering on me more than anything else. I supposed I was grateful for my daughter being able to lean on her when necessary, but my uneasiness had not waned much at all.

As we almost reached the gathering hall, a servant suddenly crossed our path and stopped. For a moment, I expected it to be the servant that had guided us, who was nowhere to be found, but then I registered whom I was looking at.

"Um, hey," Macy said, the tips of her hair completely alabaster as she shakily smiled. "Natakia, it's been, uh, a while, yeah?"

Natakia completely stopped, the air of the hallway becoming frosty as I felt my daughter's Mana begin to saturate the air. It was potent and efficient, the first hint at how powerful my daughter had become.

"Oh." Natakia's words were cold and dismissive. "It's you."

When two plateau hawks meet, there is no more dangerous place to be than in between them. I was struck dumb by the threat I felt in the air from my daughter, all focused on Macy.

"Natakia." I began to pull at my words to try and make sense of this hostility.

And yet I found myself on the wrong end of a chilling glare, my daughter speaking to me with finality. "I'd suggest you stay out of this, Dad. This isn't any business of yours."

I blinked at the frostiness, but also the fear hidden in her words. There was an attempt to mask it, by way of some enchantment, but it was not quite as expertly honed as I believed Dalton's was.

"I wanted to, you know, see you," Macy said, swallowing hard. "It's been so long, and . . . Have, uh, have you been doing well?"

Natakia's expression was immaculate, as if she'd barely even registered Macy's words. "I have a party to return to. If you're so interested in my well-being, bring drinks next time."

And then she continued on, soon passing the frozen Macy as if she were nothing to concern herself with. I followed, placing a comforting hand on Macy that she startled at before running off back to where she'd come from, almost tripping over her attire.

"Natakia," I said as I strode up next to my daughter, "what happened?"

Macy had said that Natakia had left but had never mentioned that such a rift of hostility had been opened between them. Was Macy even capable of spurring such hatred? I hadn't thought her to be.

My desert flower relaxed for a moment before regarding me with suspicion that made my heart hurt. A moment passed and she shook her head, a pain in her gaze, one that only came from betrayal.

"Friends are supposed to be there for each other," Natakia said as if that explained everything that I had seen. Esmeralda was suddenly by her side, her hand slipping into my daughter's easily.

11

In an odd turn of fate, it was easier for me to settle my mind on the subject of Dalton's suspicions than it was to consider the twists involved in tearing my daughter apart from her childhood friend.

Rejoining the gathering in full, my daughter resuming her public persona of grace and class, I was beset with the realization that I had done little throughout the night to aid in my son's investigation. My talk with Jorge had been short-lived with Penelope arriving, so there was little to make of it.

As I considered just how easy this would be for Lydia, I glanced at my daughter as we ventured farther into the large room, full of many who would have something to gain. For once, I did actually have the assistance of a powerful diviner, but hesitation struck me.

Did I ask my daughter to aid me in such an endeavor moments after our reunion? Did I really deserve her assistance after causing such heartache to all those around me for so long?

"How can I help, Dad?" Natakia laid a soft hand on my shoulder, and I felt the breath I'd been unknowingly holding release itself, her gaze much gentler than it had been moments before.

After I recovered my surprise at the offer, I smiled warmly at my daughter. "I suppose I shouldn't be surprised at your perceptiveness, Natakia."

She was so much like her mother, knowing me more than I knew myself at times. Natakia looked thrilled at my words before her excitement was smoothed over by professionalism.

"Dalton is concerned about recent attempts on his life," I said, Natakia assuming a guarded expression at the mention of her brother, but I could still feel concern from her. "He suspects the other higher members of House Tribus, but I have a hard time believing that."

I kept my words quiet, barely above a whisper that my daughter could hear. There was no telling who was listening in, but I hoped that there were far more interesting conversations to keep an ear on at the moment.

"I'll find them." Natakia's eyes twinkled. "Esmeralda and I have a lot of experience at this kind of game."

A game? A discomforting way to refer to it, but I supposed that years spent among the vipers of House Velbrun could give one such a disconnected view of things.

"Thank you." I placed my hand on hers, gratitude welling up within me. "You and Dalton have done wonders in my absence. I'm glad I can trust you with helping him now."

Her excitement dimmed for a moment before she nodded and walked off into the crowds, Esmeralda alongside her. There would be time for more conversation later, but for now, I had a woman to find.

I could cast aside all doubts on the names of my friends after I spoke with Caitlyn.

High Lordess Tribus of Alwur was not a hard woman to find, with Caitlyn having her own entourage from Alwur keeping most of the rest of the party away from her. Rather, Caitlyn took more personal audiences throughout the showing, with some of the other lords of House Tribus benefiting from her counsel.

This late into the evening, her skin was wrinkled and blotched with age, but there was a wisdom in her gaze as she spoke confidently to each brave soul willing to drink with her.

"Rakta," she spoke, eyeing me up like I was a puzzle. "I'm glad we get to speak once more."

The crone was a blunt and wise form, Caitlyn's demeanor that of a village elder this late in the day, but without the empowerment of her **Threefold Stance**, the wisdom wasn't quite as potent.

"Yes, it's been quite some time," another familiar voice piped up, the youthful face of Julian Carnline stepping into sight, the trusted attendant of Caitlyn Tribus since we had met.

Julian had been the one to originally lead me to the steps of Lordess Caitlyn Velbrun's estate so many years ago, but it had been quite some time, even before my nightmarish slumber, since I'd had the opportunity to speak with him.

"Julian." I nodded, noting that for all the years that had passed, he certainly hadn't seemed to age a day. "I'm glad to see you're doing well."

The young man chuckled, looking amused for some reason, before Caitlyn spoke up. "I can tell you came here for a reason, Rakta, beyond pleasantries. Let's hear it."

Ah, of course, she certainly wasn't in the mood for small talk right now. It would be best that I not waste the time I had before she became more irate.

"My son has concerns, Caitlyn," I said, taking as firm a stance as I could with my words alone, "that his life is being targeted by those politically closest to him."

Caitlyn raised an eyebrow. "Straightforward as always, but there's little I can say to remove any suspicion of me in his eyes. What are your thoughts?"

"I simply wish to help my son in any way I can, but I have my doubts about where his suspicions lie." I kept my gaze on her, letting my Vitae percolate through the air immediately around me. "Have there been any attempts on you? Or any strangeness within your lands that could be connected with Dalton's situation?"

"Other than the denizens of the forest becoming more irritated the farther we creep into their protected lands?" Caitlyn's words were drier than Ruskan sands. "I've had no attempts on my life that Julian here hasn't discovered the orchestrator of. He's quite good at finding the source of such skullduggery."

I glanced at Julian. "I don't suppose there is anything for you to add?'"

"All attempts have been made by lowly merchants or jealous nobles from other families within the empire," he said irreverently. "Poison is the current trend, especially in these parts. I'd say the only physically vulnerable high lord of House Tribus would be High Lord Jorge Tribus."

He certainly lacked the same physical aptitude and combat training that Caitlyn and I had back before my slumber. Dalton struck me as capable of fighting off attempts on his life as well.

"I see, but the question persists." I looked at Caitlyn. "Are you in any way related to these attacks on my son?"

"An understandable question, but an insulting one." Caitlyn took a drink of her wine. "Your son infuriates me, Rakta, but there is more risk in me attacking him myself than paying others to do it for me."

There was an uncomfortable amount of honesty and anger in those words, but they gave me relief nonetheless. "I believe you. I need to speak to Jorge once more. Thank you for your time."

"Of course, of course," she said, before turning to another member of her entourage and beginning to mutter about something that had little business for my ears.

As I turned to depart, I was stopped as a hand grabbed my wrist. I tensed instinctively before I looked back to see Julian had caught me before I could leave.

"One last thing." He smiled. "Could you say hello to Noelle for me? I haven't had a chance to greet her this evening."

It was a strange but innocent request that I swiftly acquiesced to. There was something strange about Julian, a familiarity that was building up in my head that I couldn't quite place. And yet, it didn't feel like it was toward Julian, but rather a different sensation . . .

"What!?" Jorge paced around in the private room, sweating profusely as his hands wove together. "I could never do anything like that! I mean, yes, I'm not, well, entirely unfamiliar with them, but that's not the same as saying I would do such a thing to your son! The most I've ever done is oust a rival or two!"

Jorge had not taken the idea of Dalton's accusations well. In fact, he seemed genuinely angry at the very idea, with a heavy edge of fear in his words. The idea that Dalton thought him the perpetrator behind the attacks was, well, terrifying to the man.

He approached me with desperation in his eyes that, if I were anyone else, would have made him ultimately more suspicious. Jorge had little calm when accused of heinous things.

"Oh, Rakta, you have to believe me! I would never want to hurt your son! I mean, sure, has he plagued me from the moment he assumed his position with ever-increasing standards, and has Niers's growth suffered from that? Yes!" Jorge blinked, thinking back at what he just said for a moment, before continuing. "I would never try to hurt him though!"

I put my hand on his shoulder. "Jorge, calm yourself. I don't think you did it."

"But Dalton does!" Jorge went back to pacing. "And if he thinks I made an attempt on his life, he'll make an attempt on mine! No, not an attempt, a success! Why do you think his list of suspects is so short?!"

Dalton had not shared many of his suspects, but the list hadn't seemed small. The idea that it had been even longer before my son had . . . shortened it made me somewhat uncomfortable. Few fathers would be proud of their child's propensity for assassination.

I shook my head. "I'll speak with him, I promise. That's why I'm here speaking with you, to clear up this misunderstanding and get to the bottom of this."

Jorge swallowed, nodding, before he sat down into the plush chair of the private room we had cordoned ourselves off to for this conversation. Noelle was the only one of his entourage present, but she had said very little.

"I can't believe he thinks my gifts are poison," Jorge said breathlessly, exhausted after worrying so much. "I sent him the same wine I used to send you, the same stock and all! Someone must be poisoning it on the way to Gelvurt!"

While that was what I'd thought initially, as well, it wasn't quite as simple as that. I had examined some of the wine myself, in preparation for today, and it was quite clear from the aroma alone that it had been poisoned. That said, none of the wine bottles had any signs of being tampered with or opened beforehand.

Dalton had used magical means of detecting the poison within the wine bottles after he'd found the taste of the first poisoned gift to be strange. So either there was some spell or technique being used to tamper with the wine or the stock itself had been infiltrated.

And, furthermore, it wasn't a poison I recognized, even with my **Scourger Bloodhound Technique**. It smelled bitter and earthy but was nothing that I had encountered before.

"This is still the wine you keep only for gifts, correct?" Jorge had made a practice of building up collections of valuable luxuries to appease and sustain relationships.

"Yes." He nodded. "Dalton and I don't . . . Well, we don't see eye to eye quite as often as you and I did back in the day, Rakta. I thought it'd be best to start treating him like a foreign power just, well, just in case."

I suppose he had valid reasons. From what I understood, Dalton treated most with far less warmth than I believed friends and family deserved, but that was neither here nor there.

Before he could answer, Noelle spoke up for the first time, standing up as she did. "May I be excused, High Lord Tribus? I believe it is improper for me to stay."

Jorge blinked before nodding. "Of course, of course. Thank you for your time, Noelle."

With that, she gave a respectful curtsy to the both of us before beginning to make her way toward the door of the room.

"Ah, Noelle," I said as she made to leave. "Julian Carnline from Alwur wished to pass along his greetings."

She paused, her head tilting in confusion. "I see. Perhaps we will have time for introductions later on in the evening."

And with little else said, she left the room, leaving Jorge and me alone. Jorge seemed to be gathering his thoughts to continue aiding me with my investigation, trying to narrow down the suspects.

I, however, was taking a brief reprieve from the topic of my son's shadowy foe to consider the strangeness of Julian's request if he had never met Noelle. Perhaps he had simply heard of her attendance? I suppose that the Depth of Death could still be a novelty in their period of reconstruction.

"My wine," Jorge spoke up, "is imported from afar, from House Montae. I keep it under lock and key, and I go down personally to collect it! I certainly don't trust Quentin to fetch it, that oaf . . ."

My mind was elsewhere as he continued to rant about all the precautions he took to keep his collection of luxuries safe from outside interference. At this point, it was certainly not Jorge, but . . .

"How long has Noelle been in your service, Jorge?" I hadn't had the opportunity to question him about it the last time we had spoken.

"Oh." Jorge stroked his chin. "About a year now, I think. The Depth of Death is regaining its popularity after the queen gave them land. Noelle has been furthering the faith in Niers since her arrival! A temple may even be in our future; we already have a garden for their faith."

"That's wonderful," I said, considering that for a moment. A garden dedicated to the Depths of Death was certainly an interesting idea. "Why did you bring Noelle to this party? It certainly seems to be a strange place for a disciple to be."

Jorge waved a hand through the air. "I suppose she simply wanted to see all that Gelvurt had to offer! Noelle has always been a sightseer."

Something clicked in the back of my mind at that, words slipping from my lips without thinking. "She requested to attend?"

I wasn't sure if Jorge had come to the same conclusion as I because I was suddenly a blur in the wind, feeling my Vitae burn with exertion as I realized that so much made sense if I put aside my guilt for all I had done to the Depths of Death.

At risk of making them a scapegoat once more, I'd forgotten that for all that had been done to them, it would make sense for them to hold a grudge.

A grudge that Noelle was planning on taking out on my son.

12

The Depth of Death was a monastic faith dedicated to Kalfrein, the god of endings, and the Creed of Demise. It was often mistaken as something apocalyptic in nature, as if the Depth of Death wished for all to end, but that was hardly the case.

Kalfrein, and the Creed of Demise, spread a teaching of respecting the end and all those who met it. Temples, from the one that I had been to long ago, were often morgues in their own right, with many funeral proceedings being left to their expertise and faithful dedication.

However, the Depth of Death was not without its fangs. Often magic and martial techniques were passed down to followers from their god, but Kalfrein had sought to give his people a different kind.

The black lotus was a beautiful flower grown in the inky-black water gardens tended by those of the faith. They did not grow without Kalfrein's permission, and so they were exceedingly rare. A rarity only matched by their potency when made into a poison, one that had been a distant memory until now.

The candle flames in the hallways I dashed through were put out by the speed of my **Great Wind Sprint Technique**, the blistering speed I moved at taking a toll on my Vitae.

"She left," I said to myself, landing on a wall, before kicking off to continue down a new hallway. "She had to have known we were close, close to finding out the truth."

Because my son was still alive after the poison, she must have come here to deal with him more personally. Had she even known I was awake? That I would be one more obstacle in her way?

I passed by many alarmed guests on my way but paid them no heed as I searched for my son throughout the crowds. He was nowhere to be found. When was the last time I had even seen him tonight?

I suddenly stopped, breathing heavily, as I found myself in front of the larger gathering. All of them chattering and drinking as my son's assassin was on the loose.

"Where is my son?" The Vitae in my voice echoed through the crowd, and I saw a few uninitiated to any magical or martial ways taking a knee at the force.

"Out of breath, Rakta?" Penelope of all people stepped out of the crowd before she turned her head to the crowd. "Give us some room."

With those words, most scattered, and those who lingered were aided along by those with more sense. I felt my hairs standing at attention as Penelope turned back to look at me.

"Did you see where he went, Penelope?" If there was anyone who would have the mind to keep track of where everyone went, it would be her.

"Maybe you should stop coming to parties," Penelope said, frowning. "First the Rose Gala, and now your son might be in danger . . . That's a bad pattern to continue in your old age."

I took a hard breath at that, feeling the sting of the comment. If Penelope was not going to tell me where my son had gone, then I would continue my search elsewhere.

A large surge of Mana suddenly pulsed, stopping me in my tracks, and I tensed as I watched a bright-blue energy suddenly originate from Penelope then spread throughout the room around us, stopping mere inches from the edges of the room where the crowd had retreated to.

The light dimmed, but there was still a shimmering force around us. She watched on silently as I went to the shimmering edge and placed my hand against it, feeling a solid weight behind the air.

"You've trapped me," I said, feeling the weight of the implications fall on my shoulders.

Penelope nodded, tilting her head. "The question now is, what can you possibly do to change that?"

"You keep me from my son when I believe him to be in danger?" I couldn't help the dangerous edge to my words, the gall of Penelope to waylay me. The sheer absurdity of her being in league with the assassin was the only thing staying that conclusion.

"You say you've acknowledged your weakness, Rakta, and yet you still act as if you have the strength to protect others," she said, the same blue glow as before beginning to surge through the metal of her limbs. "I can see it now. You'll go rushing off to save everyone, probably even go look for Daka. And you'll die."

"Release me," I said, my Vitae beginning to stir. "I do not want to fight you."

Penelope shook her head, watched by the people of the empire all around us. "I gave you a chance to accept your weakness and find strength in my gifts. This is the only way you'll understand the necessity of advancement, Rakta."

Settling into my **Grace Stance**, igniting my Vitae with my **Instinctive Reflex Technique** and **Skip Dash Technique**, I readied Crow against its creator and my friend.

"No matter how strong or weak I am," I said, "I will never allow my children to come to harm."

Penelope was the smartest of us; that was always one of the unmistakable truths of our adventuring party. While there was often debate around campfires about the strongest of us or the most skilled, none could mount a challenge against the academic dominance that Penelope had, although Lydia tried.

In a true fight, however, where nothing mattered but victory, intelligence was only one factor at play. And while at first I thought my greatest handicap would be merely knocking Penelope out . . .

"You've gotten better at teleporting." I kept my breathing even, letting my Vitae enhance my body as best I could without pushing it over the edge.

Penelope's body was aglow with Mana, the metal canister on her back making a small whining noise as she frowned. "And you've never been slower."

I tightened my grip around Crow, acknowledging the truth of her words. Vitae enhanced the baseline of an individual's physical capabilities. I was nowhere near slow, but compared to a decade ago . . .

And yet, there was one thing different between Penelope and me.

Feeling the burn of my **Swift Throw Technique**, I sent duplicates of my weapon into the air, keeping on the move as Penelope flashed in and out of existence, appearing in different areas throughout the improvised arena of the great hall. Each axe merely went straight through where she'd been, hitting the wall behind her.

I could sustain myself for the moment perfectly fine, but there was no chance of using my **Dancing Star Stance** without tiring myself out quickly. Instead, I merely continued to throw, keeping my eyes on Penelope and only Penelope.

"Are you trying to tire me out?" Penelope teleported right behind me then flashed away in the brief moment before the haft of my axe would have impacted the back of her skull.

If I had more time, then that would be my plan, yes. I wasn't in the mood to entertain the question, however. I just had to keep my eyes on where she was and continue throwing.

Penelope extended a metal hand as she appeared a few paces in front of me, a ball of glowing light appearing in the palm of her prosthetic. I had only a fraction of a moment to skip to the side, barely dodging out of the way of the beam of light that passed me by before it dwindled mere inches from the wall around us.

"Would you even have the Vitae required to heal from a direct blast?" Penelope shook her head in disappointment. "I'd have to patch you up, Rakta. Who is going to do that on the road?"

Another axe was all I answered her with, keeping my eye on where she was going and moving to reorient myself correctly. Penelope's teleportation device was one of her magnum opuses, allowing her to quickly move in a high-speed fight that could cost someone their life.

It was costly, however, very expensive depending on the consecutive uses and distance traveled, but it seemed many of those issues had either been dealt with or that the canister on her back was exactly what I suspected it was, some kind of large container for Mana.

I dodged another blast, keeping my eye on where Penelope flashed away from and quickly noting where she arrived, moving once again into the proper position to throw.

The crowd around us was quite the peanut gallery, with many cheering and applauding while others were barely able to follow what was going on. It was wondrous how a barrier made them confident enough to stay so close.

"Your accuracy is worse too," Penelope said, dodging another of Crow as it blurred by her, hitting the wall behind where she stood.

She was the smartest of us all and I would even go so far to say the smartest mind that the empire had ever produced. Whatever inspiration that Shawn had brought from Earth, it was no simple task to realize it on Derra. The hours she spent tirelessly working, I could see in my heart of hearts that this . . .

Penelope was hurting and had been hurting for a long time, I believed. With every criticism, I could feel that same genuine concern I felt before. To have seen her fellow CADs be killed, to watch Shawn die, to see me fall, for everyone I was sure she had lost since that night, she had had enough.

"Penelope," I said, pausing and dropping my techniques as I let my Vitae rest for the moment. "Zactrik getting away wasn't your fault alone. You aren't any more guilty because you were the one to survive."

She stood, her strange mechanical gaze giving little away, but I could tell by the shifting of her body language that what I had said struck true. I knew she blamed herself, for why else would she have made a device such as this? To keep someone contained?

"I'm sure if Zactrik absorbed the Mana of these walls," I continued, remembering the wards placed around the secret chamber designed for Shawn's surgery, "that battery would just continue to supply it with even more, buying you more time to put an end to him. Am I right?"

"Perceptiveness is still top-notch," Penelope said, a touch of bitterness in her tone. "You think you have everything figured out, don't you?"

I shook my head. "No, I truly don't. Every day, I learn more about the world that's changed around me. I take another step every day knowing how little I understand but staying true to what I believe."

And what I believed was that for the last five minutes, I had been throwing my Crows at the exact same spot endlessly, moving to make it look like I'd been aiming at Penelope. That was how I knew that sustaining the wall wasn't automatic; Penelope had to consciously apply more Mana from her supply.

Because I could see the faintest crack in the wall behind my friend, right in front of one of the hallways that exited the gathering hall. She didn't think I could make a dent in it, so she wasn't paying attention.

"I do feel old," I said, even as I let my Vitae begin to well up. "I'm not strong enough to save the world again, not from the likes of Zactrik. That's not my victory though."

The difference between Penelope and me was where we found our victories.

I crouched down low, carrying Crow properly in my grip so as to not create any duplicates, and began to channel my Vitae into a technique I often had little need for. Vitae began to coil up into my legs, like a snake slithering tightly onto the branch of a tree. I felt the energy building up in my arms, almost to a bursting point.

Penelope's palms began to glow with Mana as balls of light appeared within them, both of them pointed at me as she gritted her teeth. "And what is your victory, Rakta?"

That was an easy question to answer, but perhaps the years had dulled her memories as they had mine. And yet, if the nightmare of Zactrik's Mortum could not rip it away from me, then time had little chance.

"Keeping my children safe." I released the coiled-up Vitae within my body as I rocketed forward, all control sacrificed for every last speck of might possible with this technique, roaring the words of my victory. **"Charging Bull Technique!"**

The sheer brightness of the beams of light coming toward me, some spectacular innovation of her previous blasters, nearly blinded me completely, but sight would have been wasted on me. I felt the scorching heat of the lasers, attempting to burn my skin as they grazed me, and yet the Vitae of my charge kept me as safe as it could, blunting the pain as I carried through.

And just as I'd thought, Penelope teleported away, away from any of the danger of my attack, allowing me to continue charging forward and hit the crack on the wall with the full force of my technique.

"Impossible." The sound of Penelope's disbelief was overshadowed by the sound of shattering as the cage of Mana that she had placed all around was dispelled by the sheer force of my blow, my momentum carrying me down the hall as I continued to dash away from my friend.

I felt anger as I struggled to regain my footing and stirred my waning Vitae into the much more controlled speed of my **Great Wind Sprint Technique**. Penelope had waylaid me far too long to prove a point that I was far too aware of, but I knew in my heart that I couldn't hold a grudge for long.

Any punishment I could have asked for this slight had been paid in full a thousand times over by my dear friend. Few in the world deserved to be driven to the brink of madness as I felt Penelope had.

For the first time, as I ran toward the only place I could think of looking next, instead of wishing that Lydia were here, I wished for Shawn.

13

Racing through the estate, I began to feel the pressure rise around me as I moved from the unfamiliar renovated portions of the property to the more familiar passageways that I had walked many times throughout the years. Every step, powered by the wind and my Vitae, brought me closer to my destination, that of Dalton's office.

My gaze was piercing, looking for any inkling of the darkly dressed figure of Noelle, tightening my grip on Crow with every turned corner, just waiting for the chance to stop her. Did I plan on killing her? In the brief peace that I had within the eye of my own storm, I wasn't sure.

There was no question that I owed an apology to the Depth of Death, but there was little place for forgiveness in my heart for those who would go after my children, no matter the justification.

"Perhaps how this all ends lies within her choice," I muttered to myself, pushing off of another wall as I neared Dalton's office.

And as I rounded the final corner, I felt my heart fall as I saw the doors of the office busted and crumpled on the ground, the scatterings of wooden chips everywhere as I swiftly surged forward and into the room.

And came to a sudden halt, feeling my Vitae burning at the exertion, as I took in the sight before me. Papers and documents strewn all about, Dalton's desk looking undamaged but covered in blood, and at the center of it all, Dalton holding Noelle up off the ground by her neck.

"You finally arrived, Father." Dalton glanced at me. "I was wondering how far behind her you would be. Thankfully, the magic of someone like this can barely hold a candle to my investments."

"R-Rakta?" a smaller voice called out, catching me by surprise, before I looked toward Dalton's desk once more and saw Macy hiding underneath it.

I stepped forward. "I'm sorry I took so long. I'm glad that you're both alright."

And that Penelope's interference had not caused a tragedy. I was sure there was still much to speak about with my old friend, but now was not the time for that.

"So." Dalton looked back up to Noelle. "I already got rid of your insurance. You should have known that trick would only work on me once. Do I need to have my maid here rifle through your mind to get my answers?"

Macy crawled out from underneath the table but seemed hesitant to come to Dalton's side, inching closer to my own as I approached. "I think I have some answers, son."

"Let's hear it then." Dalton squeezed Noelle's throat, her wheezing at the sudden increase of pressure lightening as he relaxed his grip a moment later.

And so I told him all I believed, that the Depth of Death had a grudge against me and that they had made efforts to take it out on Dalton. I surmised that Noelle had switched out wine from Jorge's collection with spiked bottles, noting that she'd had a year to become familiar with where he kept it.

Dalton listened, Noelle suffering in his grip as I explained as well as I could while recovering from the effort of escaping Penelope and making it here so quickly.

"That's all I know for now," I said, motioning to Noelle. "She can confirm what we know if we give her a chance."

I tried to make it clear to my son and to Noelle that this was her chance to surrender properly and tell us all she knew. Perhaps, if we were not off the mark, then this could all be resolved without further bloodshed between our family and the Depth of Death.

"Are you willing to tell us all that you know?" Dalton shook Noelle slightly, making her cough and choke as she tried to get the air she needed. I had little sympathy, but I did think it was somewhat needless.

With as much strength as she could muster, Noelle spit on the ground before us, the spittle dropping harmlessly down onto the ground mere inches from my son's shoes. It was clear what her answer was, and by the look in his eyes, it was clear how Dalton despised her resolve.

"Seems like I've arrived just in time," Natakia said as she entered the room. "I hear we need some information from this assassin?"

There was a new kind of tension in the room as my son and daughter stared each other down, the only movement being the shadow that was Esmeralda creeping in behind my daughter.

"I don't remember ever asking for your assistance," Dalton said. "I have no need for a Velbrun to get what I need."

Natakia smiled, tilting her head ever so slightly. "Dad thought differently. He asked me to help."

And then both gazes were on me, and while the power behind both expectant stares was different than before, I was struck with a familiar warmth. It was up to me to put this sibling spat to rest.

"Dalton, your sister was concerned for your safety after I spoke with her," I said, coming up to stand between them, "and there is never a threat to pride when asking help from family."

"Last I checked, she was more family with that creature behind her than anyone from House Tribus," Dalton said, staring at Esmeralda.

Natakia sniffed haughtily. "I see that this is the thanks I get for all my hard work. My brother, ever the cold-hearted brute who couldn't understand a thing if it weren't coated in opportunity."

"At least I don't throw away my toys when I'm bored of them like a child," Dalton squinted at his sister, with Macy flinching in the corner that she had taken refuge in after I moved between the two of them.

"Enough. Natakia, I suspect that you know far more of the extent of Dalton's feelings than you care to admit." I met her gaze, her own failing to meet mine for more than a moment before I turned to Dalton. "And I know that you still have a place for Natakia in your heart, Dalton."

My son frowned, our gazes matched for quite some time, before he said, "I believe we have an assassin to question. Unless the oracle of Velbrun would like to make this quick and let us get back to the gathering?"

My daughter quickly recollected herself before nodding. "Esmeralda and I were actually going through the poisoned wine bottles, and I was able to confirm with a spell that Noelle here was the one who possessed the poisoned wine bottles the longest."

This confirmed that the wine Jorge had originally stored in his collection had likely been switched out with the poisoned bottles. Divination magic was rare outside of House Velbrun but certainly useful in confirming such things.

"Good to have confirmation," Dalton said, certainly thinking the same as me, before he dropped Noelle onto the ground, putting a foot on her chest. "Attempt to cast a spell and I'll hurt you. What issue does the Depth of Death have with me?"

Noelle said nothing, merely glaring up at us. She was obviously hurt and weak from whatever fight had occurred here before I had arrived. I certainly preferred her to look like this rather than my son, but the sheer lack of any kind of wounds on Dalton did make me sympathize with her slightly.

"That's interesting." Natakia got closer to Dalton and me. "There's a lot of hate for Dad and his adventuring party, but the real reason is actually Dalton."

"I've never done business with the Depth of Death," my son stated firmly. "Otherwise I would have known about the usefulness of this black lotus they cultivate."

That was a difficult sentence to digest, but my children continued on with their interrogation even as it settled in my stomach roughly.

"No, not Dalton Tribus." Natakia was looking down at Noelle curiously, like she was an interesting bug. "No, they're after revenge against Dalton Velbrun, the Warlock King."

Noelle was the most stunned of all of us, her eyes wide as my daughter pulled her innermost secrets out from her without even the faintest hints of Mana or Vitae. It was incredible, the gift that Overseer had given my daughter, but very intimidating for those on the wrong end of it.

"That's stupid." Dalton rubbed the bridge of his nose. "I share a name with my uncle; so what? How is that grounds for a political assassination?"

I considered that for a moment, looking at my son. "I suppose you do favor him, from the portrait I saw of him."

Lydia had only managed to save a single portrait of her brother, one that had looked far different from the man we'd fought at the end of our journey. As opposed to her brother's well-kempt appearance and darker hair, the Warlock King had been a bedraggled lunatic with little care for appearances.

"Noelle here was convinced that Dalton was the second coming of his uncle." Natakia smiled at Dalton. "After all, she'd heard such shady rumors about him, not to mention Jorge never spoke very fondly of you. Would it really be that strange for High Lord Tribus of Gelvurt to be the next threat to the empire?"

For a moment, Dalton seemed actually stunned at the accusation before his expression wiped away. I sighed as my son put up a defensive front, although my daughter seemed to take some pleasure in it.

"There are plenty of threats already," Dalton said, his feelings only revealed as he put more and more force on Noelle's chest. "There's no reason to start making up new ones out of nothing."

I put a hand on his shoulder. "Dalton, you're going to kill her if you don't stop."

"Is that an issue?" Dalton's voice was icy cold.

In honesty, it wasn't. I'd killed many in the heat of battle, but the torture of a slow death was one that had never sat well with me, even when I'd considered it in anger. Perhaps my son was different, but while this was his decision to make, it was mine to advise.

"Kill her if you want, but there is no solace in torture," I said, motioning to the pain on her face. "If her punishment is death, then it's my suggestion to make it quick."

In that moment as my son considered my words, I wondered how many he had already taken, how many lives he had ended. Dalton had mentioned another assassin before. Did they suffer a slow death?

"Fine." Dalton took his foot off Noelle's chest. "I suppose it's better to keep her alive and have the Depth of Death answer for this properly. It could just be a setup to make House Tribus look bad."

With a snap of his fingers, Dalton signaled for some guards of House Tribus to filter into the room and apprehend the disciple, with Dalton, along with a quiet Macy, following them to where I assumed they would hold her for the time being. Natakia stepped up closer to me, her smile expectant.

"Thank you for your help, Natakia," I said, knowing when my children wished to be praised. "I don't believe our talk with Noelle would have been so informative without you."

She giggled lightly. "Ah, well, I was happy to help Dalton in his time of need."

Yes, she seemed quite happy to help Dalton, although I felt there was something less than selfless within those intentions. Regardless, I saw this as a success.

But there was still one more question on my mind . . .

"When we were questioning Noelle," I asked, feeling the slightest dread lining my stomach at the thought of what the answer might be, "could you tell if Jorge . . . knew about this?"

Natakia was quiet for a moment, meeting my gaze, before she smiled. "Jorge is clean, Dad. A little stupid with his friendships, but no, he didn't plan this."

That was of great relief. Now all that was left to do was convince Dalton of the truth.

After promising to speak with my daughter again before the party was over, I followed the trail that my son had left with his guards and wandered into the dungeon of the estate.

It was a new addition to the property, one of Dalton's renovations, meaning that I had little familiarity with the environment. And yet, compared to other dungeons, I could already see a difference.

While there were certainly the iron-barred cells of stone that bore that familiar bone-chilling coldness, with plenty of guards stationed to keep any dissent low and mild, there were other rooms as well. More like guest rooms, they were moderately well-kept and warmer.

"What are these rooms for?" It was the first question I had for my son when I eventually found him, talking quietly with Macy. She still seemed quite rattled by the incident earlier.

Dalton glanced at me before turning his attention back to Macy. "Make the arrangements. I'm sure."

"Of course, High Lord Tribus." Macy seemed demure but steadfast as she quietly moved past me, intentionally not meeting my gaze. It was the most professional I'd ever seen her.

Curiosity plagued me about what arrangements were being made, but Dalton approached, his attention fully on me now that Macy had left. "These rooms are for more politically important prisoners, those I believe are better to be treated well for the sake of public relations. Noelle is recovering as we speak."

That made sense. I hadn't been aware of such a practice before, but I had never imprisoned anyone, as my son put it, politically important before.

"What were you speaking to Macy about?" Perhaps the gathering had run its course earlier and Macy was to go and relieve the guests of their attendance.

"Hmm." Dalton glanced around, having eyes on only one pair of distant guards. "I'm planning to remove High Lord Tribus of Niers from the board."

For a moment, I wasn't sure if I had heard right. And then I realized that this had been a possibility the entire night, that my son would take these matters into his own hands.

"Dalton," I said, now fearing for Jorge's life. "Natakia told me that Jorge had nothing to do with this. He merely trusted the wrong person."

"I know that," Dalton said, crossing his arms.

I blinked, running my hand through my hair in confusion. "I don't understand. Why have Jorge killed if you know that this had nothing to do with him?"

"I'm not killing him because of betrayal, Father." Dalton's expression was hidden as it often was whenever I questioned him. "This has proved his incompetence, to a level that isn't fitting for his position. I can't force him to step down, but I can make way for another."

The sheer callousness in the words struck me dumb. The coldness of the act, the death of another for simple convenience rather than any sort of survival. Jorge's life had been spent developing the prosperity of Niers, and it, alongside his life with his wife and children, was to be taken from him for simple incompetence?

"That's wrong," I said, plain and simple. "I cannot imagine a world in which such a thing would be nothing less than evil and needless."

"I can," Dalton said. "Gelvurt didn't grow because of kindness, Father. Do you think that there haven't been countless others? I've paved the way for my people to be happy with the blood of the less important. You saw for yourself the benefits; well, these are the costs."

"I won't allow it," I said, struggling with the words of my son. "I won't stand by and let my old friend be murdered for such a reason."

Dalton glared before the expression disappeared, and he began to walk off. "I know. Is this when you take back your position? Throw the weight of your influence behind my opposition? I'm sure they'll appreciate it."

The distance between us grew with every step my son took, but I already felt like it had expanded further than I had ever suspected before. The actions that my son had taken, the beliefs he had, the expectations of betrayal . . .

"Dalton." I could not hide the desperation in my voice. "I don't understand. Why does it have to be this way?"

He stopped but said nothing. I was left with a yawning abyss in my heart that whispered to me that I would never understand the sheer weight of his view of the world. And yet, I felt a burning within me, one that I, for a moment, thought came from my heart.

"There's nothing to understand," he said before he took another step away, but my body moved before I realized where the burning was actually coming from.

And as my hand gripped my son's shoulder, stopping him in his tracks, I saw the burning mark of House Tribus emblazoned on the back of my hand begin to glow with a fierce light that overtook my vision.

DUSK INTERLUDE: ABIDEMI NEL

et back here!" The sound of anger and desperation was music to my ears and a salve on my soul even as I braved the foul stench of the worst that the street had to offer.

Everything had gone to plan except for the escape maneuvers. Now as I leaped over the street scrubber doing its best to clear the dry crud off the alleyway and jumped up onto a nearby container, I had to consider my options.

Technically, these were supposed to be walkways to help with walking traffic throughout the arcology, but now it was just a mess, the only mildly clean walkways being the main travel platforms. Was there even anything around to defend myself with? Nothing that'd stand a chance against a gun.

"Kei should be here soon." That didn't mean I had anywhere to escape to. A quick check confirmed that I was stuck here, the other way out of the alleyway so mottled with trash that it was basically a dead end.

A distant voice came from the mouth of the alleyway. "I think that shithead went this way! Come on!"

Damn. I took a deep breath in and stepped off of the box and tried to squeeze behind it as much as I could to hide. I needed this money. These credits were my biggest haul yet, and Kei had promised . . .

I took a deep, quiet breath as I heard the sound of breaking glass, my pursuers coming closer to my hiding spot. The two thugs were members of the Crazed Cats, a stupid name for a small group of legitimate criminals that scarred their members with whiskers on their faces.

"I can't believe you let a shitty brat swipe your creds," the larger one with an orange ponytail said, a dangerous rifle in his hand that could likely shoot a hole through me as wide as my chest.

The other one, a less-initiated member by the fewer whiskers that he had, grumbled, "I, fuck, not my fault, okay! I took my eye off of him for a second, no more!"

If they had any kind of scanning implant, it was over for me. Worst case wasn't death but recruitment. One whisker scar and I'd never be anything more than a gutter rat for the rest of my life. Once you got a scar like that, the record that came with it, it cost a lot of credits to wipe it away.

"Well, he's either here or we lost him," the bigger one said, "so get to looking."

And then they began to search the alleyway physically, with no fancy implants or devices coming out to play. That was good; that meant they were limited. Also unfortunate because my hiding spot was pretty shit and the only toy I had on me was a tracker.

"So how young are we talkin'?" The bigger one kept talking as the other began to root through the different receptacles littering the alley-way. I kept quiet, even as they kicked over the scrubber.

"Iunno," the other absently answered. "He was short."

I frowned, but any offense I took was waylaid by the sound of the thug approaching the box I hid behind. The breath I was holding was beginning to burn in my chest, my body reaching its limit.

And just as the thug pushed the box I was hiding behind to the side, the sound of my large gasp was overtaken by the even louder horn that preceded the large crashing force that blasted into the alleyway.

"Hey! Abe!" Kei screamed over the sound of the thugs' shock as her truck rampaged through what had previously been a dead end. "If you're still alive, get the hell in!"

I didn't need to be told twice, barely even once, as I dashed from my spot and jumped into the back of the truck, barely feeling the graze of heat as the thug with the rifle started firing at us. "Go! Go!"

"Don't fucking tell me what to do!" And yet she didn't hesitate, revers-ing as fast as she could, her truck leaving the thugs behind as she sped away, the force of her turning sending me tumbling into the back seat.

The truck had taken some hits, that was obvious, but Kei's smile meant everything was fine. Running a hand through her shaved violet hair, she turned back to look at me with a grin. "Hell of an initiation, huh?"

"Yeah." I felt my body relax, accompanied by the sensation of it almost beginning to give out now that the danger had passed. This was it, though; I'd finished the task. Every last objective, I'd completed it and more.

I was one of the Merry Men now, the first step to getting my family off of the streets.

"So this is the boy?" The voice was old but had that smoothness that came from most of the market vocal implants. That meant he was rich or vain but certainly could be both.

The cell I was in was cold, but I kept it warm with the heat of my anger. My hands were tight, my nails biting into the palms of my hands. It took all I had, all that I was, to not release what I felt into the world. I had no implants to keep my mood even. I had nothing to release me from my cage.

I was alone, but in a moment, that changed. The door opened to the room I had been thrown into, and a man walked in, with dark but graying hair and a slight limp that had to be purely for aesthetics. He was rich—I could tell by the cut of his suit—so the surgeries for a simple limp would have been . . . easy.

"Abidemi Nel," the man said with that same voice that I'd heard before. The guards had been quiet since I'd been taken, and I hadn't been properly booked as far as I could tell.

Whoever this man was, he wanted something from me, and I was in the position that I had little to give other than my life. Was he here for revenge? Had I stolen from him?

He came over and sat down a few feet away from me on the same bench I kept vigil on, some sort of play at being humble and condescending to my level for an honest conversation.

"A member of the Merry Men for five years, reports are that you took them from the streets and into the real game." The man was staring off into the wall, being obvious about getting the information in real time. "Disconnected from your family, but you still send money. Sister just had her first kid; quite young for that. Mother in debt to . . . That's quite a list."

"What do you want from me? Who are you?" I only needed information, that was it. The more I knew about my circumstance, the better I could respond to whatever came next.

"I'll start with introductions." He smiled, his teeth polished white. "My name is Dr. Dane Warrick. I'm a finance manager at ZehrTech."

ZehrTech. That was a big name, a very big name. One of the pillars of the Neo York City Arcology alongside Mortol Incorporated and Fayne Intelligence and the leading provider of advanced cybernetics. He shouldn't have any grudge against me, because I'd never let the Merry Men piss off someone that big.

"I've had my eye on you for a year now, Abidemi." He nodded, checking his watch. "You see, I'm a bit of a talent scout. Corporate brats don't have the right experience to make the cut anymore, you see?"

"Do you think I'd believe that?" It was an insane idea. On the surface level, this was everything I wanted. A gateway into the corporate world, no longer acting through minor-tier surrogates. And yet that was the issue—it was everything I had ever wanted.

Dr. Warrick shook his head. "It isn't a question about belief, Abidemi. Your friend Zei handed over everything she had and knew. I'm here to benefit from your intelligence and cunning just like she did, but I'm not dumb enough to throw you away the moment I have my pride hurt."

I frowned, my mind going to Zei. She had been distant ever since I had taken over the group, passed over for the position by sake of my talent. I'd trusted her, more than I'd ever trusted anyone else, and . . .

A part of me wanted to ask about what would happen if I refused, a naive part of me that hadn't quite yet gotten the memo about the hell I was in, but I ignored it. If I said no, I would be lucky to go to jail.

"What's the plan?" I finally turned to properly look at him.

Dr. Warrick grinned. "Step one, we get you into a proper school with the right papers, and step two, we start building up the connections and experience you'll need for your future job."

"That being?" My mouth was dry as I uttered the words, my anger fading as my mind began to work at the puzzle before me.

"The CEO of ZehrTech."

* * *

"It's been a while, my little Abe." My mother kissed me on the forehead as she let me into the apartment, just one of the arcology jokes of a living space they gave to the less fortunate.

"Ma," I said, smiling as I felt warmer than I had for a long time, "it's been too long. I'm sorry I haven't come by to visit in a while. It's just . . ."

"Busy, busy, busy," she finished for me, rubbing my shoulders in her age-old way of warming me up from the cold winter air of the arcology. "You don't have to explain to me, Abe. You make me proud, and DeDe, well, she keeps me company."

As if summoned by her name, my sister peeked into the room. "I thought I smelled a rat."

"That's your perfume," I retorted, my wit hiding my genuine disgust with how much of the streets I could smell on my sister. Cut from the same cloth we were, but she'd gone above and beyond in making up for my success. "How are the kids and Clark?"

She swayed into the room, looking like a younger version of our mother who had decided to give up on ever being anyone of worth. At least our mother operated a convenience store.

"Oh, you know, kids are doing good, always getting up to trouble." She snorted, like that was something to be laughed at. "And Clark's doing great! Recently got himself a job as a courier."

My mother made a noise in the back of her throat. "I've made it clear how bad an idea that is. Courier work never pays well enough for the price."

"It is dangerous," I agreed. Just last week I had an entire group of couriers get themselves killed going after a rival that had been making far too many moves for my liking.

"Oh, are you offering him a job?" DeDe tilted her head, as if daring me to offer her thug of a husband a job was going to change my feelings on couriers.

It went without saying, but no, I would not be offering him a job. The less connection I had with my family while I moved up in ZehrTech, the better. They would just be targets of the many rivals I had been making over the years.

"Didn't think so," my sister finished, looking satisfied. Something vicious inside of me wanted to prove how dangerous the courier business was by actually offering him a job, but I repressed that feeling.

"Hey, no fighting." My mother gave both of us a swat on the shoulder, "I don't get to have both of my kids here all the time, and I want to enjoy, okay? Are either of you going to tell me no?"

My sister and I shared a glance and shook our heads. "No, Ma."

"That's right." She brought us both into a big hug. The familiar smell of cleaner and cherries on my mother's clothing made me breathe a soft sigh of relief, relaxing more than I had in a long time.

If only I didn't have to also smell that horrible smoke-stained flavor of bananas on my sister, just another point in favor of my refusal to participate in any of the street-level drugs that had been pandered to us as kids. The alcohol I had access to now was more than enough vice for my life.

"So, sit down; tell us how things have been going with the job." Ma had always been supportive of my new corporate lifestyle, even if she couldn't be a part of it just yet. Not openly, at least.

"Not much I can say." Otherwise I'd put them in danger. "But it's been going well. I'm preparing a new proposal for cutting some costs, but I've already got a lot of support. Dr. Warrick and I have been working together on it for a while now."

Dr. Warrick was a lot of things that my father had never been. A man of initiative, a man of rationality, but above all else, a man that had helped me take care of my family. It had taken a long time, but in the corporate world, he was the only man I could trust to have my back.

"One day, we're going to have to meet this friend of yours." Ma smiled. "He's helped you out so much. I wish I had the money to get him a proper gift."

"Your cooking would be enough," I assured her, putting a hand on hers and feeling the wrinkles of age in her knuckles. Once I had enough surplus funds, I was going to make sure my mother lived in comfort.

For the first time in a while, my mind could rest. There was no politics here, no game to play. I could just relax and take a step back from being a member of the corporate world.

* * *

It was in the quiet and darkness before Georgia read out my recorded messages that I had a moment to think about everything that led me to this point. I was finally CEO of ZehrTech.

There was no more clever balancing of resources, no more grabs for power. I had the power. Would I have to fight to keep it? Did every moment come with the risk of losing all I had worked for? Of course.

That was the inevitable truth of the world. No matter how smart you were, how hard you worked, there would always be a danger of losing it all. Whether it came from betrayal at the hands of a loved one or the machinations of an equal, it didn't change the outcome.

Would Ma be proud of me? I could still smell the smoke and fire of her store. I had played dumb for so long, knowing that Dr. Warrick had been the one behind it all . . . In the end, I was the perfect example of never trusting anyone, no matter the evidence at hand.

Interrupting my musings, thankfully, Georgia began to read out the recordings that'd come in.

"Hey Abe, uh, it's DeDe, was just . . . calling to let you know that Clark's in the hospital. They say he, uh, he . . . There was some old shrapnel in his system that tore up a . . . a lot." The message went silent for a moment. "So, I know it's . . . I know it's been a while. I know we haven't talked much, but the bills . . ."

And on and on the message went. My sister had never acknowledged the danger of her husband's outings as a courier. The money was good, yes, but the life expectancy was horrible.

At this point, even if Clark recovered, he'd never carry out another mission, much less be able to keep having his implants repaired. He was a dead man who would push his moving corpse around just to put one more little notch on his belt.

"Georgia, send DeDe the credits she needs for the medical bills, no more, no less."

She never came and talked to me anymore. Why would she? She knew who I was, and I knew who she was; we both lived in different worlds now. DeDe had decided that the speck of filth we'd grown up in, that our father had left us in, was our home, and I'd realized that it was a fucking cage.

One I rattled hard enough until someone heard and let me out.

"Abidemi." A new message began in a deeper, darker voice. "ZehrTech Industries is yours. Now, you pay back the debts you owe us."

And then it ended. Excalibur, the group of couriers I'd paid to make the switch between Cromby and his clone, were professionals. Ones that made sure they got paid once their services were complete and extra if certain requirements, like my appointment as CEO, were met.

"Georgia, send the package to Neon and his crew. It's time to clean the board." You didn't owe debts if the man on the other side of the table was dead.

Instead of hearing a response from Georgia, however, my body froze as the dark voice from before spoke again.

"Yes, yes, it is time to clean the board. Death to oath breakers."

And in the calm before the storm, as if the world had slowed, I saw a blur of motion and felt the weight of the world take hold of me as the heat of an explosion overtook the entirety of my penthouse. And yet, through the literal heat of the moment, I felt safe for some reason.

My penthouse disappeared, and I saw the world below me, the Neo York City Arcology, hundreds of feet from where I was flying through the air. I felt a strong grip around my waist, holding me firmly.

"What just happened?" It was all I could say as whoever had saved me landed on top of one of the nearby buildings, thudding heavily onto the ground with an audible grunt of exertion.

As I was gently dropped, I stood up quickly, my implants chugging as I made sense of my situation and my vitals were reoriented to deal with the sudden surge of adrenaline. Had I been saved by a courier?

My savior rose, and recognition began to build up in the back of my mind like the dread I'd felt when the news broke about my mother's demise. A life-changing feeling that consumed me like I was being swallowed by a bottomless pit.

"Are you alright, Dalton?" My father stood up from his landing, looking scorched from the explosion that had detonated in the penthouse. The explosion that had almost killed me—no, was supposed to kill me.

"What is this?" I looked around, feeling my implants for the first time in decades. "I was supposed to die. I did die. Why am I here? Why are you here, Dad!?"

Rakta, my father, was still smoking as he stood to his full height. "I know it doesn't change anything, not really, but I could see what was about to happen. I . . . couldn't just let it happen."

My heart started to beat hard in my chest as my father smiled at me, and I felt small as he put his hand on my head. Small as I had when I'd first seen him when I was but a baby, the giant who had taken care of me when I could do nothing but glare at the world around me and curse my existence.

"There is no world where I am your enemy, Dalton," he said with shuddering breaths. "I came here to . . . to understand, and now, I think I do. Dr. Warrick, he was a . . . horrible man, and this world has trained you to distrust it. Perhaps that, no, that certainly kept you safe, but it has also kept you from truly living. Please live for those who loved and love you, Dalton. I know it's hard, but please, try to trust again."

For a moment, I thought I could see the visage of my mother standing with him, a face that had become a blur over my years spent in Derra, but now it was as clear as a picture.

And then my father fell over, and I lurched forward to grab him as the world went white.

14

As my vision faded of the world that had been revealed to me, of Abidemi's home, I felt the pain of the explosion that had ripped across my body fade as I was once again in the halls of the Tribus Estate.

Dalton, my son, was in my embrace, and I could feel his shaking form as he hugged me tight, his head in my chest. I felt immense relief seeing that he was alive and well, realizing in the moments before it happened that in the vision of his life, it was natural to see the end of my son.

I was no follower of the Depth of Death. I was not comfortable with seeing the past end of my child, even if it was preordained by history. Within the vision of memories that he and I shared, it was only natural that I saved him.

"Father," Dalton cried, well and truly cried against my chest to my surprise. "I'm sorry. Remembering just how much it hurt to be betrayed, I was always scared of trust. I hurt people because I couldn't trust them to do their jobs, to uphold their promises, to do what I thought needed to be done. It always felt like there was too much at stake, but was that right?"

I held on to him as tightly as I could as he spilled his feelings onto me in a way that he had done only once before, a night that felt like eons ago, but I remembered in my heart of hearts. I felt hot burning tears running down my own cheeks, crying at the torturous existence my son had gone through.

I knew the pain of betrayal, those who had turned to the darkness of the Warlock King or the madness of Zactrik. My mind went to the face of a merchant whom I had once called a friend, but never again.

"But you're right," he cried. "I had a chance to be different in this world. I could have trusted others. I didn't have to try and shape this world into the horrible one I came from. Why did I do that? With this gift of mine, what did I gain that I couldn't have another way? I just wanted to do right by my family!"

There was no answer I could give him, but I hugged him as someone who now understood the depths of hurt that he had gone through. The world he had come from was unkind in a way I had not ever imagined, a foundation of cruelty and decay that had been the soil for the dystopia of his society.

"There is no way to know, Dalton," I said, bringing my hand up to his head and running my fingers through his hair as he held on to me. "But it is not what we have done that we can change, only what we do moving forward. Take pride in what you have accomplished alone, Dalton, and learn from the mistakes you have made."

I let my child cry himself into silence against me as I ruminated on all that I had learned within the last moment, the burning mark of my hand fizzling out as the gift provided by Overseer went dormant once more. I had asked for understanding, and I had gotten it.

"And then, once we have shed our tears," I said, letting my tears fall alongside my son's own sadness, "we shall move forward together to a brighter future."

Our embrace lasted for some time, but eventually my son regathered himself and pulled away from me with a calmer expression. There was still much, I was sure, to say between us, but no longer did he hide his emotions from me. I could see the confusion in his eyes as he stared at his hands.

"That was," he said, clenching his hands into fists, "a strange but egregious invasion of privacy, Father."

I considered all I had seen, having watched the days go by as mere moments, but nodded. "I suppose that is, well, fair. It wasn't my intention to learn so much. I . . . I merely wished to understand."

"No, it's fine," Dalton said, breathing in and out. "I suppose this has worked out for the better, possibly. Thinking more clearly now, it's obvious that I've been working from . . . inherent bias. With you gone, with the future of House Tribus depending on me, I suppose I . . . fell back on old practices. Harder than I ever meant to."

We both leaned up against the walls of the dungeon we were still in, both of us exhausted emotionally from the night. I was also aching in a very physical way, my Vitae having not yet forgiven me for pressing it so throughout this evening.

"I've made mistakes and hurt innocent people myself, Dalton," I said, remembering my time with my tribe. "You have a long life to atone, to become more than what you have done."

"Ha, I'll have to catch up to Macy and make sure she doesn't pen that letter." Dalton shook his head before turning to me. "So, Father, what exactly was that? It didn't feel like a technique or spell."

"It was a gift like yours," I said, unsure of how much Overseer wanted themselves to be discussed, but I said as much as I felt necessary. "It was given to me the moment before I awoke."

My son considered that for a moment before he nodded. "I see. That makes sense. To think that such an ability would even exist. Do you think it could work on me again?"

"I don't know." I wasn't even sure how I'd used it then. Perhaps it had been simply the strong emotional urge to understand my son? I doubted that, with my new understanding, I could genuinely have such desire as strongly again. "Your mother in that world was kind."

"She really was." And then he pushed himself off of the wall and stood with his posture straight and with the bearing of a man on a mission. "I'm going to right some wrongs. Go enjoy the rest of the party."

As he strode off, I watched him go and felt a great welling of pride. Dalton had a hard road ahead of him, but I would walk alongside him as far as my legs would carry me.

And soon, I had faith that Natakia and Daka would walk alongside him as well.

It was as the party began to end, with the many guests of the gathering scattering to the many welcoming rooms of the Tribus Estate and their own properties in Gelvurt, that I found myself overlooking much of the city from a balcony.

The night sky was vast in its darkness but beautiful in the sparkling stars twinkling in the cosmos. The remnants of those who went to the Great Beyond, according to my wife, but my people had always seen them as the first stories of the world, each collection of stars its own indelible legend.

"Enjoying the lights?" Penelope asked as she came out onto the balcony. Any anger I'd felt toward her had withered in the time I'd had to consider her actions.

I looked down from the stars in the sky and rested my gaze on the lights she spoke of, those of Gelvurt. The shining lamps of the street, some powered by Mana while others were simply candlelit, but they made for quite the sight from on high.

"Do they look the same to you?" It was an honest curiosity. Penelope's drive to improve herself had gone further than I had ever pursued it myself. What kind of sacrifices had she made?

"I saw the world differently long before I replaced my eyes." The playful arrogance in her voice was familiar, but she shook her head. "Honestly? Yes. They're more vibrant. I can see the pulsing of Mana around some of them. The details I can see . . . My vision is telescopic. The way I see them changed, but the beauty didn't."

"I'm glad to hear that." And also quite relieved. To lose sight of the beauty in the world around oneself was a curse that I would not thrust upon any man or monster.

Nothing was said for a time, with both of us enjoying the presence of the other. We had gone through so much together over the years and had lost so many of those close to us.

"Dalton came to me earlier," Penelope said, "and told me that there would be no issues with getting the lumber my project required."

I wasn't sure what she spoke of, but then I remembered the pressing deadline that had been pushed upon Caitlyn over the last few months. And yet . . .

"It was my understanding that agreement was with House Taine," I said, looking over to her curiously.

Penelope didn't say anything for a moment before she shrugged. "I honestly thought he would have told you already. That's just a polite fiction. Officially, the wood is going to House Taine, yes, but that's only because their shipwrights have been in my employ for some time."

I remembered the ship that had flown through the air over Dalton and me as we'd walked through the streets of Gelvurt, the marvel of magical craft that I had instantly known it to be.

"Airships," I said, but felt that was not the whole of it. "Not ones for trade, though; otherwise there would be no need for secrecy."

Penelope was quiet for a moment, her arms behind her back as she continued to stare at the lights of Gelvurt, the twinkling of their brightness reflected in the lenses of her eyes.

"This hasn't been revealed to the public, Rakta," Penelope said, "but the tribes of Rusk are being gathered together into what the empire's intelligence has foreseen as an eventual war band of unprecedented numbers."

I closed my eyes, feeling the weight of the news hit me. The last great gathering of tribes had been in the time of Brota and Garrok, a bloody time of fierce warfare. Tribes had often sought to gather similar feats of unity within Rusk, but none had managed before falling apart or being dealt with by the officials of Kakrel.

"What else do we know?" Daka had headed to Rusk years ago. Had she gotten caught up in the stirring of this great gathering? Was she capable of keeping out of such struggles?

"We have perhaps half a year before the numbers get to a point that war could break out. We've reached out to the Grand Cipher, but we've yet to receive any kind of correspondence back," Penelope said. "We think that Kakrel is dealing with a different side of this. There have been increased reports of assassinations and murder within their walls, but details are few."

"And the rallying tribe?" Each attempt at this always had a powerful head at the front and center. Always compared to the might of Brota or Garrok, these attempts often failed due to that individual being killed or disposed of in other ways.

There was silence between us, something I respected for a moment, before my curiosity tugged at me to look toward my friend and ask again. "Which tribe is it, Penelope?"

The look she gave me, mechanical as it was, still had the remnants of the hesitance of her old eyes as her metal hands shifted and scraped up against each other.

"It's the Kroterruk Tribe, Rakta," she said finally. "The leader of the tribe is your sister, Natakia."

I understood her hesitance to tell me now. My tribe, Kroterruk Tribe, had grown to such power and influence that they were a growing threat to the empire? And at the heart of it all, it was my sister who led the masses of Ruskans seeking to be a part of history?

"I didn't realize she had grown so bold or powerful." Though I believed it. Before my sudden slumber, I remembered the bandits of Rusk becoming more and more of an issue. How had that been resolved? I had not been privy to such affairs, but perhaps it was time I was.

I stepped away from the balcony, feeling somewhat dizzy at the sudden news. I only wanted peace for my children and me, but the world continued to plague us with war and conflict.

"I have to think about this elsewhere," I said, unable to look at Penelope. "Thank you for your company, Penelope. I . . ."

"Before you go." Penelope's voice momentarily stopped me. "I have one more thing to discuss."

With much on my mind, I found myself wandering the halls of the Tribus Estate with a heavy weight on my shoulders. Worries that had no place being put upon anyone else within this estate.

Daka was somewhere in Rusk, I was sure of it. I would need to head there soon, or I may not have a chance to get her out of my home nation before it was lit ablaze by the coming war. Did I have the strength to do such a thing? Did Penelope's words have weight to them after all?

"Dad?" Despite my late-night wanderings having been aimless, I seemed to have been found by the one person who could pry my worries from me regardless of my feelings.

I turned around, hesitant but happy to see my daughter again. "Natakia. Did I wake you?"

Natakia was dressed in obvious nightwear but of such finery that it would have been appropriate to wear at the gathering if she'd wished to do so. She approached looking worried, an expression that grew the closer she came. "I have an alarm that wakes me if anyone passes by too closely. I suppose it reached out into the hallway . . . Are you okay?"

"I'm afraid I have much on my mind, Natakia." My daughter's namesake at the forefront of it. "Tonight has been very long, but I'm glad I got to speak with you again before I slept."

We had spoken, of course, throughout the gathering, but my daughter was quite different when out among the crowd of nobles. There was always a sense of wariness around her that I felt few recognized. She had been quite popular, of course, with many desiring her attention.

I was happy that she had the attention she wanted, even if I worried for her feelings beneath the shell she wore when surrounded by it.

"I'm glad too." Natakia smiled, coming up to hug me and rest her head against my chest. "I noticed that Dalton had a lot on his mind. I suppose you talked to him about a . . . a lot."

Dalton's last appearance at the gathering had been at its conclusion, thanking all for coming, before he had retreated to his business elsewhere. Macy had been with him at the time, looking relieved and bewildered as she followed my son wherever he went.

"There was a lot shared," I said before I hugged Natakia. "I am always willing to talk with you, as well, Natakia, anything that concerns you or is bothering you. Have you been eating well enough?"

Natakia had always been so concerned about her weight that it had been difficult to get her to eat even the lightest of meals regularly. Did she still have such an unhealthy dedication to her beauty?

"Oh," my desert flower mumbled, "I've been eating. It's a delicate balance, you know, keeping my figure. I gain weight very easily."

I'd never known her to gain weight so easily, but perhaps my lack of experience in such things was showing. From what I could tell, my daughter at least appeared healthy, so I wouldn't press her.

After answering the question, she simply seemed to enjoy our embrace for a time before she nodded. "I want to join you on your visit to Rusk."

15

I'd known that it would have taken a miracle to keep my thoughts from my daughter, but for her to show such an outright interest in accompanying me was not expected.

"You want to come with me?" I remembered faint conversations of Natakia and Daka wishing to eventually visit my homeland, but while once it might have been acceptable . . . the danger was certainly different now.

"You're trying to find Daka, right?" Natakia shrugged, looking away. "I don't want you going alone, and I certainly don't feel like going back to House Velbrun right now."

She seemed frustrated for a moment, making me wonder just what her thoughts of House Velbrun were after spending so long with them, but nodded, resolute despite whatever had bothered her.

"Let me consider it, my desert flower. Rusk is not, well, I don't believe it will be entirely safe when I depart." Although having her near was certainly tempting. I was reluctant to see her off so soon back to the den of vipers she called home.

"That's why you'll need my help," Natakia said. "And Esme will come along too."

Natakia shot me a look as my heart dropped at the idea of that person coming along with us. I gave her a somewhat helpless look, unsure of how to feel anything but trepidation at such an idea.

"Esmeralda has kept me safe for a long time, Dad," my daughter insisted, looking moments from stomping her feet in anger at me. "I thought you were going to try and get along with her?"

"I seem to remember saying that I would keep an open mind," I reminded her. "I want to see for myself what kind of person she is."

"And what better way to do that than have her travel with us? You know she's strong; you don't need any more confirmation of that." She seemed satisfied with her points.

A feeling of amusement struck me at my daughter's insistence on us traveling together, smiling as I realized that, even if I didn't allow her to travel with me, there was nothing stopping her from taking her own trip. Perhaps that was what she planned if I proved unwilling to allow Esmeralda to join.

I stepped forward and hugged her again. "I suppose I can't argue with that. If there is one thing I believe about Esmeralda, it is that she is strong."

There was much more I believed about her, but I'd share my thoughts once I had learned more about their relationship. Although, with Esmeralda here, my thoughts did go to one man in particular.

"What of your uncle?" I asked, remembering Markus to have become distant from House Velbrun's politics but otherwise dedicated to being a father to his . . . daughter.

"Oh." Natakia glanced off to the side. "He passed away a year ago."

There was a lot to the words that had been left unsaid, something angrier that I hadn't expected. The idea that both of Lydia's brothers were dead now did sadden me, more than I thought it would. Perhaps, if I had been around, things would have been different. No, things would have certainly been different.

"I'll have to give Esmeralda my condolences when we next speak." I did feel sympathy for my daughter's companion. Losing a parent was never easy, as my children were well experienced with. "May I ask how it happened?"

"I wouldn't want to talk about it without Esme here," she said, which was reasonable. "It isn't my story to share."

I smiled, hugging her tight. "I understand. I suppose she'll have an opportunity to tell me on our way to Rusk."

"Really?" Natakia's eyes glittered as she smiled up at me, tightening her hug.

I nodded, unable to resist my daughter's excitement, and we kept up our embrace for a few more moments before I gently led her back to her room and to her bed, wishing her sweet dreams.

While I was glad that my daughter was sleeping peacefully, troubled thoughts still pestered me as I continued to walk the halls of the estate. And to my surprise, they were not thoughts of Rusk that plagued me, nor were they of how Daka fared, but rather, at this moment, I thought of Julian Carnline.

I couldn't put my finger on what had me thinking about him. It was this strange feeling of familiarity, I knew that much, but I couldn't place where it was coming from.

Julian Carnline had been a companion of Caitlyn's for years now, much longer than even I had been, but despite that I had little interaction with him. In my few encounters with him, he always seemed a very relaxed individual, going on about his day with little issue regardless of what life dropped at his feet.

"Caitlyn would know more," I said, knowing that any suspicions I had, I'd need to talk with her to confirm. It was a shame she had decided to take up as a guest elsewhere in the city, for I needed to know that the sensation I felt when I saw him now wasn't just my mind playing tricks on me after Zactrik had imprisoned me for so long.

Now that I considered his relationship to Caitlyn, I wasn't sure of what his position even was. I had met him as a runner, but a simple messenger or guide wouldn't have been at the party tonight. I had never even thought to ask about what his position was or why he looked so young.

"You've got a lot on your mind, Scavenger," a voice said from behind me, that ancient title of mine being used sending a shiver down my spine. A name I had gotten before I had even met Lydia.

"Julian," I said, turning around as I recognized the voice. Lo and behold, I seemed to have summoned the man himself by simply keeping him in my thoughts for long enough.

Dressed in his casual attire, Julian looked as unassuming as usual, but there was a different glow to his eyes as he raised up a simple hand in greeting. "Have you ever prayed?"

It wasn't the question I was expecting, but it began to make a certain amount of sense as I allowed my Vitae to saturate the air around myself, feeling the power throughout the hallway. There was Primus in the air, the primal power of monsters and beings beyond mortality.

"Deep contemplation on something, it's taken as prayer in some regions of the world." Julian raised a finger, smiling. "I'm not fond of being an object of such contemplation however."

"I see." Things were beginning to click together in my head. "Then my suspicions were correct; that feeling I've had, it is not just that my memories have been confined to the corner of my mind, but rather . . ."

Julian tilted his head, waiting for my thoughts to piece together. It was like trying to wade through deep mud, but I pushed through. The murkiness of my mind was nothing like that of the years I'd spent in Zactrik's demented nightmare, that horrible obsidian sea that would always wash me away . . .

Breaking through that murkiness, I could feel my Vitae straining, but I was using no technique, nor was I stirring it to action intentionally. As the light broke and I realized the truth, I could feel my Vitae calm, like it had been aiding me in a war I had not meant to wage.

"A god," I said, feeling the weight of the Primus in the air weighing heavily upon me. A potent aura that existed at the beginning of the world, in a time before Vitae or Mana. "You're a god."

Great unfathomable spirits that moved the world through their unseen actions. Like the Depth of Death, entities that had, in ancient times, fashioned the foundation for society even as mortality blossomed upon it. Invisible but always felt like the wind or the sun, gods were never ones for personal audiences.

Except I stood before one now, realizing what I had been feeling all this time. That same power that had held my mind in place while my wife suffered alone from the knowledge of her prophecy.

"Yeah." Julian nodded. "I guess there's so much of that disgusting stuff still inside your head that it makes it a little harder to affect your mind."

"The Mortum in my head," I muttered, before I gently put that topic to the side and focused on the here and now. "I thought gods acted by way of prophecy or other manipulations in this day and age."

"Is that a touch of bitterness I hear?" Julian cupped his ear at me, as if I hadn't spoken loud enough for him to hear. I frowned, suddenly enjoying this conversation even less.

It was well within my right to hold a slight grudge against them for the suffering my wife had gone through alone. They had kept me from shouldering that burden alongside her, which I was slow to forgive.

"Who are you, and what do you want?" If they were here to further complicate the lives of my children, then I would do everything in my power to stop them.

"I am Wayward Watcher," the god said, cupping his chin. "And what do I want? Well, nothing really. You see, I'm only here because you noticed me. That's interesting, but also, I noticed you and that strange new scent on you, the same one that your kids and everyone else from Beyond has."

He spoke of Overseer's gifts—that was the only thing I could think of. The mysterious being had mentioned being known by the gods of the world, but to think that one would seek me out . . .

And I had never heard of Wayward Watcher. I was not an academic, but my travels had been fraught with many stories of the gods that had molded the world and still did so today. To think that an unknown god such as this had been existing so close to my lands and my loved ones without my knowledge was discomforting.

"I have no answers for you," I said, tensing. "You have given me little reason to trust you."

"Tricks? I haven't tricked anyone," Wayward Watcher said, motioning out to the world around him. "I am who I am. It doesn't mean that I am only a singular existence. I am as much Julian Carnline as I am Wayward Watcher. Are you not a hero and common bandit at the same time?"

"Does Caitlyn know of this then? Those close to me know my past, even if not in its entirety. Who knows of your true nature? How long have you been watching me?" There was still so little I knew.

"I'll admit, no one knows. I like it that way. I've watched mortals for so long that I had to join the show myself, but I'd hate to ruin the story. Making unnecessary waves and ruining everything"—he shook his head—"I'd hate that. So, instead, I've merely watched. I've been watching you since, well, I guess since you arrived in Alwur."

The first time I'd ever met him. To think I'd garnered the attention of such a fearsome existence so early on in my tenure as the lord of Gelvurt.

"The only reason I'm here is because I wanted to make sure we were on the same page," the god said, putting his hands on his hips. "I keep the people around me from thinking too much about me. I don't need that attention or the power that comes with it. You thinking I'm an enemy would make that difficult."

"You merely wish to be left alone?" It was hard to even believe. And yet, was it so unbelievable? I was one of the heroes of the empire, and yet even I desired peace with all the power I had.

The Wayward Watcher nodded. "Yep, no more, no less. Julian will have to disappear if it comes out, and well, that'd cause me a lot of head-ache. You've got more important things to worry about, right?"

The knowing edge to his question did not make me happy, but there was little I could do at the moment. Making an enemy of a god or, rather, another god if the Depth of Death held a grudge against my family, wouldn't have been a good idea when I was in my prime. If he wanted his anonymity . . .

"You'll have your secret," I said, breathing out a heavy breath of air. "I'll think no more of you and continue on my way. Good night."

And as I turned around to leave, wanting to put as much distance as I could between me and this entity, Julian's voice called out one last time.

"As thanks for your understanding," he said, "I think that trip to Rain-water is pretty important. I've got a lot of eyes everywhere."

Never before had I returned from a walk to clear my head with even more weighing on it. The conversation with my daughter proved one thing: I would need to be stronger for the trip to Rusk.

Sitting down on my bed, I tenderly reached up to the stump of my arm and gently felt it as the phantom sensations of burning whispered in the back of my mind. It was gone, but it never truly felt gone.

A clear memory of my failure to save my friend, the same scar that Penelope wore upon her own soul. Had we truly recognized how great Zactrik's strength was all those years ago, could we have mounted a fierce enough defense to catch him in his arrogance?

It was a question with no answer forthcoming, lost to the endless sea that was time. It was like the stories of old where many pondered the tragedies derived from simple, harmless choices. If only a single thing had changed, would I have missed so many years of my children's lives?

"Here and now though," I said as I looked over to the chest laid out on the floor before me, having been brought up to my room by Penelope's servants, "I can make the choices to keep something like that from happening again."

Slipping from the bed and falling gently to one knee, I clicked open the locks on the chest and lifted the top, the faint smell of oil spilling from the contents inside.

And within, dimly lit from the single candle beside my bed, was the metallic sheen of an arm of black metal with an orange-bronze lining wrapping around the joints of the prosthetic. Penelope had told me that it was a blend of a flexible, reactant alloy of her own design and a rare kind of metal called vitanium, able to absorb and hold Vitae.

A new arm that she had made for me after she had perfected it. She had made it years ago for me, under the belief that I'd wake up one day and need it.

"Thank you, Penelope," I said. "I won't let what happened to Shawn happen to anyone else."

16

The day after the gathering, I decided it was time to finally begin my own preparation for the trip to Rusk. I had done all I could in Gelvurt, and while the comfort had been a nice reprieve, every moment I wasted was one more step toward the area exploding into conflict before I got there.

"Natakia is going with?" Dalton seemed deep in thought as he listened to my plans, much of his focus still on the documents laid out in front of him on his desk.

In the time since we had last spoken, Dalton had begun to take small steps to change how some of his operations were being run. The foremost change was, to my knowledge, his plans to eventually use his ability to supplement whatever timber Alwur was able to provide for Penelope's project.

That and discussions had begun with Caitlyn and Jorge to hear out their concerns and begin to rectify some of the more major issues. It was all a process, however, one that Dalton couldn't be away from in its infancy.

"Yes," I said. "I'd ask you to come, as well, but I know that you're busy. After Natakia and I find Daka and resolve whatever issues we can in Rusk, we'll be heading to the Mana Wastes."

"The Mana Wastes." Dalton paused from reading, looking up at me. "You'll be going after Doh then? I seem to remember she asked for supplies to head out in that direction as well."

I nodded. While I did not understand what exactly had drawn her to that area, by all accounts she was under the belief that she was on the trail of finding something that could have released me from my night-mare. I owed it to Dresden and Macy to do the same for them once my family was reunited in full.

"Anywhere in particular?" His keen interest was appreciated; it was always good when my son lent his full focus to a conversation.

I thought back to what Dresden had told me. "I believe my first stop will be Rainwater. Doh mentioned the city to Dresden before she left on her journey."

"I seem to remember the same." Dalton stroked his chin. "I've done some business in the area, but nothing notable comes to mind. The distance means that I've done most of my trading through other lords and substitutes. It's been for the best, considering the criminal element of that area."

"Yes, I'd imagine there are plenty from criminal backgrounds there." The Mana Wastes were generally lawless as a rule, with their strange environment rich with valuable exotic ores that few sovereign powers could hold on to for long. "Any particular group I should be aware of?"

There was always some kind of power struggle in places where the rule of law did not set a definite and respected hierarchy. Generally, there were either smaller groups vying for power in those areas or a singular one that had successfully staked their claim.

"The Diving Bells," Dalton said after a moment. "I believe they were the ones I did business through. The only thing of note is their interest in some of the archaeological sites surrounding Rainwater."

Interesting, but as my son likely thought himself, probably not entirely related to our interests. Still, it would need to be investigated during our search for Doh. Perhaps her interest had lain in those sites?

"A good place to start for information," I said before a thought occurred to me. "There is one thing I'd like to ask you, Dalton."

If my daughter was going to be joining me on my journey to Rusk and Rainwater was our destination afterward, an idea occurred to me. One that felt right, but even so, I felt some hesitation in bringing up.

Having my son's full attention, I put aside my caution and pressed forward. "Does Macy have time for a trip?"

"Absolutely not," Dresden said, glaring at me as we sat opposite from each other in his living room. The warmth of the nearby fireplace did little to defrost the chill of my old friend's gaze. "I won't have my daughter falling to the same dangers that Doh did."

This was not unexpected. When I had sat down to discuss my idea with Dresden, I already knew that the possibility of the man giving his blessing to such a venture would be difficult, almost outright impossible. And there was little I could think to say to convince him otherwise.

Or rather, as a father myself, I felt hesitant to try and persuade him of the benefits of letting Macy join my travels as we made our way through Rusk to Rainwater. Still, I was not the only audience to Dresden's decision.

"Dad," Macy said, rubbing her hands together nervously, "I think I should go."

"Of course you do," Dresden said, his glare fading as he turned to his daughter. "I've wanted to go after Doh before, too, but it's too dangerous."

"Then, well, you should come with us." Macy glanced up at her father before looking down again. The tips of her hair flickered from white to black, a seemingly conscious attempt to not appear as nervous as she felt.

Dresden frowned. "Don't you think that's what I want? Leaving Gelvurt after an attempt on the life of High Lord Tribus though . . . I can't, and neither can you."

Macy's face shifted for a moment, both her expression and her features, before she silently stood up and left the room, leaving Dresden and me alone. The fireplace crackled and popped as we sat there in silence.

"I'm sorry for reopening this wound," I said. "I can't promise I'll even find Doh, and it was cruel to put you in such a position. To have to refuse your daughter's search for your wife . . ."

"No, she's wanted to go for a long time, even before you woke up. Your waking is just the biggest opportunity she's had, well, we've had in a long time." Dresden sighed, rubbing the back of his head.

"I remember a captain of Gelvurt taking a leave of absence once before." I looked around the room, enjoying the pleasant quality of the home. The Booker family household was an old property that had seen a lot of love. "I don't think Dalton would keep you here if you requested it."

In fact, Dalton may appreciate more guards accompanying my group, but I desired to keep my traveling party small. Large groups only attracted the wrong kind of attention in Rusk, and the safer routes that I knew of weren't kind to them either. And yet, I would not reject Dresden.

"Ha, I know that." Dresden sighed, looking away toward a nearby portrait of the Bookers. Doh smiling alongside a happy Macy and Dresden, along with Dresden's late mother who had passed away a year before Doh's departure.

I stroked my chin. "Then why the hesitance in accompanying us?"

"We talked about this before, Rakta, but the worst-case scenario isn't . . . finding Doh dead." My friend rubbed his eyes. "If we find her, but she doesn't remember us . . . I hope you find her. I want nothing more than for you to bring her back, but I don't want Macy to see her like that."

He had shared this sentiment before, but I could tell that this was far deeper of a request. Going out to find Doh, bringing her back, that was easy to do and to agree to, but this sounded different . . .

"If I find Doh but she doesn't remember anything," I asked slowly, "do you want her to return?"

Dresden looked away. "I can't answer that. I'm too afraid to even search for her myself, even let Macy search for her, how is it my right to decide that? No, I'll leave that to you. I'm sorry, Rakta."

"There is no need for apologies, Dresden," I said. "I'll do my best."

In the end, I'd not only had the Bookers' best interests in mind. I'd thought that Macy traveling with us would make for a valuable opportunity to understand the rift between my daughter and her childhood friend, but those were selfish thoughts. That wasn't worth tearing this family apart further.

"The galewind horses will get us through the flat plains without issue," I said, dragging my finger across the landscape of Rusk. "After that, however, we'll have to continue on foot through the Cragged Fields."

"I don't see why," Natakia said, delicately taking bites of her breakfast. "We'll be traveling a lot longer without the horses with us. Not to mention the return trip . . ."

"The Cragged Fields will have fewer bandits, and the fauna there is easily huntable," I said, marking out the path we would take through it, "but the terrain is treacherous to carriages, even ones pulled by galewind horses."

The Cragged Fields were also called the Travelers' Cemetery, with many poor and ignorant souls having ridden through it believing themselves to be the first to conquer the environment. Many of the safe routes I knew were from the intermittent salvage missions that had taken me there.

"Past that, we'll continue on our way to Kakrel," I said, drawing a line from the Cragged Fields to the only fully developed city and capital of my home nation.

"I've never been to Kakrel," Natakia said, finally looking more interested in the planning of our trip. I supposed it had been rather dry up until now, but I wasn't sure if there was much to be excited about.

"It is a beautiful place," I admitted, "although a rigid center for law and uniform thought. The Grand Cipher employs a severe number of restrictions based upon the parables of our nation to keep the people in line."

"Ah yes, the Grand Cipher." Esmeralda gently retrieved Natakia's plate, although it was my opinion that my daughter had plenty more to eat. "I remember hearing that they were an immortal existence."

"Some believe that," I said delicately. "Others believe that the Grand Cipher is simply a title passed down from one inheritor to the next, done in secret to sustain the belief of immortality."

"That's what you believe," Natakia said, easily pointing out my true thoughts.

"I have my doubts whenever immortality is brought up." I glanced at Esmeralda, my daughter giving me a warning look of her own at my idle thoughts.

The Grand Cipher was a storied figure, having appeared after Garrok's passing. There had been a time of great upheaval after the death of the legendary figure, but in the last moment of Rusk unraveling, the Grand Cipher appeared as a new rallying point for those who desired a true capital for the nation.

Only those who had passed a series of trials could gain an audience with the Grand Cipher without being the representative of some other great nation. I had never had the opportunity to meet the figure, having been reluctant to revisit Rusk for such a purpose after I was, admittedly, strong enough to receive an invitation.

"So," Natakia began, "why go to Kakrel? Do you think Daka went there?"

"Penelope spoke to me of the empire's recent troubles in reaching the Grand Cipher," I said, doing my best to speak little of the rising turmoil within the nation. "She asked me to visit the capital and learn more about the nature of Rusk's recent silence."

I paused for a moment, thinking about how much I wanted to say. The back of my hand burned as I looked on at the markings of Kakrel on the map before me.

"Daka is there," I added. I knew not of her situation, but the gift that Overseer had given me was seemingly pointing me in that direction. I would trust the judgment it made.

Natakia put a hand on mine. "Dad, how can you know for sure?"

Her question was pointed, as if she knew that my knowledge came from a place beyond the realm of Derra. That I was not simply making an educated guess but, rather, that I had been given this information from a source that even I barely comprehended.

"A question for another time," I said, "but we must continue our preparations. Dalton is providing all the supplies we'll need, even a coachman for our travels."

With my gentle refusal to answer her any more than that, Natakia seemed displeased as she stood up and walked away from the table. I supposed I would eventually have to speak on my font of knowledge, but in my heart of hearts, I knew that I had little understanding to give.

Perhaps my children deserved to know the identity of the one who had gifted them a second chance as my younglings, but I had little idea how to approach the topic.

As I readied myself to continue my preparations alone, I felt a gentle hand rest on my shoulder before I felt the faint wrongness of my daughter's companion flicker against my Vitae. I tensed, resisting the urge to move away from the foul feeling.

"Don't worry, Rakta," Esmeralda whispered with a tone laden with barely hidden desire, "Natakia is just at the age where so much is confusing."

And with that, she left to follow Natakia, leaving me truly alone. I felt deeply uncomfortable, the weight of her hand only slowly leaving my shoulder as she departed from my view. It was not often that I let myself acknowledge that, while Natakia had inherited much of her mother's appearance, Esmeralda was growing into an almost spitting image of her.

Like a thief in the night, Esmeralda had stolen many of my wife's features throughout the years, and now I was left with having to deal with that familiar smile filling me with dread and unease.

17

After a week of preparation, I had finally said farewell to a majority of those who had supported my travels to Rusk. I had thought that I would be leaning much on the goodwill of my son, but many of the lords and lordesses of House Tribus had put forward the necessary goods.

And while my son was the one who had procured the use of the galewind horses for my journey, it had been High Lordess Caitlyn Tribus who had provided some valuable water crystals enchanted by members of the Auqkers from Alwur, a near-unending source of water. In Rusk, such a thing was priceless.

"I wish you well on your travels, Rakta." Caitlyn smiled.

While Jorge had returned to Niers after the gathering, Caitlyn had remained to finalize some new agreements with my son on some of their prior arrangements. A sign of positive changes to come.

I nodded in thanks. "It'll certainly be more comfortable with the crystals you provided. Our travel can now be a lot more independent of the usual routes taken near desert oases."

Such routes were much more frequently plagued by bandits or tribes taking advantage of the sources of water themselves. The less interaction we had with such groups, the better. While not all tribes would accost us, it wasn't a risk I wanted to take with my daughter alongside me.

"It was the least I could do." She took a sip of her drink. "Your son and I have had a lot more fruitful discussions since the gathering. He's even revisiting cost-cutting measures he implemented for Tribus Academy."

That was good to hear. I'd heard word that some of the decisions made by the council of the academy were being revisited as well. There were many who could get their jobs back.

"I'm glad that it is working out well." It was a slow process, I was sure, but my son had done a great deal in the time I had been away, so I was confident that any changes and improvements to his system would be just as expedient. That was just the skill that my son had.

"There is still a lot to resolve before we know for certain that things will get better," Caitlyn said before she shook her head. "I have hope though. It's been a while since I could say that and mean it. There's talks of getting new benefactors for the academy and everything. We just have to work out the screening process."

A lot of good steps forward, but the whole of the journey was still ahead of them. I understood that sentiment very well. With all the support I had, I was similarly hopeful of our trip to Rusk but knew that much couldn't be prepared for.

"How much longer will you be staying in Gelvurt?" With my return and the gathering keeping her in the area, I was sure that Alwur was missing her and vice versa. My thoughts almost went to Julian Carnline, but I intentionally corralled my mind elsewhere.

Taking another sip of her drink, Caitlyn grumbled, "I'm guessing another few weeks. I'll have some time to visit Alwur, but I have to be here. Jorge should be returning, as well, once he sorts out the mess with the Depth of Death."

Ah yes, that was quite the situation. It had been difficult to do, but I had requested leniency for Noelle. Targeting my child, I could never truly forgive it, but it was due to the decision of my group that the Depth of Death had been persecuted as enemies of the empire for so long.

Even in my parental anger, I knew that while Noelle had acted out of a ludicrous idea that Dalton was the reincarnation of his uncle, although perhaps not as impossible as others thought, it originated from pain and trauma that I had been a cause of. The least I could do was cushion whatever retribution awaited them.

"When do you leave?" Caitlyn had taken my introspective silence as a chance to ask the question I'm sure many had on their minds.

I thought about that for a while before answering. "Tomorrow morning."

Having helped my son and guided him away from a darker path, I was now set to continue on and do the same for my daughters.

"If we haven't heard from you within a month," Dalton said as we waited for the carriage to pull up, "I'll be sending the best CADs I have on retainer to find you."

"I don't remember you doing that for Daka," Natakia said, giving her brother an innocent smile.

My son frowned. "You rarely left your bed. I doubt you remember much beyond the walls of your room from that time."

Natakia gave a slight huff, the first sign that this was going to devolve into something far less familial, and I stepped in. "Let's not let fighting ruin our farewells. We appreciate the help, Dalton. Right, Natakia?"

"If it ever comes," Natakia said before meeting my waiting gaze with an impatient glance. "Yes, I do appreciate it. Thank you, High Lord Tribus of Gelvurt."

They were far too formal of words for family but obviously chosen intentionally by my daughter. I supposed one could not force the time apart from each other to disappear overnight.

She and Esmeralda were both dressed beautifully for the road, resembling escorted guests rather than travelers planning to wade through the dangers of Rusk. Still, any worries about the attire of my entourage were waylaid by the floating mirror dancing through the air around Natakia.

My daughter still glanced at it from time to time, but now I could feel the Mana in those faint looks. Lydia had often used a mirror for her own divinations, and Natakia had followed in her footsteps. Any dangers that came upon us on the road, I doubted we would truly be taken by surprise by them.

And no matter what Esmeralda wore, either of flesh or cloth, I still had the scars on my Vitae to know what dwelled beneath.

"Natakia," Dalton said, looking unbothered by his sister's formality, "I never took the opportunity I had to get you a present when you came of age. Before you leave, I'd like you to have this."

He took a small box out of his robes and handed it over to Natakia, my daughter reluctantly taking it from his hands, but she didn't open it. "I appreciate the late gift."

"It's just a way to get ahold of me if something goes wrong in Rusk," he said before nodding at me. "I'd give you one, as well, Father, but I doubt it'd match your eyes."

I chuckled. "I take no offense. If Natakia is nearby, then nothing has gone wrong. I'll send a letter once I arrive in Kakrel. They have swift couriers there."

And not, I reminded myself as my son agreed, the kind that would do the dirty work of corrupt CEOs and other company men. An innocent profession had become quite drenched in blood on Earth.

"The carriage is coming." Esmeralda's quiet words broke up our familial chat, all of us turning to watch as the carriage provided by one of the local lords approached, pulled by the beautiful emerald galewind horses.

We watched in silence at the light striding of the horses, the trained magical beasts of burden having been a great boon in the past for me and the Continental Adventurers of Derra. I wondered, faintly, if the rise of Penelope's airships would one day make these majestic animals merely a novelty to have.

"I don't appreciate you inviting Macy," Natakia suddenly said, whispering so only I would hear it.

"Natakia," I said quietly but with a firmness in my words, "Macy deserved the opportunity to help find her mother. No matter your past, you should recognize that."

Natakia frowned but said nothing more as the coachman of the carriage pulled on the horses and had them come to a complete stop. It was a large stagecoach carriage with enough space for our supplies in the back and plenty of room inside for sleeping in the nights. The carriage was everything we needed, sturdy but not so resplendent as to attract the wrong sort of attention.

Just having the galewind horses would mean that most would recognize our value, but there was also value in the anonymity of not having any of the colors of House Tribus adorning the carriage. For our purposes, it was perfect.

"Are you ready?" Dalton asked, not to us but, rather, the coachman. The older man nodded, saying nothing, and I assumed he was simply one of Dalton's trusted men. His hair was white from age, and he was dressed in a finely tailored robe made for travel.

Natakia sighed, looking like she wanted to say something, before she silently motioned a hand toward Esmeralda, who opened the carriage door for her and helped her inside.

"Father." My attention turned once more to Dalton, who stepped up to give me a hug that I swiftly returned. "I still have business to attend to here, but should I finish before you return, I'll meet you in Rainwater to aid in the search for Doh."

It was a sudden offer, but not one that I would ever consider declining. "I'll be waiting. If we're all together, I have little doubt about finding her."

After a small smile from my son, he shot one last look at the coachman of the carriage before nodding, turning abruptly, and heading back up the stairs of the Tribus Estate. And yet, before he got too far up the stairs, he stopped and turned back around.

"Bring them back, Father," Dalton said. "Gelvurt is far too big a place for just me."

I smiled and nodded, waving a hand as I clambered onto the carriage with a heart full of my son's wishes. It was a heaviness that I could carry until the end of my days.

I thought back to the prosthetic still resting within the chest stored in the back of the carriage alongside all our supplies. Hopefully, it wouldn't be needed, but I was glad to have it.

As the familiar forests of House Tribus began to fly past us at a brilliant rate, the galewind horses kicking up a storm behind us, I found myself alone with my thoughts as Dalton's coachman proved to be a poor conversationalist. He said very little, focused on his job, and yet he struck me as familiar.

I hadn't even gotten a name out of him, which was suspicious. Dalton seemed to have implicitly approved him for this task, so I had little initial doubt, but after an hour on the road, I was beginning to wonder if perhaps there was some kind of trickery afoot.

"How long have you worked for my son?" Perhaps my son had an easier time trusting the silent type of worker, the kind who did their task and no more.

The old man hummed. "I have worked for him for some time."

A vague answer, and I noticed the faintest twitch of the old man's hands as they gripped the reins. He was nervous, I gathered, but the reason was beyond me. It couldn't simply be that I was the father of his lord, right?

Natakia and Esmeralda were still in the carriage, a faint pulse of Vitae confirmed that, although the simple technique wasn't quite so easy to use with my flagging reserves. Although, Esmeralda's presence was more of a void than the detection of life that the pulse was supposed to detect.

"Is there," I asked carefully, "something wrong? You've been nervous for some time. I promise, this will be as safe a trip for you as possible."

The old man relaxed for a moment, but I glanced up as I saw a flash of something change. As soon as the coachman had untensed, a single bang of his white hair had suddenly darkened slightly for just a moment.

Recognition hit me as I settled into my seat, saying nothing more as the coachman simply nodded and gave no true response. There was far less mystery to my companion's anxiety now.

It was hours later, near the border between the Certillian Empire and Rusk, that the carriage came to a halt as it was time for a small break. There were certain precautions to take now that we neared the sands of my homeland, mostly anointing some of the carriage with a collection of sprays that would deter pests.

While Natakia and Esmeralda relaxed and I did my work, the coachman stayed near the carriage, and I found myself watching as his form shifted slightly, dropping an inch before resuming his original height.

"It is a bold move running away from your father like this," I said, carefully dousing my cloth in alchemical solution before picking it up and scrubbing the wheels of the carriage.

The coachman looked over as he suddenly coughed with a higher-pitched voice than before, "I, um, I'm not sure of what you speak, Rakta."

"Even bolder was the form you took. I suppose it was to distance yourself as much as possible from your real identity?" Doh had spoken once before about her own tactics of obfuscating her appearance.

For a moment, the coachman said nothing before his form deflated into the inky-haired, black-pupiled appearance of Macy, her face naturally coloring with embarrassment as her traveling attire now hung loosely on her smaller build. "When did you notice?"

"Hours ago," I said, going to the next wheel. Doing this with a single arm was difficult but nothing that required me to bring out Penelope's prosthetic.

"So." Macy came over nervously. "Does that mean you're going to let me stay? You wouldn't have continued on knowing it was me if you didn't approve, right?"

That was a difficult question to answer, one I had been considering for quite some time. I already knew the benefit of having Macy with us, but Dresden had been clear about his feelings on this matter. And yet, did I have it in me to stop this young girl from trying to find her mother?

"We need to talk about your mother, Macy," I said before walking over to let Natakia and Esmeralda know that the "coachman" and I needed a moment of privacy.

Natakia didn't seem surprised at all.

18

The closer one got to Rusk, the drier the air was. The lack of moisture in Rusk was due to the assortment of mountain ranges that closed it off on most sides. There was little opportunity for cooler ocean air getting far into the Ruskan desert.

The growing dryness in the air, that was what I let my mind linger on as Doh's daughter considered the question that had been on my mind since Dresden had offered his fears to me.

"I know she might not recognize me," Macy said. They were quiet words but firm with resolve. "If something happened to her memories, then . . ."

Doh had told me once that she had only learned memory magic due to a stroke of luck, a traveling magician having shared their knowledge with the young shape-shifter. Of course, she also didn't remember much about the person, either, forgetting about them being the price of learning.

If she hadn't ever learned it, Doh would never have become the woman I came to trust and cherish. Dresden would never have found his love, and Macy would never have existed.

"Then I have to be the one to bring them back," Macy finished, her fists tight.

It was an admirable goal. "Is that possible?"

"Oh, uh." Macy stumbled for a moment, not looking quite as confident as she had a moment before. "I don't know. Probably? Maybe. It's a definite maybe."

For all their expertise in it, Doh and Macy very rarely had the air of the masters of magic that they so often proved themselves to be. Still, if there was anyone who could do it, it was Macy. She was the only memory magician I was aware of, and she had been taught by the best.

"Doh told me once that the memories lost due to your bloodline are gone irreparably," I said, pulling on some of the tidbits I'd learned from her after so long. "It isn't like forgetting that memory magic can help; it's something more than that."

I was sure she knew this, as well, but if we wanted to find a solution, we had to be on the same page regarding our obstacles. Even if this proved fruitless, I still preferred to think of Doh as alive rather than dead. For as impossible as it seemed, memories were far easier to return than life.

"That's right." Macy nodded. "As we mature, it's like parts of our minds just . . . start working differently. Mom said that it was because the doppelgänger in our blood attacks the concept of identity and long-term memories in our head. That's why we have to depend on our magic to retain any of that at all . . ."

That was far more detailed than I remembered Doh's expertise with her condition being. Perhaps Macy truly did have a method of returning her mother to her right mind if she was without her memories.

"They still go somewhere though." Macy sighed. "But not a place where normal memory magic can really reach. There's a god that Mom started to study to try and help you, the Lady of Yesterday."

Some believed that, along with their gifts to their followers through spells and techniques, gods had inspired mortal advancement into adapting the abilities of gods into abilities powered by Mana and Vitae. If there was a god connected to memories, they would certainly have capabilities beyond Macy or Doh.

"Getting the aid of a god is a dangerous thing, Macy," I warned, feeling a sense of tension at the very idea. "If they even respond at all, some gods ask for much more than they give."

Macy shrugged. "I know that. Mom never called on her, either, but maybe she should have? What if that was the answer to waking you up? Then she wouldn't have had to leave."

"I can't imagine what your mother's plan was, Macy, but keep thinking of what you're capable of before you settle on requesting help from a god." Neither Doh nor Dresden would forgive me if their daughter was hurt while under my protection. Nor would I ever forgive myself.

"I will." She nodded, then nodded again even harder. "I promise."

With that, and Macy's resolve as firm as it could be in the face of her mother's possible fate, I stood up and offered her my hand. "I'd be happy to let you join us."

She smiled and took it strongly, pulling herself up with it.

Riding out into the Ruskan deserts was a return to home that I had not expected to enjoy as much as I did, with the sand whipping into the air on either side of the carriage as the galewind horses sped forward and the sun beating down on the back of my neck as I draped some cloth around my head to keep cool.

"It's so hot, Dad," Natakia complained, covering her own head in a cloth similar to mine after I'd shown her how. While Macy had pretended to be our coachman, knowing her true identity had encouraged me to offer to give her a break and let her sit in the carriage where it was magically cooled.

I'd thought that, maybe, it would be a good chance for Macy and Natakia to speak, but Natakia had taken that same opportunity to join me instead.

"I'm sorry, my desert flower," I said, tugging on the reins with my hand. It was a new experience, keeping the reins taut with only a single arm, but not impossible. "Rusk is unkind to those used to the milder weather of the empire, I'm afraid."

"At least you can get out of the rain back home," Natakia grumbled before leaning back in her seat beside me and watched alongside me as the horizon separated the land and sky in the distance.

The scenery reminded me of the stories my people had about the gods of our lands. Ruskans rarely deified anything, believing gods to be great spirits rather than the true divinities that other cultures thought them to be. Still, my people believed in their great power and the war that had been waged between them.

The horizon was a product of that war, a skirmish between the Earth Below and the Sky Above. No matter their sibling bond, they had fought to destroy each other before a ceasefire had been called at the behest of the other warring gods.

"It's not going to happen, Dad." Natakia spoke up, breaking the silence that had naturally fallen between us as we rode through the desert sands.

"I'm afraid that much could fail on this trip," I said lightly. "You'll have to be more specific."

"Macy and I," she said before she frowned. "And Daka."

The former I had expected her to say, but as she brought up her sister, I frowned. "Dalton said something similar. That none of this would be worth it."

"Dalton probably thought I was a lost cause too." She sniffed. "Just because I had better things to do than watch him play Monopoly from my bed."

I didn't know what Monopoly was; understanding Dalton hadn't brought forward such fine details as that. And yet, she wasn't wrong about what he had voiced at the time.

"He never stopped thinking about you or Daka," I said, smiling, "and neither have I. You have all done great things while I've been gone, but I still don't know why you left, Natakia. What drew you to House Velbrun?"

It had been at the forefront of my mind since I had first heard of her disowning House Tribus and returning to the blood ties of her mother. I was sure she had a reason, but it was hard to soothe the feeling of betrayal that lingered in the corner of my heart. House Velbrun had tried to take them away for so long, and Natakia had willingly gone with them?

"I know what you're thinking," Natakia said, but I had no shame for my thoughts. I wanted to understand and rid myself of these feelings, but for the time being, they were all I had. "House Velbrun had the answers I needed. You always said I was a lot like Mom."

"Your mother was not fond of House Velbrun, either, Natakia," I said, taking my eyes off the road for a moment to glance at her with confusion. "If you intended to learn more about her, then there was no worse place to go than back to her family."

Markus had once told me that House Velbrun had wiped away much of the histories regarding Lydia and Dalton Velbrun, both of them considered black marks on the family. One had attempted to conquer the empire in his madness and the other had simply abandoned the title of oracle.

"I learned plenty." My daughter crossed her arms. "They taught me the same magic that Mom used. They told me I was just as much of a protégé as she was."

"I don't deny the truth of that either," I said, although I'd yet to see her full capabilities with it, "but you've always seen more than I could about people, Natakia. You saw through the lies of a monster that fooled us all. I'm worried about the people whom you've surrounded yourself with."

Natakia squeezed her eyes shut at my reference to that night, which I regretted bringing up, before she looked away. "Maybe if you'd been awake, you could have stopped me."

I flinched, holding the reins tight enough that the horses began to slow down before I realized what I was doing and relaxed my grip. She was right, of course; that was certainly something she had inherited from her mother. It was a difficult and raw medicine to drink, but it was the truth.

The reason why my children had walked down these dark paths and had been vulnerable to the dangerous influences of the world was because I had failed to be a father and protect them.

"I'm sorry," Natakia said, sounding shaken. "I shouldn't have said that. I don't, that's not what I think, but . . . but I want you to know I'm fine. I had Esmeralda, she kept me safe from . . . from all of that. I'm an entire faction on my own, Dad. I'm not owned by any of those old assholes. I'm . . . I'm the Velbrun Oracle! Even among the Velbruns, I'm untouchable!"

She said it with a forced excitement, but one that seemed so genuine for a moment I was sure that even she believed how happy she was. Was she truly free? It was not that I doubted my daughter, but House Velbrun had fooled many over the years.

"I'm glad to hear that you were safe, my desert flower, but safety isn't all that I am concerned about," I said solemnly. "You were once adamant about not having gone down a dark path, but I know so little. Tell me of your time in House Velbrun. Not of the gossip or parties, but of you, Natakia."

She stared at me for a long time before she nodded and rested on my shoulder, holding me tightly as she began to weave her own stories as the sky began to darken and evening neared.

* * *

As the crackling fire at the center of our campsite roared, I was beside myself with thoughts as the girls slept within the carriage. Tonight was my vigil, my Vitae stirring as I prepared myself for the hours of midnight considerations that now pestered me as Natakia's stories twisted through my mind.

My daughter had spoken of being filled with a desire to be more than she was, of having ventured from House Tribus as she saw it falling more and more under her brother's sway. She spoke of a House Velbrun on the cusp of crumbling in on itself, the entire empire seemingly an enemy against it.

Natakia Velbrun, the Velbrun Oracle, had almost single-handedly, save for the aid of Esmeralda and Markus, spurred the faltering lords and high lords of the house into action. They built up new connections within the empire, reorganized their hierarchy, and even stripped some of their useless high lords of their titles and influence.

Natakia's gift and her talent for divination had made her the greatest asset that House Velbrun had, and even though few were truly allies, none could go against her without her already knowing their plan in advance.

"To think that my daughter would have the whole of House Velbrun wrapped around her finger," I said, looking into the flame. "And yet, was it all truly to understand Lydia more? To follow in her footsteps?"

"We had a suspicion, you know," a familiar voice whispered behind me, surprising me out of my thoughts. Esmeralda walked out from behind me and sat down beside me, her shoulder bumping mine. "A suspicion that only Natakia could confirm."

In the flickering light of the campfire, it was even harder to remember that this thing before me was not Lydia. It was only as the flame licked at just the right angle that I saw that glint in her eye that Lydia had never had. Something that was no longer truly human.

"What do you mean?" I asked in a whisper of my own. That unease was back once more, only intensifying the longer Esmeralda held my gaze with her own.

"My father and I had always thought something was strange." She moved in closer, pausing for a moment as if to gauge my reaction. "Strange about Lydia's death."

I blinked, feeling something cold grip my heart. "What do you mean by strange? What did you find out?"

"We couldn't have done it without Natakia, you know," Esmeralda said and licked her lips. "That Lydia Velbrun, the last Velbrun Oracle, was poisoned to death."

And with that, she moved forward and tried to kiss me.

19

When my wife told me she was pregnant, we knew that, in the den of vipers we were in at the time, there would be no mercy for life that had yet to fully bloom. My wife and I had many enemies, and there were plenty who would sabotage our younglings in the womb for the simple fact of my heritage.

And that's why my grip on Esmeralda's neck was iron tight, my Vitae pumping as I held her an inch from my face, her eyes wide as I glared deep into her soul.

"Is that what you told Natakia?" I felt a rage bubbling up within my stomach as I realized that this creature before me had poisoned my child with lies.

For months, Lydia and I checked every single bit of food, every gift, even the clothes that we wore for the tiniest hints of poison. We found several, each and every perpetrator punished as much as Lydia's quickly waning influence would allow.

Lydia's failing health had been a conglomeration of the adventurous life we had led, putting a strain on her body. The curses that we had overcome, the venoms we had endured. Lydia was not poisoned during birth for we had not allowed it, but rather, she was poisoned by the hazards I had failed to keep her from.

"Even if I were to believe that Lydia and I failed to keep ourselves free of the machinations of others," I said, standing up with Esmeralda in my grip, "I would never believe that coming from you."

I felt the sudden pull on my Vitae as Esmeralda's Mortum bit into my physical energy and began to pull from it. I threw her away from me, her body ragdolling across the sand of the Ruskan desert.

"Ha, I tried to contain myself, Rakta." Esmeralda's voice was filled with wanton desire. "I really did, but the way you look at me, that searing hatred, mm! I'd rather you love me, love me like you did her, but that's . . . that's not necessary . . ."

She picked herself up off of the ground, her limbs cracking and breaking like no true bones existed beneath her veil of flesh, before she was staring at me with dangerous sapphire eyes that glowed in the firelight and sclera as black as the abyss.

I held Crow in my hand before I truly recognized the threat before me. Esmeralda was a being of Mortum. None of my techniques would ever harm her unless it was indirectly. She would simply absorb my Vitae until I was a husk.

I stood brave, not letting a thought in my head cross my expression as I tried to figure out how I was going to defeat her. With my reserves, I couldn't even attempt to even the playing field with **First Dance Stance**, and there was no telling how much stronger she had gotten since our last fight.

As the light of the campfire began to dim, as Esmeralda was truly beginning to suck away the light with her dark existence and a fight seemed all but inevitable, the door of the carriage opened.

"Hmm . . . What's going on?" Natakia looked weary but mostly awake as she looked around, seeing the both of us. I wasn't sure what instinct had connected us, but Esmeralda and I both relaxed quickly in tandem, my weapon put away as her eyes shifted to be their normal coloration.

"Nothing, darling," Esmeralda said, almost purring. "Rakta and I simply heard something and got a little spooked."

For a moment, Natakia rubbed her eyes, staring at Esmeralda before glancing at me. She frowned, looking concerned for a moment, before looking back to her companion. "Dad said he was going to handle the watch tonight. Come back to bed."

"Of course." The demon smiled, looking positively innocent as she walked away from our encounter as if nothing had changed. As if we each had not been prepared to murder the other on these sands.

And there was nothing I could do to alert my daughter to the danger of her friend without inciting Esmeralda to violence, a violence that I could not deal with.

No, I realized, that wasn't true. I couldn't deal with her at the moment, but it didn't have to stay that way. I had a way to deal with the foul existence. I just needed time.

I went to the supplies in the back of the carriage.

Natakia was staying close to Esmeralda now, barely leaving any time to continue our conversation or to tell her about Esmeralda's duplicity. It would crush her. It was possible she wouldn't even believe me, but there was no doubt about it.

I knew that Esmeralda lied because such a thing would not have escaped me. Any poison or technique or spell that would have afflicted Lydia during her pregnancy had been obstructed. It was almost a mockery of my wife's ardent battle against the complications during birth to misconstrue her death as poisoning.

With all due respect to the beliefs of my wife and her people, I would rather believe in the Great Beyond than any conclusion drawn from the words and evidence spewed from Esmeralda's mouth.

"You look like you have a lot on your mind, Rakta." Macy seemed far less her anxious self on the open road, away from the pressures of the estate. She was also quite good at keeping the horses on task. "I, uh, I got some real good sleep last night. Although I feel like something happened?"

"I do have a lot on my mind, Macy," I said, unsure of how to even continue the conversation. Did I make Macy my confidante? Did I not risk threatening any kind of reconciliation between her and Natakia if I did so? And yet, did Macy deserve to know the danger of traveling with us?

Macy nodded, looking expectant for a moment, before turning back to the road. "Okay, cool. I've got a lot on my mind too."

"Macy." Her attention was quickly back onto me, despite her own thoughts. "Why does Natakia carry such dislike for you now? I remember you being such great friends."

"Yeah," Macy mumbled, "I remember that too."

For a moment there was silence between us, the only noteworthy sight on the open road being that of a jar snake diving back into his hole at the sound of our approach, before Macy spoke up again.

"I guess it all started with the Rose Gala, you know?" She seemed uncomfortable but persisted in telling the story. "It was terrifying, for Natakia most of all, but she was saved by Esmeralda."

I remembered that. While I had dealt with the pooka-blooded Petur, his brother had been targeting my daughter. The only reason she still lived was Esmeralda's intervention.

"She was scared, but then she came to me, and we talked, and . . . I remember it going well?" She shrugged. "That was a long time ago, but that's when I got sick, and Mom took me home, and . . . then you got hurt. Natakia wouldn't leave her room to eat or anything when she got back and wouldn't open up to me after that. Not for a long time."

I felt my heart lurch, remembering Natakia's words the day before. I couldn't imagine my daughter wasting away in her own room. Scared of the world? Fearful that she was next? Alone with no one whom she could open up to? What fresh misery had I allowed to befall my desert flower?

"And then . . . No." Macy stopped. "I'm sorry, I don't know if I can really say any more. She started going out more, started writing to Esmeralda. I don't know who started that, um, but . . . I don't like talking about Natakia's stuff like that . . . Sorry?"

For a moment, I was frustrated, but it was soothed by the genuine loyalty Macy still had for my daughter. Whatever happened on this trip, whatever we discovered, I believed in a brighter end with her here.

"No, thank you for telling me as much as you could," I said, putting a hand on her shoulder. "I'm glad my daughter has a friend like you, Macy."

"I, uh, don't think we're friends anymore, Rakta." Her face scrunched up, a sad glint in her gaze that she focused on the road.

I shook my head. "Natakia believes that, but I know better. Friendship doesn't always end when one side thinks it has."

A friendly smile popped into my head, one that I had almost turned away from because I was so guilty for turning to him in my time of need when I had done so wrong by him and the others. A smile that had helped me without question or expectation of reciprocation.

"You really think so?" Macy asked, looking at me with unshed tears in her eyes.

"Macy." I squeezed her shoulder gently. "I know so."

As Macy found comfort in my words, I took comfort in her story. While she had spared the details of it, I now knew that something had happened between them, something that I would have to ask Natakia about.

Hours later, I noticed something that broke up the sandy dunes of Rusk and channeled Vitae into my eyes as my vision enhanced and narrowed into the distance. A familiar landmass was near the horizon, a sign of incoming trouble.

"Alright, this is our first serious stop," I said as I had Macy slow us down, pointing to a nearby mesa up ahead. "You'll want to ease the horses until we get about a hundred feet out. Stay with the carriage and let the others know that I'll handle this."

Macy nodded but looked confused. I realized that while my daughter had simply not paid much attention to my preparation for the trip, the young shape-shifter had never been privy to any of it.

"It's fine. This is to be expected. I used to know the people here. If they're anything like I remember then it's better to pay the toll instead of trying to go around," I said, clambering off of the carriage.

The Mattuk Tribe, which in Certillian would have translated to Mesa Den Tribe, was a strange merging of ideals derived from the teachings of Garrok and Brota. Garrok devoted himself to uniting Rusk within a single city, a true nation inspired by the sights he had seen afar, while Brota believed that the heart of Rusk lay within the nomadic nature of its people.

As if attempting to keep in line with the spirit of both, the Mattuk Tribe made their home within this large mesa, a sacred ground of their tribe that was large and filled with many underground tunnels. The Ruskans within would move throughout their home as the seasons changed, forbidding the entrance into the off-season parts of their home.

The Mattuk Mesa, oftentimes referred to as only the Mattuk, was a landmark of the nation because of one simple fact. The familiarity the tribe had with the local area was so finely tuned that their oldest members could tell when others intruded upon it.

"I'll have to practice my Shahis on my way up." I chuckled but felt an undercurrent of fear suddenly blossom in my chest. Did I remember enough to speak it right?

As I began to make my way toward the Mattuk, a hand wrapped around my own. I turned to see Natakia, who giggled as she joined me. "I'd like to see more of Rusk myself. I remember a fair bit of the Shahis you taught us."

I smiled at that, remembering those lessons faintly. I'd taught them far less than I had intended to, but they had such varied interests. It was hard to make time for a language that they would likely rarely use. Thinking of it like that did not lessen the sting I felt at such disregard for my own culture.

"There are far more beautiful sites in Rusk, but I suppose the Mattuk Tribe is a safe tribe to meet." I'd made sure to bring a proper amount of sil for their toll with some to spare just in case they had gotten greedy with their prices. "Esmeralda . . ."

I doubted they would react well to Esmeralda if they took an interest in her. Bringing her along would likely incite a fight and nothing more.

"She'll stay with the carriage." Natakia rolled her eyes slightly. "I suppose she'll keep your little friend safe while we go and handle this."

Little friend? Was she speaking of Macy? I frowned, but Natakia was already walking toward the mesa, her mirror gracefully following her and floating in swirls around her. I sighed, following her.

Our approach was idle and relaxed, neither of us wanting to spook anyone watching us from afar. I was curious as I looked around, wondering when a member of the tribe would approach us. Rarely would outsiders such as us go unaddressed for as long as we had.

"Natakia, wait," I said, gently grabbing her with my hand before I knelt down and felt my Vitae stir as I channeled it into my **Scourger Bloodhound Technique**.

As darkness overtook my sight, and silence plagued my ears. My smell enlightened my suspicions with truth as I pulled back from the technique as soon as I could, feeling the faint burn of Vitae lingering in my nostrils. "I smell blood, old blood."

And a lot of it.

20

Making our way through the winter entrance of the Mattuk, I had Natakia carefully follow behind me. While I wanted to send her back to the carriage, her magic would be indispensable in figuring out what had happened here if there were no survivors.

Dried blood was splattered across the walls like the paintings I'd seen in some of the most ancient of Ruskan sites. There was less untarnished cave wall than there were sections coated in Ruskan remains.

"Dad, there are bodies," Natakia pointed out, gesturing up ahead. I grimaced, having noticed the same. There were many, both men and women. They died while fighting, but they hadn't been struggling against a wild beast of the Ruskan deserts.

These bodies were old, already scavenged by man and beast for what they offered in death. And yet, these wounds were clearly made by manufactured weapons. They were too clean to be of any beast beyond the sabretooth wildcat, but those rarely operated in this region and never killed so many.

"There are no traces of any recent animal activity," I said, having looked around for any other different kinds of markings on the walls. "I think this much death has frightened off any predator from taking refuge within these caves."

"Who did this?" Natakia asked, but there was a tinge of dread in her voice, the kind that came when one was scared of whatever answer they might be given.

"I'm not sure," I said, "but these bodies are in the winter part of the Mattuk, that means these are at least a year old. Probably not much longer than that, otherwise the bush rats would have eaten the bones."

We traveled through the caves, carefully twisting through each corridor, and found even more death with every passageway we entered and left. There was no life here, save the bugs and a few small pests.

"Dad," Natakia said, sounding distressed, "I want to leave."

I embraced her, hugging her head into my chest with my arm as I tried to calm her down. "Soon, Natakia, we're almost to the chieftain's chamber."

I'd only ever been there once before during a funeral ceremony that I had been invited to due to the friendship I had cultivated with a young man from the Mattuk. He had died in a fight against a sandworm, buying time for the others of his tribe to retreat.

"If there are any answers for who was behind this, they'll likely be there." If they weren't, then I'd have to ask Natakia to pull on her own divination expertise.

Farther in we traveled, with Natakia getting ever closer to me the deeper we went, until the passageway began to head upward and I breathed a sigh of relief as we finally reached the center point of the Mattuk Mesa. Where the Mattuk people could freely live year round and gather frequently to share their stories.

For countless generations, this place was the home to the lives and stories of all from the Mattuk. The finely engraved carvings on the walls, almost a homage to the architecture of Kakrel, had been expertly and passionately made over years. One could almost feel the energy stored by the Storytellers that had worked their magic here.

And it was now a place marred by death with the bodies of men and women scattered about. These were old, too, picked clean to the last weapon on them but with fewer signs of scavenging. I supposed the usual suspects wouldn't have traveled this far into the Mattuk with all the easier food.

"Dad, please." Natakia sounded like she was close to tears.

Swallowing hard, I turned to Natakia and hugged her tight. "I want you to wait here and keep your eyes closed until I get back. I just need to walk through that cave."

"No, no." She shook her head. "If you're going, then I am too."

I nodded. "I'll hold on to you. I'm here. Nothing here can hurt you while I'm here."

And so, together, we entered the chieftain's chamber of the Mattuk Tribe, and a gasp escaped my lips as I saw the splattered mess of blood at the center of the circular room. A crass bird swirling through the air painted in blood on the ground with the ceremonially dressed corpse of the Mattuk chieftain at the center.

The symbol of the Kroterruk Tribe, my tribe. My tribe had done this.

With what I knew from Penelope, the sight of my tribe's symbol tarnishing the floor of this chamber should not have surprised me, but the sheer amount of death that had led us to this room struck me dumb. What reason could there have been to do this to the Mattuk Tribe? Had they warred?

There were no corpses outside from what I had seen, however, no expectation of a fight. The Mattuk people would have surely seen a war band of this size coming and gone out to defend their home, yes?

"Can we leave now?" Natakia was barely looking at the room, but she shivered as I held her.

"Yes." I swallowed. "Yes, we can leave now. There's nothing more for us here. We'll learn more outside and away from . . . all of this."

I held Natakia as we departed from the Mattuk tunnels, leaving quicker than we had arrived. Once we were back in the hot sun and dry air of the open Ruskan desert, I sighed in relief. My daughter, too, looked relieved at finally having left that horrid place.

"To think that my tribe did this," I muttered to myself. "I never imagined that their warring would go after those like the Mattuk."

"Were they peaceful?" Natakia asked, her gaze still on the small cave opening of the tunnels we had just left. "Did they . . . deserve this?"

"No," I shook my head. "They assaulted those trespassing on their land without paying the proper respects, but while I would not call them peaceful, they were not barbarians. They had a great respect for their land and considered it disrespectful to not pay homage to that sacredness."

Another thought occurred to me as I thought back to our search of the caves. While we had seen plenty of women and men, the bodies we had found were all of warrior age or older. My tribe had likely taken the children away. Perhaps that had been the reason for all of this.

"Natakia, I'm sorry you had to see all of that." I focused on my daughter first and foremost, bringing her into an embrace that she reciprocated tightly.

She shook her head. "I wanted to come. I just, I didn't . . . I didn't expect that . . . I should have used my magic to see, but, um, I . . . I just didn't think it would be . . . like this . . ."

I held her tight as she shivered against me. "I'll take you back to the carriage. Whatever answers are here are not worth your distress."

"No, I . . ." Natakia gripped onto me tightly. "I have to do this. I want to help . . ."

"You do not need to help, Natakia. You need to stay safe and sound." I began to guide her away from the tragedy of the Mattuk people and back to the carriage where, hopefully, no similar tragedy had occurred.

We were halfway back to the carriage when Natakia muttered something against me that I barely heard but felt an instant alarm at. I looked down at her, my mouth dry. "Natakia, what did you just say?"

Natakia tore herself away from me, looking distressed as she stomped away. There was no grace in her steps as she floundered for the strength to repeat herself. Her gaze flickered from me to her mirror, the familiar comforts of her own appearance helping little as she seemed to simply get more upset.

"Natakia, calm down," I said, approaching gently. "Whatever it is, there's nothing to fear here. You are safe, Natakia, my desert flower."

My daughter rubbed her eyes, looking at me with such distress that I almost looked around for some kind of enemy. It was like she was having a tantrum but out of fear and anxiety. An attack that I had no medicine or protection for.

I needed something to calm her, something that could break whatever emotions held her. I struggled for a moment before I felt something unearth itself out of something dark and inky in the back of my mind and begin to flow from my lips before I even realized it, as my Vitae began to stir at my words.

"There once was a man of great power," I began, feeling the story begin to pull at the spirit of Brota still within the words. "They called him many names throughout his life and after, but Brota was the name his mother gave him."

Natakia looked confused for a moment, her focus coming back to me as she listened intently, her breath still coming at a fast, sporadic pace. She approached, listening as I continued.

"Disheartened by the death and destruction, Brota stood atop the highest plateau he could find and sought answers from the world around him." I held Natakia and slowly sat down in the sand of the desert, gently dragging Natakia down to sit with me as my children so often did when I told stories.

"And the world answered with the desert sands, pushing and pulling at his body," I whispered, feeling Natakia hanging off my words. "And so, Brota allowed it to move him as it wished."

"The first Ruskan dance began," Natakia finished. She took a deep breath, looking like she had come back to herself as her breathing evened out.

Briefly, we sat in the comfortable silence between us, the telling of the story of Brota having calmed both my daughter and me. It had been quite some time since I'd gotten such relief from the stories of my people.

"Dad," Natakia said, sounding tired but determined. "Daka is working for your sister."

I closed my eyes and let the pain of that revelation flow through me, another mark of my failure to add to the tally. I nodded and hugged my daughter, just as I should have done years ago.

Getting back to the carriage, I motioned for Natakia to go inside as I told Macy to take the helm of the carriage on her lonesome as I took a seat inside myself. I needed to speak with my daughter more about what she knew.

Esmeralda had her arm around my daughter, who sat across from me within the carriage. Natakia was far less anxious and panicked than she had been before, but she still seemed comforted by her companion's embrace. The way they interlocked together, with stray whispers of comfort spilling from Esmeralda's lips, I could plainly see the familiarity between them and internally sighed.

Daka's situation aside for the moment, it was clear that my daughter had grown dependent on Esmeralda's poisonous words. Even if

Esmeralda were not as difficult of an opponent, dealing with her had to be delicate. She was like a bee that had stung my daughter. I would have to remove her carefully so as to not have the stinger tear off inside of Natakia.

"Natakia," I said, clearing my thoughts on the subject and returning to Daka. "What do you know about your sister?"

Natakia adjusted herself, moving away from the fullness of Esmeralda's embrace and turning to me. "I, well, I don't know as much as I could have known."

"Go on," I said encouragingly.

"When"—Natakia huffed—"when Daka left and Dresden went after her, I didn't . . . I didn't know where she was going, but she said goodbye and said, said that she was going to find the rest of her family."

She played with the hem of her dress, looking far less than the picture of grace that anyone beyond her trusted few would ever see. I disliked seeing her in such distress, but for all I knew, Natakia held the answers to the questions I'd had about Daka's state since I awoke.

"When I learned enough divination magic," she continued, "I, well, I did get curious. I looked for her with my magic, and . . . it was like a slasher film."

"I'm sorry?" I had no idea what a film was, but I vaguely remembered something from Dalton's memories that seemed somewhat similar.

"It, no, nothing." Natakia shook her head. "I saw her . . . killing people, Dad. She had this mask on, but I was sure that it was her . . . But I think she noticed?"

Noticing divination wasn't an easy thing to do. It required a finely honed Vitae to detect the subtle fluctuations of the kind of scrying that the Velbrun s' staple magic used. Even I had some difficulty detecting Lydia's scrying on me when we'd first started training my sensitivity to it.

"And then I couldn't do it anymore," Natakia mumbled. "Every time I tried, my mirror would just . . . go white."

"I'm not surprised," I said, leaning back in my seat, unsure of the emotions welling up in my stomach. "Once you are aware of such an attempt, like scrying, it isn't difficult to flood the air around you with enough Vitae to disrupt the spell. Your mother showed me how."

And yet, I had never taught my daughter how to do such a thing. Either she had been taught by another or she had intuited the solution to being scried upon by herself.

"Thank you," I managed after briefly getting lost in bittersweet pride. "I know it must have been hard for you to talk about this. I'm sorry you had to see your sister that way."

"Sorry? Dad, Daka is . . . She's murdering people, attacking and killing them!" Natakia narrowed her eyes. "I told you this was a . . . a waste of time. Daka isn't just going to come back, Dad!"

I shook my head, still grappling with the idea of Daka falling to her darkest fears. So many times, we had spoken about her fear of becoming a murderer, of killing another, but now she had been turned into what she had been terrified of.

"She's done wrong, Natakia, but just because she has fallen doesn't mean that we leave her where she is," I said, looking out of the carriage window. "Daka is in a dark place right now, but it's my responsibility to correct that and make right what is wrong for all my children."

"And what's wrong about me?" Natakia suddenly asked, bitter. "How are you going to right all my wrongs, Dad? Have I not done well enough? Are you going to make me leave House Velbrun? Is that the wrong thing that is so important to fix?"

"Natakia." I found myself momentarily lost for words. The sudden turn of the conversation from her sister back to her had jarred me. "I want only the best for you."

"You don't get to decide what's best for me." Natakia frowned. "Dalton was hurting people, killing them, too, and so is Daka. They were doing bad things. I was doing good things. I was . . . I found the person who killed Mom, Dad. I did that. I'm not on a dark path."

I stared helplessly at my daughter but could say very little to that. Esmeralda smiled at me from beside my daughter. For as quiet as she had been, I felt as if I were hearing her words through my daughter.

"You already know that, though, but you don't care. Because nothing I do will ever be enough for you." Natakia looked away, the conversation truly dead in the water as we rode in silence.

21

For days we traveled through the Ruskan desert in quiet conversation. Natakia and I barely shared a word, leaving Macy to keep me company as we sped toward our destination.

We talked of the scenery and of some Ruskan tales that I had the heart to share at Macy's request, but nothing could keep my mind off of the rift between my daughter and me. Natakia had always been insecure, I knew that, but now it felt like less of a child's concern and more of a deep-seated issue.

There had been moments when my daughter thought she couldn't compare to her siblings and had felt abandoned by my lack of focus. With Daka, I could train, and with Dalton, I could study.

I shared very little with Natakia, from her magic to her interest in the finer details of the life of a socialite. Doh had been far better at appealing to that interest than I, for Natakia and Macy both.

She was Lydia's daughter, and I lacked all my wife's exceptional talent to find that common ground with my most charming of children. I just didn't have what it took.

And yet, I still had to try.

Those were the thoughts crowding my head as I felt a bump in the road, the carriage jostling. I looked up from my inner turmoil and saw the signs of desert sand intermixing with rocky sandstone.

"Macy, slow us down, but don't come to a complete stop yet," I said, making a motion for her to rein in. Even with the abilities of the galewind horses, the rough terrain we were approaching wouldn't make for a pleasant ride if we didn't slow down.

We had arrived at the Cragged Fields, a part of Rusk near Kakrel that was the source of the sandstone that the capital used to produce their impressive architecture and walls. Now, it was a rugged spiderweb of multiple unconnected canyons that few tribes entered due to the unsafe passageways.

It wouldn't be long before we would come up on the lip of some of those canyons. We would have to keep aware to make sure we didn't unintentionally approach too swiftly.

Macy looked around. "How close are we to Kakrel from here?"

"Not far, but going through the Cragged Fields will take us a few days," I said, remembering the times my father and I would traipse through these passageways. "It'll open up east of Kakrel, giving us a good vantage point of the capital."

"I'm a little nervous," Macy admitted, rubbing the reins with her fingertips as she held on tight. "If the Mattuk Tribe was . . . attacked, then what could we find at the capital?"

I didn't have an answer for that. Kakrel was the only settlement with walls in Rusk, but that didn't mean that it was impregnable. The fiercest defense that the capital had was the Royal Cipher Militants, a force loyal to the Grand Cipher and composed of some of the fiercest warriors of the sands.

When I had left my tribe, Kakrel had been one of my possible destinations for such a reason, but my tribe had been far closer to the border of the Certillian Empire at the time.

"We'll just need to keep alert and prepared for anything," I said, doing just that as we neared the edge of the first canyon of the Cragged Fields.

Shedding the supplies we wouldn't need for the rest of the trip, such as a large portion of the sil that I had thought would be going to the Mattuk Tribe, getting ready to leave the carriage as we set out on foot wasn't very difficult. I would be carrying most of our supplies, helped by Esmeralda, but with Macy and Natakia doing their fair share with some of their own rations.

Penelope's prosthetic was now in a smaller carrying case that I gripped with my single available hand. It was somewhat disquieting to have no hand free to defend myself, but I put those worries aside.

It should have been a simple transfer from riding in the carriage to setting out toward the entrance to the first route I knew, but nothing had been simple since my daughter had stopped speaking with me.

"So, you'll be taking the carriage back, right?" It was the first thing my daughter had said to Macy since the beginning of this journey, confronting her in front of the carriage.

"Oh, uh." Macy stumbled on her words. "I, no, I'm coming . . . coming with . . ."

"So you're fine with the horses going back alone? Do you think they're going to make it back? Because of your little trick, we don't have anyone to get them back to Gelvurt, do we?" Natakia's tone was practically venomous, tearing into the young shape-shifter.

I approached, frowning. "Natakia, what is the meaning of this?"

"What do you mean, Dad?" Natakia sniffed, looking at me in mock surprise. "I'm just concerned for the horses. I'm not even sure why we let her tag along in the first place, but that wasn't my decision."

Macy flinched back, looking at the horses with uncertainty. The galewind horses looked unconcerned, but for as intelligent as they were compared to other horses, they were still animals.

I looked down at my daughter and frowned. Her lips stiffened as she met my gaze, not backing down in the slightest at my disappointment in her attitude.

"The galewind horses are faster than most predators in Rusk," I said, knowing only a few that could catch up to them when they were unshackled from the carriage. "I'll tie their feed bags onto them and send them back in the direction of Gelvurt. Even if they don't reach home, they should be fine."

"Ah, well I guess it's alright then." Natakia shrugged. "Anything to keep Macy around, hmm?"

"Natakia, Macy is with us to look for her mother once we leave Kakrel." I frowned, wondering what was going through my daughter's mind. "Even if I didn't have confidence in the horses' survival, I believe that they are a small price for giving her a chance to find her mother."

"Oh, so mothers are important now?" Natakia narrowed her eyes, and I could feel the intent now. There was no point to these words or, at least, no point I could see beneath the intention to cause pain.

I sighed, "Natakia, if you wish to hurt me with your words, know that you have. I wish I understood where this anger came from, but I fear that these worries you have do not only come from within."

Natakia frowned, glancing at Esmeralda as I did the same. The monster was primly watching our conversation, tilting her head in curiosity as our attention turned to her.

"You said that you'd give her a chance," Natakia said accusingly. "I love her, Dad. Esmeralda and I are together! She's been with me when you weren't! Maybe I should just take the carriage back if it's so important to have Macy be here! Obviously you don't care if I am . . ."

The words bit into me, and I felt a great stirring of anger in the pit of my stomach. Natakia knew not of what she spoke, of the person she spoke, and to imagine that Esmeralda had tricked my daughter with love of all things . . . What poisoned whispers did she speak into my daughter's ear when I was not around? What idle suggestions were given?

And now, my daughter thought I did not want her around? As if I did not love her as immensely as I loved Dalton and Daka? I had said all the words I had to say to share that love with my daughter, and they had not been enough. What was there to even understand when my daughter spoke the words of another?

"So it is either Macy or you?" I asked, looking at the carriage.

Natakia seemed hesitant for a moment before Esmeralda was suddenly behind her with a hand on her shoulder. That touch filled my daughter with confidence in her ultimatum.

Macy spoke up. "Rakta, I . . ."

I walked over to the side of the carriage and reached down to grip tightly onto the back-most wheel of the vehicle, placing a foot against the side of it as I kept my other foot firm on the ground.

"Oh my." I heard Esmeralda purr and detested whatever pleasure she got out of my building frustration.

And then I ripped the wheel off of the carriage, feeling my anger flood my limbs as I felt the enchanted wooden frame crumble under my greatly enhanced strength. Following through, no words shed as I broke the carriage, I silently tied the feed bags onto the galewind horses and set them free back toward the border.

"Everyone stays," I said, firm in my statement. "Let's get moving."

While I had little desire to speak after such an incident, it was my responsibility to guide the group through the passages of the Cragged Fields, motioning toward weaker parts of the path that would likely fail to hold much weight and giving out other warnings as we continued on. It was difficult to keep the dullness of my voice from weighing too heavily in my words.

As the anger had drained away from me, I felt the burdens of my own mistakes bearing down on me. Would Natakia have joined this trip if I had refused for Esmeralda to come? Would Esmeralda still be as much of a guillotine hanging over me if I had brought guards?

Now, though, I only had one answer to my predicament, and I couldn't be sure if it was ready yet. It had to be ready before we reached Kakrel.

"The only beasts that we have to worry about are the cipher bats," I said as I ducked underneath a piece of sandstone and began to head toward the next open-air pathway, the desert brush of greenery gently swaying in the dry wind.

"Cipher bats?" Macy asked, the only one who seemed to be desperately making an attempt at any kind of conversation as we moved.

"Yes," I said, somewhat tired of the questions after the long day. "They aren't native to Rusk, but the Grand Cipher had them brought to our lands many years ago. They drink moisture from those they get their fangs into."

There was peaceful quiet for a moment before Macy spoke up again. "Why would they . . . do that?"

"Well." I made a quick check of our environment, making sure that, despite her silence, Natakia was alright. There was no doubt that she was sulking as she followed, looking quite upset. "I believe the bats were supposed to be pets. The usual story says that a scorned lover freed them on his departure from the palace."

Any further question that Macy had was cut short as I heard the telltale signs of the very beasts I spoke of. The fluttering of leathery wings in the distance, the subtle vibrations in the air. Cipher bats were excellent hunters, despite being as blind as others of their species. They had a special echolocation, one that detected sources of water, whether they be rivers or unlucky travelers.

"Everyone stay still. I'll handle this." I put down the carrying case for my prosthetic and unsheathed Crow before creeping out from the small tunnel we had been traveling through. I peered out into the brightly lit canyon, looking down and up, before swerving my head side to side.

A small flutter of movement caught my attention, and I saw the bustle of a single cipher bat, the furry winged monster perched on a nearby branch poking out of the side of the sandstone wall. The shade it took refuge in was enticing, I supposed, for an animal caught out in the sun for too long.

A single cipher bat could make a husk of a man within minutes, but a single one was not what I was worried about. As the cipher bat made a small chirping noise, I heard the distant sounds of other chirping noises elsewhere farther into the canyon. There was a swarm of them nearby.

"Don't notice us," I whispered to it, hoping that it would simply pass and nothing else would need to be done. There were more important things to do with my Vitae than waste it on killing such a creature.

And yet, it chirped once more, and I felt the subtlest of vibrations hit my skin, my sensitive Vitae rippling as the Primus came into contact with it. Without a moment of hesitation, with my **Swift Throw Technique**, I sent a single axe flying through the air.

The cipher bat had just turned to me, sensing the moisture in my body, when the axe took its head off and the body fell uselessly down into the deeper parts of the canyon.

I waited a moment before I heard the fluttering of the other cipher bats and felt confident that none had remained after noticing the absence of one of their number.

I returned to the group and motioned for them to follow. Our journey to Kakrel was almost over and yet had only just begun.

22

The Cragged Fields were rarely frequented by the people of Rusk, but it had once been a thriving area simply due to the desire for the sandstone in the region. When Kakrel had less and less demand for stone, the supply was left here to erode in the wind.

Before us was a prime example of that, one of the many quarries within the Cragged Fields. We stood above the large expanse of cut stone, parts of the canyon wall having been shaved down by way of tools and the power of Vitae and Mana. It was like a part of the area had been stolen overnight.

And the drop in demand had been so sharp that I was not even surprised to see the stray square boulders, the building blocks of Kakrel's society, now left to gather dust and be eroded by the wind and time.

"This is a good placc to make camp for the night," I said, looking up into the sky and noticing the sun dropping lower and lower toward the horizon. As familiar as I was with this terrain, I was far from trusting my knowledge to guide us through the night in such a dangerous area.

With this having been an area where many Ruskan workers had scraped at the stone of the earth e n masse, I was less worried that there would be severe hazards here not marked in some way.

"I'll, uh." Macy dusted herself off as she took off her backpack. "I'll get the tents set up."

I nodded. "I'll handle the cooking then."

There was enough brush around that getting a small fire going would be easy, and we had enough supplies to keep it at a cooking level for a while.

"And what about us?" Natakia suddenly spoke up, having said little in the day. She looked tired but determined to throw her hat into the ring.

"Join me in collecting brush for the fire." Despite our exchange of words, I would never decline having my daughter accompany me. Even if I was to spend that time with Esmeralda as well.

Natakia stared at me for a moment before she looked to Esmeralda. "I'll be fine with Dad. Stay here."

"I'd like to accompany you, actually," Esmeralda said, smiling at me. "I think there's something romantic about a night like this."

"We can be romantic later. Just stay here." Natakia was slightly blushing at her companion's words before moving to follow me. Esmeralda's smile dimmed, but she said nothing and made no move to disobey.

I was surprised that my daughter had sought to come with me alone, but I was appreciative of it. Perhaps we would finally have the chance to have an honest conversation.

"Brush, was it?" Natakia smiled, a glint of a plan in her own gaze.

It was peaceful walking through the night. While the dry air of the desert in the day was as comforting as it was tiring, the chilly breeze of the dry cold did little but soothe my spirits as I helped Natakia walk down a steep incline that was common in the Cragged Fields.

"I don't like getting into arguments with you, Natakia," I said as she found her footing. "I'm sorry about the carriage, and . . . you are right in that I wasn't there for you, but now that I am . . . I don't want to spend this time fighting."

"I know you don't, Dad." Natakia seemed glum. "I know you just want the best for me, but you don't . . . you don't get it. I know Esmeralda is scary, but . . . she told me that you didn't believe her about Mom."

"Natakia, your mother was not poisoned." There was no doubt about that. "Why do you believe that she was?"

"There was evidence. There was a jealous midwife. Esmeralda and Markus told me all about it," she said, a fervor building up in her words. "I can't read Esmeralda, not well, but Markus was telling the truth. He believed every word of what he told me, and the evidence . . ."

I sighed, rubbing my chin before bending down to look for a good fire starter. "Tell me about this evidence."

"Lord Hubrick Velbrun of Venil." Natakia seemed eager now, as if I were only now just listening to her. "He was the culprit. We found traces of poison on some of Mom's old clothing, and I used my magic to track the poison used back to the original stock! A stock in Hubrick's collection! He even admitted to it!"

For a moment I wasn't sure what to say, but I knew that I had to say something. My daughter was eager to have me congratulate her, but I couldn't do so without acknowledging the truth of all of this.

"Natakia, I . . ." I paused for a moment, gathering my thoughts as Natakia waited with bated breath. "I can see why your magic was necessary, your expertise, with Markus being far less proficient and Esmeralda only capable of using Mortum, but this . . ."

"Why aren't you proud of me? I solved the mystery of Mom's death! I got the person who took her away from us!" Natakia gritted her teeth, quickly getting worked up. "How could you still be thinking about whatever mistake I made when we did this right! We succeeded!"

"I already knew that Lord Hubrick Velbrun attempted to poison Lydia, Natakia," I said, running my hand through my hair. "That's why you've made a mistake."

"You . . . You already knew?" Natakia blinked, looking at me, before she shook her head. "No, that doesn't make sense. If you knew, then you would have done something about it!"

"We did do something about it. Lydia used the remains of her influence to oust him to Venil," I said, remembering the day that my wife and I had discovered his dislike for Ruskans. "The poison he used, I'm sure there were remnants on old clothing, but they were thrown away for a reason. Lydia never wore them. I knew they were poisoned even before she did."

The poison he had used, veiled pepper, was a contact toxin that made the body slowly but fatally overheat. It was a dangerous plant, but one that had a strong scent that would have likely been covered up by perfumes if we had not limited Lydia's use of those for that exact reason. Lydia had kept me from murdering the man for his attempt, as she had kept me from hurting many others, and had instead pulled on the few strings she had left.

"But that was only weeks before she died," Natakia said desperately. "The timeline fit! The poison would have killed her during childbirth! It would have . . ."

It was in that moment that I saw that vindication in her eyes, that confidence that she had avenged her mother's death, fade, and in its place were guilt and regret.

I approached my daughter and hugged her tight, pressing her against my chest. "Natakia, you did not kill your mother."

"Then why," she cried against me, "why did it happen? Why can't I have a mother who loves me?"

"Your mother loved you, Natakia. Loved you more than anything else in the world. Her children were her world," I said, holding her tight. "She had a choice. The complications with your birth, all of you, it was either her or you, and I have never doubted her choice for a moment. She loved you more than life."

I had often wished for Lydia to be here but always for the children. I missed her with all of my heart, and I still felt the scars of grief, but she lived through our children and always would.

Natakia cried into my chest, and I held her tight as we took solace in each other, my heart beating against my chest as I finally felt like my daughter and I had connected since my awakening.

And yet, a scream cut through the moment like a hot knife.

"Was that"—Natakia's voice was hoarse—"Macy?"

The wind whipped against my robes as I sprinted, my **Great Wind Sprint Technique** surging within me as hard as I could push my Vitae as I dashed toward the scream. I had quickly outpaced Natakia, but I was confident that she knew the way and was in hot pursuit herself.

"Esmeralda!" I screamed as I erupted into the dirt of our campsite, blasting away the nearby tents with the force of my arrival and kicking up sand into the air around us.

She was paces away, teetering on the edge of the canyon we were camping on. Esmeralda was smiling over her shoulder at me, her eyes alight with amusement as the squirming Macy struggled in her grip, her hair as white as snow in her fear.

"That's too bad," Esmeralda tutted teasingly. "I thought you'd be a little slower in your old age. Not that it doesn't look good on you."

Macy's face was pale as she struggled to get small gasps in and out, flailing over the edge of the canyon, empty air all that was below her. Her clothes were torn, obviously signs of the brief but loud struggle that had even alerted me to any of this.

"Put her down." I readied Crow, unsure of what threat I truly posed at the moment but posturing anyway. "I won't ask a second time."

Esmeralda blinked before she smiled, and I leapt toward Macy a moment before the Mortum-powered monster threw Doh's daughter into the open air of the canyon. I dove past her, barely dodging an attempt to grab at my feet, as I spiraled through the air toward Macy's terrified visage.

I threw Crow to the side and pulled on my Vitae, activating my **Skip Dash Technique** and **Instinctive Reflex Technique**, and dashed down toward her. "Macy, grab my hand!"

Her panicked gaze was uncomprehending, never having been in this situation before. I could tell that the fear of the moment had well and truly taken her. She made a mad grab for my extended hand but fell short.

Dresden's face as he thought of the danger his daughter would be in if she came with me flashed across my mind, and I resolved myself as I continued pushing my Vitae. I pushed downward even more with a quick use of my **Air Dance Technique**, reinforcing the air under my feet into a solid force as I kicked off it down to the canyon depths below.

"Rakta!" Macy cried out as I blurred below her, reinforcing my legs as well as I could with my Vitae as I flipped myself over and hit the first ledge of the canyon, the solid ground cracking as my legs dug into the sandstone below me.

Her screams echoed in my ears as I realized, with great terror, that I couldn't properly catch her, cushion her fall as fast as she was descending, with only a single arm. I had mere seconds to consider this as Macy fell closer and closer.

I tightened my chest, feeling Vitae burning in my stomach, before taking a deep breath and channeling the Vitae into that breath as I felt my throat burn at such a crude usage of physical energy. And yet, as I blew up into the sky, the great breath I felt leave me shot into the sky toward Macy.

"Ah!" Macy startled, suddenly held aloft by a breath of air, a mere dozen feet above the ground, before the breath left me entirely and she dropped roughly once more.

Ignoring my exhaustion, I caught her as she fell, much more easily with one arm now that she wasn't falling quite as fast as before. "I have you."

"Um," Macy said, her sense coming back to her slowly, "thanks."

"I need to get back up there and finish this," I said, putting her down and doing a quick check for predators. "You'll be safer down here."

"Wait, take me with yo—" Macy called out, but I was already jumping back up toward the campsite with a plan in mind.

This was the night that Esmeralda died. Once and for all.

23

As I arrived back on the scene of Esmeralda's inevitable betrayal, I noticed that the attention was not entirely on me as I figured it would have been.

Rather, in the bright light of the full moon, Natakia stood before her so-called friend, a conflicted expression on her face as she faced down Esmeralda. "I never asked you to do that."

"Did you not?" Esmeralda tilted her head. "I saw the looks you were giving her, Natakia. The looks that only I see. You didn't want her here; you wanted her gone."

"Not like that," Natakia said, but she seemed uncertain. "I wouldn't want that. I would never want that."

"Darling," Esmeralda purred, "you've wanted it before, just like you've wanted other things. Things that I got for you, gave to you."

"I've never asked for you to . . . kill someone." My daughter struggled with the words, looking positively sick at the idea.

"Oh, is that so? I wonder, then, why all of House Velbrun fears you. Do you really think it's because of how valuable you are as the Velbrun Oracle? Or maybe, just maybe, it's because anyone who bothers you, gets that look from you, just . . . suddenly . . . disappears . . ." Esmerelda began to approach my daughter with a swaying of her hips.

Natakia stepped back nervously, but the monster continued to move toward her. Her hands were out, as if gently beckoning her to come to her.

"Stay, stay away," my daughter said.

The monster didn't stop at the sound of my daughter's voice, but she did pause at the clicking sound that almost echoed in the clear night from the carrying case I had picked up from my things.

"Esmeralda," I said as I grabbed Penelope's prosthetic from out of the case, looking at her as I held it between my arm and side to begin undoing the ties and knots that held my robes around my stump. "When I first thought I killed you, I was sorry that none would ever truly know your story."

"I think my story is quite well told at this point." Esmeralda had turned her attention to me, and to the object in my hand. "Is that what you've been toting along all this time? Natakia wouldn't tell me anything at all about it."

"It was a gift," I said, grabbing the prosthetic properly now that the robes of my right side were untied. "And you're right. Your story has been told by this point. A parasitic parable that has brought nothing but pain to the tales that you subsist on."

"Hurtful." She giggled, eyeing my new arm up. "I'll have to take a bite out of you for that one."

I turned toward Natakia. "Macy is safe. Go get somewhere safe yourself."

With that, I placed the end of the prosthetic up against the stump of my right arm and felt the familiar feeling of its suction onto the flesh. I felt the pins and needles as the metal began to interlock with my Vitae, the musculature and nerves of my body, before the black metal of the arm tensed as I clenched my new hand into a tight fist.

Esmeralda moved away from my daughter as my desert flower moved away herself, looking frazzled by the suddenness of this all. I could feel the disgust rising in me as Mortum filtered out into the air.

"Do you really think getting an arm back is going to even the odds, Rakta?" Esmeralda seemed genuinely curious, the sclera of her eyes filling with the inky blackness of Mortum. "While I enjoy your taste, you're not quite the feast I remember from all those years ago."

"My friend thought the same," I said as I felt the final connections being made with my new arm. The bronze lining of the arm began to glow as I reached into it with my Vitae.

Objects couldn't sustain physical energy like certain enchantments and materials could sustain spiritual energy. Vitanium, however, was as valuable as it was for a very good damn reason.

I felt the kind of absolute rush of Vitae flowing through me that I hadn't in a long time. I felt my limbs move easier, my breath came to me in healthier and faster puffs of air, and I felt the strength of the world reside in me once more as I began to stir this new river of Vitae into something usable.

"You're glowing." Esmeralda suddenly sounded hungry, insatiable.

"I've been putting my Vitae into this arm every chance I could get." I was somewhat lucky that she hadn't attacked later on in the night before I had done so again.

I got down into my **Dancing Star Stance**, feeling my old techniques come to me easier than I even remembered. I was right to not wear this all the time. It was a seductive amount of power, almost addictive. And yet, tonight, it would be useful.

I gripped my new arm with my hand of flesh and felt the hot metal underneath my fingertips, glaring at Esmeralda. "With this hand, I'll be tearing you out of my daughter's story tonight."

I wove around attack after attack in the moonlit night, blurring past each attempt to lay a finger on me as Esmeralda's arms whipped out in black ichorous appendages, tearing through the air that I left.

I hadn't had a chance to retrieve Crow from where I had thrown it, but I could feel my Vitae, alive with the dancing of my people, pull at the axe around me, stuck somewhere in the canyon. I flipped out of the way of a whip before using the **Air Dance Technique** to flip once again as a second whip came to slash at me.

I darted through the air, keeping my eyes on the monster at the center of focus, and saw the glint of metal that flew toward me as I smiled, dashing away from an attack as I snatched my axe out of the air, the metal warm in my grip. And then, flaring my Vitae, I roared with exertion as multiple axes began flying through the air toward Esmeralda.

"Ah, you finally got your weapon back!" She screamed, barely moving at all as the axes tore into her dress and dug deep into her body before shattering as they were drained away. "Going on the attack is bold! And delicious!"

Esmeralda leaped up into the air, a deluge of ichor launching her in the air toward me as her arms resolidified into giant scythes that she began to swipe at me with. It was a blur, my **Instinctive Reflex Technique** working overtime as each blow could have been fatal had it not been for a last-second dodge.

She was fast, as fast, if not faster than she had been that horrifying night I had fought her alongside my friends. And yet, even with all that speed and all that strength, as I began to truly see her movements, I realized that I was fighting a monster that had never met her match.

A monster that had never trained a day in her life.

Had someone like Shawn or Dresden been blessed with the speed of Esmeralda, then I would have been outmatched without question. And yet, her blows were sloppy, telegraphed. Perhaps it was the enlightening amount of Vitae flowing through my veins, but every move she made, it began to be little more than a pattern.

"You should have gotten Markus to train you before you killed him," I said before I flipped over a blade and kicked Esmeralda down into the ground below us, where she splattered into a huge mess.

I stood in midair, solidifying the sky below me, and watched as the mass of ichor began to put itself back together again, the bubbling mess croaking out. "How did you know?"

"I didn't," I admitted. "Natakia told me that he genuinely believed Lydia's death was by poisoning. You knew that Natakia couldn't read you, not like she could read him, but when he realized the truth, a truth you probably kept from him, you couldn't let Natakia learn it from him."

The blob of Mortum shot up toward me, Esmeralda looking much like she had that night as she roared up at me in hunger. I doubted I'd done any significant amount of damage to her, but merely made her hungry. I could barely feel the drop in Vitae from the moment I'd kicked her, but I was sure she'd nibbled at me.

If I was the same man from that night, then this battle was already decided. Alone, I had no techniques that could hurt her easily or significantly enough without it simply feeding her.

"Thank you, Penelope," I said and stared down the rampaging Esmeralda as she flew toward me before I wove to the side and twisted my body as I met her charging attack with a metallic haymaker, the glow of my arm burning bright as Esmeralda screamed in pain, her form blasting away.

She hit a small standing stone, splattering over it for a moment before her ichor reconstituted itself, her eyes gleaming at me. "You . . . I felt that . . . You actually hurt me . . ."

"I can't take credit for that," I said, rubbing my metallic arm. "A friend did a lot of work testing metals that could hurt Zactrik, alloys that could burn the rot of death away. She told me that the special metals that Derra had to offer, they're old. Older than some gods, primordial even."

Older than Mana and older than Vitae. The special qualities of the metals like duplinium and vitanium didn't use mortal energy to interact with the world.

"I'm afraid I can't say what Penelope's special alloy is, but I want you to remember that this wasn't made to kill you. It was made to kill something much stronger than you."

And then I truly went on the attack.

Esmeralda wasn't prepared for the defensive, her evasive maneuvers fast but clumsy as she truly attempted to dash out of the way of my attacks as my metal fist plowed through every attempt she made to throw up some protective shell of ichor. And with every touch, she shook in pain.

I could feel the weight of my blows with my prosthetic; it practically felt like my real arm had returned, and I could feel the impact. I could feel it actually doing something to Esmeralda.

"Stop!" Esmeralda screamed as I rushed at her again, punching her in the face as she whined, a grating and eldritch noise that hurt my ear drums.

She slithered away, skirting around the rocks of the canyon around me. At this point in the fight, the environment was no longer suitable for a campsite. The clearing had been shattered, debris everywhere from the force of both of our attacks.

On top of a large spire of rock that jutted into the sky, Esmeralda reformed, looking haggard as she growled at me, "I . . . I have new tricks too! I don't care if I never get to eat you again!"

I kept my Vitae fluctuating underneath my skin as I waited to see what she did, unsure of what kind of tricks Mortum truly had. Esmeralda put her hands together, and I could see frustration building on her face before she smiled, her cheeks pulling wider than any normal face ever could.

"Yes, yes, that's it," she screamed, and I felt a powerful pulse of Mortum between her hands. "**Sacrilege Against Space!**"

In the palms of her hands, an achingly familiar sphere of death appeared that seemed to warp the air around it, pulling it in with this great weight that I felt in my bones as it formed in her hands. Esmeralda seemed unaffected by her own attack, lofting the orb into the air gently before grinning at me.

"**Black Hole!**" The orb blasted down toward me, faster than I had expected as I moved out of the way. The weight of the effect of the orb was almost crushing as it zoomed past me, digging into the stone of the canyon, and I watched as it shattered the area around it, where even the orb had not touched.

"I can do that again." Esmeralda looked at her hands, as if seeing them for the first time. "I'm learning so much, Rakta. I think I figured it out!"

I surged forward at that, not wanting to give her time to figure out any more of Zactrik's horrid abilities, but she dodged out of the way, her movements more controlled now as her hunger and fear gave way to curiosity of her own abilities.

"I can make more of them!" Esmeralda cheered as another dark orb appeared in the palm of her hand, looking like a giddy child as she threw it at me once more, the weight even heavier than before as I dove out of the way. "I'm going to get you, Rakta! I'm going to rip that arm off you and beat you to death with it!"

As she threw out orb after orb, I realized that the orbs weren't exactly disappearing quickly. In fact, Esmeralda was seemingly, almost unintentionally, surrounding herself with the crushing weight of her sacrilege, which began to slow me down more and more as she moved faster and more controlled.

I finally had the ability to hurt her, and yet even my enhanced speed was slowly being chipped away at. And with her current mood, her movements were too erratic. She wasn't dodging the same as she had been a moment ago, and I didn't have the time to pin down this new pattern.

As I considered my options, Esmeralda suddenly appeared in front of me, an orb in hand that I had expected her to throw. "I'll try it this way too!"

The orb sank into my chest, and I could feel a phantom of pain sweep through me . . . And then I dodged it, dashing away with a precise **Skip Dash Technique** that saved my life.

What?, I wondered to myself before I watched Esmeralda dart at me once more, but I realized that it was not Esmeralda I was seeing, but rather . . . an afterimage of her. No, not an afterimage. A future image, a minor vision of the future that showed me exactly where Esmeralda was going to attack from.

This was divination magic. Natakia was helping me fight Esmeralda with divination magic.

"I see," I said, dodging a future image of Esmeralda and sending her flying with a straight punch to the face, the orb in her hand dissipating as her focus was lost among the pain of my blow. "Your mother would be proud. I know I am."

As Esmeralda oozed back into a fighting stance, looking bewildered at the sudden turn of the fight, I took a deep breath in and let my Vitae circulate before letting a long breath out. My daughter was giving it her all; so would I.

I began to move in harmony with the world around me, the sky blurring as I was the tornado. My Vitae was that of the stars and the moon and the void between. I was the world and the world was I.

For that was the way of the **First Dance Stance**.

"It's time to finish this."

24

Esmeralda screamed with every strike as I ruthlessly pursued her across the battlefield, the powerful magic allowing me to see her every move in advance, giving me a familiar control over every aspect of the battlefield. I'd often battle with great foes, but never were they easier than when Lydia aided me.

Divination magic in the heat of battle was difficult and dangerous. It was a rare art with House Velbrun often appealing to the logic of foresight winning a battle before it occurred, not in the midst of it.

Lydia, however, had been a power multiplier and clever adversary. When her magic coursed through the veins of our group, the rhythm of the fight was in our hands. What did a difference in strength and speed amount to when the future was on our side?

"And the future is on my side tonight." I smiled, feeling my daughter's energy surrounding me and aiding me with every strike, the power of the **First Dance Technique: Twister Through the Valley** empowering every blow.

"Rak—" Esmeralda's plea was cut off as I smashed her face once again with my metallic fist before I reached out and grabbed her by the throat and slammed her against the wall of the canyon, the force of the wind behind my fist multiplying its power.

I dashed back, putting distance between us for a moment, catching my breath. The pull of the **First Dance Stance** was immense, more than my arm could handle for too long.

The monster was leaking, and her ichor was much less potent now, her body beginning to smoke into terrible-looking black gas that seemed to pain her to see. "No . . . I don't want to die . . ."

I walked up, her ichorous body shifting in fear as I approached. I raised my hand up into the sky, the twisting cyclone around me encouraging me to bring it down with all the force I had, to finally end this, when I heard my daughter cry out. The wind stilled around me, losing the edge of anger it'd carried.

"Wait! Dad! Please!" Natakia screamed, running closer to us, far too close to be safe. I paused my blow but kept my eye on Esmeralda, any movement, even the slightest twitch, being the trigger for her downfall.

"Natakia," I said through gritted teeth, "stay back. I am not done yet."

"You beat her, Dad," Natakia cried. "Please, don't kill her . . . I know she's done horrible things, I know, but please . . . I can't watch her die . . ."

Beaten and as close to death as I'd ever personally seen her, Esmeralda smiled up at me in some parody of victory, her treacherous hand still having some grip on the heart of my desert flower. I growled down at the monster, feeling the weight of my blow ready to end this, whatever my daughter said.

"Please," Natakia cried out again, pulling at my heart, "she's the only one I have left . . ."

The despair in her voice ground at my resolve, the delusion that my daughter was so deep seated in that she could not see the truth before her. The truth that whatever affection this thing had, it was only a vehicle for her own desire.

I tried to find the words to say, to convince my daughter of the truth that she would never be alone, that she would always have those who loved her, like me, like Doh, like—

"That isn't true!" Macy screamed suddenly, my attention going to her for just a moment; I returned it to Esmeralda before she had a moment to get any ideas.

The young shape-shifter's clothing was torn, her fingers raw, and her knees scraped as she stood at the edge of the canyon that she had just climbed. After her powerful objection, she slumped, hands on her knees.

"Ha ha," Macy panted. "I've never . . . I've never climbed that much before . . . I thought I was going to die. By the gods, what was I thinking?"

Natakia seemed to recover from her shock sooner than I. "Macy, what . . . Did you just climb back up here? That's . . . You could have gotten hurt!"

That was an understatement. Had she fallen and hit the ground at a bad angle, there would have been little to be done in healing her.

"I know, but." Macy breathed in and out, regathering herself. "What you said, that isn't true, Natakia. I'll . . . I'll always be there for you."

"What?" Natakia seemed even more shocked at that than Macy's physical achievement.

"I've always thought you were the most beautiful person I'd ever seen, the most talented, the most charming," Macy said, her words almost running together as she tried to piece her feelings together. "I'm sorry. I'm sorry I couldn't do what you asked me to do, but I've never hated you. I know . . . I know you know that. You've always known just how much people care about and love you, so why don't you believe them?"

"She's—" Esmeralda tried to say something, but I shot her a warning look that quieted her instantly. I'd kill her before she got a full sentence out if she tried to ruin this moment.

"Then why? Why wouldn't you help me?" Natakia was close to tears, and I wished that I was in a position to turn around and comfort her. "You knew I was in pain. You loved me, so why . . . why wouldn't you help me?"

"It was because I loved you . . . What you asked, I was scared. I didn't want to give you fake happiness through modified memories, Natakia. I wanted to give you real happiness by . . . being together with me." Macy sniffed, sounding close to tears as well. "I wanted to go back to how we were before, when you made every day of my life brighter, but I was selfish, and I . . . I couldn't make your world bright like you did mine."

My daughter had asked Macy to modify her memories!? That was an extremely discomforting idea. To think that Natakia had gotten to that point . . .

"No, you did make my world bright! You were the reason I started getting out of bed after Dad was hurt . . . You were the one who kept me eating." Natakia almost sounded mystified, as if only now reexamining her own thoughts and feelings.

"Then why did you leave?" Now Macy began to sound angry. "I would have gone with you. I . . . I would have followed you anywhere!"

Natakia's response was slow and unsure. "Because I . . . Because I . . . You left me after the Rose Gala, and then I started writing with Esmeralda. She's the one I was writing to then. She's the one who brought up making happy memories and told me about . . . about Mom's death . . ."

It was as she said the words aloud that I could hear the building clarity in her voice. Like the more she spoke, the farther she walked out of a long, dark tunnel.

"Esmeralda told me all the things that I always wanted to hear." Natakia's tone was crushing. "She told me how pretty I was and how smart and great I was . . . She sabotaged people who said bad things about me. She made them disappear. She made the world around me happier . . . But that isn't love is it? That's . . ."

I glared down at Esmeralda as I spoke up for the first time in all of this. "Manipulation."

"Dad's right. It was all just manipulation," Natakia cried. "I'm sorry, Macy. I'm sorry, Dad. I didn't want this. I just wanted to be . . . to be the center of someone's world."

There was silence for a moment, except for the crying of my daughter behind me, until I heard the sounds of Macy walking near her and the sound of my daughter's crying becoming muffled.

"I . . . I don't know about this center-of-the-world stuff," Macy said, tears in her voice as well, "but I'd really like to be friends again, and uh, we could try on those dresses that always . . . fit you more than me."

"They looked great on you, too, Macy," Natakia mumbled back. I could hear the faintest hint of a giggle in her voice, the tiniest sparks of friendship blossoming between them again.

I felt the burn of Overseer's gift on the back of my hand, but it seemed that such a gift wasn't necessary here. All my daughter needed was a chance to see the friend she always had waiting for her, even in her darkest moment.

"Now," I said, having kept my eye on the final issue in all of this, "I believe there will be little love lost in the world with your end."

Esmeralda had shrunk in on herself as Macy and Natakia made up, each revelation between them, unmarred by her toxicity, breaking her control one truth at a time. Now she was simply a puddle of ichor that had the barest familiarity to my wife.

"If I had a choice to do it all over again," she said, smiling something horrifically human, "I wouldn't change a thing."

With that, I let all my rage unleash upon the monster before me, my fist coming down with the force of all the lives that she had taken in the name of keeping her horrid existence and lies alive.

"So," Natakia said, "she's really gone, huh?"

I nodded, an arm around both Natakia and Macy. "Yes, she's gone."

We all looked a mess, each and every one of us having gone through a hell of a night. Much of my clothing was either ripped and torn or stained by ichor, while Macy had torn her outfit climbing up the side of the canyon. Natakia, almost as if a second gift of hers, seemed mostly unharmed except for the sand and dust that covered her from head to toe.

"She was a bitch," Macy said, looking more exhausted than either Natakia or me. I suppose she was the one who had truly gone above and beyond her limits tonight.

I, on the other hand, had pulled back from the source of Vitae within my arm, letting my reserves return to their normal capacity. The remnants of Esmeralda had turned into smoke and faded away with a horrific scream that I dared not remember too fully.

There was a great relief in my heart now that she was gone and Natakia finally seemed . . . not entirely fine but on the road to recovery.

"I guess I was on a dark path," my daughter said, sighing. "It just . . . felt so nice. I really thought I was finally doing something important with my life, but it was all . . ."

She gestured in the air, like something she was holding on to was taken by the wind. Natakia stared out into the sky, as if wondering if it would come back to her.

"Everything you do is important, Natakia," I said, hugging her close. "The importance of a thing is not self-evident; our hearts and minds give it importance. I would rather you live a life of skullduggery than pursue something simply because you thought it gave your life meaning."

So many things in my life were important because of the love I felt for them. My children, my wife, they were all important to me. Doh and Dresden, Orion and his family, my adventuring friends . . .

"Mom always said that one silver lining of our curse"—Macy sounded half-asleep—"was something about truly knowing the importance of the memories we make because of . . . being at risk of losing them."

"Have you done your nightly routine yet?" Natakia was suddenly more alert, standing up and staring down at Macy.

"Oh, uh, not really." Macy scratched the back of her head. "I should, uh, do that . . ."

Natakia helped her up, and they began to wander over to the remnants of our campsite, getting ready for whatever rest they could manage in the aftermath of my fight with Esmeralda.

As my worry for Natakia began to drain from me, I felt my fears of Daka's predicament begin to take root in the fertile soil of peace that they had left behind. What darkness had befallen my little warrior?

"Dad," my daughter called out, chasing my thoughts away, "could you move this rock off of Macy's tent?"

I hesitated for a moment before standing up. There would be plenty of time to worry myself sick about all that Daka had done. For the time being, I deserved some rest, and so did the girls.

In the peace of the night, as we all slept in the scavenged remains of our tents and the stray scraps of comfort they provided. I had almost found rest when I was approached.

"Dad," Natakia mumbled to me, "are you still awake?"

She sounded unsure, but there was a resolve in her voice that piqued my interest. What resolution had my child come to? And about what?

"I am always awake for you, my desert flower." Of course, I was a very light sleeper. I had stirred from any thoughts of sleep the moment I heard the rustling of her getting out of her bedroll.

There was silence for a moment, and I opened my eyes to see her looking down at me. Even covered in the debris of the night, she was as beautiful as her mother in the light of the moon.

"I want you to understand me, Dad," she said, placing a hand on my shoulder. "You wanted to, right? I could tell that it was important, that it was . . . It was maybe how you spoke to Dalton."

She wanted me to understand? For a moment I was confused before it registered what she was truly asking. Natakia wanted me to use the gift I had received to peer into her life, to understand her as I had with her brother.

I sat up out of my bedroll, hesitant. "Why do you want that, Natakia? It isn't an easy thing to do. Dalton lived out much that I'm sure he could have done without. I can understand you without . . . that."

"I want you to see, though." Natakia seemed unsure now. "I want . . . I don't want to hide who I was or . . . Really, it's just too painful and weird to talk about. Please, I want you to see it."

I was unsure, but I felt the burn of the symbol on the back of my hand. If my daughter desired to be understood, then it was my desire as well.

"Alright, Natakia, let us try," I said as I held out my hand for her to take. With a small breath of preparation, my desert flower grabbed it, and the world was overcome by a familiar white light.

DUSK INTERLUDE: EMILIA HEATHERTON

There you are." Light hit me as my blanket was pulled off of me, making me whine as Allie's face popped into view. "Come on, Em, you can't hide out forever."

"I don't wanna go." I wrapped my arms around my legs, my knees up to my chest. Dad had said that we were going to go watch dancing today with all the music, but now we're going to some crummy party."

"Mom said there'll be lots of pretty dresses though!" Allie tugged at me, trying to pull me off the bed. "I know you like the pretty dresses!"

Well, yeah, I did, but I didn't want to admit that I did. Mom's friends had made oinking noises the last time I wore one. "I don't like them, stupid."

"Don't call me stupid." Now my sister was pouting. I didn't like it when she pouted. Everyone always talked about how perfect it was. They were always talking about my sister.

"Then don't be stupid," I said, feeling a hint of pride at outsmarting her.

Allie stuck out her tongue before pulling on me again. "Come on, it'll be fun. Mom's in a movie! She's a big superhero! And Dad said we'll go see a show tomorrow, so it'll be fine!"

I scrunched up my face, but it did sound nice to go see Mom being cool on-screen. I could even talk to her about the movie afterward! That sounded like a lot of fun actually.

"Okay," I said, letting Allie pull me out of bed. "I'll go, I guess."

My big sister ruffled my hair with a big grin, which she knew I hated. Getting ready, I looked over at my closet. Mom had said we needed to dress up really nice for tonight, but I wasn't sure what that actually meant. She was never really happy with what I wore, so maybe I should just go ask her?

I opened my door and walked out into the hallway, going toward my parents' room. As I got closer, I could hear Mom and Dad talking through the door. I wasn't supposed to eavesdrop, but it was rude to interrupt, so I just stood there and listened until they were done.

And maybe, just maybe, I got a little closer to listen in.

"Absolutely not," Dad said, sounding like he wanted to yell but wasn't for some reason. "You know I'm not fond of your new age shit, Martina. I don't want it near our kids."

"Look, deny the health benefits if you want, but you can't deny the networking opportunities. Our daughters aren't going to be anyone important if we don't help them out." Mom didn't sound very happy either.

I heard a loud thud. "Alassandra is already auditioning for commercials, and you've got Emilia going to dance and gymnastics. How much more do you want from them? They're still kids!"

I fidgeted at the door, feeling like listening in was less and less of a good idea. Maybe I should just go ask Allie what to wear? Mom always liked what she wore.

"The dancing was your idea, Roy. Don't put that on me," Mom sighed, frustrated.

Dad huffed. "Emilia likes dancing. At least when you aren't comparing her to all the other girls up there on the stage with her."

"Of course I compare them. Do you think I should just ignore how tubby our not-so-little girl is compared to all the other dancers? Honestly, Roy, I think I pay more attention than you do."

"She's only nine, Martina! She's just losing her baby fat a little slower than the other girls . . ."

I wasn't sure what my dad said after that as I walked away back to my room. I sat down on my bed again, my vision going weird as I felt my cheeks begin to scrunch up. I wasn't going to cry; I refused. Mom said I was an ugly crier, so I shouldn't cry.

"Hey, you said you were coming." Allie popped her head back in. "Why aren't you getting ready? Do you need help?"

"No." I rubbed my eyes, wanting to cry even less in front of her. Allie was a pretty crier, the kind of crying that would get boys to do what she wanted. That's what Mom had said.

Allie stared at me for a moment before putting on a big smile. "I'll get you something pretty to wear. You can wear that really blue dress with the flowers."

"Mom said—" I stopped, remembering exactly what Mom had said the last time I'd worn that dress, my favorite one.

"Mom"—my sister came over and gave me a big hug—"doesn't always know best. Now come on. I wanna see how cute you look with makeup!"

Another shitty day at school, another shitty dance lesson. I didn't like being covered in sweat. It just made me feel grosser than I already did most of the day.

Charlene had been a huge bitch today, tripping up during pairs like I couldn't tell what she was doing. Maybe I wasn't all pretty and petite like she was, but I wasn't an idiot. Of course, the dance instructor was an actual idiot. She thought I needed to take a break after Charlene complained about me stepping on her foot.

"If I ever actually step on her foot, she'll know it," I said, frowning as I put a fresh pair of clothes on in the changing room of the dance studio.

Everyone else was mostly gone by this point. I didn't like to shower until there was less chance of other people seeing me. The other girls could be mean.

As I walked out into the studio room, looking around for my bag and the instructor, I noticed that not everyone had left yet. It was one of the girls who didn't say much, with frizzy blonde hair that I remember the rest of the group talking about. Apparently she was really annoying.

And was she really playing a video game all alone in the studio? What a weird girl. Where were her parents?

"Oh, hey." Oh shit, she'd noticed me. "I thought I was the last person here. Mom said I could just chill until the next lesson got here."

I guess I had nothing better to do than talk while waiting for my ride. Mom was supposed to pick me up, but she'd probably send some of the help. Ever since Dad had gotten sick, she'd been too busy to be around much at all.

"Uh, yeah." I shrugged. "Your mom?"

"Yeah, she's the instructor. Didn't you know that?" Obviously not or I wouldn't have asked. I didn't realize the dance instructor had her own kid dancing with us.

I came over and picked up my bag. "You should be better at dancing if you're her kid."

I wasn't actually sure if she was bad or not. I didn't like paying attention to all the other dancers, especially when they laughed when I messed up.

"Maybe." The girl shrugged before going back to playing her game. "Oh, hey, do you play video games?"

"No." I used to play some older games with Dad, but we hadn't had a chance to do that in a long time. Mom had tried to get me to play some kind of fitness game a while back. "What are you playing?"

"*Princess Towers*," she said shamelessly. It sounded like a little kids' game. She was thirteen, right? The same age as me? How could she play a game with *princess* in the title?

Glancing up at me with a smile, she teasingly boosted the volume of her game. I scrunched up my face at her smile but realized that the music was . . . pretty cool. It had a nice electric beat but with an elegant feel.

"What's it about?" I sat down, my curiosity piqued for now. It wasn't like there was anyone around, and maybe the instructor would be nicer to me if I was nice to her weird daughter.

"So, there's this kingdom full of towers, and at the top of each one is a beautiful princess that you, the hero, have to rescue!" She started to show me all the art and the action and the dialogue, some of her favorite romance scenes and her favorite princesses . . .

And an hour later, I was hooked and had a new friend in Lucy. I didn't even care that Mom had forgotten to send anyone to pick me up, but by the time Allie came by in her car, I was ready to tell her all about it.

The only light in my room was the computer screen that I stared aimlessly at, unsure of what to even do. It was technically morning, but I hadn't gone to bed since the news of Allie . . .

I swallowed hard, reading some of the messages I had gotten from some of my friends online. There was so much love and support, but it all felt . . . It was like I was weightless. I couldn't feel a thing as I tried to take comfort in all their kindness.

"Allie," I mumbled, clicking on the tab I had opened on her Instagram. Pictures of my sister done up in all the pretty dresses that had never fit me but were made for a model like her.

She didn't even like having her picture taken. Wasn't that crazy? It was something only I knew. Mom, too, I guessed, but she didn't seem to remember half the time. Allie liked being the center of attention, but ever since she'd started going to shoots, having pictures taken was just . . . work.

And so I didn't have a lot of pictures of her. She didn't work while she was home. We just hung out together, and I told her about the new games I'd been playing recently . . .

I refreshed the page and saw the post I'd been looking for. Posted just a few seconds ago, a press release from our family's publicist about Allie . . . About how she wouldn't be working anymore. It had all the condolences to my family, asking for fans and readers to keep us in their hearts and prayers.

"Fuck." It was finally real. That was sad, wasn't it? It took a press release to finally make my sister's death feel real. The funeral was soon, far too soon. I'd barely come to grips with what was happening.

Was Mom okay? She'd left the house as soon as she got the word. I'd barely gotten the news out of her before she was gone. I was just alone with the staff, and . . . and that was it . . .

"First Dad"—I sniffed—"and now Allie?"

Dad had wasted away in front of my eyes, and I couldn't do a thing about it, and now Allie had died no more than a few streets away from the house? Just because she was a little drunk? I couldn't handle that. Someone who shone as brightly as Allie had died just like that? Leaving me in a big house with little in it.

A ding came from my notifications, a message from Lucy. Ever since she'd moved away, we'd only gotten to talk about video games through voice chat. And now she'd seen my message and was reaching out, wanting to talk about it.

What was there to even talk about? There wasn't anything I could do or say to change anything. I sighed, rubbing my eyes as I put on my headset and called her.

"Hey, Lucy," I said, feeling a numbness growing in the back of my mind that began to almost hurt.

I could barely hear Lucy over the sound of the pounding headache I had, but she listened to me for hours as I talked about everything, complained about the world, and felt just a tiny . . . a tiny bit better . . .

I just had to get ready for the funeral. I needed to talk to Mom about all of this.

No matter how little I ate, no matter how much I got outside, nothing I did would ever be enough. That was what I realized as I sat alone once more at the dinner table, a single candle lit just for me by one of the servants.

Mom was gone, having left on a retreat yesterday. She'd refused to take me with her, no matter how much I wanted to go. She said a lot of things to me, a lot of things she didn't need to say.

I think she just wanted to.

"Thank you for the meal." I finally remembered to thank the chef, but I was pretty sure she couldn't hear me at this point. It was a nice meal, smelled and looked good. Something with chicken? It was hard to focus on the specifics, but it was a pleasant-looking meal.

It made me sick. Just thinking of eating, of wasting all the work I'd put into being there for Mom, of being loved. I'd spent months trying to lose weight, but I was never skinny enough. Fasting, purging, protein shakes, exercising until I wanted to die, nothing was enough.

If I started eating, I might not be able to stop.

My online friends had said I needed help when I'd told them what I was trying to do, whom I was trying to be. I'd opened up to them, the only friends I had, and they thought I was crazy for trying to be someone I wasn't.

I didn't talk to my friends anymore. Best part about only having online friends? They can't bother you if you block them. They can't tell you that you aren't meant to be anything other than a freak.

Popular, loved, the girl in the spotlight. Not for Emilia. Those spots could never be filled by an ugly girl like Emilia. I'd give anything to be beautiful, to be at the top of the world like Allie.

Mom had yelled at me when I'd tried one of Allie's old dresses on. I didn't blame her. I'd looked at myself in the mirror just before she caught me and barely kept myself from throwing up.

I was so hungry. I could probably take a few bites, maybe even eat the whole dinner if I tried. If I felt bloated later, I could just deal with it then.

And then . . . I didn't know what came after that. I felt so cold. Just like the moon would when the sun went out. There would be no more light, no more warmth. Just a craggy surface that the people of Earth decided to visit a handful of times and then never set foot on again.

My eyes caught on the lit candle. In a daze, I watched the flame, the only warmth in the room. It danced, free of care or concern. Just like the sun, people loved it and feared it.

I wanted that so much. So, so much.

But the sun was gone now, and the moon was just overstaying her welcome.

I decided to eat after all. I'd take it slow and cherish each bite. I ate more than I had in a long time, feeling content even as my stomach started to hurt.

Once I was finished with my meal, I went out of my way to thank the chef again before heading upstairs but not to my room. Mom had a medicine cabinet where she kept all her diet pills, even the stuff that was clearly not over the counter.

"I'm sorry, Allie," I said, opening up the cabinet. "I couldn't shine like you did. I shouldn't have even tried."

As I grabbed up the first of the bottles in the cabinet, about to twist the top off, a dark-skinned, strong hand fell on top of my own, stopping me. My breath hitched as I looked up and saw a stranger looking down at me with a solemn gaze.

No, not a stranger. I felt my world falling out from under me as I remembered all of this. It was just . . . It was just my past . . .

"You don't need these," he said, pushing the bottle back down into the cabinet and pulling me close. "You never needed these. I'm sorry the world made you feel like you did."

"Is this . . . I didn't think . . . This was a bad idea." I sniffed. "I'm ugly, Dad. I'm not bright and shiny. I'm not your favorite. I'm no one's favorite. Look at me. How could I be?"

"You'd be surprised how much we see about ourselves that others don't," he said, his fingers combing through my hair. "Love isn't about favorites. It is something that is shared in different ways among different people. You are deserving of love not because of how pretty you are, Natakia, but because you are you, and that is the most charming thing about you."

Hot, wet tears spilled down my cheeks as I hugged him back tightly. A dark fear tugged at my lips, moving my tongue outside of my control. "You don't think I'm fat?"

"People have used that word to hurt you for a long time," Dad said, pulling back to smile down at me. "I think that you're beautiful, Natakia. Nothing can change that. I know it's a long road with the life you've lived, but don't judge yourself by the words of others. Love yourself as others do. Like I do."

"I love you, too, Dad!" I wrapped my arms around his neck as I felt the bathroom around me fade out of existence. Maybe I could never shine like the sun that Allie was, but as Dad and I returned to Derra, among our ruined campsite, I looked up at the full moon in the sky.

I had to admit, it was beautiful in its own way.

25

After the turmoil and revelations of the night prior, it was almost too peaceful of a morning as we set out with the remnants of supplies that we had left. Esmeralda and I had, unfortunately, destroyed many of our rations as well as amenities like clothing.

"I'm going to miss this dress," Natakia sighed, holding up the scraps of a viridian gown that was now far more useful as a rag than a piece of clothing.

Macy walked alongside her closely and smiled. "It was a nice dress. But, you know, Rakta brought money with him, so . . ."

Natakia eyed me up, and I felt a chill at the look in her eyes. I chuckled it away. "I suppose we're all deserving of a shopping trip when we arrive in Kakrel. You should have your own Ruskan atan."

Had I been there for her coming-of-age celebration, I would have likely gotten her one. An atan was a traditional gift for a girl on her way to becoming a woman. Although, the atans of Kakrel would be different from the ones of my tribe. Not that I was particularly eager to pay homage to my tribe at the moment.

"When we next stop," I said, continuing the conversation as we hiked down a steeper incline of the canyon, "I'll do some light hunting to supplement our remaining rations. I'm sorry you both went hungry last night."

Macy shook her head. "I was too tired to eat last night."

"Yeah," Natakia said, but her attention was elsewhere. At the mention of last night, she looked solemn and lost in thought for a moment before she shook her head. "I'd appreciate a good meal."

I smiled, turning back to the path and keeping an eye on the dangers it had to offer. We wouldn't travel long before our first rest, but the fight would have caused any nearby prey to vacate the area. And, of course, there was the matter of how dirty we all were.

I was sure Macy and Natakia would appreciate a chance to wash in the upcoming river only a few hours ahead of us. By the time they were clean, I would have a meal ready for them.

"You know," Macy said, stepping over a large rock, "the Grand Cipher, how exactly are they immortal? I mean, do people think they use a special technique, or is it something to do with monster blood?"

"Well, there are certainly those who believe that they are simply long-lived, but there are those who sit somewhere in the middle of that belief and my belief that they are different people," I said, somewhat hesitant to go into further detail.

Natakia spoke up. "You told us about that back when we were kids, didn't you? The story of the Cipher Scrolls."

I glanced around instinctively, eyeing up the surrounding area for any potential eavesdroppers. That story was as much a scary story meant for children as it was a political powder keg in the right ears.

"Yes, you've remembered well, Natakia," I said, smiling despite my concern. "I suppose there is no harm in speaking about them. You see, in Ruskan culture, stories are where our souls live on after our flesh fails us. We pass on our stories orally because to write them down is to trap the souls, and Shahis, the language of my people, has few written applications."

I remembered when the Storyteller of my tribe had first regaled us with the story of the Cipher Scrolls. There was little fondness within the respect that the tribes of Rusk paid to the capital, but that story in particular was the epitome of how the tribes felt about Garrok's legacy.

"The Cipher Scrolls are said to be the stories of the life of the man who would eventually become the Grand Cipher, from his first breath to his last." The man had no name, or rather, it was said that his name was only written within the scrolls themselves.

Macy hummed. "So your people believe that his soul is trapped inside of the scrolls?"

"Well, yes." I nodded, Doh's daughter having caught on quickly. "But that isn't the end of it. Do you remember why most people in Kakrel dislike the story?"

Natakia was looking at herself in her floating mirror, making sure her hair was done up right. "Because it's said that whoever reads the Cipher Scrolls becomes the man who wrote them. That's how the Grand Cipher is said to remain effectively immortal."

I glanced back and saw Macy's face pale at the very idea. I was sure that she, more than either Natakia or I, knew of the inner workings that went into replacing an entire mind with that of another.

"That isn't true, though, right?" Macy fretted, looking as if someone had stepped on her grave.

"It is true as any story," I said but slowed down slightly to place my hand on her shoulder. "I've never seen or heard any evidence of it personally. It's better to simply put it out of your mind."

There was no telling if the tales of the Cipher Scrolls were true, but worrying about them would not change reality. I doubted that, real or not, we would have any business with them.

The crackling of the fire and the smell of cooked meat surrounded us as we sat around the cave that we had settled into to rest and dry after washing up in the nearby river.

"By the gods, I didn't know a coyote could smell this good." Macy was holding her stomach as if keeping it from jumping at the cooking meat as she stared down at our food.

Natakia was looking down at it with a little more dubiousness. "I, uh, I didn't know it could either."

My daughter seemed nervous for reasons beyond the novelty of coyote meat. I thought back to what I had seen in my vision of her and respected that, whatever inner turmoil she faced, it would take time to conquer it. I would support her every step of the way.

"Honestly, it'd be better with spices, but unfortunately, the only herbs around here require much more preparation than one can do out in the wild like this," I said. I had found a bushel of graytoad, but it had been a long time since I'd properly dissected it, and I didn't want to poison the girls.

"I remember Zao once said that Rusk had the most exciting spices," Natakia said fondly. "I think he meant potentially deadly."

"I'll have to prepare some sunset cactus juice for the both of you if I see any along the way to Kakrel." I chuckled. It was only now, without the shadow of Esmeralda over us all, that I was able to enjoy spending the time I had with my daughter and her friend.

And as Natakia and Macy continued to talk about this and that, their friendship slowly recovering, I stood up and went over to the carrying case for my prosthetic. Opening it up, I looked down at the metallic arm, remembering the might that it had allowed me to wield.

It had given me the edge I needed to defeat Esmeralda; no, it had been the only reason I had been able to win. Perhaps I could have escaped with Natakia and Macy, but the chances were slim. The only reason I was alive was because of Penelope's gift.

It was discomforting to use a strength that was not my own, but I quieted such thoughts with the gratitude I felt to have it. It had given me the strength I needed to win, but it would not give me victory if I depended on it and it alone.

"I need to continue my training." I had a few more days before we reached Kakrel. There, I would find my daughter and sister, but I could not know how that meeting would go.

I had never considered that a reunion with my little warrior would come to violence, but I believed Natakia and what she had seen. Daka, my daughter, slaying many when there was a time when I thought she could never be capable. Now that the shadow that Esmeralda had cast had dissipated, I was left to contemplate the shadow cast by my sister.

"We're going to stop Daka, right? We're going to get her back?" So deep in my contemplation, I had not even noticed Natakia's approach, but her soft words pulled at my heart.

"We will," I said, turning back to her. "I promise you that."

"What is our plan when we get to Kakrel?" Natakia came over to look down at the prosthetic as well. I gently closed the case, feeling something akin to embarrassment at my prosthetic being seen.

That was a very good question, but not one that I could answer completely. "I have a few ideas, but our goals are to find Daka and figure out the state of the capital. How we do that, well, it'll be up to what we find once we get there."

"Oh," Natakia said before her mirror floated around to face us both. "Do you want me to scry ahead and get an idea of what's happening?"

For a moment, I felt slightly sheepish at not having considered that idea beforehand. I nodded. "I think that is a very good idea."

As we made camp once more later that night, having found another cave to protect us from the elements and the usual predators, Natakia set up a divination ritual to view the capital from afar.

I wasn't surprised when the ritual wasn't all that complicated as Natakia focused in on the floating mirror that sat flat between the three of us. Macy seemed quite curious about how all of this worked, but I'd seen Lydia perform this very same spell many times.

Divination magic was mostly dependent on the use of a focus, either that of a pool of water or specially tempered mirrors that were prepared in advance. Natakia's floating mirror, a fine gift from Penelope all those years ago, had certainly proved of high enough quality for this type of magic.

I wondered, absently, if Penelope had had an inkling that my daughter would have a talent for divination. It certainly wasn't out of the question.

That said, as Natakia focused on her spell, I thought about the advanced spell she was using. Scrying on a person was a task of varying difficulty, mostly due to the nature of the target affecting the clearness of the image, but the spell that Natakia poured her Mana into was different.

"Let us see the truth, a world away," she intoned the words of magical power. "Open thyself, **Ocular Orb**."

And before us, the mirror flashed a bright-pink light before the light suddenly transformed into a depiction of the capital city of Rusk and home of the Grand Cipher, Kakrel. It was no mere picture, of course, but rather a direct view of the sky above the city.

"This is difficult to pilot, so no sudden movements, okay?" Natakia said before she pulled with her hands and the view on the mirror began to zoom in closer to the city.

Ocular Orb was a brilliant spell that created a pilotable invisible viewing orb that could patrol the area that it was created in. It could not reach from nation to nation like certain other divination magics could, but it had more protections from the usual counters to divination and more freedom to investigate.

We were still many miles from Kakrel, so Natakia's ability to project the orb so long a distance was a testament to her skill.

As Natakia piloted around the whole of the city, I began to see the signs of things being amiss within the capital of my home nation. There were signs of fighting in the streets, bloodstains along the sandstone buildings, and while the flags emblazoned with the symbol of the Grand Cipher flew over the walls, they did not fly alone.

"That's the same symbol as the one we found at the Mattuk," Natakia whispered. "Dad, that's . . ."

It was the Kroterruk Tribe, flags of a dancing bird flying throughout different parts of the city. Kakrel had become the site of a conflict once more, and my daughter was somewhere among it all.

Natakia continued to search throughout the city, and there was no doubt that the armed forces of the capital were defending themselves from skirmishes led against them by the people of my tribe. I felt a grim recognition befall me as my daughter's magic showed us fallen soldiers from both sides.

After a time, I couldn't bear to see any more, and little would be gained from pushing myself.

"Get some rest," I said to the girls as I motioned for Natakia to end her magic. "Thank you for your help, Natakia. I'll have a plan for us by the morning. It seems shopping may be somewhat difficult."

Their good moods had been dulled by the sights that had been before them through Natakia's magic. They both made ready for bed, and I did the same, but not before I charged my prosthetic with the spare Vitae I had from the day. From all I had seen, one way or another, I would need it.

26

It was a long-held belief that the tribes of Rusk were loose bands of like-minded individuals, having been bound through the generations under some common cause or another. While that was true, there was far more power in the bonds of a tribe than simple history.

The Kroterruk Tribe was one of the twelve tribes that had been gathered by Brota to fight against the aggression of Garrok, a facet of the story that, today, was mostly used to embolden the younger members of the tribe. That blood was strong, though, and very difficult to forget or hide.

Those tribes were more than just gatherings of Ruskans. They were sacred families whom Kakrel never forgot to pay their respects to, and vice versa, the foundation for the diplomacy between the chiefs of Rusk and the Grand Cipher.

"Alright, move along." The words of Shahis spilled beautifully but roughly from the lips of the Kakrel guard standing before the entrance to the city. "Next guest, please attend."

Having left the Cragged Fields and finally arrived at the outskirts of Kakrel, I was unsurprised to find that in the areas still controlled by the men of the Grand Cipher, the security was very tight. I saw plenty of guards, of both martial and magical prowess, watching each visitor as they approached.

And with them, I could tell, was a Storyteller. He was an old man who stood in the back, his white dreads falling to his shoulders as he eyed each attending guest. He wore a long beige shawl that spilled over the deep rustic-brown cloth of his tunic and pants. The man was barefoot but had clean feet.

I knew why he was here and what he was looking for. The stories hidden within each of us. It was said that a Storyteller could tell a man's past by simply hearing him speak and move.

"Move along," the guard spoke again, motioning the visitor along through the gates. "Next guest, please attend."

I realized that it was finally my turn and my turn alone. I had asked Natakia and Macy to wait a few paces behind me to separate our arrivals slightly. Just in case this did not end well.

"Thank you for the honor of attendance," I said, pleased that I had fallen back on my Shahis far easier than I had expected to. Perhaps it was simply too beautiful to forget?

"Reason for attendance, guest?" The guard looked me up and down. I supposed with my torn clothing and missing arm, I looked less like a respected traveler and more of a merchant who had been targeted on the road.

I met eyes with the Storyteller watching and said, "I've come to find my daughter and see the troubles that have come to my home. I've been away for quite some time."

I could see the recognition in the old man's eyes. There was no doubt that he saw the stories of the Kroterruk Tribe within me. If he said something, pointed out my connection to the tribe, I doubted that I would be met with much kindness within these walls.

For a moment, the guard seemed curious before he glanced at the Storyteller, who simply shook his head. I felt a welling up of gratitude toward the old man.

"Move along," the guard said, motioning me in through the gate. As I acquiesced to the gesture, I noticed another smaller figure behind many of the guards at this gate into the city. A scribe of sorts, furiously writing down something, before she glanced up at me for just a moment before going back to writing.

An interesting sight to see. I wondered if she wrote in Shahis or was using Nevian, the more universal language of Derra. I put that thought to the side as I continued on, paying it no more mind.

As I walked through the gates, my stride slowed to a crawl as I listened out for any issues behind me. Natakia and Macy were coming in together, and if I had made it through, I was sure they would too. Macy had even shape-shifted into a young Ruskan girl to waylay any interest in her foreign ties.

Soon enough, I heard the sounds of approach, my gaze turning back to see Natakia and Macy, both looking relieved at our peaceful entrance, but a third figure had joined them.

The Storyteller.

Having entered the capital of Rusk, I would never have thought a week ago to be under the threat of a bloody battle breaking out anywhere we stood, but I would have further been surprised by a Storyteller approaching us so earnestly.

The old man had motioned for us to come off to the side of the street and into a nearby alleyway between two large and ornate sandstone buildings, one of which I recognized as a garrison.

"Have no worries, traveler." His voice was aged and croaky. "I merely wished to pay my respects and to truly meet the man with such a storied past."

I bowed my head in respect. "I thank you for your interest, Storyteller. I am merely cautious for the sake of my daughter and her friend. Interest is dangerous in Kakrel from what I've heard."

Macy seemed unsure of what was going on, likely owing to her lack of teaching in Shahis, but Natakia seemed to be following along just fine, nodding with what I said.

"Of course, you are wise to have such caution," the Storyteller said. "I am Canon. I am a member of the Garrokian Storyteller Troupe. Could I add your name to the stories I've witnessed?"

The Garrokian Storyteller Troupe was where Storytellers who lacked a tribe or who aligned themselves with the philosophies of Garrok gathered and prospered through community and communication. As Garrok had been a Storyteller himself, it was popular for budding practitioners.

I had heard many foul words said about them, but most differences lay in the stories they told. If memory served me correctly, most Garrokian

Storytellers limited themselves to the One Hundred Tales that had been approved generations ago as the foundation for Ruskan storytelling.

"I am Rakta Tribus, elder of House Tribus," I said, feeling honored despite my caution to have a Storyteller so interested in me. "I have been called Dancer and Scavenger within the Certillian Empire as well as being known as Slayer of the Warlock King."

Natakia side-eyed me at how open I was suddenly being about my identity, but it was only proper to fully introduce oneself to a Storyteller. I supposed that old habits truly died hard.

Canon smiled. "I have heard word of you before, Rakta. I heard the truth in your words as you spoke your goals. I'd like to be of service to you and your companions."

"Not that I do not appreciate your offer, Storyteller Canon," I said, somewhat surprised by the forward nature of the vaunted weaver of words before me. "But do you not serve the guards here? I had thought you were aiding them in discovering others from the twelve tribes."

He nodded. "I was, but I can feel a story coming to a great climax around you and your family, Rakta. Be done with titles and ask for any aid you wish."

I was unsure of what to even ask for that would not come across as rude to the man before me. Perhaps it was the young boy from Rusk who tied my tongue into a knot, but it was difficult to treat this man as someone I could simply ask anything of.

"Somewhere safe to sleep and clean up would be a nice start." Natakia's beautiful Shahis broke through the silence my lead tongue had caused, her amused smile at my hesitance plain to see. "I'm Natakia Velbrun, by the way, the oracle of Velbrun."

I frowned, reminded that, for all intents and purposes, my daughter was still a Velbrun. Admittedly, however, my family had been among the Velbruns for years. It would not bother me now.

"Ah." Canon smiled, nodding in greeting before he stroked his chin as he looked at my daughter. "Yes, I believe that can be arranged, my young oracle. Follow me. We'd best hurry before we get caught up in some encounter of chance rather than one of fate."

And with that, he began to go farther into the alleyway he had brought us into, taking us away from the main streets of Kakrel and toward the spiderweb of stairways that led farther into the capital of Rusk.

Built on the foundations of an ancient mesa, Kakrel had been carved out by its people for generations, with much of their city derived from the very sandstone the mesa had formed out of, with many stairs leading down and up to the various different levels of the city. The Grand Cipher's palace was the very top of the plateau of the mesa while we walked around the lower ends of the city, near where most markets prospered.

"Canon," I said, still unsure about referring to him so informally, "I am curious as to where you lead us. It is not toward the chambers of the troupe, is it?"

As grateful as I was for the help, it was in my best interest to be wary of any aid until I understood what was going on in Kakrel. To go to the heart of some of the most powerful magicians within Rusk, I would be a fool not to have some reluctance.

"I'm afraid that is impossible, Rakta, for the chambers of the Garrokian Storyteller Troupe have been destroyed in totality," he said, as if he were simply commenting on the increased amount of dust on the stairs that we walked up.

Natakia spoke up, equally as shocked as I. "Destroyed!? Aren't Storytellers some of the strongest in Rusk? How did they destroy your chambers?"

"Well, the structural integrity of our chambers was not quite as spectacular as our magic." Canon chuckled to himself, but there was a somber edge to his words. "I'm afraid that many of the Storytellers were injured, some killed. It's been a horrible few months, you see."

"Was it the Kroterruk Tribe?" I asked, frowning. I'd once heard the architecture of Kakrel was strengthened by the Vitae of the workers who had carved and built it. It was no mere building.

Canon nodded, seeming to think for a moment before shaking his head. "There will be time to discuss the state of things. First, allow me to soothe your fears. We are soon approaching my own home."

And with a turn around the corner, he gestured toward a quaint sandstone abode, with a beautifully carved domed roof nearly two floors in height. The glazed glass on the front seemed to have some brief Shahis lettering inscribed onto it, the notes for *books*.

"You live in a bookstore?" Natakia said what I, admittedly, was thinking. It was the teachings of Storytellers that discouraged the writing of books and maintaining oral teachings!

Canon grinned. "I suppose I am a bit of a heretical Storyteller. Don't tell the others. They'll either hate my collection or that I still have a roof over my head."

Canon's home was, as he said, filled to the brim with books. I had never seen, no, ever imagined finding such a collection of storybooks in Rusk. It was simply unheard of!

Of course, there was a precedent for libraries; they were collections of encyclopedias and scholarly texts of other nations written in Nevian, but most I knew from my home nation even shied away from the written stories of other cultures. And our host seemed to take great delight in our, mostly my, confusion.

"I'm sure you have questions." He motioned at the shelves of books on every wall of his home. "I assure you, I'll take no offense from your thoughts."

"Do you not believe that these books have trapped the souls within their stories?" While it did not do much but cause me discomfort, I truly needed to know what wisdom or irreverence had prompted this collection.

"I thought the same myself once upon a time," Canon said, picking up one of the stray books, "but in my old age, I realized that the discouragement of writing our histories, our stories, down seemed . . . well, not to be disrespectful to the beliefs of my peers, but ill-advised."

He walked over to another part of his home that, beyond the many books that were scattered about, was quite orderly and clean from all that I could see.

"I wrote these myself." He picked up one book that lacked the hard cover most of the other books of his collection had. "I feared a future that had forgotten these stories, our people no longer around to tell them. At the time, my thoughts were that I would rather my ancestors be caged than forgotten."

"And now?" It was a decent reason, but one that was antithetical to the faith a Ruskan should have in the stories of our people. Our stories persevered through the strength of our nation and the pride we had in them.

Canon seemed thoughtful for a moment before he pointed at another similar paperbound volume on the shelf near him. "I wrote the tales of Brota and Garrok in that one, but there are those who still share their story elsewhere."

"You don't think you're caging them at all," Natakia said, her finger sliding down one of the spines of the books on the shelves.

"You're exactly right, Natakia." He grinned. "Just as I have a place to sleep and rest when I am tired from travel, I believe these books to be a home, a resting place for the spirits, when they are exhausted from being told. A place to recover their strength."

I had never heard thoughts like these before, but I could feel the genuine love and wisdom from the Storyteller. Perhaps it was not my place to question his interpretation of the spirits or our resting places. I thought about Dalton's museum and how it paid homage to my life and stories.

Would that be where I went home when my stories were done being told throughout the nation? I had never thought much about the endless existence of being remembered through stories told.

"I suppose it is a sound decision." I had not the time nor energy to truly dwell on the topic. "Thank you for offering your home to us, but you spoke of knowing more of the state of Kakrel."

Canon nodded before gesturing to the table in the center of the room. "Sit and I shall pour some drink for all of us. It is not right to weave a story with dry lips."

As he went upstairs to his kitchen, I looked at Natakia and Macy before I sat down and began to wait. Natakia and Macy soon followed, with Macy speaking for the first time since we'd arrived in Kakrel.

"So," she began, "who is he, and why are we here?"

27

By the time that Natakia and I had explained what was happening to Macy, who had naturally just gone along with us wherever we went, Canon had returned with a small platter of drinks.

I smelled the familiar sweetness in the air as he set down what looked to be ordinary water, if with a somewhat pinkish hue to it. "It seems we will enjoy some Ruskan delights after all."

"Is this," Natakia sniffed at the rim of the cup, "cactus water?"

"Ah, you can't truly trace your ancestry back to Rusk until you have tried the favorite drink of the dunes, can you?" Canon chuckled, offering a drink to Macy as well. "And one for our changing friend."

I raised an eyebrow but wasn't surprised that the Storyteller had read into the nature of Macy. Natakia seemed somewhat alarmed, but I raised a hand to calm her worries. "Our friend Macy does not speak the Ruskan tongue."

"Ah, well, you might want to have her change back to a less local appearance, hmm?" Canon smiled. It was a good idea. It would be far stranger for a foreigner to be in Kakrel than a Ruskan who was ignorant of Shahis. I passed his words along to Macy, who transformed back into her usual appearance.

"So," I said after taking a sip of the fresh and relaxing sweet water of the desert, "what do you know of Kakrel's state? It seems open war is happening between the tribes and the Grand Cipher."

Canon nodded, taking a sip of his own drink. "Oh yes, very much so. Unfortunately, the Kroterruk Tribe has gathered many other tribes, both smaller ones and of those of the twelve tribes, under their banner, through a combination of diplomacy and force."

That was concerning. Then perhaps the attack on the Mattuk Tribe was simply the response to any tribe that didn't join up with my sister's plans.

"How much of the city is controlled by the tribes?" Natakia seemed focused, as if she were trying to pick apart this problem as swiftly as possible.

"Oh." Canon stroked his chin. "I'd say about a quarter of the city is firmly in the hands of the Kroterruk Tribe, with another quarter being where most of the conflict is going on. The Grand Cipher has been putting down defensive lines farther back from the fighting, so I believe that the tribes are gaining ground."

Natakia frowned. "I don't get it. How did the tribes even get this far in? It isn't like they caught Kakrel off guard, right? Shouldn't there have been more of a defense?"

"Just as evenly as Brota and Garrok once fought, the tribes going against Kakrel should have been an even match, yes." Canon nodded.

I understood the implication and the sinking feeling that came with it. "Something, no, someone has upset that balance."

"The leader of the Kroterruk Tribe, Natakia of the Teeth"—he glanced at my daughter, who frowned—"has a deadly and powerful warrior on her side. One who tore through the first line of Kakrel's defense in a single day and paved the road for the Kroterruk Tribe's growing control."

That sinking feeling became a yawning abyss in my stomach as I sighed, looking away. There was no denying the truth of it all. My daughter had become the instrument of my sister's violence.

"Dad." Natakia laid a hand on my shoulder. "We'll get her."

It was a salve upon my soul to hear those words from my daughter, but the sadness I felt for my little warrior . . . What had she gone through to push her this far? Why seek family in Rusk?

"I have trust in your strength, Rakta. Perhaps now would be a good time for you to get a lay of the land yourself?" Canon asked, taking another sip from his drink.

I nodded, taking solace in the others' belief, before standing up. "I believe that will be my next course of action. Natakia, can you stay here and use your magic to learn more?"

"Of course, Dad." She smiled before beginning to fill Macy in on what the plan was.

"Then"—I turned to Canon, the old man finishing the last of his drink—"I'll trust their safety to you, Storyteller Canon. May I?"

"You may." He smiled before leaning in. "But only on one condition."

"Name it." He was already doing much for us. I didn't have much room to argue about conditions. His home would be a safe place for the girls, and having the aid of a Storyteller was . . . well, exceptional.

"What would you say about your daughter learning to tell a story or two?" There was an excited gleam in his gaze as he smiled at me.

Having borrowed a cloak and fresh clothing from Canon, I wove through the crowds of Kakrel with much on my mind. I kept my head on a swivel, looking for signs of the Kroterruk Tribe, but I was unsure if I would find much until I reached the parts of the city being fought over.

And as I kept an eye out, my mind went to Canon's condition or, rather, his offer. The idea that he believed my daughter to have the potential to be a Storyteller, I had been caught by a fit of pride.

I had given him my blessing, but it was well and truly Natakia's decision alone. While I would never forsake her for refusing the offer, it took all I had to not encourage her heavily.

"Move out of the way." A Ruskan merchant bumped into me, looking like he was in a hurry. Not much respect for a man with only one arm in Kakrel, but I was blending in.

Especially compared to how I often blended in within the Certillian Empire, which was not very well at all. Among this sea of my people, I was just another Ruskan, which . . . was quite nice. There was no prestige or title that gave me special privilege here.

There was a hustle and bustle to the crowd, but I could see the nerves. My heart went out to the people of Kakrel, there being no place for them to go while the heart of Rusk slowly bled to death. I could tell the merchants from other nations, even a few lucky tribesmen not swept up in my sister's madness, were trying to make their profits and leave as soon as possible.

My only concern was that I had not brought my prosthetic with me. It was a powerful tool and weapon, but one that I did not want to use recklessly. I would rather have to go fetch it than use it unwisely when I was supposed to simply be scouting out the streets.

I approached a poorly dressed man sitting on the corner of the road, taking out a silver sil and placing it into his offered hand. "Where might I find where the Kroterruk Tribe is causing the most trouble?"

"Huh?" The poor man seemed confused for a moment before he pointed down the street. "Take those alleyway stairs next to the bakery up to the next level. I heard some ruckus is being caused a few streets west of there."

With that he returned to business, holding his hands out toward those he thought might be the next to offer him some coin out of the goodness of their hearts. I went on my way, as well, grateful to the men and women who knew these streets better than anyone else.

I followed the directions I'd been given and began to slow my approach as I started to see the signs of old conflict. Destroyed storefronts, cracked stone, and ample amounts of dried blood began to dot the scenery as the scent of copper replaced the perfumed masses of the marketplace.

When I heard the sound of metal on metal quickly approaching, I ducked into a nearby alleyway with a quick pulse of my Vitae enhancing my speed. I watched as a few members of the Royal Cipher Militants marched quickly in the direction I had come from. A retreat of some kind?

I heard the distant sound of an explosion coming farther down the road, from where the militants had come from, and took a deep breath as I began to make my way toward it.

"Daka." I sent a whispered prayer to her wherever she was. "Don't be at the center of this."

It was a standoff as I finally arrived on the scene, creeping along hidden by the debris and general clutter of the streets and alleyways. The site of the explosion was clear, a larger building that had a gaping hole in its side, fresh smoke and a faint smell of brimstone in the air.

"This is your one chance to surrender, Kroterruks!" The man at the forefront of a large battalion of militants roared at the destroyed building. A quick count gave me thirty men, each of them looking like accomplished fighters with their shields and spears in hand.

The man at the front of them was a large-chested fellow with very little armor, but I could tell that his skin was as well-defended as it could be. Instead of a spear, he wielded a large claymore-sized blade with the curved edge of a Ruskan sword. He wielded it in one hand, an impressive display of strength.

From the fresh ruins of the building, a voice called out. "Those of the Kroterruk will never surrender to the Garrokian scum of Kakrel!"

It was hard to gauge the odds without knowing the forces hiding within the building. There very well might not be a fight at all if the true goal here was escape.

"You all heard them." The man frowned. "By orders of the Grand Cipher, there will be no more Kroterruks in Derra by the end of this month."

And with that he reared back, his muscles twisting as the faint smell of brimstone in the air suddenly intensified. With a roar, he slashed his large blade through the air, and I watched as a visible amber scar was cut into the sky before it streaked across the street toward the building.

And moments before it impacted against the building again, likely bringing it to a crumbling pile of stone and rock, a blurring projectile suddenly sliced through it.

The street was rocketed by the premature explosion, the militants feeling more force from the blow than they had been expecting as the leader held up a hand and glared at the display. The speed of whatever had disrupted his attack had been too fast for me to perceive without having been prepared with my Vitae.

Smoke, sand, and dust filled the street, obscuring the view I had from my vantage point. And as it began to fade, and the thunderous echo of the explosion had died down around them, the silence was broken before it could begin by the sound of jaunty whistling.

"By the gods," one of the militants said, taking a step back with sudden terror on his face. "Mushak Ark, you said she'd be distracted!"

Another militant had similar feelings as the whistling pierced the air. "Garrok flows through our veins. May his tales give us strength."

"It seems even after all this time"—Mushak Ark frowned, as he readied his blade once more—"we're still underestimating the depths of your strength, you faceless demon."

From out of the ash, a figure emerged covered from head to toe in blackened leather armor. Not a hint of her skin showed except for her fingers wrapped around the curved pommel of a pair of hand axes, each one looking sharp and jagged. That and her eyes.

A pair of eerily gleaming, big blue eyes, as bright as the sky, that seemed to stare unblinkingly ahead at the militants. They shone out from behind a leather helmet that was only a bit lighter than the rest of her attire, with the middle of the helmet coming down to protect her nose.

There was no doubt now. I was seeing the dark path that Daka, my little warrior, was on. The only questions now were how did I bring her back? And what had brought her to this?

"Ha ha!" That same voice from the building echoed once more but closer now. Other figures moved out of the smoke falling around my daughter, a dozen tribesmen with a weasel of a leader pointing a dagger out toward the militants. "Are the fine men and women of Garrok scared? What were you talking about again earlier? Surrender?"

My daughter had stopped in her tracks, watching the militants like a hawk. Her gaze was unflinching, but for a moment, I saw her glance straight at me. I held my breath, watching and waiting, before she turned back to continue gazing at the militants.

That jaunty whistling hadn't stopped, Daka slowly bringing her axes into a familiar stance, that of the **Dancing Star Stance**.

"Men," Mushak Ark said, "it's time to fall back. Retreat to the next defensive line."

The weasellike tribesman took a threatening step forward. "I don't think so! Go get 'em!"

He gestured his hand toward Daka, as if trying to urge her forward, looking confident until he noticed that my daughter had not moved an inch. The militants took the chance to flee, each of them quickly retreating to where I assumed the early group had done so prior.

"Hey, what's wrong with you?" the leader of the pack of tribesmen asked. "They're getting away!"

Mushak Ark was the last to leave, watching the interaction between Daka and the supposed leader of this small band of Kroterruks. "We'll meet again."

And then he was off, wisely retreating in the face of an enemy even I would not want to risk my life against. A terrible thing to think about one's own daughter, but I could tell that Daka was dangerous, more dangerous than any martial artist or fighter I had ever done battle with before.

As the militants retreated, I took my chance to do so as well. I'd learned as much as I could, more than I had expected, but for as much as I wanted to walk out and hug my daughter, there was still too much that was beyond me. Hopefully, Natakia would have more answers.

28

Arriving back at Canon's home after doing my best to remain undetected by the hostile parties in the area, I found Macy paging through one of the many books of the Storyteller's collection.

"Oh." She looked up, noticing me. "Welcome back. Natakia is upstairs with Canon. He asked me to keep an eye out for you. How'd the search go?"

"I found Daka, but . . ." I couldn't hide the weary expression on my face. Remembering the wide blue eyes that saw so little, I found myself unable to properly give words to the feelings boiling within me.

Macy scrunched up her face. "It's that bad, huh? Well, did you talk with her? Does she know you're here in Kakrel?"

"I think she saw me for a moment, but she paid me no mind. There were others from the Kroterruk Tribe with her. I thought it unwise to approach until I knew more or I could get her away from the others." Or, perhaps, that was simply the excuse that I gave after my fear had taken root.

With that, I walked up the stairs to find Natakia and Canon sitting at a circular table in a small bedroom, with an adjoining kitchen through an arched doorway. The Storyteller seemed to watch with rapt interest as Natakia's eyes glowed with the power of her magic, her mirror gleaming before her.

"I'm back," I said softly so as to not interrupt unnecessarily. I went over to sit down beside Canon, joining him in watching my daughter's efforts in discovering more about the situation.

Canon smiled at me, offering a fresh glass of sweetened cactus water. "Welcome back. Your daughter has been doing a wondrous job at deciphering the plans of Kakrel and the Kroterruk."

Relief and pride cooled the turmoil within me as I nodded, grateful that, through Natakia, the simplicity that Lydia brought to all plans had once again returned. I patiently waited for my daughter to finish, preferring to hear the good news from her directly.

Soon, the glow in her eyes dimmed, and the reflective surface of her mirror lost its magical luster. Blinking the power out of her eyes, Natakia looked momentarily surprised as she saw me. "Dad? You're back already?"

It had taken some time to familiarize myself with Kakrel and home in on the correct area of the Kroterruk's activities, but I supposed it hadn't taken me as long as it might have.

"Yes, I found Daka." I sighed, tempering my daughter's interest with a dour look. "I'm afraid it isn't good. I saw very little of my little warrior in the fighter that confronted the militants of Kakrel."

Natakia swallowed hard, nodding. "I wasn't sure about whom we would find, either, but . . . we'll get her back. I mean, Daka never wanted to hurt people . . ."

I frowned at that, remembering many of the conversations I'd had with my eldest daughter in her darker, more introspective moments. It was not just that she did not want to hurt people. There was an edge about her that seemed almost fearful of doing so. As if it would have been a return to an old shame.

"We'll reason with her," I said, nodding. "My main concern is my sister, but we can speak more after we've discussed what we've learned. In my search, I learned of Mushak Ark of the militants. He seems to be a respected leader and a skilled combatant."

Canon spoke up, having finished his drink. "Oh yes, Mushak Ark is one of the Grand Cipher's most trusted warriors. The title of mushak is only given to those with great valor and wisdom."

"He seemed wise enough to leave a confrontation that did not bode well for him or his men," I said, stroking my chin. "I'd thought he might recklessly pursue conflict."

"That might have something to do with what I learned about the

Grand Cipher's plans," Natakia said, bringing out some parchment with Nevian script written on it. "You should take a look at this, Dad."

I dragged the parchment closer. My daughter had seemingly pieced together the scraps of whatever military strategy the militants were using by way of some overheard conversations from lower-rank guards and her own natural gift. Giving up part of Kakrel seemed to actually be a part of some larger plan, something that Natakia couldn't put together without investigating the right people.

"Canon, do you know anything about this?" I looked to the Storyteller, who shook his head.

"Unfortunately"—he shrugged—"I'm not trusted with the finer details of war. I aid the guards when requested, but I've had my fill of direct conflict. I would rather keep myself away from any sensitive information, although I'll make an exception in aiding your efforts."

I was still unsure as to why, but I would not question him for now. Canon had spoken of the story surrounding us soon reaching a climax, but the more I dwelled on that reasoning, the less comforting it was. The climax of a story was not always pleasant.

"I just got more info on the Kroterruk Tribe as well," Natakia spoke up again. "Actually, a lot more. I found where they're mostly based. Apparently they've taken root in the chambers of the Garrokian Storyteller Troupe."

I glanced at Canon, but he seemed to be equally confused as to why that would be the case.

"Those were mostly destroyed. I wonder why they would take such an interest in the ruins." The Storyteller stared down at his empty cup. "Perhaps there are secrets there that are beyond me?"

"Whatever the reason, that gives me a destination. Natakia, it'll be up to you to find out more and mark out a route for me. If Daka sleeps there, then I may have an opportunity to speak with her alone." That and I may have a chance to speak with my sister and end all this madness.

I did not want to hurt my sister. She had protected me from death in my youth, but her violence had corrupted my daughter, and I was feeling very unforgiving toward her. Hopefully, we could settle this as siblings and not as enemies.

* * *

We had been in Kakrel for days now, biding our time as Natakia and I continued to get more and more information from the surrounding area. My daughter had taken up Canon on his offer to learn of his magical traditions, but after my excitement had waned, I grew uncertain at his interest.

Storytellers took apprentices when they were very young, the youngling recruits often being stripped of their familial ties. I was both comforted and curious about Canon's simple teachings for my daughter, which carried none of the traditional isolation that such a path often required.

In the evening hours that Canon taught Natakia the beginnings of his magic, I took the time to teach Macy some of the basics of Shahis to keep her from being completely ignorant of the conversations around her.

And to keep my mind off the growing anxiety I was feeling about the state of Daka.

"I just don't know if I've got the pronunciation right." Macy scratched the back of her head. "Like, there are beats between words in . . . everything else, but Shahis is just . . . Everything flows together so seamlessly. How do you even tell what the words are and when they end?"

"You just have to train your ear, Macy. There are some dialects of Shahis that are even difficult for me to understand sometimes, but once you understand the distinct words and tones, it'll be far easier." It didn't help that Macy was just a tad tone-deaf, not really as talented with music as Natakia was.

Macy and I were studying in the first-floor bookstore when our lesson was suddenly interrupted as Natakia came stomping down the stairs without her usual grace. "Dad! Dad!"

"Nataka, what's wrong!?" I jumped to my feet, darting to my daughter with worry.

She grabbed onto me. "Dad, I was scrying on one of the nearby militant garrisons west of us and suddenly got whited out by a big source of Vitae! I think Daka is doing something outside of the contested area!"

And if it was happening at a garrison, that meant that it was likely not going to be peaceful. I nodded, squeezing my daughter's shoulder tight. "I'll go and see if I can stop her."

Daka had killed many, yes, but I knew in my heart of hearts that she lost more of herself with every death. It was my responsibility to make sure that when she was finally back in her right mind, that the burden of guilt and regret was as little as possible.

"Take your prosthetic with you." Natakia seemed firm on the subject.

I sighed. "I don't want to fight Daka. I wasn't given that arm to even the odds against my own daughter."

"Dad," she said, "how are you going to stop her if you can't even touch her? Do you think she's in a state to listen to you right now?"

What was the solution then? To beat up my own child until she came to her senses? The thought of even having to truly defend myself against Daka left a sour taste in my mouth.

"I can't control Daka's actions, but I will not bring a weapon of that magnitude to our reunion. If she fights me, then I am more than capable of escaping if nothing else," I said, confident at least in that.

Daka had years of training, and her gift had certainly made her strong, but there were a few tricks that I had up my sleeve. I did not think I could beat her as I was, but that was fine.

"Well then," Canon suddenly said, having slowly descended the stairs, "go forth and see how your wayward child responds, Rakta."

Natakia did not look happy at my refusal to bring my prosthetic, but I knew she was simply concerned for my safety. Nodding to the Storyteller, I turned and walked out of the home and onto the streets of Kakrel, beginning to stir my Vitae into action.

Daka was up to something, and I needed to put a stop to it.

Dashing over the streets and buildings of Kakrel was an interesting sight. I moved fast, the burn of my Vitae noticeable as my **Great Wind Sprint Technique** carried me forward, but in the dark of the evening I was sure that few spotted me.

The garrison that Natakia had pointed me toward was quiet as I arrived, and I noticed the guards at the front of it were still alive and breathing, with little tension between the two of them.

I was crouching on a building on the opposite side of the street below the garrison, hiding behind a tall chimney that rose from the domed roof. Confident in my stealth, I took the time to examine the surroundings of the military facility.

* * *

"Something isn't right," I said, looking through the windows of the building. The windows of the second floor were mostly dim, but there was still movement inside.

The sound of combat would have been obvious if a full-on attack had occurred, but . . . not if Daka were here in secret. An assassination attempt? Natakia hadn't mentioned any important officials here.

Pulling my Vitae into my eyes, I saw the world brighten and intensify as I examined everything more closely. I moved from building to building, trying to get a good view of the garrison.

That was when I noticed a single open window or, rather, a melted window in the back of the garrison. It was high up, on the second floor, and there was no light in the room.

"If I'm going to stop Daka," I said, preparing my Vitae, "I'll have to go in there myself."

With a few careful but tiring uses of my **Air Dance Technique**, I made my way stealthily to the melted window, pushing back the curtain and peering inside as I caught my breath and my physical energy recovered.

It was an office, no, a courier space. I could see the many messages and scrolls of the militants scattered about. Someone had been looking for something here, or rather, Daka had been looking for something.

Not seeing my daughter, I crept in through the window and began to examine the room more closely while staying as quiet as possible. If I were found here, there would be no convincing the Royal Cipher Militants that I was here for purely benevolent reasons.

Firmly in the garrison, I noticed that there was some light spilling in through the door to the hallway. The hanging slats covering the entrance blocked it out slightly, but it was why this room was not pitch-dark.

Crouched low, I looked around the room, and I was alone. Daka had either already gotten what she needed and left or she had gone farther into the garrison. There was only one way to find out.

I stirred my Vitae into action and pulled it into my senses, my **Scourger Bloodhound Technique** activated, and I began to sniff around the room. I quickly pulled apart the unfamiliar scents of others who had frequented the room and the smell of paper and ink before grabbing onto the familiar scent.

One that was now soaked in blood and leather but was still undoubtedly my daughter. And it was very powerful—far too strong to be a scent that had merely been left in her departure from the room.

I dropped the technique and opened my eyes, meeting a pair of wide blue eyes that met me on equal level, Daka crouched low as she saw me.

"Daka?" I asked, instinctively filled with joy to be face-to-face with my little warrior after so long stuck in the hellscape that had been Zactrik's punishment.

And yet, that punishment paled in comparison to my daughter whispering to me in perfect Shahis, "You're not real. I know you aren't."

And then the hanging slats of the room were thrown open as the familiar form of Mushak Ark stepped into the room, his curved blade drawn and pointed at the both of us.

29

There was no time to consider the lack of belief that my daughter had in my very existence when it was only through the sharp draw of Vitae that I was able to dodge the blow that came slicing at the two of us.

Daka spun through the air, faster than even I, and already had both of her jagged hand axes drawn as she began to slash and strike out at the mushak, his large blade deftly parrying the blows with precise maneuvers that kept his blade in the right place to deflect the consecutive strikes easily.

From the force of my dodge, I planted my feet firmly on the wall for a moment, watching as Daka suddenly flashed forward even faster than before and went for a killing blow at Mushak Ark's neck.

"No!" I dashed forward with the use of my **Skip Dash Technique**, Crow in hand, and deflected the blow as I got involved before noticing the large swing of the mushak's sword coming down to cleave us both. "Stop!"

I kicked out at him, the force of the enhanced blow sending him back as his sword simply grazed the side of my shoulder. Daka seemed stunned for a moment, looking at me, before her axes were suddenly flying through the air toward the militant leader, his blade barely coming up to deflect one as the other lodged deep into his shoulder.

"You Kroterruk scum!" he roared as the metal in his shoulder did little to slow his pursuit of us, his blade glowing with a familiar heat as the smell of brimstone filled the air.

Out of pure instinct, I initially reached out to push Daka out of the way of the attack, only to find her having already flashed away from my side and out of the line of the mushak's attack.

As my Vitae screamed out, I used my **Instinctive Reflex Technique** and **Skip Dash Technique** to dodge out of the way of the searing scar of an attack that surged below me as I jumped up, hitting the ceiling of the room awkwardly but by no means having the time to fully escape the explosion.

The searing attack hit the wall of the courier room and detonated with a powerful force, sending me flying as I instinctively coated my body with Vitae to protect myself. I could feel the struggle of my Vitae to keep my body from being burned but gritted my teeth as I hit the ground hard.

My cloak had been burned away by the explosion, left in tatters, and I knew that if I didn't leave soon, my face would be known as an enemy to the whole of Kakrel.

I noticed Daka jump out of the ruined hole in the side of the room, and for a moment I thought to leave with her, to follow and speak with her. And yet, she hadn't even thought I was real. Would she even pay attention to the words of a figment of her imagination?

Mushak Ark walked into the room, his form a shadowy blur through the debris of his explosive attack. The sheer force of the explosion of his blow had been impressive. I would not fare as well against a direct hit.

Pulling at my Vitae before the smoke of the attack disappeared completely, I coated my hands and body with my physical energy as I began to pull at the ground below me. The **Burrowing Mole Technique**, an old favorite of my daughter's, tore through the sandstone of the building as I dug down to the first floor.

There was a scream as I dropped down onto the table of a uniformed guard and quickly knocked him unconscious with a swift punch to his face. I did not wait even a moment to dig farther into the ground and away from the garrison.

The swift but harrowing battle at the garrison had made my adrenaline spike, but there was still very much the matter of what my daughter had intended to do there in the first place. I was sure it wasn't a coincidence that she had entered through that room.

After getting away from the garrison, I had spent some time moving around Kakrel to throw off any attempt to track me. There would be no benefit to getting followed back to Canon's home.

I had just arrived at a small private park, with soil and trees that would have otherwise been impossible to come by naturally in the majority of Rusk. I was sure the water in the small pond at the center of it was likely connected to the oasis of Kakrel, their major source of water.

It was a good place to take a moment to breathe before I turned around and began my twisted route back to Natakia to see what she had discovered while I had . . . ultimately failed at my mission to talk to Daka. Our reunion would have to wait for another time.

"Who are you?" Daka's voice surprised me. I made to turn around, but I felt the cold steel of metal against my neck. "Don't . . . move. Just tell me who you are. Why do you . . . look like that?"

Look like what? Did Daka think that I was some kind of impostor? Perhaps it was the height of naivety, but I could not bring myself to feel fear even as my daughter held a blade against me.

"Daka," I said calmly, "it's me. You know that it's me. Your father."

There was a moment of silence before the tension behind the blade lessened slightly, yet a mere moment later it pushed even harder into my flesh, biting into me. There was a burn as it pierced my skin, and I realized that these blades . . . were poisoned. And not weakly so.

"You're lying. My father . . . He died. He died years ago." Daka's voice was cold, but I could hear the hard edge of fear in her voice. Why was she afraid? What was she afraid of?

I stirred my Vitae, counteracting the poison as it tried to get into my bloodstream. It was a countermeasure that would only work for so long. "I woke up, Daka. I'm here for you."

I did not want to rush Daka into believing me. This was a tremendous revelation, I was sure. Hopefully, however, she would remove the blade from my neck, and I could stop burning Vitae to continue living.

As if answering my silent but very fervent wish, the cold metal suddenly left my flesh entirely. I felt relief, letting my Vitae recover from the dance with death that it had been performing alongside whatever powerful poison was on her blades.

"Thank you." I turned around, expecting to see my daughter, but she was no longer there. I looked around, having not even heard her leave. I was alone in the park, my reunion with my daughter cut short.

I stood there for some time, as if waiting for her to come back, but with every second I gritted my teeth more and more, tightening my fist as anger began to build in my stomach. A terrible rage that wanted to be unleashed against the world and my own failings as my daughter fell through my fingers again.

"Ha." I tried to breathe out the anger, trying to do anything to control the anguish that I felt. A hand put up against my face, I rubbed my eyes before staring toward the twinkling stars of the night. "I need to get back. Natakia will be worried."

With that, I waited for only mere moments more, looking around for any trace of Daka, before beginning to head out. My daughter, among all her other talents, seemed to be quite the expert at stealth.

"How did it go?" Natakia greeted me as I entered Canon's home, looking relieved to see me, but I could tell that she hadn't missed the tatters of my cloak or the cut on my neck. I hadn't thought to circulate my Vitae into healing it.

I simply embraced her, holding her tight. "Daka did not believe I was real at first. When I convinced her of who I was . . . she left. I'd thought it was the moment I had been hoping for, but I was wrong."

She hugged me back, and I felt quite useless. Natakia hugged me even tighter, which dragged me from my thoughts slightly, but I was still mired by the failure of the night.

"I'm fine, Natakia," I said, putting my hand on her head. "I was not seen . . . At least, I was not recognized. There will be more chances to speak to Daka and decipher how she ended up like this."

"The conclusion of a story is often self-evident if one understands all the parts that precede it," Canon said, putting away some of the books that Macy and I had been using for her Shahis studies.

Speaking of the young shape-shifter, I looked around. "Macy . . . ?"

"Asleep," Natakia said. "She was pretty tired, and there wasn't much point in her staying awake. So, what do we do now?"

Daka had been fearful during our reunion, that was evident, but I still didn't know why. I had some ideas, but they were difficult to definitively believe. As Canon said, it was likely that we simply needed to know more. And I knew exactly how to learn as much as I needed.

"Natakia, wake up Macy." I began to change out of my burned clothing, circulating my Vitae to finally heal the wound that Daka had given me and the remnants of burns on my arm.

Soon, Macy had stirred, although she seemed somewhat confused as to why she was needed. I was going to need Natakia and Macy for this plan of mine, each of them having a different part of the solution.

"What do you need us to do, Dad?" Natakia seemed as curious as Macy, although as she looked at me, recognition entered her gaze.

I nodded, sure that her gift had enlightened her to my intentions. "There was a man, some kind of leader for the Kroterruk band that I saw facing off with the militants. He spoke to Daka with familiarity."

"He's our target then?" My desert flower looked determined.

"He's a softer target than my sister," I said, "and we don't have the time to wait anymore. While it's difficult to believe, Daka may inform my sister of my presence in the city."

The last we had met, my sister and I were nearly equals in battle. With my prosthetic, I could likely outlast her, but that wasn't a battle I wanted to seek out until absolutely necessary.

"Macy, I need you to grab the memories of the man I saw and show them to Natakia." I waited for Macy to nod before I turned to Natakia and said, "I'll trust you to find him for me."

She nodded, and with the plan formed, I settled myself into allowing the memory magic to pull at the right image, keeping my thoughts as clear as I could.

"And I told the mushak straight to his face," the weasel man barked out to the small crowd of Kroterruks around him, "I told him that I'd bury him so deep in the ground that no one would even know his name!"

The tribesmen around him laughed and guffawed, all of them enjoying a raucous night of entertainment in the depths of a half-ruined tavern that was quickly being drained of every last drop of alcohol it had.

Perhaps it was because of the fine spirits that were slick on his tongue, but his storytelling was crude and lazy. I supposed that the audience wasn't exactly encouraging any fine renditions of the man's battle experience, but I had little reason to reserve my thoughts.

Chattak, a trusted member of the Kroterruk Tribe, but everything that Natakia discovered had painted the picture of a Ruskan capable of making friends with the right people and looking out for himself. My sister didn't necessarily trust him to win any battle, but he was a source of morale for the larger group.

I didn't recognize him, meaning that he was a new member, perhaps from a different tribe that had been swallowed up by my sister. The same went for the rest of the crowd. I counted about a dozen of them, but none of them stoked any familiarity in me.

Taking a deep breath, I stepped out from around the corner I had been hiding behind and walked out into the open. "Excuse me, my ears caught wind of your stories outside."

The crowd was slow to grow tense, but tense up they did as I wandered into their notice. I wore a heavy cloak, another one that I had borrowed from Canon at his insistence. The hood fell low on my face, keeping my identity somewhat obscured as I slowly walked forward, keeping an eye on all of them.

"I brought an offering," I said, holding up a bottle of fine drink that I'd purchased earlier that day. "I offer it in return for a story of my choosing."

"Who are you?" Chattak frowned but certainly seemed interested in my offering. "What do you want?"

"I want to hear about the Whistling Demon." I hated calling Daka that, but it would do me no service to speak her true name in this crowd. "I'd like to know who and how she came to be."

Chattak eyed me suspiciously before his eyes began to count the men and women alongside him, the liquid confidence in his veins emboldening him further. "I think we've actually got some questions for you, old man. Give us the drink and maybe we'll make them gentle."

"Even Brota shared a drink with Garrok before he passed," I said, swishing the contents of my drink around. I had hoped that they would see reason and I would be saved from an unnecessary struggle.

As the crowd began to draw their weapons, I sighed and put the drink down onto a table beside me and took off my cloak, revealing my metallic prosthetic arm. I couldn't bear to tear another of Canon's cloaks.

30

Surrounded by moans and groans of pain, I held Chattak off of the floor by the scruff of his tunic and carried him over to the only still-unbroken table in the room after I had dealt with the crowd.

"Sit," I said, putting him into one of the last remaining chairs in the establishment. "I would have liked to hear your stories told willingly; now you will tell me everything you know by force if required."

Chattak was not a strong fighter, and his people, slow with drink, had been even less of a concern. The most difficult part was making sure that none had a chance to yell before they had been knocked to the ground and punched into unconsciousness. Although, I wasn't sure all had survived.

"You." The man was woozy, swaying as he stared down at the table. "Who are you?"

I sat in the chair opposite him, placing the undisturbed drink to the side. "The more I tell you, the less chance there is of you surviving. I do not wish to kill those of the Kroterruk Tribe right now. I simply want to know more about the one you call the Whistling Demon."

For a moment, he looked close to simply passing out. I had punched him once, early on in the fight, with my metal fist. It seemed like that had been enough to knock him down, and he was still teetering on the edge of unconsciousness.

"Okay," he slurred, "I'll tell you . . . what I know. She was just a girl. I think she came to the tribe about five years ago? She was dirty, hungry, and desperate, but she called us . . . family. She said she needed help killing a man, killing monsters. Natakia took her in, and the next time we saw her . . . she was a monster on the battlefield."

Had my daughter come to the Kroterruk Tribe in search of aid in revenge against Zactrik? How had that turned into aiding them in preying upon the other people of Rusk?

"She's been fighting for the Kroterruk Tribe for five years?" I asked, somewhat mystified. That was a long time to be among the dangers of the Ruskan desert.

Chattak swallowed hard. "I, yeah, she . . . Yeah. She's powerful, stronger than our leader, but she listens to her. I don't know why. People have said it's because they're family or something. All I know, she changed everything. She protected us when tribes attacked; she killed when we went raiding."

He made a drunken motion with his hands, as if to invite my imagination to take over for him. So Daka became the pillar of strength for my tribe. At such a young age, that was impressive but . . . It was very distressing.

"She doesn't talk to anyone, doesn't drink, doesn't come to any sort of celebration," he continued. "The only one who is able to get anything out of her is Natakia. Otherwise, she's like a great spirit. Deadly, mysterious, beyond the scope of the tales . . . Our tales . . ."

Chattak started to slump, and I let him, having gotten as much as I thought possible from the man. Hearing from someone who had known my daughter during all of this, I could begin to understand more about where her mind had been during all these years.

Daka had left three years after I had fallen asleep, and the portrait I had seen of her was angry. Perhaps she had taken my state as a personal failure and had decided to seek out a place to become strong? Then why did she run away from me? Why did she think I was dead?

Did she now think of me as some sort of specter coming back to haunt her for all the death and destruction that she had caused in the pursuit of helping the Kroterruk Tribe?

"Thank you, Chattak," I said to the unconscious man. I left him the drink, not really caring about it at the moment. I had far more important thoughts clouding my mind.

* * *

Once Daka had asked me if she would ever have to kill others. I had told her that it was always a choice, even when life seemingly gave you no other. She had said then, if my memory had served me right, that she would never be a killer.

"So Daka came to your tribe to try and protect them? Or fight for them?" Natakia seemed to be wrestling with the idea as well. "Your death was never rumored. Most believed that you were simply retired or were resting. Never dead. Why did Daka think you were dead?"

"My sister may have told her that I was dead at a certain point. I can't be sure, of course, but I would not be surprised if she had. It may have given her more control over Daka," I said, eating some of the food that Canon had cooked for us. It was delicious and perfectly spiced with local herbs.

It reminded me of Adoabi, a chef I used to visit at the capital. It had been quite some time since I'd last heard from him or had the chance to sit down at his shop. I hoped he was doing well, if he was still alive.

Natakia munched on her meal, although taking smaller bites and looking more hesitant with each one. Macy was encouraging her quietly, smiling at every bite.

"So," my daughter said between bites, wiping her mouth primly, "I think I know what the Kroterruk Tribe's plan is. The chambers for the Storytellers were pretty old."

"Somewhat of an understatement." Canon smiled, motioning for her to go on.

Natakia shrugged. "Yeah, but, anyway . . . I was reading some of the stories Canon wrote, and there was one that I thought was pretty interesting. It was about the Grand Cipher's love life—"

"*Love Within the Palace*," Canon said, looking fond as he spoke the title, gesturing into the air as if imagining the story before him. "A timeless classic that brings a touch of humanity to our Grand Cipher."

Natakia huffed, giving Canon a look. I patted her shoulder, comforting her after being interrupted one too many times. Our host was certainly excitable when it came to the tales that he'd spent his life weaving.

"Anyway," Natakia continued, daring the old man to interrupt her again, "I noticed that in the story, it talked about the Grand Cipher sneaking out to see their Storyteller lover. And there's one part that talks about tunnels from the palace to their chambers!"

"Tunnels . . . That would mean that the Kroterruk Tribe targeted the Garrokian Storyteller Troupe to get access to those tunnels. Canon, did you know about this?" I turned to look at the old man, who simply shrugged his shoulders.

"We've often searched for those tunnels ourselves, but wherever they lie, they are not easily found." He stroked his chin. "Although, perhaps, the destruction that was caused to our chambers wasn't just to force us to seek refuge elsewhere."

I understood where he was going with his logic. "They could have used that to destroy parts of the chamber that were concealing the tunnels. They may be trying to dig out the tunnels now to gain a direct route to where the Grand Cipher is staying."

Canon took a deep breath and exhaled. I understood the sentiment. The idea that the Kroterruk Tribe's main goal was to assassinate the Grand Cipher was a very heavy one. In all the stories I knew about Kakrel, no one had ever succeeded at assassinating the leader of the capital.

"We'll have to stop them," I said. "Killing the Grand Cipher doesn't end the war; it starts it. The whole of Rusk will be subsumed by outright war. The street-level conflict now will have nothing on the power struggle that will ensue, not to mention if other nations get involved."

The Storyteller stood up and stretched, the sound of his back cracking echoing out throughout the room, before he sighed and stood straight. "Rakta, do you think you can beat your sister? Given the opportunity?"

"Yes, as long as I have the aid of my prosthetic. It will allow me to fight evenly with my sister long enough to beat her," I said, confident of that.

"And your daughter," Canon continued, "can you reach her? If given the chance?"

I felt the burn of the gift I had received from Overseer and nodded. "I can. As long as I can find her, I can reason with her."

"Well," Canon said, "then I believe it's time for us to set this story straight and true. Do you trust me and any aid I can gather, Rakta?"

He stood much firmer than usual, looking as serious as I had ever seen him in the time that we had spent living in his abode. For all the questions that I had about him and his beliefs, there was no doubt that he had taken care of us during our time in the capital.

"I trust you, Canon. You have been teaching Natakia well and have given sound counsel. If you have aid that you can call upon, then please." I certainly could not go against the whole of the Kroterruk Tribe by myself, even with Penelope's gift.

Canon nodded, looking at Natakia and Macy, before smiling. "Well then, I'll go and let Mushak Ark know that he can finally come inside and chat."

"So," Mushak Ark said, his wound from Daka having been properly healed and a ceremonial shawl covering his armor as he sat down before me, "you are the famous Rakta the Dancer, the traveler from afar whom Mushak Canon has spoken so fondly of this last week."

"Yes," I said, glancing at Canon. "I was unaware of his prestige, however. I thought him simply a respected Storyteller. Not a mushak of Kakrel."

"I'm sorry for the slight duplicity, Rakta," Canon said, looking properly apologetic. "I approached you out of genuine interest, but I was quite sure that if I had been open about my position, you would have been . . . far less receptive of my aid."

I had not intended to pick a side in all of this, but with this revelation, it seemed that I certainly was on one now. Perhaps I always had been? It didn't sit well with me, but I put my discomfort aside for now. If we could benefit from the Royal Cipher Militants, then we would do so . . . until we couldn't.

"I'm sorry, Dad," Natakia said, looking uncomfortable. "I realized it pretty early, just after you went searching for the first time, but . . . Canon asked me to keep it secret. If I had thought he meant any kind of harm, then—"

I held up my hand, smiling to comfort her. "It's fine, Natakia. I'm sure Canon had his reasons. I don't need to know everything, and even in hindsight, Canon's aid has been invaluable."

Besides, Canon was effectively Natakia's teacher at the moment, possibly more so when this all was over. I would not disparage her for keeping her teacher's confidence.

"Your daughter's intelligence has also been invaluable," Mushak Ark said, motioning to Natakia. "Canon told me that while only some of her information has aided you, much of what she has learned has been passed along to us. We've been hitting the softer parts of the Kroterruk Tribe's territory, and the results have been exceptional."

"My daughter is exceptional," I said, proud of my desert flower, before I seriously considered the man before me. "Before we speak of our plans, I want to make my expectations clear. My daughter, the Whistling Demon, is not to be killed. I will handle her."

"Your daughter is the Whistling Demon?" Mushak Ark's eyes widened, looking clearly alarmed. Canon looked moderately sheepish for a moment.

Ah, he had not passed that information along. Appreciated, but I wished I had known about that omission before I'd made it so transparently clear. "Yes, she is. I have been indisposed for years, and she has gone down a dark path. I can only promise my aid if I am the one who handles her."

"You expect us to allow you to simply take her from Kakrel without even the slightest punishment?" Mushak Ark frowned. "That is the height of lunacy."

"And yet, they are agreeable terms," Canon said, looking pleased with himself even as Mushak Ark gave him a dirty look.

"You do not speak for the whole of Kakrel, Mushak Canon," Mushak Ark said.

Canon retrieved a scroll from his robes that he passed over to Mushak Ark, the symbol of Kakrel emblazoned upon it. "No, the Grand Cipher does."

"What is that?" The very idea that the Grand Cipher had knowledge of what we were doing was disconcerting. I had never met them, and for a moment I felt the lopsided amount of information between us very vividly.

As Mushak Ark unfurled it and read it to himself, his face scrunching up, Canon turned to me. "A conditional pardon of the Whistling Demon's crimes. She'll never return to Kakrel, but as long as she leaves with you, she won't be pursued through legal or extralegal means."

Mushak Ark looked disturbed at what he was reading, and after a shared glance with Natakia, who seemed surprised at this herself but convinced of Canon's honesty, I nodded. It was a good deal, more than I had expected. It was honestly somewhat disquieting in its generosity.

"Why go so far for my daughter and my family?" Canon had done much for us. It was hard to believe it was out of simple interest in the story that we wrote with our actions. That was far too like the detached interest of a god than a man of flesh and blood.

Canon came over and laid a hand on my shoulder, smiling. "I had a brother once, Rakta. We never agreed on anything; in fact, quite the opposite. Still, even when I left the tribe, I never let go of those family bonds. You look a lot like him, you know?"

It took a moment for his words to truly sink in. My father had never spoken of a brother, had never once even let slip an implication of it. And yet, as I realized the truth, I could see the resemblance. The way that Canon smiled, the way that his brows furrowed while deep in thought.

"Does my"—my lips were dry—"does my sister know?"

"I doubt it," he said, shrugging. "That said, I think it's time Mushak Ark tells us how best we can be of use to him and this strategic strike on the Kroterruk Tribe."

31

I realized that, just moments ago, I had been at the receiving end of familial kindness for the first time in many decades. Canon, some long-lost uncle I had never known about, it was . . . It was truly indicative of the state of my life that after such a revelation, I had not the time to celebrate.

Rather, I stood among the tops of ruined buildings and destroyed structures deep within the Kroterruk Tribe's controlled area within the capital of Rusk. Mushak Ark had said that his militants would be marching to this destination soon, and that meant that it would be my time to act.

I stood a mere block away from the ruins of the chambers that once held the Garrokian Storyteller Troupe. In lieu of any proper blockades to obstruct movement within their territory, it seemed that the Kroterruk Tribe had simply let debris from their attacks naturally cordon off the area.

"He said there would be a sign." I continued to keep an eye on the skyline. Back at Canon's abode, Natakia and Macy were safe, being guarded by militants and the Storyteller himself.

Mushak Ark and his men would be a distraction for the larger part of the Kroterruk Tribe's forces, who would mobilize once word spread about the incoming militant forces. It was my job to move in and reason with my daughter before she went to aid them and deal with my sister if it came to it.

Dealing with my sister . . . Canon had asked me if I was capable, but I wondered if what he had truly been asking had nothing to do with power and everything to do with strength. Would I be able to reason with her as well? If it was all for naught, would I be forced to kill her? Or would I leave her to the mercy of Kakrel?

Canon had managed to obtain a pardon for my daughter, but no such thing had been sought for my sister. If she were left to Kakrel, would she be simply executed? What punishment would she face?

Dwelling so heavily in my thoughts, I almost missed the bright shining light that streaked through the sky above the war-torn streets of Kakrel. It glowed with the same amber color as Mushak Ark's powerful strike as it brightly sparkled for all the world to see.

And while all saw it, it was meant only for me.

"It's time," I said, taking hold of Crow firmly with my prosthetic. "I've got to go down there and find Daka quickly before she runs off to help the rest of the tribe."

A voice cut through my actions. "Let's not be too hasty, brother."

I felt a great outpouring of Vitae behind me, which had somehow been hidden from my senses until just as she'd finished speaking. I turned to face Natakia, my sister, for the first time in decades.

"You haven't changed, Natakia. I was never clever enough for you." Once upon a time, those words would have been said playfully, but now the grimness between us had soured them.

Natakia of the Teeth stood before me, standing on the same half-destroyed rooftop as I did, a long, jagged coil of bladed chains dangling from her ready grip. She had aged far better than I had. The gray in her hair was scattered, her tangle of curls tied up into a tight ponytail, and her body still looked lean and healthy.

She had certainly not spent eight years wasting away in a nightmarish coma nor had she been plagued by the scars of Mortum on her Vitae. I was somewhat envious, I had to admit.

"I'm afraid my niece doesn't want to see you," Natakia said, letting her chains begin to loosely fall to the ground. "She's scared that you've come to slay the monster that she's become."

"I have come to speak, Natakia, to give you a chance to call this off. I see no reason for this attack on Kakrel. You threaten the balance that Brota and Garrok struck years ago," I said, readying myself as well.

My sister shook her head. "Still a traitorous coward who can't understand the value of power. We seek victory, Rakta, victory where Brota failed! And when the Grand Cipher burns and their scrolls along with them, then we will finally build a Rusk that Brota would be proud of!"

Scrolls? Did she speak of the Grand Cipher's Cipher Scrolls? I was unsure if my sister truly had evidence of such things even existing, but I was not here to verify her claims.

"Dragging my daughter into this when she sought your counsel." I shook my head. "I cannot forgive you turning her into what she feared becoming. And yet, I offer it again: Do you yield?"

"You truly ask if I yield?" Natakia seemed genuinely offended. "I am Natakia of the Teeth, the chiefess of the Kroterruk Tribe, and you, brother, are simply a crippled fool who has come here to lose everything."

Emerging from around her were other Kroterruk warriors, looking far more skilled than the ones who had surrounded Chattak. Spears and axes were pointed my way, the collective Vitae radiating from them all toward me being quite impressive.

My sister and I were quite alike. We both sought victory, but my victory was far different than hers. She stood in the way of me reaching Daka, of pulling her out of the darkness . . . I had been trapped in darkness once.

"No, sister, I've already lost everything once before to a monster that was beyond even you and me," I said, getting my **Dancing Star Stance** as I felt the Vitae of my arm erupt through me. "I am on a journey to get back all that I once had."

There were six warriors alongside my sister, and something told me that was not a coincidence. There was a familiarity in these warriors, in the way they moved. The most telling thing, however, was the hatred they had for me as they struck out with their Vitae-empowered blades.

My sister had barely moved as the fight began, her bladed chains instead moving for her as the metal of her weapons grew into a large steel snake, the almost living weapon attempting to crash into me and cut me in half. It was the **Dancing Star Stance**, much like my own, but with my sister's unique touch.

The warriors moved in tandem with the bladed snake as it followed me through the air, my **Instinctive Reflex Technique** and **Skip Dash**

Technique working hard alongside my **Air Dance Technique** to retain my aerial superiority.

The Kroterruk warriors actually carried themselves through the air toward me, holding on to the bladed snake and letting its movements shoot them up toward the sky. It was obvious that my sister and these warriors had fought together for a long time, confirming what I thought.

Sending out a deluge of Crows with a quick **Swift Throw Technique** toward the warriors, I dropped down and got close to my sister, flipping over her bladed snake's attempt to slice me in half.

"These warriors," I breathed out as I parried a blow from a spear, hooking the haft with my axe before pulling the warrior into a fierce punch that left them staggering. "They are from the last time we met?"

"They've been wanting to thank you for a long time for letting them live," Natakia said, looking all too pleased to give her warriors a chance to do exactly that.

That confirmed it. I didn't have much time to dwell on it consciously, but my mind pulled for the memories regardless as I fought the warriors, pulling on the gathered source of Vitae invested into my arm to keep up with their movements.

The last time that Natakia and I had met, it had been while I adventured with my friends and Lydia. We'd been on a mission, but the details were somewhat obscure at the moment. We had collided with my tribe, my sister had the reins, and many of them had died against the onslaught of my group's strength.

I empowered Crow and cut through the entire wooden haft of the greataxe that had attempted to slice my head off, my blow following through as I sank the edge of my blade into the side of the woman wielding it. "They're trained well, Natakia, but I have fought more in quality and quantity before."

For all that Rusk had prepared me for the dangers of the world, it still paled in comparison to the exhausting battles of the war against the Warlock King.

Natakia seemed to be unsure of her warriors' chances, as well, as she began to finally move forward, her bladed snake becoming quicker and deadlier with its movements. As the tide of the battle began to change, I swiftly knocked out two of the warriors who had come at me.

"You will finally fight?" I asked, somewhat out of breath. While I could read the attacks of the warriors and the bladed snake, they were still quick and couldn't be simply dodged every time.

Natakia unraveled a second coil of bladed chains. "I will."

She unleashed the chains into another bladed snake, one that quickly began to attack in tandem, rearing up into the sky before simply spearing toward me. I ducked, dodged, and wove through the attacks, making my way toward my sister as I felt the nick of a spear catching me in my side.

The instant burn of pain from the poison on it made me wince, my Vitae instantly going to contain the toxin and erode it away, but not before I felt a few more nicks from other weapons. I couldn't ignore my sister's blades, but in the wake of focusing on her, I was unavoidably more vulnerable to her companions.

"It is always poison," I grunted, feeling the burn of the weapons that sliced into my skin, ruining another perfectly good cloak from Canon.

I jumped toward my sister before I blurred as I instead jumped back, letting the warriors who had shot forward to strike at me as I attacked Natakia leave themselves wide open. No longer having the luxury of taking it easy, three simulacra shot forward from Crow as I threw toward the distracted warriors.

With meaty thunks, the axes buried themselves deep into the back of the skull of each one, three of the warriors falling down, surely dead. It was a dark day to be shedding the blood of my own tribe, but they had made their choices, and now so had I.

"Natakia," I said, "please. This doesn't have to continue. You're right, I am not as strong as I once was. I can't be sure that you'll survive if I am to defeat you."

There was only a single Kroterruk warrior still standing alongside my sister as she scowled at my words. "I am against you, Rakta. You should have no concern for this life of mine. Do not cover for your own weakness with some foolish notion of mercy!"

For a moment, I thought that it was time to do as she asked and put away these thoughts of mercy. She would not appreciate them. Even in her darkest hour, she would spurn my attempts to save her life. Natakia, for just a moment, was right. We were enemies; we were against each other.

She had made her choice, and I had made my own.

"We always get to choose, even if the world makes us think otherwise," the words coming from my lips unbidden. "No matter what we chose before, we can choose again and choose something different."

I bore witness to the blinding speeds of the dual bladed-chain snakes that ripped through the ground heading toward me and pulled on my Vitae, dashing to the side and leaping as they shifted to try to catch me unawares with the lagging length of their chains.

Leaping high into the sky with the aid of my **Air Dance Technique**, I began to fill the air with Crows, letting my axes begin to dance as I focused on deflecting Natakia's enlarged chain snakes with the force of the Vitae in the duplicates of my axe.

And then I saw the moment, through all the fighting, the moment that one of my axes sank into the leg of the last warrior. The moment that Natakia took her eyes off of me and looked toward her warrior in concern.

"Charging Bull Technique!" I said, filling my body with Vitae as I suddenly shot down through a hole in her defenses, barely dodging through the blades of her chain snakes, before coming face-to-face with my sister with the full force of my Vitae-enhanced charge behind a vicious haymaker. "Natakia!"

And then everything suddenly blurred as an incredible force knocked me aside, the Vitae of my attack dissipating as I hit the ground hard, barely able to flip back onto my feet as I skidded across a nearby roof.

As the dust settled around where my sister had stood, I felt my heart drop into my stomach as Daka stood in front of the standing form of my sister, her expression as pleasantly surprised as mine was grim.

She said nothing, her wide blue eyes staring through me, and I knew that wherever she was, she wasn't on this battlefield right now. There was an emptiness in them, tinged with something primal, instinctive.

As Daka unsheathed her hand axes, a jaunty whistle began to echo over the rooftops from her lips.

32

As my daughter got ready to fight me, in the depths of whatever madness had taken her, I felt something welling up in me. Revulsion at the idea of fighting my own child in this way.

"No," I said, plain and clear. "I will not fight you, Daka."

Instead of the dark leather attire she'd worn before, Daka stood before me with simple bandages covering her fists, her leather helmet and bracers being the only armor she wore. I could see her hair was a mess underneath her helmet, and I felt a great affection remembering all the times I had combed it.

"You don't have a choice." Natakia smirked.

And with that, Daka flew toward me, and while I quickly attempted to dodge, she immediately showcased how completely she outmatched me in a test of speed. I grunted as I felt a kick to my side nearly throw me off the roof I was on before she grabbed me by my collar and threw me over her shoulder and back onto the roof.

I felt another kick, this time at my back, sending me flying toward the bladed snakes of my sister, who had quickly regathered herself at Daka's intervention. I gritted my teeth, pulling on the welling up of Vitae in my arm, and used my **Skip Dash Technique** to jump up and over my own impending death.

I pushed off of the air as I tried to reorient myself and shot back toward the ground, barely dodging to the side as Daka came crashing past me once more, her gaze trained on me.

"Daka! It is me!" I called out, but realized that despite her prior recognition no mere words would drag her from whatever mindscape she had walled herself up in.

I flipped over another attempt by my sister to cut me in half, throwing a few Crows in her direction to keep her bladed snakes preoccupied in defending her.

With that, I darted toward my daughter, beginning to go on the offensive as the mark of House Tribus on the back of my hand began to burn with my desire to understand what my daughter was going through, to understand what was driving her to do all of this.

And yet, in a frustrating mirror of all the deadly blows that I had evaded in my life, Daka nimbly dodged my pursuit. I could recognize, vaguely, the techniques she used to evade me, but there were plenty that I had never seen used as masterfully as she used them. In one moment, she was invisible, and in the other, there were three of her.

Insubstantial copies, dashing beyond my reach, and even getting me with an ankle-breaking trip that I had to quickly recover from, Daka was proving to be every bit of the warrior I'd thought she might one day be. The frustration and sadness I felt at seeing my daughter this way warred with the respect and pride I had.

Deflecting her attempts to strike me with her hand axes, parrying them with my own blade, I could at least count myself superior in experience. While she was fast, brilliantly so, she was not quite as fast as Esmeralda and still had enough wasted movement that I could waylay her attempts to cut me.

"Twisting Chain Technique!" Natakia called out, her bladed snakes suddenly whipping into a combined cyclone of bladed chains that headed straight toward me.

It was fast, far too fast to dodge completely without having seen it coming, and I felt the skin of my stomach get shaved as I dashed to the side. The burn of poison began to pain me, making me draw more and more Vitae to fight off the effect. It was potent; a lesser fighter would be dead by now.

The troublesome combo of my sister and my daughter continued to assault me. Perhaps I could have managed to evade either one alone, but Daka's attacks were too fast and novel, and my sister's capabilities were far too flexible.

Focusing on one at a time invited the other to try her hand at tearing into me, and I was not sure how much longer I would last if I did not change something soon.

I deflected a blow from my daughter with the back of my metal arm, reaching out to grab her with my gift before she darted away expertly. While she couldn't know how my gift worked, Daka certainly was capable enough to know to evade any attempt I made to grab her.

As we fought, I was vaguely aware of explosions in the distance. The Kroterruk Tribe and the Royal Cipher Militants had begun to fight in earnest. Without their chiefess or my daughter, I didn't give the tribe warriors favorable odds against the likes of Mushak Ark and his soldiers.

"Daka," my sister yelled over to my daughter, obviously thinking the same, "finish this! The Kroterruk Tribe is going to lose, and our people will die if you don't finish this now!"

Even in the lingering pain of my sister's onslaught, I shouted, "This can all be over by your call, Natakia! You started this. You can end this!"

"The only thing ending is the mockery of our nation with the burning of Kakrel! Beginning with the Grand Cipher and their regime!" My sister grinned, her bladed chains returning to her and wrapping around her defensively.

Before I could respond, Daka landed before me, meeting my gaze, and I felt hope that I had finally jogged her out of my sister's insanity. And then she fell back into a stance that made my heart skip a beat. One that I felt immense fear and pride at seeing my daughter so masterfully maneuver her body into.

Briefly, I could feel the wind still and the sky itself turn to watch as the clouds began to vibrate with Daka's Vitae. The air felt electric, like it was a point of no return, but there was a control within it that sought to tame the primal power of nature . . . no, not tame. To ride with it and be carried by it.

For that was the way of the **First Dance Stance**.

"**First Dance Technique**," my daughter intoned, flatly, "**Twister Through the Valley**."

The force of the blows that rained down on me dwarfed the weight of the attacks that I had felt before. The cuts and bruises that had been carved into me by my daughter and the force of the storm behind her were tearing chunks out of my Vitae.

Every blow, I pulled harder and harder on the source of Vitae within Penelope's gift, but even the week's worth of physical energy that I had channeled into it was slowly coming to the end of its usefulness. There was only so much aid it could give.

A solid punch to the face threw me into the air, landing heavily on top of yet another destroyed roof, before I felt myself slip and fall onto the debris-covered streets of Kakrel. I felt Crow fall somewhere beyond me, out of my grip and away from the battle.

"She's very strong," I said, wiping the blood off my face, slowly standing up as I felt the wear and tear of the fight. I had promised Canon that I could handle our family, but it seemed that I had overestimated my capabilities. Perhaps if I had been more ruthless I could have ended Natakia faster . . .

Daka landed in the street, the vicious, angry air twisting around her hands and feet as her eyes glowed with the power of her Vitae. It was like seeing a dark mirror of myself in my prime.

Natakia watched on from the top of the building behind Daka, looking self-satisfied as my own daughter prepared to strike me down. Did my sister intend to celebrate my death without even an ounce of regret?

As I stretched and got back into a fighting stance, I considered that it was not the only time I had seen a sibling strike out at another. I had a new appreciation for the strength that Lydia had, to endure the pain of having to be the downfall of her brother.

It was a strength that I wished for at this moment. I did not want to fight my sister, not when there was so much left unsaid between us, and I certainly did not wish to hurt Daka.

And yet, as the wind blew around me and Daka blurred toward me with the incredible speeds of the cyclone that was at her beck and call, I breathed deeply in and set my gaze toward victory.

The edge of Daka's axe clashed mightily against the solid metal of my arm, and I felt the world around me stir as another beckoned for it. My Vitae blended into the world around me, and I saw my daughter hesitate for a moment as she felt my Vitae meet hers.

For while a lone dancer had a beauty truly unique to themselves. It was when the hearts of two dancers blended together that the true majesty of Brota's legacy was revealed.

"**First Dance Technique**," I said, falling into my own **First Dance Stance**, "**The Stand of the Unconquered Plateau**."

She blurred around me, her axes attempting to cut into my skin with the force of her cyclone, but a breeze could not make a mountain bow. I felt my Vitae burning as I weathered the storm of her assault, the highly defensive technique increasing my physical fortitude more than it ever had before.

I looked up at my sister, where she watched stunned on top of the building before me, and gritted my teeth with rage and purpose. My technique did not only grant me the stalwart blessing of the mountain but also its strength.

Slowly lifting my foot, even as Daka tried to knock me off of my feet with her repeated blows, I slammed the full weight of my strength down into the ground. A crack exploded into the ground, stretching out toward the building that Natakia of the Teeth had rested upon in comfort for far too long.

"Get down here!" I yelled, beginning to move with the weight of the world as my sister, shocked by the suddenness of my action, nearly slipped and fell as the building below her crumbled.

Before I could make it to my sister to finally end all of this, I felt Daka's punch slice into me with a force that finally gave me pause. I reared back, the pain of the attack echoing through my bones, but I managed to reach out and grab at my daughter's weapons, pulling them from her grasp and shattering them.

Daka was breathing heavily now as well, her hands aglow with the Vitae she had been surging into her weapons to allow them to pierce the thickness of my current defenses. I could feel my body begin to strain, and soon I would be pulling at something far more important to keep my power alive, my very life itself.

As my sister became entangled by the debris of the building that had collapsed beneath her, her cries swallowed by the stones and dust falling in on her, I turned my attention to my daughter.

Natakia would not be held down by simple debris for long. She was far too strong for such a thing to be her end in this fight. And yet, maybe, it gave me time to find victory in the darkness of defeat.

"Daka," I said, tossing my cloak to the side as my techniques faded away, "if I do not reach you, I want you to know that not for a single moment do I hold hatred in my heart for you. I love you, now and ever more. I hope that when you see the light, you understand that this does not always have to be who you are."

I had been a bandit once, had killed many, had felt that same numbness in my heart as lives were ended by my hands. Perhaps, to those I had ended, I would never be more than a murderer, but to those I had saved, I was a hero.

No story was simple; no character in any tale was ever only a single thing. I would not have my child define herself as the worst that she had done and never seek to be better.

She had paused as I spoke and I felt a brief moment of hope that she had finally come to her senses, but that was snuffed out as she blurred toward me with her fist raised, a clear intent to kill.

And yet, I was relieved.

For all that my daughter had changed, she still threw a punch just as I had taught her all those years ago. As I lashed out with my hand, I grabbed the punch, feeling my bones break as I used all the remains of Vitae to survive the blow, and Overseer's gift burned as it had finally found purchase upon my daughter.

Even as I felt pain begin to blossom through me, the world gave way to a bright white light.

DUSK INTERLUDE: GEORGE DERBY

The only proper way to wake up was to the smell of bacon. I opened my eyes and felt the cool autumn air through the crack in the window I always liked to leave open. It helped the air flow, and the smell of the outdoors did me good when I got a mite glum.

Kicking off of my bed, the old springs of the mattress aching and groaning underneath me, I hopped out of my room and into the restroom to use the loo and give myself a freshening-up. I was still a bit dirty from the game of football with the lads I'd had yesterday.

After a quick scrub, to keep Mum from harpin' on me for tucking into bed while covered in a fine layer of dirt, I headed downstairs to finally get some grub.

"I can't believe the budget passed." Pops seemed mighty surprised as he read the daily paper. He lightly tapped his finger against the story on the rag. "A war budget against poverty, David said. I'd never thought it'd see the light of day."

Mum meandered over with breakfast, taking a short glance at it. "I think it's good to see some of the money going back to the people so hard at work to earn it. Better than that . . . What were they plannin' to do?"

"Tariffs." Pops shrugged. "Woulda made breakfast a whole lot more expensive, o' course. Glad they saw sense. Hope the king lives long enough to give it his blessin.'"

Oh yeah, the good ole king had been sick for a while. The paper hadn't been particularly optimistic about his chances. Still, it was all political mummery to me, but Mum's nosh was good, and I sat down to enjoy it. Her cooking could make any day start as a good one.

"So, George." Pops put down the paper. "I hear you're still runnin' with that Dawson lad. I was talking to Mabel from across the street, and she was yammerin' about seein' you pickin' on a poor boy."

Miller Dawson, my best friend since boyhood and a hellion for anyone who looked at him wrong. He wasn't a bad kind of lot. He just stood up to people who looked down on 'im.

"Miss Anderson just saw the wrong end of things," I said, glancing between my pops and the delicious bacon being scooped up and over onto my plate by Mum.

Pops frowned. "That'd best be true. Those Dawsons are trouble, not a lick of good in 'em. Surely got a bit of those Irish in his family, that Dawson Sr. keeping so deep in the bottle as he is."

I stayed quiet, not even daring to share a glance with Mum as Pops jumped from talking about my best mate to his father to the greater whole of things going on like he always did. I'd seen my fair share of 'em myself, the Irish, but Pops seemed to only see 'em at their worst.

"I was thinkin' of going out with my mates after school, Pops," I said, trying to cut him off before the bacon started tasting sour in my mouth.

He shrugged, giving his blessing at a whim. Pops was a good bloke, workin' every day at the factory to keep us fed and warm. It was just mighty hard to know what was on his mind, really on his mind.

As the risk of him going off on a tangent about everything going wrong and right with the world, from the Irish to the Germans, lowered, I turned back to breakfast.

I wondered what craziness Miller was gonna be up to today.

"So, Georgie, gonna be on the make this year, or are you still tied down by the football?" Miller chuckled, all our lot hootin' with him as they had a grand time on my account.

Ole James and Carter Henway from down the street were giving a good laugh during it all, even though they'd said that they wouldn't put up with Miller's shit anymore. Not that I blamed 'em. Miller had a way about him that made you want to laugh at his jokes.

Just something temptin' in his eyes that made you wanna smile or something like that. Pops would probably call it some kind of devilry, but Miller was as devout as Mum.

"Football still has me," I said, shrugging and smiling. "Don't got time for a bird."

"That's a right shame. You got the makings for a popular fella. I had a bird come up and ask me about you just the other day. She was a beauty too," Miller said.

I wanted to ask him all he'd said about me, but I shrugged. "I'll always have these looks. My pops kept his looks past twice my age."

James said something about not looking pretty when the factory was done with me, but I didn't pay it any mind. The others laughed. Miller gave it a light chuckle, but I was proud of my pops. He'd done well to keep safe from all the disaster that befell the less careful.

"I don't blame Georgie." Carter shook his head after they all stopped laughing. "The birds are going crazy, smashin' windows all for the sake of gettin' to run things. It's right mad."

Miller shook his head. "Nah, I like 'em spirited. 'Sides, they got the right idea. If you want something, you gotta take it. Smash and grab, lads! From gin to votes, yeah?"

The way Miller put it made it sound a lot more adventurous than it really ever was. I'd not thought it very wise to go causing so much ruckus in the night, but we'd been all the way over on Oxford Street.

In the dark, we probably just looked like a band of those crazy suffragettes that Carter had been yammerin' about. I hated givin' them any more of a bad name though. Mum had said some kind things about a lot of those ladies, saying they were doing God's work.

"Talkin' about football's got me wantin' to play. How 'bout it, lads?" I asked, trying to steer the conversation away from any more talk of smashin' stuff.

My mates were all up for it, Miller taking up the reins of team captain and picking me first. It was only right, of course; we were best mates, and no one ran faster than me.

"When Britain first, at Heaven's command, arose from out the azure main . . ." The musical echoes of patriotic fervor were peeling my ears as Miller dragged all the rest of the blokes off our streets and me to the alleyway that crossed over to Melvin Avenue.

It was war, proper war. That was what all the papers were saying, the big old print on the side of the road. England had declared war on Germany over its treatment of Belgium. Pops had been grim, lookin' little pleased as Mum had been at the news. She'd dragged me out onto the streets to take part in all the revelry at the announcement.

I wasn't sure what to make of it. I'd read about it, war that was. Never seemed like a fun thing, but so many of my blokes were excited about heading off to fight the good fight.

None more so than Miller. The gleam in his eyes had never been stronger as he got us all together in a circle, slapping us all on the backs as he chattered about his chance to shine.

"Ah, for king and country, right, lads?" Miller laughed, looking thrilled at the news of a war. "I'd say, we should've gone to war a long time ago, give us something to actually do instead of the lousy shite all the pram-pushing teacher fucks would rather have us wasting our time with!"

I took a sniff of the air as he slapped me on the back and smelled the gin on his breath and his clothing. God above, Miller was already sloshed properly, wasn't he?

The Henway boys were lookin' a mite nervous, James speaking up in lieu of his older brother. "We're right worried for our mum. Not sure if our uncle'll be joining up or not, but someone has to look after 'er."

Ah yeah, Henway Sr. had come down with a bad sickness recently. It was still up in the air if he'd even make it to the winter, much less get through the chillier weather.

Miller seemed a bit peeved at the Henways for not going along with his elation, pointing a dangerous look at them. "You gotta let God sort that shite out. That's outa our hands. All we need to worry about is gettin' in line to join up with the military."

I was an adult in my own right now, but I still lived under Pops's roof. I wasn't sure if he was wantin' me to go out and get myself involved right out of the gate. He'd been talkin' about a job for me at the steel mill. Surely that'd be a fine way to support the good fight?

While I was in my own head, I'd hardly noticed Miller's expression flattening for a moment, like it always did when he was thinkin' his most dangerous thoughts. Before I could dissuade whatever notion was twinkling in his eyes, he smiled in a way I couldn't argue with.

"My trusted blokes, I know a German bloke down in Richmond. He's got a mean scar, and he's shot me a lotta dirty looks before." Miller grinned. "What say we go and get some practice in, eh?"

Nobody said no strongly enough, everyone expecting someone else to talk some sense into Miller. A lot of them were waiting for me to say something.

I wasn't strong enough to say no. All I could do was watch from the sidelines as Miller and the others went on to beat the shite out of a fella whom I'd never met. There was cheerin' from the crowds, the song getting louder and louder, but no one came to stop us.

Was this what war caused?

I got out of there before the coppers rolled up to see what was going on, and I kept my distance for a long time, unable to take my mind off of Miller's face while he kicked that man on the ground.

The next time I heard anything about him, he'd gone off to the war.

I didn't volunteer, but when the conscription began, I wasn't saved by any sort of physical ailment like my father had been with his nearsightedness. Nor had I worked long enough to be seen as essential at the mill. I was a bloke ready and physically able to serve my country.

I'd resisted the temptations of Kitchener for longer than any of my mates, but I'd ended up at the same place they did. In front of an officer, signing my papers and getting me fitted for my uniform.

"For king and country," the officer said, giving me a nod as he handed me my things, with all I needed to get sent off to the war.

I didn't have the chops for study work, couldn't get the tribunal to see me off away from the front line, nor did I have what it took to be a medicine lad. Truly for king and country . . .

"Hey, mate," a voice broke my fugue. "You're looking knackered already. Not excited to go and get your arse blown up?"

Glancing up, I blinked as a cool pair of blue eyes met mine. Another bloke, same height as me, same build. He had a cocky bent to the way he stood, looking like he knew something I didn't. He reminded me of Miller, a fair bit too much to be right honest.

I looked around, still knee-deep in the school that the military had taken roost in, plenty of other conscripted lads with their heads down and their moods dour. No one was quite fond of being here.

"Name's Toby Johnson," the fellow conscript said after I didn't answer. "I thought I'd bother you for just a moment. See, I don't have the time, and you seem like a bloke who kept the time."

I looked around, wondering what gave that impression. "It's gotta be around noon, yeah?"

"Oh, so you can't say for sure?" Toby, no, I'd rather think of him as Johnson asked. I really didn't want to get too attached to the fella. Still, it was annoying how he said it like he'd expected better.

I pushed forward. "I got somewhere to be. Go bother someone else with your shite."

"Oh, didn't realize you were all that important. Places to be and all that, eh? Come here to try and weasel your way out of the war? You don't look sick, but you'd have a chance convincin' me you're dumb." Johnson grinned like he was just messing around, but it pissed me off.

Pushing past the asshole, I left the school grounds and ignored all the other sorry lots surrounding the square. I felt numb, and it followed me all the way back home where I let my pops know that I'd be leaving soon.

Mum cried, though I couldn't tell if it was joy or fear, but Pops just wished me well and said that he was proud of me. I didn't know what there was to be proud of.

I didn't want to go to war.

The sharp, steel-coated whistle reverberated through the trench. Even as the sound of explosions hit the ground no more than a couple yards from us, the clamoring of the soldiers broke the momentary silence as none wished to be at the wrong end of the rifle of a friend.

"If any man flees in your direction," the officer had yelled, "you shoot him! A coward doesn't deserve to live! For king and country!"

The man in front of me climbing up the ladder mere moments before I did fell down dead, a shot ripping through his helmet as he almost landed straight on top of me. I knocked him aside, blood that wasn't mine mixing with the dirt in my mouth, and I started running, as fast as I could, trying to get my legs and eyes to work in the dust and gloom of no-man's-land.

I pumped my legs with everything I had, my rifle up and shooting at every single living creature I saw. At some point, I barely saw the difference between friend and foe. There was no difference in hell.

I hated this. I hated everything.

That didn't matter to my king or my country though. They didn't see me; they saw the weapon in my hand. The enemy didn't see me; they saw the weapon in my hand.

I was just a threat, to be used or killed. No tears were ever shed over the end of a threat. People celebrated in the streets to send me off to die. Miller had almost killed an innocent man over being so excited to die. My country had killed . . . had murdered Johnson for realizing that we were sent here to die.

There was no pride in this. I wanted to play football. I wanted to see my pops. I wanted Dad. I wanted Derra. I didn't want to be George anymore. It was all war around me. How many had I killed? How did I even stop killing?

I'd been given another chance to be something else, but I couldn't change the killer that I was.

And then something hit me, as it always did in this eternal cycle of hell, a loud, concussive explosion that sent fire and brimstone through every inch of my body. Or it would have. It was supposed to.

If a strong, warm grip hadn't pulled me aside, dashing away from the explosion mere moments before it detonated in the dirt beside me, the mortar shell a football field away as it erupted.

"What?" I asked God and whoever had saved me. "What's happening?"

And then a voice spoke, a familiar voice that I couldn't believe was real, I couldn't believe was somehow with me in the mud and shite of this hell I had been fighting in for eternity.

"It's alright, Daka," Dad said, his grip warm and strong. The embrace of a hero but not one meant for me, not one that was appropriate for a monster.

I sputtered, trying to wrench my way out of his grasp. "I'm not Daka! Daka was . . . Daka was supposed to be good, to be just a . . . just a . . ."

A second chance? An escape? I didn't know what she was anymore, but she didn't deserve to be George. She didn't deserve to have all the blood I'd earned on her hands.

"You are good, Daka." The certainty brought tears to my eyes. The sheer gall of Dad to . . . to think that I was still good. It was insane. I was insane.

"You don't get it, Dad," I said, holding up my hands to him as shells continued to rain down upon us, but it was as if the world had forgotten we were there. "I've killed so many . . ."

Dad looked down at me with none of the fear and disgust that I had expected, that should have been there. I met his gaze, and all I saw was a deep sadness that made me feel even worse before I noticed the love.

The warmth of love, a silent promise that no matter what I had done or who I was, whether I was Daka or George, he would always love me. A promise that had kept me afloat in my darkest moments when I felt like I was drowning in the sea of all that I'd been through.

A promise that I had thought had died and gone away, leaving me to be consumed by darkness and blood all over again.

"Dad, help me," I cried, feeling tears spill down my cheeks and catching the dust and blood from all I had seen and been through.

"Of course, Daka. You are my child, and nothing could change that." I fell into his embrace, and he pulled me tight. "I have been right where you are, wondering if I could ever be more than a monster. It takes time, hard work, and while you can never rewrite the stories you've woven before, you can always be a part of new ones."

I cried even harder, hope burning in my chest. "I was so angry, and Dalton and Natakia . . . They were so busy and sad, I didn't know how to help them. I . . . I thought if I found your tribe, I would go after Zactrik . . ."

The monster had taken my dad away from me, the monster that I thought was worth giving up all that my second life had given me. And then Aunt Natakia had said so much had to happen before that, that we needed the might of a nation to take down Zactrik.

"My sister used your hate, Daka, your desire to protect. She gave you only the choices she wanted you to make," he whispered to me, somehow heard even over a shell going off feet away. "You are so precious to me, so strong and so skilled. You have all the choice in the world. You always have a choice."

Aunt Natakia had used me? No, that wasn't right, was it? She'd made everything seem so simple, even as it got harder and harder to think clearly. I was just another threat for her to use, though, wasn't I?

"What if I'm not? What if I keep making the same decision?" What if Dad was wrong? What if I was destined to keep being the monster that tore families apart? The hope in my chest began to dim, the sound of the war around me getting louder.

Dad chuckled, and I was almost stunned at how he could find anything humorous right then. His fingers ran under my helmet and through my hair, the warmth of his palm soaking through my scalp.

"Daka, this war is not you." His words were somber and kind. "You don't crave violence, but you have been fed it and nothing else in your pain. I have faith in you because you remind me of myself. Change isn't easy—it never was for me—but stay true to love, and it will find you."

Did I not crave violence? It was like I was surrounded by problems that only violence could solve. My body was always so tense, and it came so easily to me. Was this truly how Dad felt? Were we that alike?

He continued, "I made many mistakes in my life. Even after I left my tribe I was not instantly a hero. It was only after I found love in Lydia, in my friends, and you and my other children that I became the man I am today. So no matter what happens, no matter what choices are before you, temper your hatred with love."

There was so much more to say, so much more I wanted Dad to know about all I'd done and why I'd done it and all I'd felt every second I thought he was dead, but the world suddenly became white.

The bloodstained battlefield of no-man's-land fell away and was replaced by the sand of Kakrel and the dust in the air, kicked up in the battle between Dad and me. I swallowed hard, realizing that I had tried to kill Dad. I had almost murdered him.

"Da . . . ka . . ." I looked up from my thoughts, noticing with a sudden icy dread that my hand . . . My hand was warm and wet, as Dad's voice croaked before me.

My hand was half-lodged in his chest, his hand gripped around mine as it had been when he'd gone to try and stop my attack. He hadn't . . . hadn't had a chance to dodge . . .

"No," I said, feeling my blood run cold even as his life felt warm on my fist.

I saw his Vitae, his warm and brilliant Vitae, beginning to dim, and I surged forward, activating every technique I knew for healing as my cursed reserves were finally of use to someone who deserved it.

The **Flesh Stitching Technique** that I had picked up years ago, the **Blood Recovery Technique** that I had watched a healer perform moments before I slew him, the **Healing Flesh Technique** that Dad had taught me . . . taught me when I was just a little kid.

"Don't die, Dad," I said, pumping every bit of Vitae that I could. "Please, I can't be good if you're dead. I . . . I'll just get inside my own head again . . . Please . . . I love you. I can't watch you die again!"

"Daka," Dad said weakly. "You being good . . . It isn't because I'm there to keep you in line. You . . . You can be good because of the love . . . love between us, and no matter where I go . . . that love is always there."

His body relaxed, and I would have panicked as he lost consciousness if I couldn't see his Vitae slowly beginning to pump harder and healthier through his system. His arm, his metal one, had been like a beacon of Vitae before, but now . . . now it was so small . . .

"I'll be good, Dad," I cried before determination entered my heart, "but I'm not going to let you die!"

As my Vitae continued to supply Dad with more and more healing, memories of healing techniques passing through my fingertips, I heard shifting in the debris behind me before a familiar voice started talking.

"What are you doing? Healing him?" Aunt Natakia scoffed. "We've got more important lives to save, proper Kroterruk lives. Come on, Daka."

I felt a rage building up in me at the very idea that I'd leave my dad to die. It mixed with the guilt in my heart of ever letting it get this far, igniting into something . . . something familiar and repulsive.

Hatred. I hated the woman behind me.

<h1 style="text-align:center">33</h1>

Eternal darkness. An obsidian sea. An ebony existence that threatened to consume me and all that I was composed of. How long was I to suffer? Why was I back in this damnation?

A light, a voice. A beacon that suddenly pierced the darkness that chained me.

I gasped, suddenly awake, feeling the warmth of someone's hand in mine. My eyesight was blurry, but it quickly cleared as sleep left me. I was in a room, small but cozy, in a bed covered with a viridian quilt.

"Where," I asked, my mouth dry, "am I?"

The hand in my grip tightened, and my gaze was drawn to the young woman sleeping at my bedside, her head half on my chest. Without her helmet on, I was able to marvel at how my little warrior had grown, the curls of her hair still falling near her shoulders.

The bandages around her hands and arms were clean and unstained by blood. Instead of wearing the Ruskan embroidered cloth from before, she wore a Certillian tunic with the sleeves cut off.

As I felt the peace of the moment, many of my worries melted away with my daughter sleeping hand in hand with me. It allowed me to feel the ache in my chest. Taking a deep breath, I grunted as I felt the deep pain that echoed through. A wound that I could feel was . . . stable but serious.

I remembered now. Daka's memories, that war that had been greater and more terrifying than anything I had ever seen before. Zactrik's horror had been monstrous, but the war . . . It had been utterly human.

To think that my children had all come from such a horrifying world. Perhaps Derra was no better, but for all that my world was familiar with violence and death, Earth seemed to be even more so despite the lesser dangers of their natural world. Where they lacked Mana and Vitae, they built weapons of war that had been unthinkable in scope before I bore witness to them.

And when I had returned to Derra, Daka's attack had gone through, and I had been incredibly injured by it. I had thought I had once again abandoned my children, but I was still here. Another gift? I was grateful.

"Dad?" Daka slowly stirred, her blue eyes lacking the empty glow that had haunted me for so long. She met my gaze and seemed to start, smiling in relief. "Dad! You . . . You're awake!"

"I am," I said, smiling as I squeezed her hand in mine.

The relief on her face faltered as tears came to her eyes. "Dad, I'm so bloody sorry. I . . . I hurt you so bad, and . . . and . . ."

"Daka, I told you, nothing you could do would make me love you any less," I said, pulling her toward me gently and bringing her into as much of an embrace as I could manage lying down, injured, and with no free hands. Admittedly, not a great hug.

Suddenly the door to the room opened, and Macy came in, holding a platter of food. "Alright, um, I got some solid stuff for you, Daka, and, you know, some soup for—Rakta! Rakta awake! Natakia, Dalton, your dad's awake!"

She put down the platter haphazardly, running out of the room as she screamed out for my other children, and I blinked as I heard my son's name. My son was here? Where were we?

It felt like too important of a question to simply let it linger in my thoughts.

"Daka, where are we? Are we still in Kakrel?" I was beginning to feel like I had been out for longer than I had originally thought. I hadn't lost more years with my children, had I? It felt far more likely than I wanted it to.

Daka had barely glanced at Macy, the slightest tense in her form when she saw the maid, but she looked back and shook her head. "Uh, no. We had to . . . leave pretty quickly. Natakia apparently sent a message to Dalton? He was already nearby with an airship, so . . ."

"How long have I been out?" I was going to need some time to digest the fact that I was on an airship and that we were actively flying through the air right then. It certainly didn't feel that way. Everything felt very stable. Almost as if we were on the ground.

Before Daka could answer, Natakia came in, her mirror floating about, and she too looked relieved as she saw me. "Dad! Oh, thank goodness, I knew you'd wake up eventually, but . . . there were a lot of possibilities."

Gone was her traveling attire, Natakia instead wearing an elegant pink dress as she walked into the room. Her hair was done up, as well, and she looked far more comfortable dressed to the nines than she had covered in sand and dust while on the road.

As my youngest daughter walked up alongside the eldest, I could feel the tension or, rather, the awkwardness as they shared a brief glance with each other. Daka looked away in shame, with Natakia seeming unsure what to say either. Both of them soon focused on me again.

"I'm glad you're safe, Natakia," I said, feeling more relief the more of my children were in the same room with me. "Daka was just about to tell me how long I'd been out."

"Oh, um, about two days," Natakia said, looking at Daka, who nodded in confirmation. That was a good answer. The nightmare I had of Zactrik's darkness . . . I set such thoughts aside for the moment. And yet, I noticed Natakia's gaze saddened as she swallowed hard.

I nodded, attempting to dispel both of our discomfort. "I'm glad to hear that. It seems that I missed quite a bit. You got into contact with Dalton?"

As I said his name, my son entered the room, as well, looking as put together as I remembered him being the last we'd spoken. His hair was up in a ponytail and his official garb dyed in the blue and brown of House Tribus, and he had a familiar satchel at his side. Penelope's bag of holding that she had gotten for him so many years before.

"I gave her that gift for a reason. I was certain that something unexpected would happen in Rusk," he said, sounding stoic as he approached. His gaze was a scalpel, dissecting my health as he neared.

Distantly, I remembered that Dalton had used his gift to purchase the knowledge and expertise needed for Shawn's surgery back before the disaster had happened.

I smiled. "I suppose I have you to thank for my recovery?"

"Not just me," he said, glancing at Daka, who looked uncomfortable. "Daka here has been using her techniques to keep your heart beating long enough for any recovery to actually take place. When I arrived in Kakrel, you were being kept alive by her and a local alchemist."

That was . . . extraordinary. Sustaining the life of another without overdoing it through the use of Vitae required precise levels of control and ample reserves.

"That's amazing, Daka," I said, looking at my little warrior. "Thank you."

Daka's expression was less than accepting of the praise. "Dad, don't thank me. I'm the reason you were hurt. I don't deserve gratitude."

"You are also the reason I'm still here," I said, keeping a firm grip on her hand. I felt that, of all my children at this moment, she needed it the most. Daka frowned but made no further arguments.

I sighed, feeling the weight of curiosity still plaguing me. "Now, I'm sure plenty has happened while I was asleep. Could I get a summary?"

The Kroterruk Tribe had retreated and fled from Kakrel once their leader and strongest warrior had left them vulnerable to the militants' attack. Once I had been recovered, Natakia and Daka's reunion had been a tense affair at the sight of my injured state, but they had worked together to keep me alive.

While Daka had been sustaining my physical energy and consciously keeping my lungs and heart, which had been . . . very injured by her attack, working, Natakia had sent for Dalton. He had been flying through the area, halfway to Rainwater, when he received the message and diverted course.

"You say this isn't one of your ships, however?" I asked my son. Apparently, this was an expensive model, even for someone of his wealth. The speed we were going at, we'd arrive at Rainwater within a few more days.

Dalton nodded. "I mentioned to Penelope that I would be heading to Rainwater myself. She offered her ship on the condition that she would accompany us."

"Penelope is on the ship?" That was shocking but quite a pleasant surprise. That did explain where my prosthetic was. I hadn't seen it anywhere in the room. My friend must be doing maintenance on it.

Natakia smiled. "Yes, although you wouldn't know it by walking the halls. She's been stuck in her own special workshop ever since we got on board."

That did sound like Penelope. I would have to visit her and keep her company once my injuries allowed. My friend had gotten far too used to solitude in my opinion.

And yet, another thought crossed my mind as I reviewed all that I had learned. I was proud of my children working together, relieved to be alive, but one thought kept coming up, and I had no answer to it.

"What happened to my sister?" I asked, my gaze crossing from each of my younglings before falling onto Daka, the one who, by all regards, should know the answer more so than anyone else here.

She sighed, looking incredibly uncomfortable. "I . . . almost killed her, Dad."

For a moment, there was silence in the room. I had my thoughts, but I kept them close to my chest. It felt like there was far more to the story than simply that. Natakia looked like she wanted to answer, as well, but kept quiet after glancing between her sister and me.

"She mocked me," Daka continued, "for healing you, said that there was . . . there was more important stuff to do, people to kill. I . . . got so angry at her, Dad. She was the one who . . . I hurt her. I didn't kill her, but I did hurt her, Dad. I'm so sorry."

Knowing that my sister had been attacked by my daughter wasn't a pleasant thought, but it was one I could accept. My daughter's anger wasn't magically gone, nor ever would mine be. "You restrained yourself, Daka. That's what matters. I'm sure that many would have rejoiced over my sister's death, but I am proud of the decision you made because you made it."

Daka sniffed, holding my hand even tighter. Perhaps my sister would be killed eventually, but I was relieved that it was not my daughter who had done so. She already had so many scars on her heart.

"The militants recovered her when they brought you in," Natakia spoke, adding more details as Daka digested my words. "Canon said that he'd be doing his part to make sure her punishment was proper and carried out . . . He didn't say it, but I think he's going to try to keep her alive."

I considered that for a moment. "Natakia of the Teeth assaulted and destroyed many of Kakrel's historical sites. I doubt leniency will be easy.

A pardon, conditional though it was, for Daka was already immensely surprising."

Daka nodded, looking like she shared my thoughts on the pardon. I wondered what her reaction to the pardon had been once her mind had cleared. I doubt she though she deserved it.

"If you don't think you deserve that pardon, Daka," Dalton said, taking the words from my mind, "then you should work hard to become someone who does."

His clear and concise judgment made my daughter blink before she nodded, a glimmer of determination in her gaze. I nodded to my son, appreciating and agreeing with his advice.

A second chance was not always given because of how deserving one was of it, but rather, sometimes it was given in the hopes that one would one day be deserving of it in the future.

"Well," I said, breaking the silence that had fallen upon us at my son's words, "it is unfortunate that I could not say farewell to Canon, but I suppose there will be time in the future to do so."

I still had many questions about my father and Canon's departure from the tribe and why I had never heard about him before. I'm sure that Natakia still had much to learn from him as well.

"I'm just glad that all of you are finally here by my side, safe and sound," I continued, meeting the gaze of each of my precious younglings. "It's been so long since I've felt the peace that I do now. All of you have grown so much while I was . . . was away, but I love you all so much."

I wouldn't allow myself to be taken from them again, whether it was in Rainwater or anywhere else. My place was guiding my children, and I would not be torn away so easily as last time.

34

Now that I was awake and could consciously manipulate my own Vitae alongside my daughter channeling her own physical energy into my wound, as well as Dalton's own expertise, my recovery was relatively swift. A scar on my chest was preferable to being dead.

My recovery wasn't over, but I was able to walk around most of the ship, usually with one of my children keeping me company as we spoke about all that had happened over the years and in the past weeks.

Dalton told me about the closing of the deal that he'd made with House Taine or, rather, with Penelope and the representative of the Donns of Neve visiting Gelvurt. The bank, he'd told me, was inevitable. A boon for the community and his coffers.

Natakia and I had shared much about the parts of Kakrel that we wouldn't mind visiting again, with Natakia talking about the fashion that she had seen but had little time to enjoy. She and Macy had been talking much about ideas for their next visit, and it seemed they were rebuilding their relationship.

And, of course, Daka and I were spending a lot of time together. With no other business to attend to, Daka stayed by my side and worried over my injuries more than most healers did during the war. I'd had to convince her to let me start doing some light exercise, compromising with just some daily stretches.

With my newfound freedom from my bed and with Daka beside me, I was able to finally pursue some of the conversations that had been on my mind for a while.

"Are you sure about this, Dad?" Daka looked unsure, her hands shaking slightly. "You said this could get violent, and if it does . . ."

I put my hand on her shoulder. "I was being humorous when I said that . . . mostly. Just remember that we are all friends and family here. There is no fighting between friends and family."

My daughter was constantly worried that she was on the edge of falling back to where she'd been just a short time ago. I was somewhat at a loss as to how to help her beyond simple encouragement. There were limits to my wisdom, but at least I could give endless support.

"Okay, just be careful." Daka swallowed hard and opened the door for me. I had wanted to knock but shook my head and went inside.

It was a small room, as most were on the ship, with a simple bed in the corner and a table for amenities. A guest room that was somewhat less luxurious than my own but was still plenty comfortable.

"I hope you know," the resident of the room said, "your injuries aren't going to make me take it any easier on you, Rakta."

I sighed, feeling the force of the glare being laid upon me. "I have no intentions of using my injuries as any sort of shield for my actions. You have plenty of reasons to be angry with me, Dresden."

The guard captain of Gelvurt, premier swordsman of House Tribus, and patriarch of the Booker family, Dresden was tightening the laces on his boots as I came in. Standing up off of his bed, Dresden crossed his arms, looking unsure as to where to even begin, but the longer he took, the more frustrated he became.

"I told you, multiple times, that Macy needed to stay in Gelvurt," he said, as if trying to clarify that had indeed happened, which I nodded at. "Okay, great, so tell me, Rakta, were you unaware that my daughter had snuck away on the carriage, or did you just not care?"

"I discovered that Macy was our coachman the evening that we left from Gelvurt," I said, unwilling to omit any truth. I couldn't say I regretted my actions, but I knew they were disrespectful to my friend.

Dresden shook his head. "I'm sorry? You knew that soon? So you actually let her go with you when you absolutely could have brought her back . . . What the hell?"

"You spoke of fearing Doh not remembering you or Macy, but when I spoke to her about her mother's memories, she was determined that if anyone could bring them back, it was her," I said, remembering my reasoning then. "And of course there was the matter of Natakia . . ."

It had been my instincts pulling at me, but I'd had suspicions that having Macy there would help my daughter and the hold that Esmeralda had over her.

"My daughter endured a lot of heartache because of your daughter, Rakta. I'm glad they're getting along, but that wasn't your risk to take. You had no right to . . . I heard about what happened at the canyons," he said, his fists tight.

I nodded. "I apologize for putting your daughter in danger. You're right, it was not my place, and I should have tried harder to convince you if I felt so strongly about it."

Dresden watched me for a moment, and I was unsure of what more I could say. I had plenty of reasoning for my actions, but at the end of the day, I had put my friend's daughter in danger. He had every right to be angry at me.

Despite his anger being pointed at me, I could tell that Daka was looking more and more irritated at my side. She had been quiet, but she wasn't looking at Dresden very fondly either.

"Daka," I said, quietly but firmly, "he has every right to say what he wants. I would have many words for any who put you or your siblings in similar danger."

My daughter stilled, looking ashamed for a moment. Dresden shook his head, his fingers going through his hair. I wondered how much he had heard about Daka's escapades in Kakrel and Rusk.

"Macy's practically begged me not to hold it against you, but this isn't going to be the last time we talk about this. If my daughter had been hurt, it would have been your head. You know that, right?" He looked at me, a hopeless anger in his eyes. There would have been nothing he could do about it.

"I know," I said, sighing. "I treated your daughter as my own, protecting her with every fiber of my being. That doesn't change what I did, but know that I did my very best to not treat your daughter's life carelessly."

Although, I had left her alone with Esmeralda. I had grown complacent, thinking that she would only attack me or, at least, that there would be more signs before the attack. If I had been even slightly slower . . .

Dresden seemed exasperated. "Despite everything, I can still believe that. I came here, officially, to guard Dalton, but I'll be helping in the search. Even if I don't agree at all with how she did it, with what you allowed, I still think that if we're in the area, we owe it to Doh to look for her."

That was everything I needed to hear. Trading a few more words, I eventually departed alongside my daughter, whom I considered for some time as we left.

Did Daka still see those with the strange Vitae of those with monster blood as the enemy? How did she feel about Macy? For all the scars my daughter carried, that worried me the most in some ways. The idea that she harbored ill thoughts toward some for simply . . . existing.

As we continued our walk, having departed as amiably with Dresden as my actions allowed, I could tell Daka was still troubled, an expression on her face that lingered as we shared a private moment in one of the many hallways below the deck of Penelope's airship.

"Dresden's anger was not malicious, Daka," I said, sure that his aggression still weighed on her mind. Simple anger was far from true intention to harm me, which I'd found less and less evidence of as Macy's father had a chance to vent his frustration at me.

Daka was quiet for a moment before she shook her head. "I . . . know that. Mostly."

I gave her time. I could tell that I'd been somewhat mistaken as her troubled expression flickered, looking momentarily distracted by my words. Whatever was on her mind was of a different matter, one that I would be patient to hear.

"Do . . . you know how, uh, Winfred's been doing?" Daka rubbed her arm, looking unsure as she asked the question. My little warrior had little of the boisterousness that I was familiar with from her youth, but this question seemed to be touched with even more nerves than usual.

Winfred, or rather, King Winfred Certimov-Hanchett had been a dear friend to Daka when they were both younger. I had to admit that in all my time awake, I had only spared a few moments truly asking about the state of Shawn's family, too concerned for my own.

"He's become king, but I know little beyond that his rule has been far from easy." I couldn't imagine the headache that the turmoil of encroaching civil war surely caused.

"Wow." Daka blinked. "King? Winfred is a king. That . . . I wish I'd been there for him. Maybe I should have run away to the capital instead of Rusk."

It was an interesting thought. I certainly would have been comforted upon waking up to know that Daka and Winfred had kept each other company during my absence.

I reached over and hugged Daka to my side as we walked, comforting her in the sudden embrace. "I am sure that he will be happy to see you if you'd like to visit him. I'm sure he could use a friend right now."

Daka sighed, some of her nerves melting away as she leaned into the hug. "I'm not a very good friend, Dad. Winfred doesn't need a . . . someone like me around."

I could tell she still had much to think about, but it lightened my heart to hear her talk of Winfred. Another person who knew Daka for who she was and not the scars she bore would certainly be only a boon for my daughter.

"Are you ready to go back to your room?" Daka seemed to be eyeing me carefully. She was no doubt measuring my Vitae as it fluctuated, weaker now as I pushed myself on the walk. Daka wouldn't let it get too low, but it was far wiser to simply rest soon.

"Almost." I said, chuckling as my little warrior shot me a suspicious glance, as if I were trying to trick her. "Only one more stop, I promise."

I needed to get my arm back.

"The Vitae-Containing Mortum-Killer Arm is back to one hundred percent effectiveness," Penelope said, handing over the prosthetic case to me. I raised an eyebrow at the name but was amused at her familiar naming scheme. It certainly had lived up to its title, however.

Penelope's special workshop was the largest room on the airship and likely the reason all other rooms were so small and minimalist. The workshop was filled with magical devices that I had never seen before, impressive machines that whirred with energy as they manufactured materials.

Daka, proving that some things never changed, was poking at instruments and tools while Penelope and I made some idle chatter as she finished examining my prosthetic.

"It was quite useful in dealing with Esmeralda," I said, still somewhat discomforted by Penelope's mechanical gaze. "Will you finally tell me what your special alloy is made out of? The fact that it can hurt beings like Zactrik so deeply . . ."

Penelope seemed to consider my question for a moment. "It is quite expensive, a mixture of a rare metal that absorbs sunlight and releases it on hard impact and an even rarer material that was once used in ancient resurrection rituals."

"Resurrection?" The act of bringing back the dead to true life was an art that had been lost for centuries. The only remnants of the ancient rituals and the cultures that used them were vague limericks and stories.

"Yes," Penelope said. "While we still lack the evidence that any such rituals were possible, my understanding of Mortum led me to pursue materials with strong attachments to the concept of life. The purple diamond dust of Pintyre is a key ingredient to my alloy. I'm glad it has an effect on the real deal."

For the sake of my sanity, I wasn't going to question whether or not Penelope had been confident the prosthetic would actually hurt Esmeralda or not. It had been my assumption at the time, but now I felt more like a successful prototype.

"Could you make me a weapon like that?" Daka was suddenly nearby, looking eager, before she remembered herself and backed away. "Ah, actually, maybe that isn't . . ."

I knew that she had a vested interest in taking Zactrik's life. It had been what had pushed her to find strong allies within Rusk. And yet, a new weapon maybe wasn't the best idea at the moment.

"No," Penelope said, continuing on even as my daughter's face fell. "The material is prohibitively expensive, and I don't have any more to spare. You'll have to make do with those I've already made."

I nodded before realizing what exactly my friend had said as she went over to a wall and pulled a lever. A part of the room shifted to reveal an assortment of weapons, about a dozen of them, all with the similar black metal and golden-bronze outlines of my prosthetic arm.

There were two swords, a halberd, an entire quiver of arrows, and an assortment of other weapons. Daka's eyes were wide as she went over to the collection, me not too far behind.

Her attention was on a pair of gauntlets that were hanging off a durable length of thread wrapped around one of the hanging forks all the weapons were held on.

"Pick one," Penelope said. "You never know when Zactrik will show his disgusting face."

As Penelope walked away, leaving Daka to look at all the weapons, something in her words piqued my interest. While she tried to sound casual, I felt there was much more meaning in them than she truly intended to express.

I followed her to the worktable, and something began to itch at the back of my mind. "Penelope, while I am grateful for you being here, I am still unsure as to . . . why you joined Dalton on this trip. You even used your own personal airship. Why? Are you here simply to aid us in finding Doh?"

It had felt like that before, back in Gelvurt, with her aid simply being for the sake of my children and Macy's mother, but now it felt different, a new urgency in her actions.

"What," I asked as she seemed to consider my questions, "is waiting for us in Rainwater?"

My friend's time was important; that was very clear. The brightest mind of the empire coming to help find a long-lost friend in the Mana Wastes? I could explain it by offering Penelope's general good nature and kindness, but that didn't feel right this time.

Penelope stilled, threading her metal fingers together, before she turned to look at me. "I was the one who told Doh about the possible answers to your malady residing in Rainwater."

"What?" I was entirely unprepared for that.

"Rainwater was founded on a nexus point, sometimes referred to as a ley-line crossing. It's a powerful area where powerful rituals could be conducted, and much history remains undiscovered," Penelope said, not really answering my question yet. "I heard that Doh was trying to contact a god, so I told her what I knew."

I stroked my chin, feeling somewhat frustrated at just now knowing this, but it still wasn't what I had originally asked about. "You sent her to Rainwater, fine, but does that mean you are here out of a sense of responsibility for her going missing? If you knew, then why not before? Why now?"

"I didn't send her empty-handed. I've been slowly seeding places of power with a device I created to react to high levels of Mortum. Doh was given one of them and was told to put it somewhere in Rainwater." Penelope's voice was even, but her body was tense.

And yet, she didn't have to waste her words after that. I understood the implication within what she spoke. Penelope wasn't here to save Doh at all but, rather, because of that device.

"There's Mortum in Rainwater then?" We only knew two beings who were capable of using it, and I had slain one of them mere weeks ago.

Penelope nodded. "I have reason to believe that Zactrik is somewhere in Rainwater."

35

The Mana Wastes was a kaleidoscope of paradoxical landscapes, with freshly snow-covered plains harshly juxtaposed to hot, gray deserts and strange weather dotting the area. Flying through it, really, was what put into perspective how sharply the environment could change.

"Dad." Natakia approached alongside Macy, looking disappointed. Macy's expression was dour, looking as if some great hope had been extinguished. "I tried to scry on Doh, but it didn't work."

"Interference?" Something blocking the scrying was far better than the alternative of her divination magic not being able to find someone.

My desert flower nodded but didn't seem very certain. "It feels like interference, yeah, but nothing like I've felt before. I tried a few times, and it felt different every time."

That definitely didn't sound like a spell or technique I had ever heard of. "Do you think it has something to do with Doh's shape-shifting capabilities?"

Lydia had once tracked down some doppelgängers posing as the two of us using her magic, but I wasn't sure of the particulars. It had been far simpler than trying to smell them out though.

"Natakia and I tested that out just in case," Macy said. "I took some other shapes while she was trying to scry on me, and it still worked, mostly."

"Mostly?" I was glad that the two had taken the initiative to experiment in their search. It showed that everyone on the airship was serious about the expedition.

"Yeah, Natakia would sometimes get false positives if I took on the forms of other people she knows or people who actually exist." Macy shrugged. "Sometimes the magic would show the wrong person?"

An interesting quirk, but unfortunately, it didn't give us much answer for Doh's predicament. Although, if divination magic was tricked by the concept of identity, looking for Doh when she was still alive but no longer existed as Doh . . . I wasn't going to give voice to thoughts I was sure the two girls had already considered.

"It was a good idea," I said, smiling at the girls. "I'm sure the two of you can find more to divine as we approach Rainwater. Penelope said that we'll be arriving in less than a day."

The two girls nodded before heading back down below deck to their rooms. Hopefully they could find more answers or, at the very least, leads. All that we had at the moment were the Diving Bells.

If Zactrik truly was in Rainwater, then we needed more information than just that. I didn't dare ask my daughter to scry on that monster, however; there was no telling what kind of counter he had to it.

"Thinking about our arrival?" Dalton was suddenly next to me, having come up with a mug of ale that I took appreciatively. "It's been on my mind too."

"There'll be much we have to do with little time when we arrive," I said, looking uncertain at the hundreds of feet of empty air below us.

He nodded. "I'm sure, but we have efficient means of reaching an answer. I received a gift from the Donn who visited Gelvurt, a sizable monetary one. If there's anything that you think we'll need in Rainwater . . ."

"I'll let you know," I said, unsure of what would truly aid us the most. Now that my children were with me and safe, Overseer's gift paled in comparison to those of my children. I was not so much envious as I was afraid that such power would be necessary to actually defeat the monster that was Zactrik.

When I had let my children know of the coming danger, they had been incensed. Natakia and Dalton had obviously been putting a lot of thought into how to deal with him, but Daka was now training on a dummy at the back of the ship with her new gauntlets.

I hadn't asked where her axes were, but I imagined that they likely had never left the spot I'd thrown them in my battle with her. Perhaps it was for the best. Those were weapons from a past she wanted to distance herself from quickly.

"I think," I eventually spoke up again once I thought about it, "your ability to adapt through your gift will be a great asset. Instead of preparation, I think you should simply keep an eye out once we're in Rainwater. You're familiar with the organization that runs the city, yes?"

"I've done business with them before, albeit indirectly." Dalton nodded. "They're thugs but tamed ones. I believe their leader is a woman named Harrow. She's credited with the Diving Bells' rise to leadership in Rainwater."

We'd likely be doing business with them again, it seemed. Hopefully they did not have connections to Zactrik, but if he was there, then either he was after whatever the Diving Bells had or they had been working for him in some capacity for quite some time.

"Well then, we'll be on our best behavior and see if they offer us any answers to our questions," I said before turning back to go below deck myself and get some rest.

Rainwater was, appropriate for its name, always surrounded by the dark-gray skies of rain clouds, a near constant downpour on the people who called this city their home. It had no walls but instead rested on a large island within a massive lake that was only a day's travel from the nation of Prayers, an ancient stone bridge the only thing that connected it to the shores of the Mana Wastes.

"Prepare for descent," Penelope said to some of the workers who began to scurry across the airship, with levers being pulled and all sorts of magical apparatuses being observed for issues.

Looking down at Rainwater, which seemed to be mostly built from the remnants of some ancient ruins as its foundation, I turned to Penelope. "Does Rainwater have a dock for a craft of this size?"

"Not exactly," she said. "They have an old harbor that we'll be using instead. This airship has the capabilities to land and launch from aquatic environments, so there will be no problem."

As the airship began to descend, I could see the harbor she spoke of. It was certainly old and seemed popular with smaller ships that seemed far more appropriate to the lake than the galleon-sized craft we were arriving on. Daka was silent beside me, looking as interested as I was in how the landing would go.

Macy, however, stood alongside her father, with Natakia and Dalton keeping them company as they made their own final preparations. Penelope had handed out umbrellas that she had quickly fashioned on the way over, meaning most of us weren't completely soaked by the heavy rain.

Penelope had also offered her anti-Mortum weaponry to others in the group, with Dresden grabbing himself a longsword that was similar enough to his own and Dalton wielding the halberd expertly enough. Natakia and Macy had both grabbed daggers, but neither looked like they wanted to be directly in a fight.

"Dad," Daka said, still looking down at the harbor. I had taken my eyes off of it for a moment to look over at the others on the deck of the ship. "There are people in the harbor. I think they're waiting for us."

My prosthetic arm was firmly in place, with as much Vitae as I could spare over the last few days invested into it. It wasn't much, nowhere near the amount I'd needed when fighting Daka and my sister, but hopefully it would be enough to aid in whatever offensive we operated against Zactrik.

That meant that I had enough to spare to enhance my vision as my daughter had and peer down through the heavy rain to see the vague forms of people waiting in the harbor below us.

There were a handful of them, all of them looking quite heavily armed and armored from afar, but details were few with the distance between us. I nodded at Daka, who looked nervous. "I'm sure we can handle discussions peacefully."

It was certainly what I hoped. I had little fear for our ability to defeat them, but causing a stir wouldn't help our goals. I was also reluctant to have Daka near unnecessary fights. I knew she was scared that she would react dangerously to threats.

"The criminal element of Rainwater won't be an issue," Penelope said, twisting and tightening her metal hand on the joint of her similarly metallic wrist, a bizarre sight.

Well, at least we were all confident in our own ways.

* * *

"Rainwater ain't accepting any new guests, certainly not ones from the sky," the gruffest armored thug said, looking wary of us but unwavering in his response to our request to debark from the airship.

The Rainwater men had not been kind upon our arrival. They hadn't thrown anything at our ship or made any crude comments toward our group, but there was a general air of aggression around them. These were capable warriors who would fight us if we did not retreat.

I coughed, motioning to my group behind me. "We have business in the area. I'm afraid we must insist that we speak to a representative of the Diving Bells. A friend of ours—"

"We're representatives of the Diving Bells," the man interrupted me, "and the boss lady has said that none enter and none leave. So take the opportunity before things get bloody."

"Dad." Daka's voice was tense, her hands shaking. "They want to fight us."

Before I could quiet my daughter's nerves and possibly find an avenue here that didn't require instant violence against these thugs, Natakia stepped forward.

Holding her umbrella gently and tossing her hair back, she smiled at the thugs. "I doubt there'll be any need for that. How about fifty gold sil for each man here willing to look the other way? Guests are one thing, but paying guests? I doubt your boss will have an issue, and we don't know any of your names if she does."

The thugs seemed caught off guard by the sizable offer. While fifty gold sil wasn't much on the explosive salary of an adventurer, it was quite a bit for thugs who likely made most of their money from theft.

"Make it a hundred each," the head thug brought back after a moment, each of them looking positively eager to get their hands on that kind of money.

Natakia nodded. "I think that's more than fair . . . Dalton?"

My desert flower looked over to her brother expectantly, her lips in the slightest of pouts. Dalton blinked before he shook his head and took out a couple of sacks of sils from his bag of holding that he expertly tossed to each thug in turn.

"There will be no more where that came from," Dalton said, more to his sister than any of the thugs. Natakia shot him the slightest of teasing smirks.

Mollified, the thugs seemed far more interested in their new wealth than us as we began to disembark from the airship, all of us getting a lay of the land as we looked around.

"I have a read on where the Diving Bells hang out," Natakia said, taking a glance at her floating mirror. "I think that's where we'll find their boss."

Penelope nodded. "We'll get information out of Harrow and then continue with our search. Everyone be on the lookout for Doh or Zactrik."

It was somewhat disquieting that, for all Doh's importance to us, it would be far easier to find Zactrik than it would be to find her simply by sight. Macy put a hand on her father's shoulder, Dresden taking a deep breath before giving her a smile.

"Your mother's been waiting for us, Macy," Dresden said. "Waiting for much too long."

Leaving the airship manned by Penelope's men and women, whom she seemed to trust to protect the ship, we began our venture to the headquarters of the Diving Bells. While Rainwater, circumference wise, was not a large city, it made up for its diameter in depth.

As we began to make our way down flights of stairs that carried us below the first layer of streets above, it was strange to watch the water from above flowing all around us farther and farther down. I was not sure where all the rain went, but Rainwater had certainly found a way to manage the sheer volume.

And not only was the city bizarre, but so too were the people of Rainwater eye-catching in their own ways. Brilliantly colored hair like that of the rainbow, skin that seemed to be slightly transparent, body parts that were slightly smaller or larger than normal, and much more made every citizen unique.

Mutants of the Mana Waste, although I believed there was a far less insulting term for them. I, unfortunately, was not aware of it exactly.

And while the whole of our group glanced around in interest at all the strange architecture, some of which was old and refined while other examples were new and unique, such as a statue of a four-headed man in the middle of a park with red grass, Penelope seemed to be far more comfortable here.

"You are quite familiar with the people of the Mana Wastes," I said, sidling up next to her as we continued to follow my daughter.

Penelope glanced at me, or rather, I assumed she did as she turned her head toward me before looking back to the road before us. "I've been here many times. I've done plenty of trade for rare materials here, and I regularly visit Zerota's family to make sure they're doing alright."

I remembered Zerota, the CAD who'd come from the Mana Wastes and one of Penelope's trusted companions after our original group broke apart. She had been one of the many casualties at Zactrik's hand that tragic night so many years ago.

"We've never really spoken about that night beyond the fight with Zactrik," I said distantly. It had been, in the grand scheme of it all, just a few short hours in the night when it had all happened.

"We have our priorities," she said, "but yes, there were many beyond Shawn whom we failed to save. Whom I failed to save."

I put a hand on her shoulder. "I told you before, we share that burden of defeat. It will be different this time."

"It will," Penelope agreed before she looked over to our left. "Your daughter is giving dirty looks to the people here. You'd best fix that."

I looked over and noticed that, yes, Daka was in fact giving many of those she passed strange looks with barely hidden fear and aggression. Sighing, I thanked Penelope before heading over to my stressed daughter.

"Daka, calm yourself," I said, putting a hand on her shoulder. She looked up at me, shame taking her again as she regained herself. I was sure she wasn't entirely aware of what she was doing, but this was no place for such hostility.

While strange in appearance, the people of the Mana Wastes were often quite kind. Though their cultures were varied and strange, most I had met who had ventured from their lands were decent and good.

"I'm sorry, Dad." Daka sighed, trying to regather herself. "The people here, their physical energy just looks so . . . odd, and that makes me feel . . . threatened."

It was a similar sentiment to what I'd heard from her before when she was a child. That sense of otherness that made her see even those close to her, like Doh or Macy, as oddities to be feared.

"Being aware of threats is important, and your sight is valuable, Daka," I said, "but you must keep yourself from relying on it. Filling your heart with worry of threats and danger leaves little room for acceptance and understanding. These people are just like you, despite what they look like."

Daka nodded, obviously agreeing with me in her rational mind, but retraining something as deep and traumatized as the heart, the instincts, was much more difficult to do.

"Just hold my hand and focus on me," I said, offering my hand, which she quickly took. I kept my gaze ahead, watching for dangers, as well, and kept a close eye on Natakia as she continued to lead the way.

36

Four layers down into the depths of Rainwater, we arrived at the headquarters of the Diving Bells, but it was quite obvious that we had not arrived in secrecy.

Men and women obviously aligned with the Diving Bells loitered outside what looked to be a tavern but with a far larger structure connected at its back. It was as if a tavern had been joined structurally with a warehouse, which certainly gave the impression of importance to whatever was in there.

"I count twenty-one potential participants in any hostile encounter," Penelope said. "I don't see anyone bearing the self-importance of a typical gang leader though. Harrow must be farther inside."

While Penelope had voiced it efficiently, I had seen more or less the same. No one here bore any sort of marking or iconography that made me think of them as leadership material.

"They don't look particularly strong," Dresden said, nudging Macy and Natakia behind him. He kept his words low, so as to not incite combat by way of hurt pride, but we heard him all the same.

I nodded. "I'll approach. Get ready for a conflict."

"Dad, should I fight . . . if it gets to that?" Daka looked unsure, her hands shaking. I wasn't quite confident she was ready for that and there was certainly no reason to test it for a lot such as this.

I placed a hand on her shoulder. "Natakia and Macy—go protect Natakia and Macy. Dresden may get caught up in the fight, but someone needs to pay attention to our less combat-oriented members."

It was a tale as old as time, making sure that the right people were protected because not everyone was built to be dodging and tanking techniques and spells. I was sure that if Natakia supported us with her magic, then this fight would be quite easy.

Dalton simply had his arms crossed, and I was mostly unaware of his capabilities but was confident he could at least take care of himself in any kind of struggle.

After the quick assessment of our advantages and who was to do what, I approached the large group of Diving Bell thugs and nodded my head at the first to meet my gaze. "Hello, my name is Rakta Tribus. I am here seeking an audience with Harrow of the Diving Bells. We've come for information."

"She's busy," the thug instantly spoke up, looking positively thrilled to deny me. I looked around and found similar satisfaction all around.

I shook my head. "I'm sure that's true, but our business is urgent and cannot wait. Please, we will be walking through that door. It is only a matter of how many here wish to stand between us and it."

I allowed some of my Vitae to flare, and in sync, so did Daka and Dresden. The sudden wave of Vitae washed over the thugs alongside my threat, and I watched as a few tried to fight back with a weak flare of their own, but they faltered, and many of the thugs scattered.

"I count twelve potential participants in any hostile encounter," Penelope said, as if adding on to how outmatched the warriors of this criminal organization were.

Before the remaining thugs could either scatter or attack us out of desperation, the door of the tavern flew open behind those that opposed us. A woman clad in soft pastel-colored tunics, many of them barely concealing the skin underneath, walked forward with confidence.

"Come on, come on." The woman made a grand gesture forward. "I think that we've all made a big deal about nothing more than a couple of outsiders wanting a little chat."

With bright-green hair and eyes that seemed to flicker with the colors of the rainbow, the woman was obviously a local, even if one disregarded the hooves in the place of her feet.

I tilted my head at the newcomer. "Are you Harrow?"

I would have thought her to be somewhat rougher as the others in the group had tended to be. This woman seemed more appropriate for a stage production or other kind of performance. Not exactly the type I had expected to walk out of the tavern.

"Oh." The woman shook her head. "No, no, no. My name is Rauzin, I'm Harrow's assistant. I'm afraid she is truly busy right now, but I am a great conversationalist myself!"

"You will talk with us in her stead?" It wasn't a preferable alternative, but we would get answers nonetheless. If they weren't satisfactory answers, then there was always heading to Harrow personally.

Although, if Harrow was attempting to escape in the time bought by this Rauzin, then we may lose our chance to actually speak to her.

Rauzin nodded with a put-upon wisdom. "Oh yes, I am your humble servant."

"Who is Harrow having business with?" Penelope's tone was crisp and unwilling to humor the woman in front of her.

"Okay." Rauzin smiled. "Now that is a question I can't exactly answer. Harrow's business is very private. You can't just barge in unannounced."

Penelope didn't look like she was going to be settling for Rauzin's responses to her questions, so I took a step forward, realizing where this was headed. "Then you'd better announce us, Rauzin."

Storming the Diving Bells' tavern was easy, with thugs unconscious, bruises or deep cuts on their bodies, all around us as we walked in. Rauzin was struggling in my grip, her hands trying to fight at my fist around the collar of her dress-like tunic.

"Let . . . Let go of me!" Rauzin was pretty short, and trying to kick me to make me let her go was not working very well for her.

I motioned for the others to begin to head toward the back of the tavern. "Harrow is in the back, yes?"

Rauzin looked like she was going to resist for a moment before she seemed to deflate and nodded. I gave a confirming nod to the others as they began to head toward the back of the warehouse.

"Seems like a legitimate business," Dalton said, looking at some of the stock behind the bar as we passed. "A debt sheet, classic for loan sharks. This place probably has quite a few debts hanging over the heads of other people in Rainwater."

After his quick check, he continued to walk with us, and we all made our way into the back of the tavern, Dresden slicing through the two large steel doors that would have barricaded most from the warehouse area. Rauzin blinked, looking at that, and seemed to become a lot less wily.

"Oh, look, they left the door open." Dresden smiled, motioning for Penelope to walk on through. I walked through, as well, with Rauzin's gaze focused on the guard captain.

Moving in, the warehouse part of the hideout seemed to be a mostly simple affair. A large wide-open space with what looked to be a lot of boxes full of valuable trade goods. Some looked like it was food and other supplies, while the rest seemed like materials.

The air smelled very thick and sterile, the kind of scent that laboratories had. That was, until a small emblazoned circle on the back of Penelope's back began to glow and that smell disappeared.

And at the very back, a metallic staircase crept up the wall and into a large room in the upper corner of the warehouse, with drawn curtains that I saw move as we entered.

"That's Harrow in there, yes?" I asked, glancing at Rauzin, who seemed dazed, before I shook her. "Rauzin, that is Harrow?"

She swallowed hard, glancing around at the others with me, her gaze lingering on Dresden and Macy. "I, uh, yeah! For sure! Sorry, this is just, like, a lot."

There was something familiar about the woman, which I would revisit once we had information from Harrow. I had my suspicions, but it was far too early to make that call.

As we took our first few steps toward the stairs that would lead us up to Harrow's inner sanctum, the door of the room flew open as another woman suddenly erupted from the chambers.

I barely recognized her without her bulbous glasses or the form-concealing clothing she often wore, but despite her now long rainbow-colored hair, her rainbow-colored eyes, similar to Rauzin's gaze, and the far more developed physique that she had, I recognized her almost instantly.

Harriet Pillops looked scared as she met my gaze, swallowing hard as she waved her hand. "Rakta, it's been a . . . really long time, huh?"

"Harriet? You are Harrow?" That all but confirmed that Zactrik had connections to the Diving Bells and likely their interest in the archaeological sites of the area. Harriet had helped cause the chaos that had ended with the death of Shawn and my undoing.

Harriet nodded, not looking like she had forgotten the last time we'd met. "I can see that you . . . all remember me pretty well."

I glanced over at Penelope and saw the anger in her body language, the slight bend of her shoulders forward as if she were about to pounce on prey.

"Penelope," I said, putting a hand on my friend's shoulder, "calm yourself or we won't get any answers out of her."

It seemed to calm my mechanical friend only slightly, but that was all we needed. I myself was feeling anger begin to rise up in my stomach at the very sight of this woman. Harriet had planned on murdering my children. That wasn't something I would just forgive.

And yet, I could bide my time and see if she had anything that would buy herself a reprieve from our revenge. While my anger was returning, it was old and not as severe as that I felt toward Zactrik himself.

"Yes, answers," Harriet said, slowly making her way down the stairs with her hands up in the air. "I've got a lot of answers, and I don't want to ask much in return for them."

"You are not in an advantageous bargaining position," Dalton said, his halberd slung over on his shoulder casually. Of course, I couldn't help but notice his interest in a lot of the goods in the warehouse.

Harriet shook her head. "No, I'm not, but I can tell you everything about Zactrik and where he's going and what I think he wants to do. That's why you're here, right? God, he's fucking ruining everything!"

Even after the betrayal, I had never seen such visceral anger on Harriet's face, her skin turning slightly translucent and colorful. Daka looked vaguely disgusted and tense watching the former trusted merchant of the Certillian Empire throw a minor tantrum before she suddenly regathered herself.

"Sorry, ha ha, sorry," Harriet said, waving her hand through the air. "I just, I built up a real life here, and now everything is going down the drain. First Zactrik and now all of you . . . I can't even look Rakta in the face right now. He definitely wants to kill me!"

"Out of curiosity, what do you want in return for your information?" It was hard to sympathize with a woman who had thrown her lot in with a monster. And yet, perhaps death was not necessary?

"One, don't kill me after I tell you everything," Harriet said, looking relieved that she was even able to list her conditions. "And two, if you can't stop Zactrik, you need to get me out of Rainwater!"

We all tensed at that, all of us feeling the desperation in her words as she clasped her hands together, as if in prayer toward us.

"What is he planning to do?" Natakia was the one to voice it, and yet there was already dawning horror in her eyes as she focused on Harriet.

"The same ritual he did to become the monster that he is," Harriet said, looking haunted, "but bigger than the first time, big enough that all of Rainwater is going to be his sacrifice."

Getting reorganized after the news that all of Rainwater would die in Zactrik's next attempt to empower himself, Penelope seemed to be the most determined to get more out of Harriet.

"Why is he attempting to empower himself again? Does it have anything to do with his absence over the last eight years? Why now?" Penelope's mechanical gaze was intense, and there was a tremor in her voice as she questioned Harriet.

Harriet was far less collected as the ball of pure Mana was held barely above the skin of her neck, ready to blast her head off at even the slightest movement. "Yes, so, he's very weak right now. That poison, all those years ago? It hurt him really badly. He . . . I guess he never recovered?"

Harriet's skin seemed to almost begin to boil, whatever ooze-based capabilities that Zactrik had given her revealing themselves at the intense heat of Penelope's magical threat.

"The golden-speckled rose injured him so badly he went into hiding?" Penelope asked, her need for confirmation seeming to grip her with a righteous fury.

The former merchant nodded furiously. "Yes! And, uh, he wants to save the world. He's always going on about killing death or something, and please don't kill me. I'm telling you everything I know!"

"Where is he?" I stepped in and put a hand on my friend's shoulder. She tensed for a moment before the sphere of Mana died down and Harriet was no longer at as much risk of dying.

"Oh, thank the gods." Harriet breathed a sigh of relief before she looked me in the eyes. "He's down in the ancient ruins below Rainwater. He's been having me drain them for years. I was done a long time ago, but he only just now came to use them for his ritual."

"This is a nexus point," Penelope said, nodding her head. "A place where the gods can be reached if you call on them hard enough. A ritual performed here would be monstrously powerful."

Dalton spoke up. "I bet he's been spending all these years coming up with a version of his ritual that could use that power correctly. Could he really use power capable of calling on the gods with the same ritual that only required a single death?"

Those were very good points. It would explain his lack of activity and why he had waited for so long. And yet, this was all so strangely timed. I had awoken as soon as Zactrik began to pursue his ritual?

Overseer had said that they had nothing to do with my awakening. Did that mean that I was freed from my nightmare because Zactrik had consciously retrieved his power from me? The timing fit far too well, more than any coincidence could explain.

"You'll need to lead us," I said to Harriet, but she shook her head. I grimaced, approaching with growing frustration. "You do not have a choice."

She shook her head again. "I don't know anything about the ruins! I've never been down there! My job was to keep Rainwater in line, to make sure the excavation continued without issue! Not go down there!"

"Then who has gone down there?" There had to be an expert on the depths somewhere among her organization, possibly one of the thugs we had dealt with in the room before? That would be unfortunate, having to heal one when a battle loomed ahead of us.

"Oh, uh, me?" Rauzin suddenly spoke up, looking pleased but also unsure if she should really be nominating herself. "I'm doing public outreach now, but I actually came from the ruins. They're like a second home to me, you know? Stonefish and all."

I sighed, looking at Harriet. "Tell us everything about Rauzin."

"Uh." Harriet seemed confused for a moment. "She's my assistant? She's definitely an expert on the ruins though. I don't think you'll have an issue with her."

"No." I wasn't sure if I wanted to ask this. "How long has she been here in Rainwater?"

At that question, many in the group stopped looking at Harriet and focused on me. Macy and Dresden both shared a look as they then turned to examine Rauzin.

Harriet shrugged. "I, uh, almost five years? Like she said, she basically came from the ruins. Like, lost and confused and—"

"Didn't know anything? Like she'd lost her memories? She probably seems like she's always losing her memories, yes?" I asked, already having felt a familiarity. "I bet she has some very interesting talents as well."

"Oh yeah. I didn't take you for the type to pick up on such things so quickly." Harriet smirked almost, as if forgetting the situation she was in, with a deep blush. That was very discomforting.

With a quick look to Daka, who nodded her head after a short glance at Rauzin, and exchanging looks with Dresden, I nodded. "I think it's very likely that Rauzin is Doh."

37

"Wait," Rauzin said, looking at Macy and Dresden. "I'm married with a kid? I'm pretty sure I would remember something like that."

Dresden and Macy were both crouched low beside the green-haired woman, looking her over as if to find signs of their wife and mother respectively. Macy sighed. "No, you wouldn't . . . That's the whole point of losing your memories."

"Is there anything you can do for her, Macy?" I asked, looking over the Booker family as they tried to bring sense back to Doh. Or at least, I hoped she was Doh. I'd feel terrible giving them false hope.

Macy seemed unsure. "I . . . Nothing quick. I need more time to figure out if there's anything familiar about us still left . . . I could maybe use that as a jumping-off point to reconnect lost memories . . ."

I was unsure if that would work. Macy had said that the memories destroyed by the blood of the doppelgänger were not ones that were simply forgotten but, rather, effectively destroyed. I didn't think that Macy would appreciate that reminder, however.

Natakia knelt beside Macy, as well, giving advice about the work-arounds that they could experiment with. If nothing else, Macy definitely needed a friend to lean on. Dresden seemed drained already before any true combat had even occurred.

"Good, we recovered Doh," Penelope said. "We don't have time to bring her back right now, if that's even possible. Zactrik isn't going to be waiting for us to begin his ritual."

Dresden shot Penelope a dirty look, but my friend ignored it easily. While I thought she could have been far more tactful about it, I agreed with her priorities.

"Actually," Harriet said, looking like she was trying very hard to be as helpful as possible, "his ritual began a couple of days ago. He's been siphoning bits of life force from people in Rainwater for his ritual. I don't know how much he needs before the big sacrifice, but . . ."

"Every second we give him puts us at a further disadvantage," I said, nodding. "Did he have any subordinates with him?"

"None. He came alone," Harriet said, looking nervous but bolder as she straightened up. "So, I'll ask this straight, do I get to live? I've been very helpful, and I am very sorry for everything I did. I'm comfortable where I am right now, and I'll even give up on you, Rakta. I'll give up on making you mine."

Penelope and I shared a look. Harriet had been extremely helpful and hadn't put up even the faintest of struggles to aid us in taking down a far larger threat. I looked to my youngest daughter to get her counsel.

"She's lying about giving up on you," Natakia said, looking uncomfortable, "but otherwise she's telling the truth."

Harriet was a little sheepish, but she seemed to know our decision to spare her before we did as her smirk appeared almost flirtatious as she looked at me.

"Harriet, we are going to let you live," I said, nodding at Penelope who gave a short, terse nod back. "If we ever see you again, that will not be the case. We will kill you without question or comment."

It was the bare minimum of mercy I would spare on her. Hopefully, she would go off and do whatever she wanted with her life far from my own. I certainly had no desire to ever make amends with a woman who had conspired against my family and friends.

For a moment, Harriet seemed to want to haggle, a merchant at heart, but she nodded. "I don't suppose I can stay here, can I? Once you've beat Zactrik?"

"No," Penelope said, "you aren't going to stay in the Mana Wastes. If you do, I'll find and kill you before you realize your mistake."

Harriet sighed, looking around the warehouse. As we spoke with the leader of the Diving Bells, Dalton had been going from box to box, seemingly checking for any valuables. Daka had been of great help in opening up some of the sturdier containers.

"Wow, my boss has never looked that glum before." Rauzin watched on from her corner of the warehouse. "So, am I leading you through the ruins or not?"

"We'll find another guid—" I said, not wanting to endanger Doh's life when Macy interrupted me, standing up as her eyes lit up with an idea.

"No! She definitely has to go!" Macy looked down at Rauzin before looking at Penelope. "You said it yourself. This is a place where you can call on gods, right?"

"Yes, but that is very dangerous," Penelope said, warning in her tone. "If your mother was here with the same intention, then that may be a reason she doesn't have her memories."

Penelope wasn't wrong. There was still no evident reason for why Doh had lost her memories other than going down into the ruins. She would have still been able to use her magic. There would be no reason for her to have lost her memories unless something unexpected had happened.

"It's the only option we have, and we need a guide anyway," Macy said, looking determined. If she thought that the Lady of Yesterday was her answer, it was not my place to take it from her.

Dresden seemed unsure, however. "Macy—"

"Dad," his daughter interrupted him, "you didn't go after Mom . . . because of me. Please don't keep us from getting her back because of that again. She's here . . . in our arms! We're halfway there!"

The guard captain sighed, exchanging a look with me. I wanted to support him, but this was between him and his daughter. Perhaps, due to my earlier interference, that was hypocritical. I couldn't stand between them, however. This had to be a decision of their own accord.

"Okay," he said after a long pause, "we'll look for another way while we go down there, but if we have to . . . I know you've been studying the notes your mother left behind. I won't take this chance from you. Just . . . be careful."

Macy seemed surprised before she smiled as tears welled up in her eyes. She embraced her father, and the swordsman was powerless to do anything but hug her back. I was not envious of his position.

I turned away as they embraced, motioning for my children to follow as Penelope readied Rauzin to journey with us. Dalton and Daka returned from the crates, and Natakia, although concerned for her friend, gave her a moment alone as she approached me.

As the Booker family steeled themselves to do whatever it took to save Doh, the rest of us steeled ourselves to put our all into fighting Zactrik. It was time to go into the ancient ruins of Rainwater.

Journeying deeper into the ruins of Rainwater, it was becoming clearer and clearer where all the eponymous rainwater that fell upon the city truly went. Chutes that had been dug into the walls and looked man-made and recent compared to the ancient stonework around us.

The rainwater flowed down the tubes of stone that descended from the upper layers of Rainwater and traveled into these chutes, emptying out into a deep reservoir away from the city. Rauzin had added that last detail, nothing of that design visible from within the ruins.

"Have you ever thought of the empire that once shone in this part of the world?" Penelope asked me as we descended farther with every minute spent on the slippery and treacherous path of the ruins.

Daka and I were keeping our footing quite well, alongside Dresden, but there were times that we had to reach out and keep the others from falling and sliding toward a more dangerous slope.

Of course, after Dalton had slipped once, he had looked irritated before suddenly displaying a much higher level of grace and control over where he stepped. Adaptation was definitely a strength.

Rauzin, proving her capability as a guide, seemed to be at home in the ruins. Her hooves seemed capable of keeping her from slipping where she otherwise might have.

Considering Penelope's question, I gazed at all the ancient stonework around us. "I suppose I have. The empire is long forgotten, but there are stories in every bit of stonework. There were living hands that carved this very chamber, hands that never knew of the endless rain that would be coming."

"It's been long thought that the fall of the empire unleashed a deluge of Mana across these lands," Penelope said, a gentleness to her voice that I rarely heard these days, "but I've wondered if that's the truth or merely what we believe possible."

"You think they wielded a power greater than Mana?" Penelope had told me that the power within the metals of the Mana Wastes was founded on the primal energy of the world.

She nodded. "An empire that wielded the power of Primus. It's hard to believe, but can you imagine what that must have looked like? Were they even human?"

"And yet, for all of their power," I said, kneeling down to run my hand over the remnants of a pillar, the stone weathered away by the water over time, "they were still forgotten."

It was almost strange to think that. An empire of such strength being entirely forgotten with no inkling as to the stories that had lived on through it. Perhaps Canon was right, that there would be a time that all stories were tired of traveling the world and would appreciate a place to rest.

"So, I have a kid," Rauzin said, looking innocently bemused by such a thing. "I really thought that would be way too boring for me . . . Wait, how old am I?"

Honestly, the exact number was a little beyond even me. Doh hadn't been sure how old she was before she wandered around a long time, and she often shape-shifted her apparent age as she wished.

"Old, but younger than me," I said, feeling the answer was fine enough. "At least eighteen years—the time that I've known you—and plenty before that, I had assumed."

Rauzin nodded, looking like she was digesting the new information about her own age, before pointing down to the next layer of the ruins. "I suggest we take the long way around; otherwise you might slip and get trapped in the locked-out zone."

"The locked-out zone?" That was a somewhat innocent-sounding name for what felt like a pretty dangerous area if we were giving it a wide berth. It looked like a particularly slippery path that seemed to be a much more straightforward route.

Our guide nodded. "Yep, it's full of this metal that makes magic and techniques really hard to use. It's pretty hard to get out of if you don't have a rope or something."

"Have you . . . ever gotten trapped there?" I tried to keep my question light, but I already felt like I knew the answer.

"Nope," Rauzin said, "not as far as I can remember."

Ah, yes, that was the answer I should have expected. Still, I was sure that area was connected to Doh's loss of memory, a place she'd be unable to keep up her mind-preserving magic. Glancing around, the rest of the group seemed to have the same thoughts.

"Yeah," Macy said, looking nervously at the area Rauzin had pointed out, "let's, um, stay away from that."

"Oh, hey, I raised a smart kid." Rauzin looked immensely proud of herself. I wondered if somehow Doh's spell work hadn't left some sort of imprint, even without the regular use of magic. With no ability to preserve her memories, Doh had said she only had vague recollections of being listless and apathetic. Rauzin seemed far more expressive than my friend had spoken of about her years without memory magic.

As we began to descend the longer route, Daka was wary and kept a close eye on all that was around us. "How much longer until we reach the bottom?"

"Another hour," Rauzin said, looking over the edge of the path we were on and down into the dark abyss below us. Somewhere down there, Zactrik was waiting for us.

As we neared the bottom of the ruins, we finally began to feel the Mortum in the air. It was a damning, toxic miasma that seemed to pry at my physical energy before shying away without finding purchase.

The siphoning was likely barely felt by the people above in Rainwater but surely had begun to weaken the young and elderly. Had I even seen a child on our way through the streets of the city? I couldn't be sure.

"How safe are we?" Natakia asked, keeping close to Macy, who hadn't left the side of Rauzin as we got farther and farther down into the depths of Rainwater.

Penelope spoke up, her words concise. "While visible to the naked eye, Mortum of this concentration level will have little effect on us, but if the ritual occurs in full, then we will likely perish."

I nodded, having assumed the same. Her words were a bittersweet salve upon the souls of our group, but there was little to be done about that. I sent comforting looks to my children, trying to reassure them, and held the hand of Natakia, who seemed the most disturbed by the idea of death.

"Alright," Dresden said, his blade drawn, "then we need to do this quick, right? Anything to know about this Zactrik before we get too close to strategize?"

A good point. I shared as much as I knew before Penelope did the same. His great speed, the sacrileges that Zactrik had used all those years ago, his ability to seemingly halt time and disturb the mind, as well as his greatest weakness beyond the weapons we wielded.

"Zactrik is a prideful man," I said, "and his rhythm can be thrown off by taunts and ridicule. However, it is risky if his abilities are turned against one of us in full rather than his attention being spread out."

We had been trying to distract him last time to give Penelope a chance to inject him with enough poison to kill him, and seemingly, we had almost done the job. Now we just needed to finish it.

As we spent some more time figuring out our plan of action. Each of us having our role to play in the coming fight, we eventually reached the bottom of the ruins of Rainwater.

38

Penelope had further explained that, even as the Mortum around us became more visible, it would still only have a subdued effect due to the nature of the ritual at this stage. That said, the blizzard-like density of black flecks of death was incredibly disconcerting.

And yet, there was a power here, that of the nexus that my friend had spoken of. As we stepped onto the lowest layer of Rainwater, the ancient ruins of a past empire, there was no doubt that this place was steeped in significance.

The stone we walked upon was almost marble white and smooth with the exceptions of the engravings of near perfection, even after the attempts of the water to erode them. The markings were geocentric, circular and all collapsing down farther into smaller circles as we approached the center.

Where the Mortum felt the heaviest and most suffocating.

"Calm your hearts and wield your weapons with confidence," I said, taking out Crow. It would not be able to hurt Zactrik in a meaningful way, but there was much to be gained from having it out.

Daka stayed close to me, her body shaking but her gauntlets steady. She was scared, and if this weren't Zactrik, I would have asked her to take leave of this fight. Dalton was frowning, but his quick aptitude with the halberd in his hand was proved by his gentle twirls of his weapon as he prepared himself.

"Alright," Natakia said, "Macy and Dresden, we'll stay back here. I'll support the fight from here, and we can keep an eye on Rauzin."

Dresden nodded, taking guard of the two young magicians who, while capable in their own right, didn't have the physical training to safely keep up with Zactrik's full speed. Natakia's divination magic would be useful from afar, so there was no need for her to be too close to the fight.

"Strike team with me," Penelope said, leading the way. I nodded to Dalton and Daka and headed with her. If there was anyone I trusted in this rematch with Zactrik, it was Penelope and the years she had spent preparing for it.

As we stepped farther into the realm of darkness that Zactrik had slowly begun to transform this site of power into, I connected myself to the source of Vitae within my prosthetic.

"Is that going to be enough?" Daka whispered to me, looking at my arm and me. Her gifted sight surely saw the less-than-impressive amount of Vitae I had managed to store for this fight with all my recent recovery.

I nodded, letting my Vitae circulate. "I will be able to do my part. I am not alone in this, so I will not fear the madness that we face."

Daka smiled, and Dalton nodded his head as he overheard my words as well. Following Penelope, we felt the beginnings of Natakia's magic begin to envelop us as we approached the center of the bottom layer of the ruins.

Zactrik, for all his power, still seemed like just a man as we approached him. His eyes closed and on his knees, the madman had his hands on the ground before him. A deep, revolting power flowed into the ground from his touch, a thick Mortum corrupting the ground around him.

"I am very disappointed in Harriet," he said, that ever-polite tone sharpened with a dark dissatisfaction. "I only needed a few more weeks, and this would have been over, and the world would be that much closer to salvation. Now, I'll have to start all over again."

A piece of metal on Penelope's foot glowed, a familiar sight, as the world around us was suddenly engulfed by the same Mana cage that she had placed me in once before.

Zactrik was trapped inside with us for better or worse.

"You won't get that chance," I said, spearheading the conversation. If there was anyone whom Zactrik would focus on, it was me. The man who was here despite Zactrik's own best efforts.

For a moment, Zactrik was quiet before he finally opened his eyes and looked at me with shock. "I'm sure I see a ghost. Rakta, you should have gone insane within my sacrilege. I destroyed your mind."

"You tried to," I clarified, "and just as your attempts here, you will fail without having gained a thing."

Zactrik stood up, the mess of Mortum beneath him beginning to withdraw from the stone of the nexus point, and he turned to look at all of us with all his attention.

"Just as your attempt to kill me all those years ago failed," Zactrik said, a small smile on his face, but his gaze was not quite as placid. I could see the exhaustion in his gaze, but also the madness and rage.

In the brief calm before the storm, I quickly settled into my **Grace Stance**, my techniques beginning to stir, right before Zactrik suddenly blurred toward me. Even lacking his cane, Zactrik's force of strength was immediately apparent as I could feel the immense physical power of his assault as he struck the air that I had just been in.

I dodged, keeping my movements efficient and trying to reserve my Vitae as much as possible as Zactrik's speed continued to increase with every attack aimed at me, his onslaught fast and strong. He was slower than before, barely giving me the chance to dodge some of his blows, but that advantage was quickly fading.

Weakened or not, Zactrik was a being that was beyond the limits of mortality, and I had to treat him seriously if I was to have a chance of surviving this. For a moment, I felt the loss of Shawn even more as there was little standing between Zactrik and I.

Daka and Dalton moved in, Zactrik's attention pointed so heavily toward me that he didn't notice as he was quickly surrounded by a triangle of me and my children.

Penelope looked deadly focused as she continued to supply the cage around us with Mana, limiting the area we fought in, while beginning to charge up Mana in the palms of her hands.

Feeling the potent Mortum in Zactrik's blows as he grazed my side with a fierce punch, feeling as if days of my life were being drained away by each touch, I dashed backward before throwing a deluge of Crows at the monster.

"Now!" I yelled as Zactrik's focus was momentarily on the flying projectiles, unable to ignore them after our use of the golden-speckled rose from last time.

Natakia's magic suddenly activated throughout all of us, and I felt my sight aligning with that of my allies as powerful divination magic bestowed us insight into our enemy but also one another.

Daka and Dalton moved as one, their movements perfectly in sync, as Zactrik dodged the first straight punch thrown by my daughter before moving to the side, barely getting out of the way of Dalton's swing of his halberd. Zactrik darted out, punching straight through the image of my son, shattering it.

The real Dalton came out of invisibility and struck him from behind, landing the first blow on Zactrik as his halberd tore into his back, a pulse of energy erupting from the wound as the monster roared in sudden pain at the cutting slash laid upon him.

I moved, quickly stowing Crow, as I charged the man, feeling the impact as Zactrik, in his unexpected pain, didn't foresee the haymaker I landed straight on him, sending him flying toward my daughter, who was ready to receive him.

"Cross Combo Technique," Daka said, her eyes aglow with her Vitae as her feet blurred and so did she as she wove toward Zactrik with beautiful footwork, her gauntleted fists suddenly too fast to see. Zactrik was stopped dead in the air with one punch, two punches, four punches, and then an absolute blur of sixteen punches that sent him flying back toward us.

Penelope, connected with us by Natakia's magic, as well, pushed the air with her palms as I watched the air crack in front of her in a very familiar way. The same way that Ulric's shatter magic tore the air apart.

"Shatter," Penelope intoned, the pressure of the air being torn suddenly exploding toward Zactrik, enveloping him with the full force of the attack and blasting him into the wall of the cage we'd trapped him in. For a moment I was stunned at the power of what was undoubtedly Ulric's magic blossoming from Penelope's person.

Unwilling to give him a moment of rest, Daka, Dalton, and I pursued him. I took the lead, charging toward him with my fist raised to take advantage of his position on the ground.

"**Sacrilege Against Time**," Zactrik suddenly said, sounding nearly desperate already, "**Broken Clock**."

The world was suddenly overtaken by gray as Zactrik's ichorous sacrilege stopped time just as it had so many years ago. Fear buried itself deep in my heart as I watched him slowly stand up.

Bruised, ragged, Zactrik unbroke his own neck as he stood up, the massive tear on his back from Dalton's surprise strike from behind slowly closing, but the damage did not disappear. We had hurt him, and he couldn't simply regenerate from the kinds of wounds we had given him.

"Why do people always make things so difficult?" Zactrik said, sounding tired. And yet it did not sound like the exhaustion of a warrior on the edge of defeat, but rather an exasperated teacher. "I'm trying to give this world a chance to be more than a place of needless death, but you keep getting in my way. Why?"

I expected him to approach me, readying myself to accept whatever attack he had up his sleeve, but instead, he moved toward Penelope.

"I'm just so confused because you obviously understand," he said, speaking with my frozen friend, even as her stuck expression of focused murder remained unchanging. "You fight the fragility of mortality just as I do, so why do you stop me? We could be sharing notes. I've never turned my epiphanies, the insight I was gifted, toward what you've achieved with the mortal frame. We could learn so much from one another."

For a moment, it seemed like Zactrik was just thinking to himself before he looked around the ruins and the cage he was trapped in. Could he leave the cage while time was frozen? It seemed like he had been unable to interact with anything during this time last we had fought.

"I've seen so much death, but I must see more if I am to rid this world of it," he said before he walked over to me, and I felt the world slowly begin to resume time. "**Sacrilege Against Space**—"

The gray was suddenly shattered as Dresden smashed through it and the Mana cage that Penelope had erected, the world suddenly flickering back into reality as I jumped away from Zactrik's attack.

"Are you all alright?" Dresden asked, his blade pointed toward Zactrik, who looked surprised at the sudden intervention and outright destruction of his sacrilege.

The cage around us quickly relit, Penelope pumping it full of her Mana. I nodded, briefly checking Dalton and Daka for any wounds and finding none.

"What just happened?" Daka looked shaken but steeled herself. "That was how he stops time? That felt . . . disgusting."

"Natakia told me something was going on," Dresden said, his blade shimmering with his Vitae. "Whatever he did, it only affected a small area, and my sword cut through it like paper."

Penelope nodded. "An outward attack that destabilized the Mortum. Good work, Dresden. You just saved Rakta's life."

"For now," Zactrik said, frustrated as he looked at all of us, our weapons, before settling on Penelope. "I suppose this is your work."

The premier innovator of the empire stared back at him. "The last time you fought us, you took us by surprise, and we still almost beat you. I didn't have to work this hard to kill you, but I wanted you to feel every blow, every wound. I wanted you to burn just like Shawn."

Her words stoked a familiar anger in me, watching Shawn disappear with a smile on his face. A hero had fallen to this monster and Zactrik had gone on to survive for years. Years that Shawn's son had lived without a father.

As Natakia's magic enchanted us once more, Dresden being surrounded by it, as well, I watched as Zactrik warily looked at all of us. Speed, strength, they were assets in a fight that he had us outmatched in, but Zactrik fought against the future now, a future that all could see but him.

I was not one to enjoy the pain of others. It was a level of sadism that I very rarely succumbed to, but as every strike upon Zactrik's person brought him more and more pain . . .

"Whatever strength you've drained from the people of Rainwater has still left you little to spare," I said, punching him in the stomach before I dashed away from his incoming strike.

Dalton appeared out of nowhere, some combination of invisibility and teleportation, and struck out from behind Zactrik once more, cutting into his legs and hobbling him. "Mortum is a good investment, but you should have diversified your portfolio."

Zactrik whirled, trying to strike out at my son, but was sent flying as Daka stepped in, a punch from her gauntlet hurling him off to the side and away from her younger sibling.

Dresden, deep in his **Iron Knight Stance**, took a solid step forward and came down with a powerful downward strike at Zactrik, nearly cutting the monster in half had Zactrik not recovered and dodged.

For a moment, he was back on the offensive, darting toward Daka with powerful and swift attacks that my daughter nimbly dodged, proving to be just as hard to hit as when we'd last fought. Brief moments of invisibility, darting duplicates, every trick in the book seamlessly used to frustrate Zactrik.

Ducking under a blow, Daka rose with an uppercut, sending the monster flying through the air before he hit the ground hard. As Zactrik picked himself up with an enraged expression, I could tell that whatever patience he had was gone.

"**Sacri—**" Zactrik spoke, the beginnings of his Mortum affecting the area, before a plume of destructive air pressure consumed him, Penelope teleporting around to get a perfect vantage point of her own.

Stopped mid-sacrilege, Zactrik cried out from the pain of the attack. Growling, his form beginning to distend and deform from that of a normal-looking human, his voice became a bubbling, gurgling distortion. "You think that this is enough to end me? That which has died cannot die again."

"Welcome to strange aeons." Dalton suddenly appeared, an overhead slash downward into the monster, but with a soft pulse, Zactrik was nowhere to be seen.

"**Sacrilege Against Self.**" The dreaded words were suddenly spoken from behind all of us, the future catching up a moment too late as Zactrik roared with power, "**Duality of Man.**"

It was only the future sight afforded to me by Natakia that kept a tendril from plunging into my stomach, giving me time to flip over it and dash away. And yet, even as Zactrik lashed out at me, I could feel fate shiver as I glanced over and saw that I was not his only target.

Nor was there only a single Zactrik fighting us now.

A second, equally grotesque being that matched the original's capabilities near perfectly from what I could surmise, roared as it began to focus on my children.

"Ugh!" A tendril of Mortum slashed through Dalton's guard, landing a glancing blow on his side that sent a chill down my spine. Daka moved in, dashing him to safety, but I swallowed hard. Natakia's magic was working harder than I'd ever felt Lydia's work to continue granting us our blessing. Could my wife have even divined the future of two Zactriks?

The original Zactrik grinned at Penelope, Dresden, and me, as my children began to fight his clone. "You couldn't even handle me before. Do you really think you'll win against the two of me now?"

"Our odds are more favorable than you'd believe," Penelope said. Her hands were balled up into tight fists, the only hint of the rage she was feeling.

Dresden and I shared a glance before dashing toward Zactrik, moving in tandem to begin cutting into him, but he swiftly began to dodge blow after blow. He was no animal like Esmeralda, no matter how monstrous he was. The longer this took, the more Zactrik learned our movements.

I flipped over a punch, feeling the weight of the blow almost implode the air below me as Zactrik jumped back, away from an overhead strike from Dresden.

I dashed toward him, kicking off of the air, to punch him before he nudged the blow aside, the weight of his touch throwing me off and to the side. I fluctuated my Vitae as I spun through the air, regaining my balance.

"Old, useless," Zactrik said. "The weight of mortality makes you all slow."

Focusing on Penelope, he seemed to pause, before zooming toward her, and it was all I could do to dash toward her as well, even as her form began to glow.

"No more running away!" Zactrik made a grab for Penelope's throat, before she was whisked away by her teleportation, leaving him with nothing but empty air. I dove in, making a swift feint toward his face, before dashing to the side and dodging around him as Dresden struck him with his blade.

Flinching in pain, Zactrik lashed out with a barely noticeable tendril that struck both Dresden and me in our midsections, the weight of the attack sending shockwaves through our skeletons as we were thrown back.

Hitting the wall of the arena that Penelope had laid down, noticing my friend reappearing from her teleportation a few paces away, I felt my back ache as I shot a worried glance toward the other side of the fight. Daka and Dalton's fight against the duplicate Zactrik.

"Don't be worried about them," Penelope said. "Your kids are ridiculous."

The awe of seeing my children move with the certainty of those with the future on their side, Natakia's magic flowing through them, was only matched by amazement of their own prowess against the duplicate of Zactrik.

Perhaps it was not a fully realized duplicate. Perhaps in some ways, it lacked the intelligence of the original and simply raged against the world as Esmeralda had. Even so, every tendril flew past my daughter, her form a blur of her own duplicates as she focused on evasion and powerful single strikes.

Dalton, not bearing the weight of the duplicate's full attention, never came at him with the same trick twice. Every time he leapt from invisibility, I saw a new spell, a new technique. And every time Dalton introduced a new technique into the fight . . .

"Daka, follow my lead," Dalton yelled out. "**Triplicate Blow Technique!**"

Daka glanced at her brother before her gauntlets flattened and glowed with Vitae. "**Triplicate Blow Technique!**"

And as her brother introduced what I assumed to be an entirely new technique to Daka, she used it with the same level of mastery in tandem with him as they both began to tear into the duplicate Zactrik.

"Rakta! Eyes front!" Penelope roared at me as I instinctively dodged away from a strike from the original.

Our fight with the original continued, and there was no doubt that the struggle between Zactrik and only the three of us, Penelope, Dresden, and I, would be a lesson in defeat. I was already feeling the beginnings of exhaustion, pulling more and more from my arm's Vitae reserves to supplement my lagging supply.

"Stay defensive, buy time." Penelope said. She had the most time to access the battlefield while Dresden and I continued to evade attacks. I trusted her insight, trying to find a moment to strike as the original Zactrik started trying to stab us with the ends of his tendrils.

For a time, it felt nothing would change, every second of the fight feeling like hours. A lash of tendril almost sliced into Penelope before our opponent suddenly howled in pain.

"What!?" Zactrik's form melted even more, looking pained even as none of our attacks had managed to graze him.

"Dad," Daka was suddenly by my side, some of her Vitae funneling into my body in the brief respite we had. "Sorry. Dalton and I took longer to deal with the clone than I thought we would."

Dalton stepped up beside me, "I spent thousands of sil on all of those new attacks. Let's see if they work on the original just as well."

Feeling immense relief, I nodded. "I have no complaints. Dresden and I are happy to have you by our sides again."

"Yeah," Dresden said, but his attention was on Zactrik. The monstrous creature had devolved from anything resembling a humanoid creature, becoming nothing more than a Mortum-obsessed ooze that began to writhe in its place.

"You, all of you." Zactrik's voice was stretched and warped, a loud keening overlaid on top of normal words. "I'll kill all of you!" The future suddenly changed, and Zactrik's form shot toward Dresden, the inky blackness of his ichorous, nightmarish body sprouting multiple new appendages that began to rain down on the guard captain.

"Dresden!" I sped forward alongside Daka, both of us attempting to strike out at Zactrik, but his speed had suddenly increased, and the limits of Natakia's enhancement were being reached. The monster dodged our attempts to hit him, continuing to harry Dresden, who was crumbling fast.

A powerful defensive Vitae meant little to the eldritch potency of Mortum, and while Dresden had gotten faster, he wasn't nearly fast enough to dodge the attacks. Especially as Zactrik began nearing speeds eclipsing that of our previous battle with him.

Even Daka and Dalton, who had fared far better against the duplicate, were not able to react in time perfectly, taking glancing blows and finding themselves unable to land a hit.

Penelope suddenly teleported behind Dresden, gripping him with her metal hand, before both of them teleported away from Zactrik's attempt to skewer him with his new appendages.

"He's too fast," Daka said, watching as Zactrik didn't let up, now following after Penelope and Dresden. He was out for blood, and we had to do something soon. Penelope wasn't going to be able to keep Macy's father safe for much longer.

I nodded. "Then we need to get faster."

Daka looked at me, and recognition entered her eyes as she smiled, excited for a moment before her face fell to a clear uncertainty. "Are you sure?"

"No father would deny his daughter a dance," I said as she and I both began to move with the moisture in the air and the rainwater that flowed through the roots of the city.

The wind and stone both sang as we danced to their rhythms, an enraptured audience as we finally moved with each other rather than against the other.

For that was the way of our **First Dance Stance**.

"**First Dance Technique**." Daka and I gathered the Vitae in the air around us together. "**Twister Through the Valley!**"

And then we rocketed forward together, my heart feeling light even as it filled with determination to finally bring an end to Zactrik together with my friends and family.

39

In perfect sync with Daka, enhanced by the magic of Natakia and the winds of my technique and supported by Penelope, Dalton, and Dresden as they harried Zactrik between our strikes, victory seemed inevitable. A dangerous assumption.

Daka and I saw through every attempt to dodge our blows, our impacts meeting at the same time. I would strike Zactrik from the front; Daka would meet me with a blow at his back. I rammed his head into the ground; Daka came down with a powerful downward double-hammer punch into his stomach.

"Guh!" Zactrik cried out, feeling the pain from every single blow. His malformed ooze tried to reform at times, but our attacks destroyed every semblance of man in his appearance, his visage crumbling into the likeness of the monster he was rather than the man he pretended to be.

As Zactrik was assaulted by air pressure from Penelope's continued use of Ulric's magic and besieged on both sides by Dalton and Dresden slicing into him, I could feel victory within our grasp.

And yet, I could feel my Vitae burning up as every attack rang true. I hadn't had the reserves required for the **First Dance Stance**, not enough to finish this battle if Zactrik's monstrous constitution didn't give up soon.

Daka, however, seemed in the zone. Lost to the power of her technique and the goal of destroying Zactrik, the sight of my daughter's prowess inspired pride even as my attacks began to falter and lag behind.

I gasped, feeling my Vitae give out and my power abandon me. Daka continued her assault as I suddenly hit my limit, the twister gathered around my limbs dissipating. Dalton was quickly by my side, looking concerned.

"Father, are you going to be okay?" He offered me a hand up, which I gratefully took.

I nodded, standing up with his help. "I'll be fine. Does Penelope have a read on how much more he can take?"

"It doesn't seem like he has much left. Take some time to recover. We'll help Daka finish this and give you a chance to catch your breath." Dalton was then gone, back into his invisibility.

Dresden fell back alongside me, looking pretty hurt as well. I hadn't been hit by as many direct blows as Dresden, but I was still feeling the times that Zactrik had gotten his hands on me.

"This future-sight stuff is amazing," Dresden said, panting. "I feel like I'd be dead a thousand times over if I didn't have it right now."

I nodded, feeling much the same. It certainly hadn't been an advantage we'd had the last time, and it shored up what would have otherwise been a disastrous lack of teamwork. I couldn't even say I was intimately familiar with how Penelope fought these days.

The battle raged on as we spoke, my eyes following as best I could to find an opportunity to aid or assist. It gave me a deeper appreciation for our systematic takedown of Zactrik, seeing it from an outside perspective.

My daughter's speed, strength, and versatility were certainly incredible, but as the fight went on, Dalton grew stronger, not weaker. New tricks, midfight investments, quick thinking, and an adept sense of tactics. My son fought consciously while my daughter fought instinctively.

And Natakia, even with her distance from the battle, allowed them to fight as one, with Penelope supporting them and striking Zactrik every time he made an attempt to use one of his powerful sacrileges.

I wondered if I'd had Shawn and Ulric here, instead of my children, we would have had as much of a chance as we did now. What if instead of my daughter's magic, we had Lydia's? It was an impossible comparison, one summoned by my exhaustion, but I was sure that it would have been no easier than what we dealt with now.

And then Zactrik, his ooze-like form erupting into a facsimile of his humanoid appearance, finally managed to hit Daka. His fist plunged into her stomach hard as she was suddenly rocketed back onto the ground. Dalton stepped forward, bringing his halberd to bear, but had to evade and abort his attack as Zactrik turned his full attention on him.

"Daka!" I yelled, moving forward, but stumbled, feeling my Vitae scream at me to stay still, to breathe properly, to recover before I strained it any further.

Dresden dashed forward, parrying Zactrik's attempt to attack my daughter on the ground, with Penelope teleporting in and snatching Daka away, her form shimmering apart before it reformed beside me.

"We need you back in the fight, Rakta," Penelope said, watching as Dresden and Dalton kept Zactrik busy for a moment before she teleported away to help them.

Daka stood up, regathering herself. "Dad, don't worry, I got this."

And with a renewed strength, twisters regathering on her limbs, she flew toward Zactrik again, but I could tell that such a direct hit . . . It couldn't be ignored easily. Healing was prohibitive for most during a fight, especially alongside such an experience as taxing as the **First Dance Stance**.

"Penelope's right. I need to get back in there." I cursed the limitations of my body, watching as my friends and family continued to harry Zactrik, but the closer he got to defeat, the stronger and faster he became. Eventually, he would simply kill us before we could react.

"Sacrilege Against Space!" he suddenly cried in a fit of desperation after having a set of his limbs torn from him by Dalton, a new pair of arms springing from his inky mass to hold a spiraling black hole of destruction. **"Black Hole!"**

It grew large, larger than I'd ever seen that horrific ability. Esmeralda's sacrilege had been about the size of her palm, somewhat bigger, but Zactrik's grew to be nearly three times as big.

I rushed forward before I even thought of anything else, using the remnants of my Vitae to enhance my speed as Zactrik shot toward Dalton, carrying the destructive sphere in his grip to utterly destroy my child. Dalton stumbled, the future having altered and changed before our eyes at Zactrik's action.

Zactrik screamed, "I'll kill you one by one, starting with you!"

I wasn't fast enough. My Vitae wasn't enough. Could my son survive such an attack? Was I about to watch another loved one die? When Shawn had died, I had been filled with such anger, but my weakness had kept me from avenging him. I couldn't be weak this time. I refused.

I felt a glow in my chest, my worries lifted for a moment as warmth filled my body.

Weakened as he was, determined as he was to get to my son, there had been no expectation of me jumping in front of the attack with my fist ready.

"Not this time," I said, plunging my prosthetic into the dark sphere of destruction, utterly engulfing the anti-Mortum metal of my arm into the sacrilege as far as it would go.

Zactrik screamed as my fist plunged through his black hole and drove itself straight through his body. I felt the pain of the black hole ripping away my skin and muscle as it neared my body, the weight of the attack trying to drag me farther in before it suddenly buckled and dissipated.

The monster dashed away, screaming in pain, leaving me to look down at the wreckage of my prosthetic. Many of the fingers had been destroyed and broken, with deep scars on the surface. I was bleeding profusely from the attack, unable to heal my wounds.

If nothing was done, I'd die in a matter of minutes. I simply had no Vitae to stem the flow of blood, nor was my body responding properly.

And yet, I looked back over my shoulder at my son and smiled. "I'm glad you're alright, Dalton."

And then I took a knee, that warmth that had filled my chest leaving me as I was left severely deprived of Vitae. Daka was swiftly by my side, and I could feel her Vitae surging through me to replenish what I had lost. I gave her a smile, her focused gaze lost in healing my wounds.

I remembered when she was just a babe and I'd had to do the same for her when she'd first tried to pulse her Vitae like I had. My little warrior was quite the healer.

Dalton was by my side, as well, looking concerned but staying quiet as Daka did her work. Soon, I felt much better, most of my wounds having, at the very least, been stanched by the beginnings of new flesh.

"Thank you, Daka," I said, patting her on the head. "You've gotten very good at that."

She smiled, her gaze unfocusing on the task and refocusing on me, a tear rolling down her cheek at seeing me alright. Dalton put a hand on her shoulder, looking concerned.

Dresden and Penelope were standing a fair distance away, looking tense but unmoving as they seemed to survey the walls of the Mana cage. I couldn't see Zactrik. The fight had seemingly come to an end.

Recovered, I walked over to Penelope, my children following, as the puddle of Mortum that Zactrik had been reduced to was scraping helplessly at the wall of force that my friend's Mana kept up even as he attempted to drain it away. It was a piteous sight, but not one that I felt any true sympathy for.

"I'll . . . kill all you," the mush said, a single small-clawed appendage scraping away at the wall. "I'll get . . . away . . . Become strong . . . Learn more . . ."

Penelope gestured me forward toward him. I looked at her before looking back at Zactrik and approached. Kneeling to the ichorous puddle with the remnants of a humanlike face imprinted on it, I felt a deep anger toward this creature, this existence before me, but I had another feeling as well.

"Zactrik," I said, standing up, "when I awoke from the nightmare you put me in, I hated you, and . . . I still do. And yet, my victory was never your death. I did not come here for you. I came here for my friends and my family . . . You were just an afterthought."

I turned to look at Penelope and motioned toward Dalton's halberd. My son gently handed it off to Penelope as she walked over, and I could see that need in her to finish this, to finally free herself of that night.

"Shawn," she said, "I loved you. I'm sorry I wasn't strong enough to say that while you were alive. I'm sorry I wasn't able to keep you alive. I'll make this world one that you'd be proud to live in."

And with that, with not even a final word for his wretched existence, Penelope brought the halberd down and ended Zactrik once and for all.

"So," Natakia said, after hugging me strongly once we'd regrouped, "is it all over? Zactrik is dead, and we can all go home?"

She hadn't been in the fight, but she had seen much of it through her mirror. I hoped it wasn't too stressful for her, watching as we fought for our lives. I couldn't imagine the possibilities that ran through her head. Our victory hadn't been assured in all of this.

Penelope was briefly silent but nodded. "I don't think it's entirely over, but Zactrik is dead. I'm sure there are plenty of remnants of his experiments, but that is an issue for another day and a larger team of combatants."

To that, I agreed. Zactrik's discarded notes had given birth to Esmeralda; there was no telling what other parts of his research and experimentation would give rise to in the future. It was a blessing that he had not sought to bring any such horrors with him to Rainwater.

"There's just one more thing we have to do." Macy stepped forward, holding Rauzin's hand. Rauzin looked a little nervous now, unsure of what was about to happen.

Dresden came over. "Macy, are you sure?"

"Not . . . yet," Doh's daughter said before she walked over to me and Natakia, her eyes only on my desert flower. "I, uh, I wanted to say some things, just in case . . . you know, calling on a god doesn't go very well."

Natakia blinked, focusing on Macy, and her eyes went wide. "I could look into the future, see if it . . . goes well? You don't have to . . ."

"I, uh, I want to. I have to try, even if it doesn't work," Macy said, "but before I do . . . I think you're wonderful, Natakia. Getting to walk with you and talk with you like . . . before, these have been some of the best days of my life. I just . . . I want to say . . ."

My desert flower blushed and hugged her. "I know. Me too."

I looked to Dresden as our daughters embraced each other. He met my gaze and seemed lost, but I gave him an encouraging nod. It was on him to keep her from this if he truly thought it was right to do so, but there came a time for every parent to let their children do what they thought was right.

Rauzin was watching the embrace, as well, looking somewhat bemused. She leaned over to me. "So, did we agree on a payment for this little trip?"

"We forced you to come with us and lead us," I said, reminding her. It was hard to tell if she was being serious or simply making a joke.

"Oh," she said, straightening up. "I thought you guys were paying me. What are we about to do?"

Macy separated from Natakia, nodding to her father. "I'm ready now."

"Okay." Dresden walked up and hugged his daughter. "You've gotten so big, you know? If something happens to you . . . I'm trusting you, alright? Come out of this safe, yeah? Your mother isn't . . . she wouldn't want you to risk yourself like this."

"I know, but I have to. I'll try to come back. Back with Mom. I love you, Dad." Macy hugged Dresden back tightly.

Natakia came over, her worry unhidden now that Macy wasn't looking. I reached out to comfort her, but paused as Daka came over and put a gauntleted hand on her shoulder, trying to give her a comforting smile. "Macy's strong. Don't worry."

"I know," Natakia mumbled before considering something for a moment. "Daka, you aren't a monster. I'm sorry I called you that."

Daka looked stunned for a moment before she nodded. She looked uncomfortable, as if she were unsure how to accept that, but responded, "I'm sorry I punched you. Family shouldn't fight."

"No, they shouldn't," Dalton said, joining up with his sisters. He'd been mostly watching from afar until then, not looking any happier about Macy's risk than the rest of us. "Hopefully, we'll remember that next time we have to deal with anything troublesome."

Sighing in relief, I came over and gave them all a big hug, my prosthetic working enough to at least grab them all up in a big embrace. "I'm glad we're all together now that this is over. All that's left is to bring Doh home."

"I beseech the Lady of Yesterday, of sound mind, to ask of thee a favor." Macy's words were filled with power as she went through the ancient process bound in delicate spell work.

Macy's Mana was floating through the air and interacting with many of the engravings on the ground in a far more delicate and humane way than Zactrik's Mortum had been moments ago. A part of me feared that Zactrik's attempt would taint Macy's own efforts, but that fear had been put to rest.

Penelope had helped her prepare the ritual, a process that hadn't taken very long and had been primarily based on the notes that Doh had left behind. From what I had gathered, the ritual to contact a god wasn't necessarily the complicated part but, rather, the research into the god in question.

"What are your thoughts on this, Penelope?" I asked, feeling the power of the nexus point being drawn upon as Macy continued to call upon the Lady of Yesterday.

Natakia and the others were standing with me, as well, all of us watching Macy try her best to call upon the god to bring her mother's memories back. Rauzin was the closest, brought over to sit next to Macy for the sake of the ritual. She seemed . . . uncomfortable but going with flow.

I suppose that, with such fleeting memories, going with the flow was how all those with the blood of doppelgängers usually acted.

"I think that it's the only chance she has," Penelope said. "Of course, that's the same thing I told Doh when she was desperate for a way to fix you. I suppose this is my fault in some ways."

"It was Doh's decision in the end, but maybe you should offer to join the next friend you send across the world to speak with a god," I advised casually.

"Shush." Natakia suddenly interrupted Penelope and me. "Something's happening!"

I turned my focus back to Macy and saw that my daughter spoke the truth. Where originally Mana was felt, a new spiral of primal energy began to swirl alongside Macy's energy.

Macy's eyes began to glow as the spiral connected to her Mana, and I knew that through this nexus point, the young shape-shifter had truly made contact with a god.

"Wow," Daka said, sounding amazed. All of us were similarly enraptured by the sight, lost in the glow that began to circle within Macy's gaze. Dresden's face was tight with worry. I placed a hand on his shoulder, trying to comfort him, but it was an impossible task.

Rauzin sat befuddled at the light show, watching the glow in her daughter's eyes. Did she even truly understand what was going on? What was about to happen?

"Lady of Yesterday," Macy said aloud, "I ask you to bring back the memories of my mother. Her blood has taken them from her, a terrible accident leaving her vulnerable without her magic to protect her."

She was silent for a moment, and I could tell she was listening to something, someone, that we couldn't hear. A conversation that we got to know only one side of.

"I agree to those terms," Macy said, a grave finality in her tone. There was a beat before a flash of light overtook all of us, and we shielded our gazes from Macy and Rauzin at the center of the ritual. For a moment I was sure I had seen my entire life flash before my eyes, but the feeling passed as soon as it came.

When the light dimmed, we all saw mother and daughter embracing for the first time in a long while.

40

That's one crazy story," Doh said, sitting on the edge of the ship as we rode home from Rainwater. It was evening, the sun dipping toward the horizon.

I nodded. "I will cherish it for a long time."

We had spent hours talking about all that we remembered, the stories of my last two months and the collection of memories that Doh had received due to the blessing of the Lady of Yesterday.

"I can't believe I've got a name like Delilah." Doh shook her head. "What a name, am I right?"

I chuckled. Macy's deal with the god had not only returned Doh her memories of, well, being a mother and wife, but also of much of her childhood. Doh had even realized her own mother's name, Macy. It felt like much more than just a coincidence that that was the name she'd given her daughter.

"How does it feel, knowing more about yourself? Do you think you're changed by the experience?" Having so much revealed, I'd imagine that it could be hard to adjust to everything, new or old.

"Eh," Doh said, "I feel like it's less of a bother and more of a boon. I mean, heck, I think I remember how to get back to my old village now. That sounds like a family trip to me! And I . . . I don't know. I still have a lot of memories from when I was Rauzin. I think those . . . those are the most difficult ones."

Rauzin aided many crimes, plenty that Doh didn't want to talk about, and her relationship with Harriet had been . . . very complicated. I hadn't pried, but I had let Doh know that I would always be around to talk about such things if needed.

"Speaking of changed . . . Natakia and Macy, huh?" Doh wiggled her eyebrows. There was an implication there that was a mystery to me.

I looked over, uncertain. "I'm not sure what you mean. They've gotten much closer since our trip through the canyons, but . . ."

"I just didn't know my little one had it in her." Doh giggled. "But I'm sure they'll figure it out. I've got to make up for a lot of other things before I get certain mom privileges back."

That felt like the biggest weight that Doh was carrying. The regret of having not been there for her family for so long, the belief that she had abandoned them. It was one I could empathize with.

"We'll be there for them from now on," I said, putting a hand on her shoulder. "I know that Macy and Natakia will both need someone with more delicate taste in clothing and fashion once we get back to Gelvurt."

Doh nodded, looking out at the evening horizon. Her gaze was solemn but light as she watched the sun begin to dip down below the skyline, her hair flowing in the wind.

"About Macy." One last thing had been bothering me. "A god does not often do things for a mortal expecting nothing in return. Has Macy said anything about . . . the terms?"

Doh shook her head. "I guess I'll hear about them one day, but . . . she's a big girl. If she's gotta go fight off some monster or do a few crazy things for a god, then . . . I'll help her out. I've got faith in her."

I nodded, somewhat less optimistic that it'd be something that simple, but I agreed with the sentiment. Whatever Macy had to face, she would not face it alone. We were all there for her.

Just like Doh and the rest of the Bookers had been there for my family.

"Thank you, Doh, for doing what you could to try and cure me." I smiled before leaving her on the deck to go down below to see my children.

I passed a blushing Macy as she left my daughter's room, paying it little heed as I knocked on the door. After a moment, I walked inside Natakia's room, finding her reading a book, one of Canon's. Off to her side was another book, *Tenon's Worldwide Monstrous Encyclopedia, Volume Eight*.

"Getting some reading done?" I came in and sat down, smiling at how at peace my daughter looked as she read the book.

Natakia looked up from her book. "Canon wanted me to know all these stories by heart . . . He said it would be good for my Storyteller training."

"That's amazing," I said, coming over to read the book alongside her. "I'm still wary of my uncle's methods, but I can't deny that he has done a lot for us in a short time. I'm proud of you working hard to learn from him."

Becoming a Storyteller was arduous, but there was no greater honor in Rusk in my opinion. To become a Storyteller meant to weave the histories of my people into reality. It was so much more than I, with little talent in the art, could accomplish with simple words.

My desert flower seemed pensive as I sat down next to her. She lightly closed the book she had been reading as whatever was brewing in her heart boiled over, and she spoke.

"I . . . learned divination magic to feel closer with Mom, but I wanted to feel closer with you, too, Dad," Natakia said, leaning against me.

Closing my eyes and feeling weak at the sincerity of her words, I ran my fingers through her hair. "You are so very kind, Natakia. I know that your mother would be so proud of you. No matter what name you bear, you will always be my most beautiful daughter."

If any of my children could sway the hearts and minds of those around them with words alone, it was surely Natakia. Her wit and charm would serve her well in her training.

"If I wanted to," she spoke again, suddenly nervous, "I could come back to House Tribus, right? I can probably work something out with House Velbrun. They've taken a lot of political losses recently so perhaps . . ." House Velbrun and Esmeralda's manipulations had tempted my daughter away from her home while I was gone, but I would not rest until she was where she wished to be, where she belonged. That pit of vipers was no proper place for my little flower to grow.

I nodded. "I'll help you in any way necessary. I'm sure your brother and sister would be delighted to have you back at the estate . . . Macy too."

Natakia blushed, and I was beginning to think I understood what Doh meant. In any case, I'd support my daughter in whatever or whomever she pursued.

"That would, uh, be really nice." She giggled. "I'm going to get back to reading. Oh, when is dinner going to be ready? I'm . . . getting hungry."

Inwardly pleased by her growing comfort with meals, I let her know. The airship had a surprisingly adept team of chefs for a mobile structure. It felt strange to have such good food while traveling so far and so fast.

"Father," Dalton greeted me as I walked in on him working on some documents in his room, obviously some Gelvurt business he'd brought on the road. "I had a question for you."

For all that had changed between us, it was almost comforting to hear the professionalism in his tone. Perhaps others would doubt my son had a heart, but I had seen the care in his actions.

I sat down, nodding. "I'm happy to answer."

"Have you ever considered retaking your position as High Lord Tribus of Gelvurt?" Dalton looked up from his work only slightly, as if it were a simple query, but his expression was unguarded. He was curious, somewhat hesitant, but seemed open to hearing what I truly felt.

"Dalton," I began, "no, I never considered taking it back from you. If you no longer desired it, then the responsibility would fall back to me, but despite my objections, you have done well. You will always have my counsel, but I trust the people of Gelvurt are safe and well in your hands."

Perhaps Dalton would still err in the temptations of profit or control, but as long as he kept his heart open to those around him, I was confident in his future. All of my children were talented, but it felt right to leave Gelvurt's future to my son.

Dalton nodded, closing his eyes. "I appreciate that, Father. I . . . I always thought that this second life was wasted on me, that I had stolen the life of another to live my own life over again with no change. I thought that I was a parasite."

"You are no parasite." The very idea hurt my heart.

"I know that now. Well, I believe that to be true," Dalton said, looking relaxed. There was a glint of determination in his gaze as he opened his eyes. "Father, I want to try and live this life somewhat differently from the one I had before. It's not going to be easy though . . . I'm glad you'll be keeping close by. I am hard on the people around me. Trust still eludes me at times, but I want to be better."

An honest assessment of himself. It was a difficult thing to admit, especially in front of another. I could feel the iron in his assertion, a will-power that could snatch victory from the jaws of defeat. Pride welled up inside me as I approached him.

"And that is the most important thing. A desire to change is the first step," I said, laying a hand on his arm. My son had a long way to go—all of my children did—but there was time, and I was here.

Leaving the room, I waved farewell to my son, passing along the time for dinner as I did.

"So, uh, where are we going to go next?" Daka looked somewhat nervous in her room. It was a bit of a mess, hardly what it had looked like before she'd gotten here, I assumed. Most of the mess was simply clothes, but there were some breadcrumbs scattered about. Remnants of a midday snack?

I tossed a ball over to her, which she caught and threw back. "I suppose Penelope will go have an audience with King Certimov-Hanchett and give the good news. I might accompany her. I never got the chance to give Tracy my condolences for the loss of Shawn."

"Yeah, Uncle Shawn." Daka seemed sad for a moment before something piqued her interest. "Wait, that's Winfred . . . Winfred is the king . . ."

Ah yes, I knew Daka had an interest in seeing her old friend again, although she had shied away from the idea before. Perhaps now, with a bit of encouragement . . .

I smiled. "Yes, Tracy abdicated the throne once he was of age to inherit. Would you like to come and see him? I'm sure he'd be happy to see you as well."

"Uh, are you sure about that?" Daka caught another throw, passing it back to me. The ball was leather and filled with sand, a toy that Natakia had picked up in Rusk. It had made for a nice gift and had a nice weight to it that made it perfect for tossing.

"Well," I said, throwing the ball, "I'm sure it won't be easy, but a friendly face would be good for the both of you. You always had so much fun together."

Daka smiled, still looking uncertain. "Yeah, I've just . . . changed a lot."

With a bit more force than she intended, she threw the ball back at me. I caught it, feeling the extra force. The notion of Winfred, of visiting him, it was eating at her.

I tossed it to the side and came over to sit next to her, letting her lean up against me. "Daka, you have changed, but less than you think. I still see the face of the fun-loving little warrior I remember training with all those years ago. If you've changed once, all you have to do is change again."

"Yeah?" Daka looked up, sounding like she enjoyed the idea of what I said but didn't entirely believe it just yet. Being something other than the soldier who had taken so many lives was something my daughter wanted more than anything. "Do you really . . . think we'll still be friends?"

I thought for a moment, remembering when I had similar doubts. "A Hanchett's friendship is hard to lose, Daka. Perhaps it will not be simple, it will likely require a great deal of bravery, but I think you'll find that bonds with others, new and old, are what reveal who we are in the end."

Perhaps Daka and I both had blood on our hands, innocent blood, but I had found myself through the love and friendship of those around me. I was sure that if I could find such clarity, then Daka would reach it herself as well. And yet, not all wounds healed so easily . . .

"Daka," I got her attention once more. "I'm going to talk to Dalton about finding someone you can talk to . . . Someone you can share things with, who can help with how you're feeling. Help you in ways that I wish I could, but am not . . . equipped to in all aspects."

I was sure there were a few people still at CAD who would help me if I reached out to them. It wouldn't be the first time the organization had helped those who'd seen too much. From the glimpse I'd had, Earth was certainly well and beyond that threshold.

"Okay, but you'll still be around, right? I can talk to you about stuff too?" Daka held me tight, and I embraced her.

"Of course, Daka. You can tell me anything, no matter what burns in your chest. I've seen a lot, Daka, of this world and your old one. Whatever you've felt, whatever you continue to feel, I want to hear it, and we can talk about it for as long as you like." I put my forehead against hers, feeling her warmth.

Daka pulled back after a while. I could still see the tremor in her brow, as if she were firmly clinging onto the comfort my words gave. "Thanks, Dad . . . When's nosh?"

I smiled and let her know, giving her one last tight hug before heading out to help prepare the food. Tonight, we would finally celebrate all that we had accomplished.

Sitting down with my friends and family, my children to either side of me, I finally felt complete victory in this moment. Before me, there was true happiness.

Doh and Dresden were laughing and chatting away like nothing had happened, with only the few rare moments of them sharing something deeper between their gazes giving anything away about how much they had missed each other.

Daka ate messily, still not one for table manners, with Natakia fondly shaking her head while giving pointers on how to eat properly. Macy was talking with Dalton about some of the work he'd been doing, the construction of the bank and how that was going.

Occasionally Macy and Natakia would glance at each other, as if in secret, and Doh and I would share a glance of our own. I understood now what she meant. I was happy for my daughter.

And at the end of the table, opposite me, was Penelope. She was taking in the same sights as me, and I watched as her expression softened more and more over the course of the meal.

"I still can't believe that you guys finally take a big family trip to Rusk and it's while I'm playing amnesiac in the middle of the Mana Wastes," Doh complained, far too loudly to be taken seriously.

Dresden nodded, looking younger with his wife's return, "I hear Natakia and Macy are going on another trip to Kakrel eventually."

Natakia and Macy both blinked, my daughter shooting her friend an accusatory look as the young shape-shifter floundered at the trip being suddenly out in the open.

"Oh, do tell," Doh tittered. "I might have to tag along to make sure you don't get up to anything too dangerous."

"Mom, we're not . . . we just want to go shopping!" Macy blushed, rubbing her cheeks. And yet, her hair hadn't changed a single shade.

There was still quite a bit to talk about in regards to the arrangements for Natakia's Storytelling training, but those were talks for much later. Not during a celebration such as this.

"Doh, Macy," Daka spoke up suddenly, having been more or less quietly enjoying the atmosphere of the dinner until now. My little warrior suddenly grabbed my hand as both shape-shifters turned to look at her.

Natakia blinked, before smiling encouragingly at her sister. I could feel Daka's appreciation for the gesture, a few of her nerves melting away.

Doh looked like she was going to make a joke, before she quieted down, seeing the troubled expression on my daughter's face. "What's going on? Feeling okay?"

Macy seemed curious as well, with Dresden watching on intently. I wondered how much he was aware of Daka's feelings regarding his family.

"I wanted to, uh, apologize," Daka said. "I, uh, maybe now isn't the best time, but sometimes . . . I'm working through a lot and . . . If I've ever made you feel like you aren't family, I'm sorry. You are."

I tightened my grip around Daka's hand, knowing how hard it was for her to say something like this with everything she was working through. It was a good step, a necessary one, and one that I was proud of her for taking.

Doh stared at my daughter for a moment before she grinned. "I knew I'd grow on you eventually. I thought it'd happen after the fiftieth mess I cleaned up, but I guess sometimes it takes a few extra decades."

". . . Huh?" Daka said, tilting her head. The rest of the table broke out into an assortment of chuckles and giggles as the moment passed and Doh began to drag Daka more and more into the conversations around the table.

Talks about the future, about heading back to Gelvurt, about what came next and everything in between. It was a fine family meal that we all deserved after these past few weeks, no, years. Finally, we were able to simply enjoy the company of one another.

Eventually, the meal had come to a close, with all now simply chatting until my friend stood up, drawing all the attention to her.

"It's been a long time since I've sat down and had a meal with people," Penelope said, smiling. The smile dimmed, however, as she looked off into the distance. "For a very long time, I didn't think I was deserving of these kinds of things. I'd almost forgotten how much better food tastes when in good company. Thank you all for everything."

Realizing that she was about to leave, I stood up with my glass of wine. "Penelope, before you go, I'd like to offer a toast, a toast to all who are with us and to all those who are not. We wouldn't be here without any of them."

"A toast." Penelope paused, her smile becoming somber. She picked up her glass as the rest of the table did, and we raised our glasses together to Zerota, to Garrick, to Shawn Hanchett, to Lydia Velbrun, and to all the rest we had lost along the way.

This would not be our final story together, I was sure, but I felt we were finally ending an important chapter. Whatever came next, I could hardly know, but I knew that I would be with my children through it all.

EPILOGUE

Many years later, I closed my eyes for the final time, surrounded by a family that had grown larger than I had ever thought possible. So many new faces, young faces, and my children having grown so much into their own . . . I was surrounded by love.

For all the destruction that prophecy had once promised, my younglings had done so many great and wonderful things. Peace across the empire and beyond, the end of Zactrik's remaining taint upon Derra . . . Even when I became far too weak to stand with them, my children had stood together.

And now, my spirit could rest easy within the stories passed down by my children and grandchildren. The stories of Rakta the Scavenger, the Dancer, the Slayer of the Warlock King, but also of the father of Daka the Gentle, the Great Donn Dalton Tribus, and Natakia of a Thousand Tales.

I found myself eager to be remembered as a part of their stories more than any of my own. The only regret I had was that I would likely never have the chance to tell them all to Lydia myself.

I opened my eyes once my final breath had left me and looked around to see a clear cerulean sky above me, the feeling of soft grass underneath my form. I heard birds chirping in the distance, the sounds of nature that were almost mystical in clarity.

"We meet once again, Rakta," Overseer said. I looked over, seeing the same violet-eyed entity that had given me a gift so many years ago. During the darkest time of my life. Overseer's gift had not burned in quite some time, but it had done its work, and for that I was grateful.

I nodded in respect. "Overseer, I . . . I was not expecting this. It was my understanding that I would never see you again. What is this?"

"I am a giver of gifts, pulling people who have much potential from their worlds and giving them a chance to live out that potential in another," they said. "You remember, yes?"

I nodded. "I've lived a full life, Overseer. What more potential do I have?"

Overseer's lips twitched upward into a faint smile, and I realized that they were not smiling at me but, rather, at someone behind me.

Before I could turn, a pair of hands wrapped around to cover my eyes, a familiar voice whispering in my ear, "Can you guess who?"

"Lydia?" I couldn't hold back the sudden emotion in my voice. My heart ached as my hands, for in this world I had both of my arms once more, went up to touch the hands over my eyes. I gently caressed them, bringing them down to kiss them. "Is that you?"

My enchanting Lydia circled around me, her hands still in mine. Her beautiful silver hair, her moon-kissed skin, her deep blue eyes . . .

"I still don't understand," I said, glancing between Lydia and Overseer. "I already received a gift. Why am I receiving another one?"

Lydia blushed, her eyes fluttering as she hugged me tight, her head falling into the crook of my neck like it had so many times before. "It's not your gift, Rakta; it's mine."

"Lydia Velbrun is going to another world, Rakta," Overseer said. "It is within your power to decline, but the gift that her soul desired was to have another chance at a long life with you."

I swallowed hard, staring at Overseer for a moment before letting my gaze fall down onto Lydia. I smiled. "I have so much to tell you, so much to ask. Another life together may be just enough time for both."

"I love you, Rakta," Lydia said, reaching up and giving me a kiss that I had dreamed about for years but never with the real weight of this one.

As light consumed us both and our new lives began, I thought to my children and the long life that I had spent with each and every single one of them. And now, they would live long and happy lives without me.

I had so much to tell Lydia about our children from another world.

ABOUT THE AUTHOR

Payton Fletcher is the author of My Children from Another World, a slice-of-life reverse-Isekai trilogy, as well as a small-town journalist. Also known as _Glasses, Fletcher first fell for the stories of his great-grandfather and the rest of his family. When he became a journalist and began to hear even more people's stories, he decided to finally put his own ideas down on paper for the world to read. In addition to writing, he spends his time walking around his downtown area, researching new ideas, reading new books, and trying to put his glasses back together whenever they fall apart. Fletcher lives in southern Georgia.

Podium
DISCOVER
STORIES UNBOUND
PodiumAudio.com